A Dangerous Kiss . . .

A smile appeared upon Victoria's lips and her heart lifted. "Ooooh. I see now."

Jack drew up stiffly, acting affronted. "Just what do you see?"

Victoria wrinkled her nose at him. "You want to kiss me, and that's why you're so upset." She knew she was treading on dangerous ground, but her heart soared with the knowledge that she had not imagined those heated looks he sometimes threw her way.

Jack battled the ridiculous urge to run from the room and escape the little temptress. He knew what would happen should they kiss. He knew and it scared him. He would no longer be able to ignore how he felt. The game would be over.

He inhaled harshly as she came toward him and flinched when she laid a hand on his chest. She didn't know, couldn't know what she was doing to him. "Miss Casey, I believe . . ."

". . . so do I." And she stood on her toes, hands on each shoulder, and kissed him, pressed her lips against his and pulled back slowly. He stood there, his body rock hard, hands curled into fists by his side, feeling he would surely die if she pressed up against him any tighter . . . and suddenly he was devouring her with mouth and tongue and teeth, and all she could feel was his mouth on hers.

Anything for Love

Jane Goodger

A TOPAZ BOOK

TOPAZ
Published by the Penguin Group
Penguin Putnam Inc., 375 Hudson Street,
New York, New York 10014, U.S.A.
Penguin Books Ltd, 27 Wrights Lane,
London W8 5TZ, England
Penguin Books Australia Ltd, Ringwood,
Victoria, Australia
Penguin Books Canada Ltd, 10 Alcorn Avenue,
Toronto, Ontario, Canada M4V 3B2
Penguin Books (N.Z.) Ltd, 182–190 Wairau Road,
Auckland 10, New Zealand

Penguin Books Ltd, Registered Offices:
Harmondsworth, Middlesex, England

First published by Topaz, an imprint of Dutton Signet,
a member of Penguin Putnam Inc.

First Printing, November, 1997
10 9 8 7 6 5 4 3 2 1

 REGISTERED TRADEMARK—MARCA REGISTRADA

Printed in the United States of America

To Jim,
who taught me how to dream

Prologue

This must work. The baby will bring us closer. She
will make Christina well, thought Jack Wilkins as
he glanced over to his wife. She was bundled up as if
it were the middle of January instead of a warm summer day. And still she shivered. Jack longed to open
up a window in their stuffy carriage, but concern for
his wife stopped him.

"Nervous?" he asked, grasping one gloved hand.

"A bit. I imagine she's . . . small." Christina Wilkins
gave her husband a shaky smile.

"Of course she's small. A newborn," Jack smiled
widely, unable to contain his excitement. He chose to
ignore the way his wife's eyes shifted away.

The carriage stopped with a jolt, and Jack stepped
down to help Christina alight. A motorcar, its engine
stuttering loudly, drove by causing the horses to shift
and Christina to nearly fall into her husband's arms.
He helped her catch her balance, wincing at how thin
she felt beneath his hands. Jack clenched his jaw and
slid his gaze away from his pale, beautiful wife to the
steps leading up to St. Mary's Hospital, where their
daughter awaited them.

"So, we've agreed on Emma Louise?" he asked,
trying to bridge the silence between them.

"Emma is fine," she said, her voice as colorless as
the rest of her. Her silky, light blond hair, blue eyes

the color of a hazy sky, porcelain skin, all added to the air of fragility she seemed to delicately hold. Sometimes Jack imagined he could reach out to touch her and feel nothing but air. Christina had been waiting to die for so long, it was as if she were slowly fading away. One day, he would look at her and she would disappear before his eyes. But that would stop now. The baby would change her, would make her want to live. It had to.

They walked into the hospital, stopping while their eyes adjusted to the gloom inside. In the spirit of frugality, the hospital kept its gas lamps turned down low, making the nun who approached them from the gloom appear to solidify and take shape like a black phantom before them.

"Mr. and Mrs. Wilkins? I am Sister Margaret. If you'll follow me."

Jack smiled, feeling like a six-year-old on Christmas morning, his excitement so great he could barely stop himself from running down the hall to greet his daughter. He turned to share the moment with Christina, faltering when he saw nothing but fear in her eyes. "We'll be fine, Christina. She'll be wonderful."

His wife let out a small, shaky sigh. "I've never even held a newborn. I don't think I've ever even seen a newborn."

Jack shrugged, dismissing her fears. "Neither have I, darling. We'll muddle through this together. We'll have your mother come over." At seeing Christina's look of mock horror, he let out a small laugh. "Fine. We'll handle Emma. How difficult can a little baby be? All they do in the beginning is sleep and eat, or so I'm told." Indeed, Jack had questioned every family man he could find about the finer points of caring for newborns. Most, he found, were totally devoid of any helpful information, having relegated all child rearing to their wives. In fact, they seemed rather perplexed that he was inquiring about such things at all.

Christina gave him a timid smile, but the fear in her eyes remained.

"Here is your daughter," Sister Margaret said, holding a small bundle that looked very un-babylike until the nun turned so that the couple could see their new daughter. Jack was the first to move, laying the back of his index finger against her cheek. His heart did a little flip-flop, and he beamed a smile at Christina, who stared at the baby, her eyes wide, as if she had never before seen an infant.

"What's wrong with her?" she whispered. The babies she had seen were cherub-faced little beauties, with soft curling hair, not this scrunched up, red-mottled thing with spiky dark hair poking out from behind the blanket she was wrapped in.

"What do you mean, dear?" the nun asked, gazing from the baby to Christina.

She shook her head. "She looks . . . horrid."

To both Jack's and Christina's surprise, Sister Margaret burst out laughing. "Oh, dear. You've never seen a newborn before. They all look like this little one. She'll look more like what you're used to seeing in just a few weeks. It's one of God's little miracles."

"I think she's beautiful now," Jack said, his heart completely stolen by the baby. "Look at her lashes. Look how long they are."

Christina stepped closer trying to find something beautiful in the bundled-up little girl. The lashes *were* long, she supposed. But, no, her new daughter could not be called beautiful. Jack moved in close again so that his head was nearly touching his wife's, and drew back the swaddling so that he could hold one tiny hand. Instead, he revealed a simple silver cross.

"The mother," Sister Margaret said with a sad sigh. "She left this note with the babe." The nun handed over the note. "Of course you are under no obligation to obey her wishes." The "but" was left dangling in the air. It is so little she wants, Sister Margaret thought, her heart aching for the poor woman. She'd seen so many young women in similar predicaments, many of whom found it difficult to give up their child even after the decision had been made. But this one had touched her somehow.

It was the first time Jack had thought of the mother, the first time he realized that perhaps she loved her child and giving her up was likely the most difficult thing she ever had to do. Jack looked at the silver cross, moved by the gesture, and read the small note: "Please keep this cross upon my daughter. It is all I can give to her."

One

New York, 1997

Victoria Ashford ran a slender finger across the line of her jaw, her cool gray eyes studying that small bit of smooth, perfect skin. Victoria had the kind of jawline that drew a man's attention, that had him wanting to place his lips there when she tilted her head just slightly. Her eyes followed the track of her manicured nail, painted a deep, deep red, stopping when she reached the puckered, scarred tissue that made up the rest of her face.

That one spot of unmarred flesh. How many times had she stared at that spot, wishing with a pain so deep it scraped her soul, that the perfection could be stretched a bit farther. She no longer wished for her entire face to be as it once was, but just a bit more, an inch or two more that wasn't covered with the horrible mottled skin that replaced her once beautiful face. Oh, and how beautiful Victoria had been. The kind of face that graced the covers of *Cosmopolitan* and *Vogue*. The kind that had women gazing at her with envy and men with lust.

"Monster."

She said the word in a whisper, watching her deformed lips in an almost masochistic way, caught up in a trance manufactured from pain and self-pity. Blinking rapidly, Victoria grimaced, more at her morose thoughts than her scarred face. "Big baby," she said aloud. She took a deep breath, wincing at the searing pain in her lungs, endless pain that would never disappear, a burning that reminded her with each breath what had happened to her that fateful day and the stupidity of the entire accident.

It happened two years before. Victoria had just signed a contract to model for Enchantress perfume, a huge contract that had all the top models in a vicious competition. But Victoria, with her face, ah, what a face, had won hands down. That her perfection had come with a soft, sultry voice had put her over the top. Weeks of fierce competition, of stress-laced meetings with her agent and the perfume company, had finally ended with a huge paycheck, guarantees of fame, and a media blitz that had Victoria completely dazzled.

High on her victory, and just a bit too much champagne, Victoria had returned to her New York apartment already planning a move to somewhere new. Somewhere exclusive and decadently expensive. She could afford it before the Enchantress contract, but now she could afford it without guilt. Twirling about her apartment, giggling, happy, she got on the phone and called her friends, inviting them over to help her celebrate. For all the time she spent alone, Victoria hated to be solitary. Hers might be the only name on her lease, but she was rarely without a houseguest.

Champagne, top-shelf liquor, catered food, was all a phone call away. Within hours, her apartment was filled with laughing people. Music played loudly, alcohol poured freely. Victoria was at her best, entertaining, the center of attention. And no one seemed to mind riding along with her.

As she put on her lipstick in a careful attempt to hide her disfigured lips, Victoria smiled at the memory despite the party's horrible ending. For it had been a party like so many others, loud and brash and meaningless. Allie had been by her side, as always, there to support her, to share her victory, her flashing green eyes filled with as much happiness as Victoria's. For they both remembered their lean days, when splurging meant taking the subway instead of walking twenty blocks. That party had been so much goddamn fun! Until . . .

She removed the lipstick from her lips as her hands began to shake with the memory of what happened on what was one of the happiest days of her life. Stupid, stupid. How could she have done such a thing? How *could* she have? But thinking back, remembering how carefree, how very high she was on happiness and liquor, it was easy to understand.

The perfume company had given her a huge bottle of Enchantress, a ridiculous bottle, two lifetimes worth of the stuff. Heaving it atop her head, laughing happily at the delighted response of her guests, she had poured the perfume over her head. Poured and poured and poured, laughing and sputtering, oblivious to a nearby candle, and then—woomph! A bright flash, screams, and suddenly, horribly, Victoria was aflame, her head a macabre torch. The stunned guests backed away at first, a reaction of self-preservation. And Victoria, panicking, not quite comprehending what had happened, began to run, screeching as if she could run from the flames that consumed her body.

Finally, blessedly, Allie had covered her with a blanket, smothering the fire, leaving behind the most awful smell of burned clothing and flesh, and sickeningly sweet perfume. It was clear to everyone standing, gaping at what remained lying on the floor writhing in inexplicable pain, that it would be better if she were dead. But she was not. Modern medicine saved her, had made her live through unimaginable physical and emotional torment. She had thought over and over, before she could speak, before even she knew the full extent of the burns: Let me die. Let me die.

But she lived.

"I'm alive." The words, rasped through a damaged throat and lips that weren't even lips, were spoken with despair. Victoria took the deepest breath her ravaged lungs would allow, to give herself resolve. Today, for the first time since the accident, she was going out in public. She had enough operations, enough plastic surgery to reconstruct her face, that with carefully applied makeup, she could pass for something human. She penciled in eyebrows with the care of an artist. She carefully placed her false eyelashes, thanking God once again that she was not blinded by the flames. She caked on foundation, special stuff meant to be used by burn victims. Nothing could be done for her nose, which had been eaten away by flames and replaced by plastic surgeons with something that only resembled a nose. Victoria sighed as she reached for the wig that hid the fact that her left ear was also gone. Her hair grew only in obscene patches, so she decided to keep it shaven and wear a wig.

Finished, she stepped back to review her work. She grimaced, then squinted her eyes. Okay. Not bad. Not horrible.

"I can do this," she said, clenching her fists. Two years of loneliness were two years too many. She was not such a brave person, she found out. To go out, to face people knowing they would want to look away, knowing they would remember how she used to be, it had been too much. Until now. Until Allie had badgered her and pleaded with her and begged her to join the living. How she wanted to. How she wanted to simply go to a restaurant with a friend and order a meal, a glass of wine. But she was so afraid, so very, very afraid.

And now she was doing it. She would pretend it was something she did every day. She would pretend her face was not something to hide but something to flaunt. Thousands of burn victims led normal lives, didn't they?

Oh, God, she thought fighting back the burning tears, I can't do this.

Her buzzer went off, jolting Victoria out of her self-pity. Allie had arrived. After buzzing her in, Victoria hastily went to the bathroom, once again studying her face to make sure all the makeup was still in place. She was back at the door, breathless, by the time Allie gave her customary two hard knocks, as assertive and sure as the woman herself.

Victoria opened the door and eyed her friend warily, awaiting her verdict. A gorgeous redhead with green eyes and voluptuous curves despite her size-six body, Allie gave her friend the smile that made her one of the most sought-after models in the business. "You look great, kiddo."

Victoria narrowed her eyes. "Yeah. Right."

Allie's smile widened. "Okay. Not great. But good enough. How's that? Let me see." And Allie took one finger and placed it beneath Victoria's chin, tilting her head this way and that. With one thumb, she smoothed out a bit of foundation. Allie was the only person other than medical personnel who could look Victoria in the face, eyeing her critically. She was the only "friend" Victoria had left, the only one who, after obligatory visits to the hospital were over, continued to return. Her parents were so horrified, so torn apart by what had happened, they still could not look at her without breaking down. And though Victoria loved her parents dearly, she had avoided them in the two years since her accident. It was too painful for her and too painful for them. Victoria couldn't bear the looks in their eyes as they beheld their daughter. Allie was the only person that could look at Victoria without pity, could touch her face without repulsion.

"That color looks good on you. But, God, Vicki, have you lost more weight? You're not praying to the porcelain god after every meal, are you?" She grabbed her friend's upper arm, wincing when she felt hardly anything but flesh and bone.

Victoria put her hands on her hips in mock anger. "The last time I wore this outfit I was still modeling, and no one thought I looked too skinny then."

"You're impossible," Allie said, giving her friend a look of disbelief. "If I didn't have to be this thin, God knows I wouldn't be. I can't wait until I can eat like a human again."

Victoria gave a graceful shrug. "I'm just not hungry." She tried to say it nonchalantly, but something in her voice made Allie look at her sharply.

"You okay, kiddo? I mean, no more thoughts about ending it all. You'd tell me, wouldn't you?"

Victoria looked away from Allie's concern, ashamed that she had frightened her friend by her near constant talk about how miserable she was. "Allie, I would never kill myself. Never. I won't kid you. Sometimes I wish I would just die naturally, just slip away." She let out a bitter laugh. "I'm so sick of feeling lousy, of hurting. I'm so sick of feeling sorry for myself. I hate what I am, inside and out." Seeing her friend's distress, she added, "This is helping. Really. Getting dressed up, putting on makeup, looking forward to something. You've no idea."

Allie gave a tentative smile. "You're sure you're okay with this? I know I bullied you . . ."

"No. I needed to be bullied. You're the only one with enough chutzpah to snap me out of this funk. Ugh. I don't know how you've put up with me."

"Me neither." But Allie was smiling broadly now. She had worried endlessly that forcing Victoria out into the world might be wrong. She wanted everything to be perfect and *normal,* knowing how difficult it must be for Victoria. Her heart ached for her friend, but she would never let Victoria know how much seeing her suffer affected her.

"Okay, skinny girl, we're ready to face the world. Right?"

Victoria smiled. "Right, Allie Cat." Allie smiled at Victoria's use of her nickname. She hadn't used it in a long time, and that she had meant she was happy.

In the taxi, Victoria felt the beginnings of panic. She had rarely left her apartment in the past two years except to travel to and from the hospital. She thanked God she lived in New York, where everything could be delivered. She hadn't realized just how isolated her existence had become and was shocked by the feeling of foreignness that swept over her at the simple act of sitting in the back of a cab.

Traffic was light, so the trip to the East Side took less than twenty minutes of white-knuckled driving.

The cab swung in front of the restaurant, stopping with a jolt. Allie stepped smartly out of the cab and headed to the restaurant's entrance, as if she were late to a meeting. She stopped suddenly, squeezing her eyes shut at her insensitivity at leaving Victoria in the taxi, probably quaking at the prospect of departing that relatively safe haven. But when she turned around ready to apologize, her eyebrows rose in surprise and admiration, for Victoria was right behind her looking determined and confident.

"I'm scared shitless," Victoria sang pleasantly, making Allie laugh.

"Here goes nothing, kiddo." And Allie pushed open the revolving doors into the entrance to Anthony's. Approaching the maître d', she flashed him her best smile. "Hello, Joel. Our table ready?"

"Miss Roberts, Miss Ashford. So nice to see you both," Joel said, nodding casually as he grabbed two leather-covered menus and led the women to the table they had shared countless times over the years. Assisting the women into their seats with practiced ease, he presented the menus with a crisp gesture. "Agatha will be with you in a moment. Please enjoy your lunch."

Very normal. Too normal. Victoria gave Allie a half smile and shook her head slightly. "Well done, Allie," she said, with just a hint of censure in her voice.

Allie looked up with mock innocence. "What?" But she couldn't help but smile. "Okay, okay. So I might have told some key people that you were coming to lunch. Shoot me."

A part of Victoria wanted to do just that, the part that lived in a fantasy of denial, that told her that with makeup and a smart suit, she could go back to her old life. The other part, though, was thankful Allie had warned the restaurant of her arrival. She had been terrified of the looks of pity and horror she was sure she would see in the eyes of others. "Thanks," she said.

She stared at the menu, unwilling yet to look around the room, to see who else was dining. Chances were she would recognize several people, and she wondered if they would recognize her. She corrected herself silently; they would not recognize her, but they would know it was her. Slowly, the quiet murmur of voices seeped through the deafening noise of her blood pounding in her ears, and Victoria caught herself smiling. She had done it. She was in a restaurant, about to eat a meal with her best friend. She hadn't felt this good in years.

"You okay?" Allie asked, leaning forward and tilting her head a bit.

"Yeah. I'm fine. Really fine. This is good, Allie. I needed this. I'm in a restaurant!" She couldn't help but widen her grin. She was so damn proud of herself.

The meal went forward without a hitch, and by the time Victoria was sipping her coffee and Allie was drinking her cappuccino decaf, the two women had forgotten that they were doing anything special. For the first time in a long time, they talked about work, laughed about old times, and even delightfully and viciously observed some of the other patrons' bad taste in clothing.

They were having so much fun, they didn't notice the skinny woman in baggy tan pants and an oversize T-shirt hiding behind the trunk of a palm tree, snapping pictures rapid-fire. The woman stood there for twenty minutes, changing lenses, changing film. And when she was finished, when she got what she came for, she slipped a hundred-dollar bill into the hand of a smiling waiter.

"So. Not so bad." Allie flipped a bit of her red hair out of her eyes so she could catch her friend's expression as the cab pulled out into traffic. She sighed happily when she saw the smile on Victoria's face. She had taken a huge chance with Victoria, she knew. If the lunch had backfired, if something had gone wrong, Allie would not have been able to forgive herself. Every outing would not be as well planned as this, and certainly, someday someone would hurt Victoria. But it didn't happen today. Thank God. And now there would be more lunches, maybe even a party someday. Easing her friend back into life would not be easy, but it would have to be done. Allie would be damned if she'd stand by and watch the only true friend she had ever had slowly kill herself. Not that she blamed her.

So many times Allie had wondered if she would have had the strength Victoria had to withstand not only the hideous reminder of the accident, but the god-awful pain she suffered along with it. Simply breathing in and out was agonizing for Victoria, who refused to take the pain medication her doctor had prescribed. Laughing was torture, but Victoria still laughed in an odd raspy way, clutching her stomach so that she would not breathe in too deeply. Allie knew there were times Victoria was almost overwhelmed by self-pity, when she truly wished she would die in her sleep. But maybe, if there were more days like today, the nearly obsessive thoughts of death would end. Allie was sure Victoria would never take her own life, for as much as she denied her Catholic upbringing, Victoria could not shake deeply held beliefs of mortal sin. But how far was wishing to die every waking minute, from actually being dead?

"I feel alive," Victoria said, and Allie suspected she'd somehow read her thoughts. Victoria let out a throaty laugh. "Actually I feel pretty damned good. You know, for a time there, I forgot. I actually forgot everything." Her throat constricted with emotion. "Thanks, Allie Cat. You've no idea what this has meant. Being normal. God! I've been so full of self-pity and so whiny! You should have slapped me."

Allie laughed. "You've been a trooper. If the roles were reversed, you would have done the same thing. Except I probably would have chickened out."

Victoria sat back, relaxed and happy, not minding even the taxi driver's mad swerves in his race with other taxis. Today was the beginning of a new life. A different and difficult one, but one that held promise. Oh, yes, she thought, I can do this. I can be human again.

Three days later she would hold a full bottle of painkillers in one shaking hand, a glass of wine in the other, ready to commit a mortal sin to escape her pain, her emptiness, her life.

Two

When Allie saw the picture in the *National Globe* while standing at the checkout stand in her neighborhood IGA, she let out a small horrified gasp. The sound led the woman behind her to comment, "Gruesome, isn't it? She used to be so beautiful."

The photo, obviously taken at Anthony's, was a cruel close-up of Victoria in the midst of a laugh, her eyes halfway closed giving her an almost drugged look. Allie thought Victoria's smile beautiful. But the photo showed a face distorted and, indeed, gruesome. Looking at the *National Globe,* she saw Victoria the way a stranger would: with pity mixed with revulsion. An inset showed Victoria the way she had been, a photo reminiscent of those old Hollywood glamour shots. Victoria had never been more gorgeous than she was on that day. The comparison was vicious. The headline was almost worse than the photo: BEAUTY GONE TO BEAST.

Tears flooding her eyes, she dumped her handbasket on the floor and pushed her way through the line, ignoring the affronted shoppers she left in her wake. Oh, how could they have done it? How could even the *National Globe* so callously played up such a tragedy? Slumping against the outside of the IGA, she held a hand to her mouth, willing the sobs to stay put. Suddenly she stood erect. What if, somehow, Victoria had seen the magazine. She would be devastated. Allie knew Victoria had her groceries delivered and knew she never bought such tabloid trash, but she had to see Victoria. Now. She could not ignore the panic she felt, the overwhelming feeling that her friend needed her. "Hold on, kiddo. I'm coming."

Victoria's copy of the *National Globe* lay on the couch next to a small pile of unopened mail, the large manila envelope the tabloid had come in beside it. She didn't care who sent it, she told herself. She was glad. Indeed grateful. For hadn't she just been kidding herself? She winced as she remembered how just that morning she'd been flipping through a catalog trying to pick out a nice outfit for her next lunch out, how she'd experimented with her makeup, thinking how good she'd looked. Breathing in painful gasps, Victoria abandoned the magazine and looked into the mirror, the efforts with makeup still on her face.

"Idiot," she screamed as loud as she could, not caring how much it hurt. "Stupid fool. Ugly, hideous fool!" She crumpled to the floor and rocked back and forth, letting out low moans of anguish. "It hurts," she sobbed, letting all the self-hatred and self-pity she'd been putting aside for days to come out at once. "Oh, God, I want to die. I want to die." For the first time, it seemed, she truly meant it. She had always held out hope, even in her moments of deepest despair, that things would get better, that something in this life was worth the suffering. But now she knew the truth. Her life would never change. She would live in pain for years. A beast. The headline was true.

It is not self-pity, she thought, it is reality. And now I am facing it. This is my life, living as a recluse, hiding from the world. Maybe others are strong enough to face the world, but Victoria found that she was not one of them. She would never be the spokeswoman for a burn center, for fire safety week. She would live the rest of her life as she had the last two: alone. To Victoria, that was not a life. No hope of falling in love, no hope of having a family. She knew, even in her deepest despair, that she had always held out the hope that she would meet a wonderful man, one who didn't care about appearances, one who would love her for who she was. And they would have children, two or three. Despite Victoria's life as a top model, she always pictured herself as a regular person, with a nice house and a big yard with a swing set in the back. But that was just a fantasy, a hurtful dream. Reality was this apartment that she would live in alone until she was old. There would be no husband. No children. Just long, empty years of endless physical pain. That was her future, and it was intolerable.

She stood slowly, calmly, taking the deepest breath her lungs would allow, and walked to her bathroom, where a nearly full bottle of painkillers was stored. She had refused to take the things, hating the foggy numbness more than the pain. Carrying the amber plastic bottle with her, she walked to the refrigerator, where a half-empty bottle of Chablis was stored. Should I leave a note? she thought idly. Should I lay the copy of the *National Globe* across my body for dramatic effect? She smiled. Maybe she would do just that and some other tabloid could run the headline: FORMER BEAUTY KILLED BY MAGAZINE. She uncorked the wine and poured a generous portion into one of her favorite wineglasses. Are you sure? she asked herself. And she felt a calmness steal over her, a sense of rightness. Yes, I'm sure. Forgive me God. Please forgive me.

Allie, out of breath and near frantic, shoved some money at the cabby and ran to Victoria's building. Pressing impatiently at Victoria's buzzer, she hit it several times, growing more and more panicky when there was no response. A teenage boy with ridiculously baggy jeans and five earrings in each ear sauntered up to the door, pushing it open almost violently, obviously not caring that he was letting an unauthorized person into the building. Thanks, punk, Allie thought as she ran through the door.

She stabbed at the elevator button, willing herself not to press the lit button again, knowing it would do no good. Finally, the telltale ding sounded, the doors opened with agonizing slowness, and Allie was on board, pressing the eighteenth floor and suppressing a scream of frustration when, as if the elevator was conspiring against her, the doors snapped open just as they were about to close.

An elderly woman stepped into the elevator, moving so slowly Allie felt the overwhelming desire to simply grab her arm and heave her forward. "Would you press ten for me, dear?" she asked. Allie was tempted to say she was in a hurry, but she found herself pressing the number and gritting her teeth. Each second seemed like an eternity to Allie, and by the time the doors slipped open on Victoria's floor, she was convinced she would find her friend in a pool of blood, the *National Globe* by her side.

Instead, she found herself stunned when Victoria answered the door almost immediately, an odd smile on her lips.

"Oh. Hello. I . . ." After expecting to find the worst, Allie was at a loss for words, finding her friend unscathed. Here she had been ready to dial 911, and Victoria was calmly greeting her at the door.

"You saw the *National Globe,* I take it," Victoria said serenely, stepping back and letting her friend in. She was not angry that Allie had interrupted her. This would give her a chance to say good-bye, to see once again the one person who had stood by her.

Allie gave Victoria a sharp look. Something was wrong. Not as wrong as she expected to find, but definitely wrong. Victoria had obviously seen the magazine and was acting nonchalant about it. She should by hysterical, crying, swearing at her for forcing her out that day. Maybe I've underestimated her, Allie thought, a crease marring her beautiful face.

"So you saw that trash. How come you're not more upset?" Allie asked.

Victoria clenched her jaw. "I am upset. Very upset. But grateful, too." Victoria gave her friend a look that stopped whatever it was Allie was about to blurt. I shouldn't have said that, Victoria thought. I shouldn't give Allie any fuel, any clue about what I'm planning.

"I know now that I'm still a curiosity. Next time we go out, I'll expect something and I'll be better prepared," she lied. "It's really sort of funny when you step back and look at it objectively."

Allie turned red. "It's not funny, it's horrid. You should sue the bastards."

And Victoria thought: For what? Telling the truth? Instead, she shrugged indifferently.

"You're trying to tell me that this didn't bother you?"

"I said it did bother me. I'd have to be made of rock for it not to bother me." She turned away quickly so Allie wouldn't see the sudden tears that flooded her eyes. Blinking rapidly, she kept her back to Allie and walked to the kitchen. "Want some wine? I was just about to pour myself some."

"No. I . . ." Allie shook her head. She had felt such a feeling of dread. She'd been so certain something was wrong. Victoria was not having a normal reaction, and the more Allie thought about it, the more she realized Victoria was trying to cover her pain. Allie followed Victoria into the kitchen, fully intending to force her to admit her anger and hurt. She stopped cold when she saw the open bottle of pills on the kitchen counter.

"In pain, Vicky?" Allie said, her green eyes narrowing dangerously.

Victoria spun around, her gaze darting guiltily to the prescription. "Yes, I'm in pain." And to Victoria's disgust, her eyes spilled over.

"Oh, Vicky," and Allie pulled her friend into her arms. "That's not the answer, kiddo, you know that."

Victoria allowed herself to be comforted for a few moments, then pulled away. "Then, what is the answer? I don't have it, or I'm sick of looking for it. Allie, I can't stand it anymore, okay? I'm sorry. I'm weak. I'm vain and shallow and a coward. But I can't stand this life anymore. I don't want to die, but I don't want to live, either. And right now, dying seems better. I never thought it would, but it does. I wish I could just throw this life away, and get a new one."

A new life. Allie shivered, remembering a former model who had wished for much the same thing. She'd gotten hooked on crack, tried suicide more times than most people who knew her could count. Allie hadn't heard from her in years, and wondered if she had finally been successful. She was not too bright and rather pathetic, Allie remembered, and so she had never given a second thought to the loony story she had spun about a Chinese mystic in Boston who claimed he could give people "a new life." The model had returned from her trip to the Bean Pot unhappy, claiming the mystic had rejected her as a client even though she'd been prepared to pay thousands for his services.

The guy must have been a quack or a crook, Allie had thought at the time, and dismissed the entire story. But now the fact that the so-called mystic had refused to take the model's money—if indeed that is what happened—made her give the craziness another thought. It would be insane to troop to Boston and visit this quack, an act driven by pure desperation. But what was the alternative? Allie had a knob of fear growing inside her that felt like an ice cube stuck in her throat; she was certain this time Victoria was serious. Maybe visiting the Chinese guy would give her hope. Maybe by the time they traveled to Boston, Victoria would have gotten over her depression. If she treated the trek as an adventure rather than as a last-ditch effort, maybe Victoria wouldn't be completely devastated when the guy turned out to be a nothing.

And if it worked? Allie smiled. Victoria would be happy again. Allie knew nothing of the mystic's meth-

ods, but if he came through on what he promised—
no matter how it was accomplished—any amount of
money would be worth it. If Victoria had anything, it
was money.

Victoria scowled darkly at Allie. "What is there to
smile about?"

And Allie told her. "He's probably a crook, but
what's there to lose? I remember how excited that girl
was, how sure she was this guy would be able to give
her a new life. She was ready to spend some pretty
big bucks. If what she says is true and the guy actually
rejected her money, maybe he's legit."

Victoria shook her head. "No way." She was afraid
to believe in something so wonderful. Her intellect
told her that nothing could change her life, and she
felt threatened by the seed of hope Allie's story had
planted.

Allie's shoulders slumped. "Why not? Why not just
visit the guy. We'll know in two seconds whether he's
for real or not."

"He probably preys on people just like me," Victoria said. But something in her voice made Allie believe she was not completely against the idea.

"No, not like you. You're intelligent. You'll see
through him in a second if he's a fake."

Victoria hugged her arms across her middle. "I'd
like to think that I am. But what if I want to believe
so badly that I do. I don't think I could stand it."

Deciding to play tough, Allie said, "You were
standing here not fifteen minutes ago ready to throw
a whole container of pills into your gut. What the hell
could be worse than that? So what if it's crazy? We
should at least find out what this guy's all about. I
know it'll probably turn out to be nothing. But if
there's a chance. Victoria, think about it. That's all.
I'm no more convinced than you are, but I'm willing
to give it a try."

Victoria let out a bitter laugh. "Allie, this is my life
we're talking about here."

"True. But you are a big part of *my* life. Get it?"

Victoria threw her friend a smile. "You're so tough."

"I gotta be where you're concerned, since you're such a wallflower."

Victoria burst out laughing. No one ever had accused her of being shy. "Fine. We'll give this Chinese mystic a visit. What the hell."

Allie was so relieved that Victoria had decided not to end her life, she almost burst into tears. Seeing her expression, Victoria shook her head. "I don't think this changes anything, Allie. It just puts everything off." She fought the despair that once again gripped her heart.

After Allie left, Victoria battled with herself over her decision to travel to Boston. She didn't want to get her hopes high, but couldn't help it. No matter how many times she told herself he was likely a fraud, she couldn't help but pray he was not. If only the man could help her. She had no idea what it was all about, but it was probably some sort of hypnosis. She could picture him now, a wizened old man with bald head and pointy white beard waving a watch in front of her face. "You are beautiful, you feel no pain," he would say. "When you look in the mirror, you will see your face as it once was."

Victoria laughed aloud at her fantasy. If hypnosis was this man's secret and it worked, so be it. She was willing to give anything a try. Anything to get her life back, even if it was only in her mind.

Three

Victoria looked up through her fine mesh veil at the ordinary office building on the fringes of Boston's Chinatown, and then down at the slip of paper in Allie's hand that contained the address of John Wing, the infamous mystic. "This can't be it," Victoria said. She had expected to walk through dirty alleys, searching for a half-hidden door that led to rickety steps and finally to the dark, smoky den of the mystic. The building she stood in front of contained lawyers' offices, insurance agencies, and doctors' offices.

Allie stared at the address, as if staring would change the fact that where they stood matched what the piece of paper said. Shrugging, she said, "We can at least look." They walked into the building, across the gleaming tile floor, and stood before a large directory listing all the building's inhabitants.

"There." Dr. John Wing, suite 420.

"*Dr.* John Wing? Maybe we've got the right building, but do we have the right guy?" Allie asked as she followed Victoria into the elevator.

It had taken Allie two weeks to find the model who had visited the mystic all those years ago. The woman was a waitress now, married, with two kids. She was apparently off drugs, a little on the plump side, but appeared remarkably happy, Allie thought. She got a little shiver when she remembered what the woman had told her. "It was the luckiest day of my life when

John Wing rejected me," she'd said. "I'd be dead right now if he hadn't."

Allie hadn't understood. "I thought you said this guy was supposed to give people new lives."

"He does," she'd said, hugging her arms across an ample bosom. "But doesn't that mean the life you have now is gone? Doesn't that mean you die?"

Allie supposed it did, and she prayed that whatever John Wing did to help people didn't mean that she would lose Victoria forever. She had thought that John Wing gave people new lives in a figurative sense, that he was some sort of psychologist or hypnotist. Never in a million years did she think he could actually create a new life for someone. The idea was absurd.

The elevator doors slid open, halting Allie's thoughts, and she looked over at Victoria to gauge her mood. With the white veil and slim white suit, Victoria looked chic and elegant and incredibly composed. "Nervous?" she asked.

"Nope. I have absolutely no expectations about this guy. 'Expect nothing, and you won't be disappointed,'" she quoted.

"I guess."

Victoria had lied. In the long days following her near-suicide, she had allowed herself to fantasize that her endless nightmare was nearly over. She would be watching some inane sitcom on TV and let her mind drift to visions of herself walking on a beach, smooth-faced and lovely, a faceless man on one side and a little toddler on the other. And then she would catch herself, disgusted that once again she had allowed herself to dream such a happy scene. No matter how strongly she berated herself, she simply couldn't stop the daydreams and that butterfly nervousness she felt whenever she dared to think: Maybe it's possible. If only, if only it is true.

She knew she was setting herself up for a terrible disappointment, one she would not recover from. She knew it, and yet she persisted. Finding the offices of John Wing so very ordinary blotted out a bit of that hope. The former model must have been stoned when she visited Dr. Wing. He had probably gently refused her money because what else could he do for a disillusioned woman who expected a miracle? He was an ordinary physician who had somehow developed an extraordinary reputation. The poor man probably had desperate, pathetic people knocking on his door daily.

Victoria's stomach clenched uncomfortably. She did not want to make a fool of herself. She did not want John Wing looking at her with pity as he carefully explained that none of what she had heard was true.

"Can I help you?" a young girl, looking barely out of high school, asked them.

"I have an appointment with Dr. Wing," Victoria said.

"Victoria Ashford?" At Victoria's nod, the young girl picked up a phone and quietly informed whoever was at the other end, that they had arrived. "Dr. Wing will be right with you, Miss Ashford."

Allie and Victoria exchanged a look that expressed both their surprise at their surroundings. Allie whispered, "Maybe we do have the wrong John Wing?" Victoria shook her head as if to say she was as in the dark as Allie.

Their attention was drawn to a handsome young man, clean-cut, wearing an oxford cloth shirt and conservative tie beneath a white doctor's smock. "Miss Ashford, I am John Wing." He walked directly to Victoria and offered his hand, only glancing politely at Allie. "If you'll come with me."

When Allie made to join them, he said, "I'm afraid I need to see Miss Ashford in private." Allie grabbed Victoria's hand and gave it a little squeeze. "Don't do anything until you talk to me," she warned.

Dr. John Wing led Victoria to a small office that contained a desk with two leather chairs positioned in front. Two diplomas were tacked to one wall, a potted plant sat beneath the office's only window, and a painting of the China countryside graced another wall. The painting and John Wing were the only *Chinese* elements in the rather stark office that looked like any number of doctors' offices Victoria had been in.

"If you please," Wing said as he gently lifted the veil from her face. The movement was so smooth and unquestioning, Victoria had no time to protest. But Wing's demeanor and slight smile immediately put her at ease. He looked at her face with the disinterest of other doctors she had visited. Victoria had left off any makeup, believing it better that Wing see the full extent of her injuries. It was a casual exam until he looked straight into her eyes. He had kind eyes, mature, it seemed, beyond his years. And there was something else about that intense gaze, something that made Victoria went to squirm in her seat and look away. But she held his brown eyes in her gray ones for what seemed like several minutes. She did not realize she had been holding her breath, until he looked away and sat down behind the desk.

"What kind of doctor are you, exactly?" Victoria asked in her raspy voice, trying to sound authoritative. "I mean, you look like a doctor doctor, but . . ."

Wing smiled broadly. "I take it I'm not what you were expecting, Miss Ashford."

Victoria smiled back, relaxing a bit. "No. I expected a wizened old man. Someone a bit more Chinesey, if you know what I mean."

Wing let out a short laugh. "Well, I am Chinese. But no, not old. I have an M.D. from Harvard and have a regular general practice. Perhaps you should tell me why you are here."

Victoria had the distant feeling that he already knew, but she was not sure whether her request for a "new life" would be met with pity or interest. Wing's face, so animated before, was now completely devoid of expression.

"Well, I . . ." She laughed nervously, her composure

crumbling. "Believe it or not, I heard you had a special talent, um, special training to help people." God, do I sound lame, she thought, cringing inwardly. Heck, girl, just spit it out. "Something to do with giving people new lives?"

"Ah, yes. I thought so." He seemed to study her, taking in every detail of her face, stopping again at her eyes. He tapped one finger on his ink blotter and took a deep breath, closing his eyes just briefly. Victoria braced herself for a kind, but firm lecture on life's realities. Finally he spoke.

"I come from a long line of, and I know how this sounds, believe me, mystics. My ancestors going back thousands of years have studied this art, rather like a religion. It is my religion. I take it very seriously. It is not a frivolous thing."

"I am not here for a frivolous reason," Victoria said softly.

Wing leaned back in his chair then. "Why are you here?" he asked.

Victoria blushed, suddenly feeling very foolish in front of this Harvard-educated physician. "As you can see, I suffered an accident about two years ago."

"I remember reading about it," Wing said.

"Yes. Well. My life, as it is, has become intolerable. I nearly committed suicide about two weeks ago. Allie stopped me in time. I'm Catholic, or at least I was raised Catholic. But I still believe in my heart that suicide is a sin." Victoria bit her lip. "That didn't matter to me. Doesn't matter to me anymore."

"Is it the loss of your looks? You were once very beautiful, but there are many people who have suffered as you have."

Victoria let out a long sigh, feeling defeat hovering close by. "That is part of it, I can't lie. But it's more than that. It's life, my life. Before the accident I really lived. I was so happy, so alive. I've thought about that, how I took it for granted. I never was down. Never. I lost more than a pretty face, Doctor. I died that day, and this life I've been living . . . I'm in constant pain. Someone who doesn't have this sort of pain, the kind that will never end, can't know what it is like. I don't mean to whine, or complain. I know how I sound, how this must look to you. I know there are people worse off than me that somehow rise above it." Failure covered her like a shroud. "Maybe I should go."

"No, Miss Ashford. I believe I can help you."

Victoria tried to stamp down the joy those words brought. "How?" she whispered.

"I can give you a new life." And his lips held just the slightest hint of a smile.

"Hypnosis or . . ."

"No. *A new life.*"

Victoria shivered. "I don't understand."

Wing leaned forward so he could gaze into her eyes again, and somehow Victoria was transfixed. "So many people come to me. Yes, people worse off than you, Miss Ashford, although you have suffered greatly. But most carry a terrible flaw in their heart, in their soul. I cannot help someone with blackness on their soul, with hardness in their heart. You, Miss Ashford, are pure of heart."

Victoria almost laughed aloud. "I'm no saint," she found herself arguing.

Wing smiled. "No. Not a saint, for even saints sometimes cannot be helped. I turn people away, broken, sad people, almost daily. People who are willing to give me anything, willing to do anything for help."

Victoria was skeptical. "Then, why me? I have, as you must know, a great deal of money."

"I have turned away clients with a great deal more to spend than you, Miss Ashford. I have explained why I can help you; it matters not whether you believe it or not. It is simply true."

Victoria couldn't help but shiver, for Dr. Wing suddenly sounded more the mystic than the physician.

"What do I have to do?"

"First," Wing said, that odd little smile hinted at, "you must die."

Four

Wing let out a short laugh upon seeing the look his news produced on Victoria's face. "I'm sorry, Miss Ashford. I tend to get a little dramatic. It's a flaw."

Victoria relaxed slightly. She suddenly wasn't so sure she trusted Wing, and eyed him skeptically. "The whole reason I'm here is so I won't die," she said.

"I realize that. Again, I apologize. I was talking in the physical sense, not the spiritual one. If we proceed, your body will die, but your spirit will continue."

Victoria frowned. "You mean like a ghost."

"Oh, no, nothing like a ghost. You will have a body, it simply will not be your own." Wing cursed himself as he watched Victoria's frown deepen. He was constantly forgetting that what was commonplace for him, was strange and frightening for his patients. How many times had his father and his grandfather before him told him that he must be more gentle with his patients.

"Let me start at the beginning. Every human has two lives, a spiritual one and a physical one. It is much more difficult to kill a person's spirit than destroy their body. In a sense, your body has been damaged beyond repair. But your spirit, Miss Ashford, is vibrant and pulsating. In the simplest of terms, I have the ability to send your spirit into a healthy body whose spirit has departed."

"You mean into a dead person." Victoria was repulsed by the idea.

"Yes, exactly."

"You mean to tell me you've done this before? That there's a bunch of people out there living in the wrong body? I find that really hard to believe. Really hard."

His finger began tapping again. "Of course it is difficult to believe. It is beyond your experience. But I can assure you that it can be done. That it has been done. My grandfather had ten clients, my father, seven. It is not common. It is, in fact, extremely rare."

Victoria was ready to walk out. This was ridiculous hocus-pocus. As disappointed as she was, she was also angry with herself for believing for just one minute that *Dr*. John Wing was anything more than a quack.

"And how many clients have you had?"

"One." He said it without apology.

"One patient. Not much experience, if you ask me," she said, crossing her arms and giving him a disdainful stare.

Wing was aware Victoria did not believe him. It made no difference to him whether she believed him or not. He had only the truth to back him up and the knowledge that he was giving it to her. "I have centuries of experience."

Ah, Victoria thought, suppressing a laugh, the Chinese mystic is back. "Really. This is ridiculous," Victoria said, finally getting angry at Wing. "You should be ashamed of yourself. It's not that you take the money. It's that you give people hope . . ." Her eyes filled with tears, and she angrily dashed them away.

"Damn," Wing said softly. If his grandfather were alive, he would berate him until *he* cried.

"Miss Ashford, please. My grandfather would blame my youth for my insensitivity, for my inability to put you at ease. I wish he were alive today, for he had a gift of communication. I was always amazed that with a single look, my grandfather could make people be-

lieve in him. It is a gift I am sorely lacking." Wing
heaved a sigh. "I suppose it *is* my youth."

Victoria looked at him through narrowed eyes.
"You can't be for real," she said. But there was something in her tone that gave Wing hope, that told him
he had not lost one of the rare people who were pure
of heart.

"I am. It is all I can say. I sometimes believe it is
a curse and not a gift my family has been given. I hurt
more people than I help. I turn away so many people,
good people who are suffering. But I must turn them
away. You, Miss Ashford, I cannot turn away. I can
offer you no proof. I can give you no names. I can
only say that, yes, I can help you. I can give you a
new life. I could make a solemn vow, but so could
someone evil who takes advantage of people. I know
it would be meaningless if you do not already trust
me."

Victoria was engaging in a battle within herself. The
guy sounded so sincere. But this spirit stuff, this travel-
ing into another body, was absurd. Wasn't it?

"You say my body dies. How will anyone know
whether I'm really dead or just my body is dead? If I
agree to proceed, how will anyone know that you have
succeeded? If you fail, obviously I can't do anything
about it. I'll be dead. I'd want justice. If it did work,
I'd want to contact Allie and let her know that it
worked. And if I don't contact her, I want her to have
you arrested for murder. And if I don't die at all, if
nothing happens, I'll slap you with the biggest mal-
practice suit this state has ever seen. Don't think I'll
be too embarrassed to do it, either. I'll do it, believe
me."

Wing gave her that smile she was beginning to hate.
"If you decide to proceed, it will work, but it is unlikely you will be able to contact anyone—at least
not directly."

"Why not?"

Wing gave a small sigh, letting the air out through

puffed out cheeks, obviously reluctant to explain his point. "You will be placed in the body of a woman who has lived, and died, sometimes in the rather distant past." Wing halted her outburst with a raised hand and a beseeching look. "I know that is the most implausible aspect of this. But you see, in some respects, it is easier to control the past than the future. If your soul were placed in the body of a contemporary woman, you might change what the future should be."

"But if I'm in the past, isn't that even more dangerous? Couldn't even the smallest thing change the future?"

"That is the common belief, but I'm afraid it is simply not so. Very few human beings have the capability of changing history in any significant way. But if we proceed, there are certain rules you must follow. Certain stipulations."

"Such as?"

"I can't marry, can't have children, can't murder anyone, can't tell anyone who I really am. That's about it. Oh, and I have to solemnly vow not to do these things."

Victoria and Allie had been sitting outside the office building in their rental car for several minutes while Victoria explained the entire procedure.

"You don't actually believe all this, do you?" Allie asked.

"Of course not," Victoria said, snorting. "But . . ."

". . . you're willing to give it a shot anyway," Allie finished.

"Well . . . yes."

"Okay. You're dead. You're in this other body two hundred years ago. Why can't you fall in love and marry and have kids? I mean, what's the point of having a life if you can't fall in love?"

Victoria gave her romantic friend an indulgent smile. "For one thing, say I marry some guy who was supposed to have married someone else and have ten kids with this other woman. By marrying me, I'd technically be preventing that marriage and those kids from happening. And that would change history. *I* can't have kids because the woman who died and who I have taken over is supposed to be dead, not popping out a bunch of kids. See what I mean? I can live a life, relatively happy, but I have to abide by the rules. I can't run for president, or start the women's liberation movement a hundred years early. It's really all just common sense."

"And what happens if you break the rules?"

"Supposedly I die," Victoria said reluctantly.

Allie placed a hand on her friend's wrist. "Oh, Victoria, I should have never brought you to this guy. I should have known it was a hoax. I'm sorry."

Victoria looked out the window blindly. "I'm gonna do it."

"What?!"

She turned her body to face Allie, her eyes bright with excitement. To Allie, Victoria looked a bit out of control. "I've nothing to lose. Imagine going back in time? Living the life of another person? At least it will be interesting. I'll be able to walk around, no one will stare. I'll be able to fill my lungs with fresh air. I'll be free, Allie."

"Even if you could go back in time, what about this life? What about your parents? Have you ever thought that if you leave your body, to the whole world it will appear as if Victoria Ashford is dead? The reason I thought of this guy was I thought he could give you *your* life back, not someone else's." Allie refused to say what she was truly thinking: She would lose her friend forever. The only difference between suicide and this craziness was that at least Allie would be comforted knowing Victoria was somewhere happy.

"So what happens to your body?"

"Dr. Wing has a plan," Victoria said slowly. "I told him I'd think about it for a couple of days. I'm not convinced, Allie. I'm not crazy. I know this probably won't work. But just think if it does? Imagine it."

"I'd rather not, thank you very much," Allie said dryly. "By the way, any idea whose body you'd be entering?"

Victoria smiled at Allie's sarcastic tone. "Not yet. I get to pick from two or three. Dr. Wing has to do some, I don't know, research I guess."

"Research."

"Yeah. Research. You know, Allie, it wouldn't kill you to be a little bit more supportive about all this. It was your idea, you know."

Allie saw red. "It was *not* my idea that you would die. It was my idea that you would get help and stick around a little while. Maybe you can be glib about leaving this world behind, but forgive me if I'm not glib about losing my best friend. *If* this guy isn't pulling a fast one. And how do you know he isn't just going to kill you, take the cash, and then tell me the transfer was successful. Hmmm?"

"I can't be sure. I can't be sure about anything. But if I die, then I'm still better off than I am now," Victoria argued. "Anyway, I'll find a way to let you know whether it worked or not. Somehow. Please, Allie, try to understand. I'm not taking this lightly. How could I? It's my life we're talking about. And I'll miss you, too."

Allie scowled, refusing to cry. She would lose her friend no matter what happened. "Yeah, well, you'd better."

Victoria smiled. She had made her decision to allow Dr. Wing to transport her, but she felt a bit better knowing Allie supported her decision. Even if it was given a bit grudgingly.

Over the next two days, Victoria, for Allie's benefit, made a great show of weighing the pros and cons of putting her life in Dr. Wing's hands. She visited Dr. Wing the day following her first visit to hear about the lives she might choose from, leaving the office full of hope. She had been given three choices—a 1920s English actress, killed in a car crash in California, a wealthy recluse who died by her own hand in 1874, and an Irish immigrant who died in childbirth in 1898. The child had lived.

Victoria chose the Irish girl, even after being told that she could not keep the child; it would have to be raised by the adoptive parents it was destined for. To keep the child would mean her death, Dr. Wing had told her, his voice stern, his eyes hard. Victoria agreed without hesitation, but a tiny part of her heart rebelled. For this child she would bear would be the only one to come from her womb, would be her only chance to be a mother. The fact that it would not be *her* body made no difference.

Having made her decision, and choosing the woman whose body she would enter, Victoria found herself becoming detached from her own life and time. She forced herself to act interested in the news, in Allie's chitchat about some war between two agencies over a model that Allie insisted looked like an emaciated twelve-year-old. But in truth, nothing interested Victoria—except a woman called Sheila Casey, long dead and long forgotten. She wanted to visit her grave, she wanted to go to the library and read old newspapers to find out what was happening in her time. She wanted to begin her new life *now*.

Two nights after her first visit to Dr. Wing, she broke the news to Allie. She might have expected a lot of things from Allie, but for her to burst into tears was not one of them.

"Please don't," pleaded Victoria. "Please don't cry." Having never seen her stalwart friend cry, never mind this heart-wrenching sobbing, Victoria was at a loss.

"Oh, God. I'm sorry," Allie said after blowing her nose loudly into the tissue Victoria offered. "It's just that I'm losing my best friend. And you don't even care."

Victoria smiled at the last dramatic statement, which was followed by another bout of sloppy tears. "Of course I care."

More sniffles. "I know." It came out "I doe."

"And it might not even work."

Allie stopped crying then, her eyes still bleak. "I have this feeling it will work, Vicky. I guess that's why I'm so upset."

Victoria could not stop the rush of happiness. It *was* going to work.

"Allie, if this works, I'll find a way to let you know. This is going to be a miracle. This is going to be incredible."

Five

It was pure hell, that's what it was. Something must be wrong, Victoria thought frantically. It hurt too much. Dr. Wing never said anything about this excruciating pain.

"It's not working, Doc," she muttered as she tried to open her eyes. She let out a groan. "It hurts." Victoria felt as if her body were being pummeled. And she was cold, so cold. She shook her head in a mad effort to communicate to Wing. Why wasn't he listening? A sharp pain assaulted her, making her double over. "Stop it! Stop it!" she shouted, desperate now and more afraid than she'd ever been in her life.

Victoria and Allie, in the car Victoria had rented, had driven to a small lake in western Massachusetts, followed by Dr. John Wing in his own car. The parking lot and the lake were deserted, for it was a raw, drizzly day. Victoria's body would be found here by an anonymous passerby—Allie—who would call the police. The death would baffle local police, for no obvious signs of death would be located. The coroner, Wing told them, would find no evidence of suicide or any disease. He would conclude that Victoria Ashford's heart had simply given out—even though it would display no signs of cardiac arrest.

Allie and Victoria had already said their tearful good-byes at the hotel, clutching each other desperately, with Victoria promising she would never forget her friend. "You're saving my life, Allie. Don't you ever forget that."

At the lake, they held hands while Dr. Wing began. He was in the driver's seat, Victoria in the passenger's, slightly reclined, and Allie knelt outside not caring that she was getting wet. The last thing Victoria could remember before the horrible pain began, was turning her head to look at her friend and smiling. Allie smiled back, but her eyes were filled with tears. And then . . . it seemed that all she had done was close her eyes, and the agony had begun.

"She's back with us." A soft female voice. Victoria sighed with relief.

"Didn't work?" she managed through a raw throat—and she wondered if she had been screaming.

"Everything's fine, dear, God be praised. You've had a little girl."

Victoria's eyes snapped open, and she searched for the soft, reassuring voice. Blinking her eyes, she finally focused on a smiling face that definitely did not belong to Allie. Another sharp pain had her crying out, and she felt a hand clutch hers. As the wave lessened, she opened her eyes again, searching until they rested again on the nun's kind face. She felt herself smile. "It worked."

The nun seemed momentarily puzzled by her odd comment. "Yes, dear. God has blessed you with a little girl. It's a miracle. We thought we had lost both of you. Father Dennis was giving you comfort when you awoke. A miracle, Miss Casey, a true miracle."

Slowly, Victoria became more aware of her surroundings, of herself—her new self. Her legs were spread and tied to wooden posts, and she saw who she assumed was a doctor busily doing something between her legs. He was frowning. "The bleeding has stopped," he said, as if he were displeased with that discovery. Victoria winced as he continued his rather rough examination.

"Ow!" Victoria let out, wincing from his probing

exam. "It's a bit sore down there, Doctor." She said it more to amuse herself than to berate the doctor, to hear her voice, to hear how it sounded in her own head. She had done it! She was actually in Sheila Casey's body. Sheila Casey, who had died one hundred years ago. Suddenly, she stilled, and everything happening to her and around her seemed to fade away. Lifting her hand, she gazed at it with wonder. It was so small! Sheila Casey's nails were cut short and were a bit grubby. The smooth back was sprinkled lightly with freckles, and she had a scar running between her thumb and forefinger of her left hand. *My left hand has a scar.*

Lifting that hand, she touched her face. Her smooth, unblemished face. Delicately, her hand trembling, she touched her lips, her eyelids, she traced the arch of one eyebrow, then the other. Beautiful, beautiful face.

She turned her head to see the nun watching her with interest. "I'm alive," she said, and she felt her lips curve up into a smile.

"Yes, dear."

The doctor had finished packing something between her legs, and stepped around the bed so he could get a look at his amazing patient. The girl had been dead. He was certain of it. He stared at her as if he could somehow see in her face the reason she had recovered. He had done nothing, for once it became clear the mother was lost, he had spent all his time trying to save the babe. This girl would have no more children, partly because he had thought her dead and had not taken the care he might have otherwise, and he told her this, gruffly and with little regret. Oddly enough, the girl seemed relieved. Or perhaps she was simply grateful to be alive, for it was impossible that she was lying there smiling and talking to Sister Margaret. He told her that, too.

"I came back, didn't I? I died." Victoria asked, sensing that the doctor was confused by her miraculous recovery.

"You appeared to have passed, yes." He shifted his attention to the nun. "I'll be heading home now. Send for me if you need me."

When the doctor was gone, the nun untied Victoria's legs, lay them gently on the bed, then set about removing the bloodied sheets she lay upon with remarkable ease. Victoria was silent while she went about the task of making the bed around her, but her mind was going a mile a minute. This is so weird, she thought. This is so incredibly fantastic! She wished she could explain to the nun the real miracle of her being alive. Another rather painful contraction interrupted her thoughts.

"They'll continue for a day or so," Sister Margaret said, noting Victoria's wince.

"When can I see my baby?" Victoria hadn't realized she was going to ask that question until it came out of her mouth.

The nun frowned. "We find it's best in circumstances such as yours that you do not see the child. It just makes it more painful for you. I'm sorry."

Okay, Victoria thought, they do things a little differently in the 1890s. A 1990s woman giving a child up for adoption would be allowed to hold her baby, even care for it for a time in order to make sure she was making the right decision.

"I have no intention of changing my mind about the adoption, Sister. I simply want to see my baby girl. She is the only child I will ever have, and I want to see her, that's all." Victoria kept her voice devoid of emotion, but her heart beat crazily inside her chest. My baby. I want to see her. I want to hold her. I want . . . Oh, God, I want to keep her.

But she knew she could not, and that thought nearly overwhelmed her. Why should she feel any connection to another woman's baby? Why should she care whether it was adopted or not? It didn't make sense. She had come on the scene after the baby had been born. And yet the urge to see her was almost staggering.

The nun hesitated. It was strictly against St. Mary's rules. Parents for the baby had already been found, and this girl had signed papers giving her little girl up more than a month ago. She knew when she signed those papers that she was relinquishing all rights to her child.

Sensing her dilemma, Victoria persisted. "Just once. Just for a moment."

Sister Margaret looked about her to see if anyone were listening. "Tonight, then. If you can walk." Then she quickly walked away, her black robes snapped out behind her in her haste.

Victoria slept for most of the day, recovering from Sheila Casey's birth and her own exhausting experience. She was oblivious to the mostly silent women in the ward, disturbed only by the smart steps of the nuns who cared for them. The packing between her legs was changed sometime around midday, and Victoria awoke, startled to remember where she was. And who she was. Although much of the day passed by in a haze, by the time the ward was murky from the night and the hospital's sparing use of its gaslights, Victoria was wide awake.

She lay unmoving for several moments as she got acquainted with her new body by moving an arm, a leg, her mouth. Her tongue investigated her new teeth, which were in definite need of a good brushing. One molar toward the back was missing, and her bottom teeth seemed to be a bit crooked. Victoria smiled. Even the imperfect teeth were amazing to her, and she longed to look in a mirror to see what Sheila Casey looked like.

Everything seemed to work and everything, oddly, seemed to be hers. She was almost surprised that her new brain was telling her new body what to do. "Hello, hello, hello, hello," she said softly, testing her voice, which came out slightly higher than her own harsh alto. It was smooth, almost musical-sounding to Victoria, who had become used to her scratchy, fire-damaged voice. Somehow that startled her. It was like hearing a stranger's voice, but it was her voice now. Just as this compact little body, still swollen from the baby, was her body.

Her hands went to her neck, where a chain lay damply against her skin, fingers searching for whatever object the chain held. When she made out the familiar shape of a cross, Victoria smiled; Sheila Casey may have been a sinner in the eyes of the church, but she had held on to her beliefs. Victoria was feeling under her hospital gown, exploring her new body when Sister Margaret approached her. Her face filled with heat as she quickly brought her hands from beneath her gown, embarrassed to be caught in such a position by a nun.

"Do you think you can walk, Miss Casey?" the nun whispered, her brown eyes darting nervously about the ward.

"I think so," Victoria said, and proceeded to heave her legs over the edge of the bed. Her vision swam for a few seconds, and she winced as a painful stab erupted from between her legs.

"You're too weak," Sister Margaret whispered, laying one hand on Victoria's shoulder.

"No. I want to see her."

"This goes against my better judgment. There are reasons for our rules," the nun said.

"I don't want my baby. I just want to see her." Victoria knew she was lying, although she was still baffled by the bond she had with a baby she'd never seen, a baby that truly was not even hers. Perhaps part of Sheila Casey was still inside her, the part that longed to hold her child, the part that caused an ache deep inside whenever Victoria remembered she must not try to keep the baby for herself. Wing told her she would die if she broke any of her vows, something Victoria forced herself to repeat as they made their way to the nursery.

They walked along a gleaming hall that smelled of wax and sickness, Sister Margaret leading the way, turning now and again to be certain Victoria was still following. She stopped by one door, letting Victoria enter first. Three little babies lay sleeping, bundled so tightly they looked as if they could not move a muscle. Their heads were covered by little caps, so only their red and wrinkled faces showed. Moving forward, her habit rustling in the silence, Sister Margaret moved toward one crib, soundlessly motioning to Victoria.

Her heart beating hard in her chest, Victoria peered over the edge of the whitewashed wooden crib at the tiny bundle. My daughter. The thought seemed to come from nowhere, and this time when a sharp pain assailed her, it was in her heart.

"She's beautiful," Victoria whispered. She was, of course, nowhere near beautiful. She was a mushed-face, mottled-red little being. But Victoria thought she was looking at an angel. "I know I can't keep her," she said aloud, more for her own benefit than Sister Margaret's.

"No, my dear. You know it's for the best. She'll be in a good and loving home," Sister Margaret said, her eyes touched with concern for the girl who looked at the babe with such love.

"When are they coming for her?"

"Tomorrow. Her new mother and father are coming for their daughter tomorrow." Victoria knew Sister Margaret was trying to be kind by forcefully reminding her that she was not this baby's mother, at least in the eyes of the law.

Victoria rubbed the back of her hand against the baby girl's cheek, smiling at how soft it was. This is the last time I will touch you, she thought, the last time your mommy will smile down at you. Victoria's whole being rebelled against the idea, and yet she knew it had to be so. She had made a bargain, and she must abide by it. Nothing could be less attainable than this little girl, she reminded herself. I have a life now, I am whole, and that will have to be enough.

But later that night when the ward was dark and silent, Victoria lay awake trying to think of a way to keep her daughter, for somehow, that is how she had begun to think of that little bundle down the hall. "My daughter," she whispered, hearing a stranger's voice. She tried to remember what Dr. Wing had told her. "The baby must be raised by her adoptive parents. Her destiny must be fulfilled," he had said. But he had not said Victoria could not see her, could not be a small part of her life.

Victoria smiled, feeling Sheila Casey's lips respond to her happiness. There was a way. God help me if I'm breaking my vows, but I have to try. Victoria gingerly made her way out of bed and headed toward the nursery, praying she would be able to pick out her baby from the rest. It turned out to be surprisingly easy; one of the babies was a boy and the other girl had a thick thatch of blond hair. A quick search of the room produced the items she looked for—a pencil, paper, and diaper pin. She pinned Sheila Casey's cross to her little girl's swaddling clothes and placed a note atop it.

Across the street from the St. Mary's Hospital, Kevin Donnelly and a young boy watched the well-dressed couple, who had entered the hospital with nothing, leave with a baby in their arms.

"Where're they from, boy," Donnelly asked the scruffy lad beside him.

"Louisville Square," the boy said, wiping his nose on a well-used sleeve. Donnelly jerked his head once and gently cuffed the back of the boy's head, pleased he had gotten that information from the driver. "Well-done, me boy. Well-done."

His thoughts then turned to Sheila Casey, the tiny little Irishwoman, who lay recovering from childbirth. It had been no easy task finding out where she had disappeared to. But now that he knew where she was, Donnelly vowed he would not lose her again. He considered visiting her, then as quickly rejected the idea. Better to keep her a bit off her guard, he decided. Sheila had managed to avoid him for a month now, and that was one month of lost wages, Donnelly figured. With her ballooning with child, the two could have scammed even more cash from Boston's good folk. She was his bread and butter, he had to admit. And the babe just might turn out to be a silver platter to lay that bread and butter on.

His light blue eyes narrowed as he watched the carriage pull away from St. Mary's. Rich folk had no business stealing their babies, no business coming to the poor side of town to take what was theirs.

Spitting out a bit of tobacco he'd worked clean from his battered cigar, the man noted the fancy carriage and the couple's fancy clothes. Beacon Hill might as well have been stamped onto the side of the forest-green carriage, he thought, growing angry. Weren't Irish, that was for sure. But they were willing to raise an Irish babe and call it their own. A flash of anger burned through him.

"Wonder how much Sheila got for the babe," he said, thinking aloud. One look at Kevin Donnelly's face told the boy it would be better to not venture a guess.

Six

Victoria swallowed a huge lump that had lodged in her throat ever since Sister Margaret told her she needn't worry about her baby girl, a very nice and very wealthy couple had adopted her. Although she tried to chalk up her sadness to postpartum depression, Victoria knew the real reason she was so blue was she held little hope that she would be able to find her daughter.

"I should be happy," she said softly, but the tears that filled her eyes spilled over. What an ingrate. I get a new life, and all I can do is cry about it, she chastised herself silently. For some reason, Victoria knew her happiness was now directly tied to that little baby she had seen only twice. Why she had forged such a tie was beyond her comprehension. It made no sense, it simply was.

Victoria knew that for the rest of her new natural life, she would search for her daughter, she would wonder if every baby she saw was hers. The chance the new parents would keep the cross on their daughter was slim. The chance she would ever get close enough to a baby to check whether it wore a cross was even slimmer. "It seemed like a good idea at the time," she grumbled to herself.

Victoria did have a plan, of sorts. She knew the adoptive parents were wealthy, and she knew Sheila Casey was not. She didn't know much about Sheila Casey, but she figured she must have been some kind of maid. In every old movie about the rich she had ever seen, the family had been served by someone with an Irish brogue. Basing her plan on information garnered from old movies wasn't the best method, but it was the only information Victoria had to go on. Since she couldn't rub elbows with the kind of rich people who had adopted her daughter, she would have to work for them. Victoria almost laughed aloud at the thought of her cleaning for a living. Even after her accident, she had kept her maid service. To Victoria, dishwashers washed dishes, the laundry service cleaned clothes, and someone else did everything else.

The next time she saw Sister Margaret, Victoria asked her how to go about getting a position in a respected household. She prayed it wouldn't be in the home of some cranky old woman who never had guests. For her plan to work, she would have to obtain a position in a home that entertained, where she could eavesdrop on conversations and determine what couples had recently adopted a child. In the right household, Victoria had no doubt that it would only be a matter of days before she could put enough clues together to find her daughter.

Four days later, Sister Margaret gave her the good news that she had found a position for her. "They're Protestant, of course," Sister Margaret said. "But they are willing to hire Irish girls if they come with good recommendations. I have assured them you are a good girl, a hard worker." The nun's voice held a bit of warning, letting Victoria know the good sister had gone out on a limb for her.

"Thank you, Sister," Victoria said, with just the right amount of meekness.

Now that Victoria had a job, she wanted to begin as soon as possible. For the sooner she began working, the sooner she would find her baby. To Victoria's frustration, the doctor continued to refuse to allow Victoria to leave her bed. "I have to admit, Miss Casey, your recovery is remarkable, just short of a miracle.

But I must insist you remain abed for another five days."

Victoria huffed out an impatient sigh. In her time, women lobbied heavily to be released from the hospital in forty-eight hours instead of just twenty-four, and here she was arguing to be discharged just shy of a week. "Doctor, where I come from women are discharged from the hospital much sooner than this."

The doctor raised his eyebrows in disbelief. "And just where do you come from?"

"New York."

"I'm afraid I don't believe that even in New York women would be allowed to get out of bed in less than a week." With that, he walked away, assuming his orders would be followed.

After the doctor left, Victoria turned her pleading eyes to Sister Margaret. "Sister, you found me a position, and I am deeply grateful. But if I don't start immediately, I'm afraid I may lose it." Seeing that the nun was considering her plea, Victoria rushed on. "I have no home, no family, no job, no money, . . . no anything. If I lose this chance, they may hire someone else."

Sister Margaret wrung her hands together in consternation. Seeing that she was about to fold, Victoria played her last card. "If you don't discharge me, I'll simply leave," she said softly, but with a determination the nun could not ignore.

That did it, as Victoria knew it would.

Once dressed in Sheila Casey's ragged dress, Sister Margaret led her to a nearby bench and forcefully got her to sit down while she disappeared in search of what Victoria assumed was Sheila Casey's only worldly goods. Poor Sheila, Victoria thought, fingering the rather stained dress she wore beneath a well-worn coat. She would probably never know what Sheila Casey was like, whether she was happy to be having a child or loved the man who gave it to her. "I'll be good to her," Victoria whispered. "I'll love her enough for the two of us."

Victoria lifted her head at the sound of Sister Margaret's smart footsteps.

"This is all you had with you," she said, holding out a small cloth bag with a drawstring top.

Looking inside, Victoria drew out what appeared to be immigration papers, a bit of lace cloth, a Mass card, and twenty-five cents. "This is all?" What was she to do with no money? She didn't even know where Sheila Casey lived so that she could get a change of clothes. She could not show up at her new job wearing the stained, ragged dress she wore.

"How did I get here?" Victoria asked, bunching up the useless bag in her hands.

"A cabbie brought you in. Said he found you on the street. You don't remember?" Sister Margaret's eyes were filled with compassion.

Victoria shook her head. "And no one has been here to see me."

"No."

Victoria was relieved but saddened that Sheila Casey had truly been alone in the world. And now Victoria was, too. Okay, girl, you need clothes; you have no money. Figure something out. But it was Sister Margaret who read the situation before Victoria was forced to spell out her predicament.

"The church has some clothing. If you are in need," she said hesitantly. "There is no sin in accepting charity, Miss Casey. The sin is in being too proud to accept it."

Victoria, knowing she had no choice, had to stop herself from jumping at the opportunity for some free clothing. A poor woman who had just borne a child out of wedlock would be humble and a bit awed by this nun's compassion, and so Victoria immediately put on what she hoped was an expression of gratitude tinged with embarrassment. An hour later, Victoria left the hospital, wearing a "new" dress and carrying a battered suitcase containing two others, one that Sister Margaret described as her Sunday dress, as it was slightly finer than the other drab things. "Ready or not, new life, here I come."

"Holy shit," Victoria whispered as she stood outside the four-story stone mansion on Beacon Street in Boston's Back Bay. One hand fingered the cold, elaborate wrought-iron gate that separated the elegant property from the street. Wide stone steps, guarded by two stone-carved lions, led up to a massive carved door that looked too heavy for a single person to open. Thick, beveled glass windows gave no hint of what the interior of the mansion looked like. "So this is what old money looks like."

Victoria was no stranger to rich people, but somehow those modern rich now seemed tacky. Victoria had been middle class to her bones until her modeling career had taken off. When she was a child, she'd thought her parents were rich. After all, the Ashfords had two cars, two color television sets, and an aboveground pool with a red cedar deck. They were the envy of their small neighborhood. But they were not rich. This, thought Victoria eyeing the elaborate stonework near the roof, was rich. It was the kind of money that bought Newport "cottages" and owned, not just invested heavily in, railroads and steel mills.

She let out a long breath, letting her cheeks puff out. "Wish you were here, Allie-girl. I sure could use you about now," she said under her breath. A horse and buggy clip-clopped by just then, empty except for a uniformed driver, a startling reminder that Allie was a long, long way away. Two lifetimes away, to be exact. But instead of fear overwhelming her, Victoria felt a rush of excitement. God, this was going to be fun!

"Hey, miss! Miss!"

It took Victoria a few moments before realizing the voice calling out was calling out to her. The body attached to the loud voice was a young girl, her cheeks blooming color, compensating for that rather drab brown of her hair visible beneath a small white cap.

"Yes?" Victoria's first instinct was to turn away, to hide her scarred face. With a flash of joy, she remembered who she was, and beamed a smile at the slight woman hurrying toward her.

"You the new scullery maid?" At Victoria's nod, the tiny woman put on a show of mild exasperation. "Well, that's what I thought when I saw you just a'standing out here gawking at the house. You needn't be afraid. It's just brick an' mortar," she said, her voice carrying a lovely Irish lilt. Opening the gate, she continued her speech.

"We was expecting you. Mrs. Loveless, and believe me, her name fits her right enough, has just begun her rantin' about where the new scullery is. You and me's to work together in the kitchen. It's low work, but it's my first. And the Grants, they're one of the few houses hiring Irish, so I've heard. I expect to get promoted soon enough. Hey, ain't you a little old to be workin' as a scullery maid?"

Victoria smiled at the young, energetic girl. It was impossible not to. "Don't tell anyone," she said conspiratorially, "but it's my first position, too."

The eyes of the little maid grew huge. "What was you before?"

"I lived at home with my mother, but she recently died," Victoria ad-libbed quickly.

"So you're an orphan," the girl said with drama.

Victoria tried not to think about her parents, who were likely horribly grieved by her "death," and said, "Yes. I suppose I am."

"Well, we can be your family now," the girl chirped. "I'm Anne Finley. And you're Sheila Casey."

Victoria's head was nearly spinning by Anne's unrelenting perkiness. "Yes, I am. But I go by Victoria, my middle name."

"Victoria it is, then. Though I got to be honest with you, I prefer Sheila. It's a good Irish name, it is."

Victoria found herself biting her lip trying not to smile at Anne's obvious pride. "My grandmother was English," she explained.

"Ahhh," she said, with almost as much sadness as she had expressed when learning Victoria was an orphan. "Well, I won't hold it against you." And she beamed another smile at Victoria.

Victoria quickly followed Anne as she walked briskly down a brick walk, turning her head now and again to make sure Victoria was keeping pace. And honestly, it was not such an easy accomplishment. Walking was not the most comfortable thing to do right now, even after all her days of bed rest, but Victoria gritted her teeth and bore the pain as best she could, praying that the trickle of blood she felt would be absorbed by the cloth between her legs.

She found herself following the girl through a door to a long hall that led to a monstrous kitchen. A huge wooden table split the room in two. Half of the kitchen was lined with counters, ovens, and a large stove with eight burners. The other half contained sinks and dark-stained cupboards stacked high with dinnerware of several types, from ordinary to what looked like fine bone china. The brick-red tile floor was spotless, even though food was being prepared by what seemed to be a platoon of workers. Pots and pans of every size hung over the wooden table from large iron hooks. The kitchen looked surprisingly modern to Victoria, similar to the kitchen in a large banquet-type restaurant where a chef she once dated worked.

"Here she comes," Anne whispered. She could only have meant Mrs. Loveless, a formidable-looking woman who marched toward the pair. She was dressed in a dark gray gown that looked to be starched so stiff, a quick movement might cause it to crack. The high neck bit into her loose flesh, and folds of skin drooped over the collar. She was not, Victoria thought, an attractive woman. In her old body, Victoria would have loomed over the woman. But in Sheila Casey's petite frame, she found herself looking up the enormous and hairy nostrils of Mrs. Loveless. They were the biggest nostrils Victoria had ever seen on a woman, and she had to force herself to stop staring.

"I am Mrs. Loveless. This is my kitchen. These are my workers. Note that no one is talking. Note that everyone is neat and clean. Note that they only speak to me when spoken to. Note that they work diligently, thoroughly. If you emulate them, you can remain. Anne will explain the other rules. Break them, and you will no longer work here. That is all."

It was only at the end of this rather ridiculous speech, clearly made to intimidate the cowed, that Mrs. Loveless turned to face Victoria and she gasped aloud. Mrs. Loveless, bless her ugly face, had been gifted with the most brilliant, beautiful green eyes Victoria had ever seen. She almost asked whether she was wearing contacts, before stopping herself.

"Are you deaf, girl?" Mrs. Loveless asked, her rather bushy eyebrows snapping together. "I asked if you had any questions."

Victoria shook her head distractedly. "I'm sorry, Mrs. Loveless. You have the most beautiful eyes I have ever seen." She said it with such sincerity that Mrs. Loveless was momentarily made speechless. She harrumphed. She cleared her throat. Her gray pallor turned the tiniest bit pink.

"I will not tolerate such personal remarks," the woman finally said.

Thinking Mrs. Loveless had turned away, Victoria shrugged and rolled her eyes at Anne. The next thing she knew, her head snapped back from the force of a blow. Holding a hand to her burning cheek, Victoria gave Mrs. Loveless a look of complete shock. She had never been struck before. "That is the last time you will show disrespect," the housekeeper said, and turned away.

Anne grabbed her sleeve when Victoria made to go after the woman, and forcefully drew her from the room and into what looked like a large pantry. "You're a cheeky one," she said, eyeing the livid red mark left behind by Mrs. Loveless's slap. "You don't want to cross her, Victoria."

Victoria folded her arms and looked out the door, directing what she hoped was a scathing look in the general direction of the already hated Mrs. Loveless. "I guess there's no labor board or anything around here."

Anne screwed up her face. "A what?"

"Never mind. But someday, Mrs. Nostrils is going to have to learn how to take a compliment." Then, thinking of how truly ugly the woman was and still feeling the sting of her blow, Victoria silently amended herself. It was likely Mrs. Loveless would not get another compliment.

Anne flung one hand over her mouth to stifle a laugh at Victoria's nickname for Mrs. Loveless. No one, ever, had made note of Mrs. Loveless' cavernous nostrils, not even in private. "I think I'm going to like you, Victoria. That is if you're here long enough to get to know." She paused, giving a cautious look at the pantry door. "I'll tell you something. But you didn't hear it from me, right? Mrs. Loveless ain't afraid of no one, but one person."

Victoria smiled, loving Anne's sense of drama. "And who would that be? Mr. Grant? Mrs. Grant?" Victoria asked, referring to her employers.

"Nah. They's pushovers. Mrs. Loveless is afraid of Sister Margaret over at St. Mary's. You *might* have heard of her. Just thought you should know."

With that bit of information imparted, Victoria knew nothing short of an act of God—or an act of Sister Margaret—would get her fired. It was a wonderful bit of information to have.

By day's end, Victoria wasn't feeling a bit wonderful. Her back ached, her hands were red and raw from washing dishes in scalding hot water and soap, which she swore must have had acid in it. Also her feet felt like they had swollen two sizes from standing all day. Whine, whine, whine, Victoria said to herself as she followed Anne to the fourth floor, where the servants' quarters were. She trudged up the stairs, holding a darkened lamp, her way lit by Anne's lamp ahead of her.

"You share a room with me and a bathing room with all of us," Anne said, jerking her head to indicate the latter. "Don't spare plumbing for the likes of us, so gets a bit nasty sometimes 'cause some of the girls are so lazy. They'll clean the house spotless but won't clean up after themselves." She wrinkled her nose to show her disgust.

Victoria entered the room, which appeared clean at the moment, and immediately noticed a full-length mirror tacked to one wall. Her heart beat crazily in her chest for a moment. *I won't look now,* she thought, *I'll wait until I'm alone. Then I can take my time.*

Victoria had lived in Sheila Casey's body for more than a week and had yet to see more than a murky reflection of her new self. Now she would be able to see with crystal clarity the face that would peer back at her the rest of her days.

"This is our washstand. Don't use anyone else's. The girls don't like anyone using their stand that ain't supposed to. We get one bath a week Saturday night, three girls to the bathwater. So if you're number three, the water's usually cold and nasty too. Not that it's ever too warm to begin with." Anne shrugged, not noticing Victoria's crinkled nose and appalled look. Lord, how she could use a nice hot shower right about now.

"I'll let you go first while I set up your bed. Don't be thinking I'll be doing that every night, now," she said, good humor in her eyes. She dipped into her apron's deep pocket and withdrew a box of matches. "Light your lamp, and I'll let you have some privacy."

Victoria took a step back, eyeing the matches as if they could somehow jump out of their box and light her on fire.

"Jesus, Mary, and Joseph what's wrong? You look like you seen a ghost," Anne said, and quickly crossed herself.

"When I was a little girl, a fire burned our house," Victoria lied. "Ever since, I've been afraid of fire."

"Ah," Anne breathed. "Then, I'll do it for you this time. But you'll have to light it yourself after this."

"No, no. I'll light the thing," Victoria said, swallowing her fear. With a trembling hand, she removed the globe, struck the wooden match, and lit the wick, eyeing the tiny flame cautiously, fully expecting it to leap out and smother her.

"There. Not so bad," Anne said, as if she were talking to a small child.

"No, not so bad."

Anne departed then, giving her some privacy. The first thing Victoria did was eye that mirror. It was just an ordinary mirror, but when she approached the glass sometime later, Victoria found herself staring at it as if it held some sort of dangerous magic. Although she had come to terms that she indeed had been transported back in time and into the body of poor Sheila Casey, seeing her reflection in the mirror would be indisputable proof. And if Victoria was perfectly honest with herself, it was a bit frightening to "meet" yourself for the first time. She hadn't thought it would be difficult. She had thought she would rush to the mirror. But now, confronted with the thing hanging so menacingly benign against one tiled wall, she was filled with unease. She had become used to her own face, for as scarred and disfigured as it was, it was still hers. Her eyes had stared back at her, her features were still discernible beneath her damaged skin. Sheila Casey's face would greet her each time she looked in

the mirror, and she wondered whether she would ever
be able to look at her reflection and see herself.

Taking a deep breath, Victoria shifted and stood in
front of the mirror. "Whoa. This is weird," she whispered, and watched as this stranger's lips moved with
the words. She stood about six feet from the glass so
that Sheila Casey's entire little body was visible in the
reflection. She looked like what her grandmother used
to call a ragamuffin: Her dress hung awkwardly on
her thin frame, bulging a bit at the middle from her
recent pregnancy.

Victoria lifted a hand to her mop of red-gold hair,
mesmerized as she watched the mirror hand follow
her lead. She had to look away. "Boy, oh, boy, oh,
boy. Okay, kiddo, calm down. That's just you in
there." Victoria swallowed heavily, watching with fas-
cination as the woman in the mirror also swallowed.
She stepped closer to the mirror, her eyes on the wide
eyes of her reflection. Despite herself, Victoria found
herself smiling. Sheila Casey had a nice face.

Greenish-blue eyes dominated her face, marred only
by dark smudges beneath them. A beautiful face, she
thought at first, with flawless skin. But after several
long minutes of studying every detail, Victoria realized
Sheila Casey had been no beauty. However, she had
a pleasing look about her, the kind of face people saw
and smiled. She looked . . . impish. That was the best
way to describe the woman who peered back at her
from the bathroom mirror. Her curling, vibrant hair,
her slightly upturned nose, the freckles sprinkled
lightly across her rather pale cheeks, all lent her a
jaunty air, she thought. Victoria's gaze drifted to her
mouth. She tested a smile, noting that Sheila Casey
had been blessed with straight teeth—at least those
that were visible. She tried a happy look, a stern one,
an angry one, a sexy one, relying on her training as a
model to practice with this new face. Somehow, sexy
just didn't seem to work, so she tried again, this time
licking her lips as provocatively as she could. The re-

sult was so comical, Victoria burst out laughing. Oh, well, she thought, no need to look sexy here anyway.

Despite her flamboyant lifestyle as a model, Victoria was an old-fashioned girl at heart, believing that one day she would fall in love and marry. Victoria had not saved herself for marriage, but she had saved herself for love. And Victoria had only been in love—or what she had thought was love at the time—once. She had foolishly thought marriage was possible. Twenty-two and completely besotted with Allen Schofield, she had mistakenly believed that when someone told you they loved you, it meant only you. But it had turned out that Allen had loved several women, not with his heart—for Victoria came to believe he had none—but with his gorgeous body. Since that disastrous affair, Victoria had steered well clear of the "pretty boys."

Unfortunately, she'd been so knock-down-drag-out gorgeous, most men without excessive vanity hadn't thought they had a chance with someone like Victoria. If they'd only known that what Victoria wanted most in the world was to curl up on the sofa with a strong man beside her and two kids snuggled in their beds upstairs, someone might have at least tried. Now, looking at her new, more ordinary self, Victoria wondered what sort of man she would attract now. Not that it mattered.

Victoria thought of her vows, and wondered what a lifetime of trying to avoid falling in love would be like, to not ever hold someone at night, to never share a sleepy breakfast with a man, to never kiss a drowsy child to sleep. It would not be the best of lives, but it would be far, far better than the life she'd just left, she told herself. But to never hold a man's hand, to feel its strength around her slim fingers . . . to never kiss him and lose herself in that delicious first-kiss feeling. To never make love. No, it would not be easy.

With a grimace for those depressing thoughts, Victoria headed to bed.

Seven

"**Y**ou, my friend, look like hell." Henry Grant said the words good-naturedly enough, but there was real concern in his eyes as he looked at his longtime friend Jack Wilkins. It had been a month since Christina Wilkins' funeral, and if anything, Jack looked worse now than he did that misty September day. Henry had never seen anything more tragic than Jack Wilkins standing before that gaping hole, his face gray, his eyes dead, holding his little baby girl, who blessedly slept through the graveside service.

Those who wept, wept for Jack, as few knew Christina intimately. His wife had kept to her room, emerging infrequently to attend various balls and social events that drew Boston's elite. It was known by most that Christina Wilkins was sickly and that Jack Wilkins was uncommonly devoted to her. Henry was among the few people who knew Jack suffered from more than the loss of a wife he loved, but from guilt that he had not done more to make her happy, to make her well. No amount of talking would make his friend believe that he had done more than most men would have. Henry suspected there was even more behind Jack's grief, but so far, his friend had suffered silently.

"I'm just tired," Jack said. "Emma won't stop crying. I've gone through three nurses in one month. Two quit because they couldn't take the crying anymore, and I fired one because she didn't want to 'coddle'

Emma and just let her cry alone in her crib. Woman had the heart of a brick."

"Babies cry," Henry said cheerfully. He and his wife had three children, all with the same nurse. "I'd lend you Gertie, but Mary would never forgive me. Anyway, they all grow out of it. Probably just colic or some such thing."

Jack shook his head. "It's more than that." It was as if Emma were . . . sad. He didn't say it aloud, but sometimes when he looked at her eyes brimming with tears, it was as if the little babe's heart was broken. He would have liked to believe she missed Christina, but in the month before her death, she had barely acknowledged Emma. She had not been ill when they'd first brought the baby home, but Christina had been unnaturally afraid to be with the baby. Though she had agreed to the adoption, Jack realized shortly after they brought Emma home, that Christina had agreed only to make him happy.

His memories of the short month they'd had as a family were painful ones. "Here you go, Christina," Jack had said gently to his wife, who lay as she did so often in her canopied bed. Emma had been with them two days, and Christina had not held her yet. In that moment, Jack, his disappointment bottomless, realized she feared the little baby being offered to her. Christina's eyes darted from the baby, helplessly up to her husband, practically begging him to understand.

"There's nothing to it, really. You just have to support Emma's head with one hand and hold her with the other. Simple." Jack held the baby suspended between himself and Christina for so long, his arms and back began to ache. "She won't break."

Jack closed his eyes and sought the patience he always saved for his wife as he watched Christina's hands fiddle with the bedsheets.

"I don't feel well right now. Maybe later," she'd whispered, staring down at her hands.

"For God's sake, Christina. She's your daughter.

Try." There was no anger in Jack's voice, just an awful resignation. "Please. Try."

"I'll just lay her here on your legs," Jack had said, and placed Emma there before Christina could protest. Satisfied that Emma would not roll off, Jack backed away from the bed, his eyes on his daughter sleeping on Christina's rigid legs. It was as if Christina had known she soon would die and was afraid to become attached to her, he now told himself cruelly. But the truth of it was, Christina didn't want Emma, and once presented with her could not even force the emotion, not even for Jack.

"Have you sent for Doc Brighton?" Henry's question brought Jack back to the present.

"He said basically the same as you. That Emma's crying is likely colic," Jack said grudgingly.

"Suzanne is still about?" Henry asked. Christina's sister had immediately announced it was her duty to care for her sister's baby, and moved in "temporarily." Henry suspected Suzanne wanted to care for Jack more than Emma, but he kept his theory to himself.

"Yes, she is. And I know what you're thinking, Henry. Don't think I don't know what that look means. But she's been remarkable with Emma," Jack said.

"And with you?"

"Yes, damn it. With me, too. She's taken care of things for me. I . . . wasn't in the best shape in the beginning, and she was there. She knows I never plan to remarry, so if you think she's hanging about hoping to become the next Mrs. Wilkins, you're wrong," he ended heatedly.

Henry gave his friend an apologetic look. Maybe he was wrong, but he doubted it. He knew Suzanne, had even, briefly, considered courting her before he met his wife. As a young girl, Suzanne had been strong-willed, as a woman she had become as unbendable as steel. Her marriage to Erick Von Arc, wealthy and twenty years her senior, was considered a wonderful match. The marriage was brief, just three years, and childless, and left her a wealthy young widow at just twenty-seven. She was such the opposite of her sister, Henry had often wondered how the same parents could have produced such different siblings. As beautiful as Suzanne was, she held no warmth that Henry could see.

What Jack needed was neither a woman as pliable as Christina was, nor as rigid as Suzanne. He ignored his friend's vow to never remarry, and Mary and he had already sat up nights joyfully developing lists of potential mates. Suzanne, needless to say, was not on their lists of prospects. Both readily agreed it was much too soon for Jack to be interested in another female, but it was time for him to reenter the world. For ten years, Jack had been unfailingly devoted to Christina, exhibiting a patience that Henry knew he never could have. It had often seemed to Henry that the two had been horribly mismatched—not only financially, for the St. Georges were ridiculously wealthy, but in temperament. Henry had never known a man who loved life as much as Jack Wilkins did, who would stop and watch a bird build its nest, and maybe climb the tree for a closer inspection. He'd done just that when they were walking along the Public Garden paths discussing Jack's latest building designs.

It was almost as if Jack had so much life in him, he had been trying to allow some if it to spill over to his sickly wife. Henry suspected Jack viewed his wife's death as a personal failure, and saw Emma's near-constant crying in much the same light.

"I'll tell you what, old pal, you bring Emma by the house this weekend, and we'll give her a dose of Gertie. If anyone can get a baby to stop crying, it's her," Henry said, slapping Jack companionably on the back. He moved his hand up to grip Jack's shoulder, giving a quick squeeze. "And it'll be good to get out, Jack. It will be good to see you."

Jack's expression immediately became shuttered, but Henry persisted. "Shall I tell Mary to expect you Saturday? Say at six for dinner?"

Jack gave his friend a weak smile. "Emma and I would be honored."

Victoria rubbed her arm where a bruise was just beginning to form. Infuriating Mrs. Loveless might have become her favorite pastime for all that the woman seemed to always be angry with her. The poor woman simply could not understand why Victoria insisted on being so nice to her, suspecting ulterior motives when there were none. Ever since Victoria had mentioned Mrs. Loveless' remarkable eyes, the woman seemed to want to beat her down and make her admit Victoria had been mocking her. That Victoria did not quake beneath her steely-eyed stare, as everyone else did, might also have been part of the problem.

Victoria had been assigned the lowliest sort of work to do, from scraping out a maggot-infested garbage pail to polishing silver that had been discovered in the attic and was so tarnished it had taken her more than an hour to clean a single setting. Humankind had advanced in the next century, she thought sourly, for at least most people had the good sense not to bother with silver settings. And how many times, when the clock was nearing midnight and every muscle in her body was aching, did she eye an unending pile of dirty dishes and wish for a nice Whirlpool to do the job for her.

But she'd take all the dirty dishes in this house rather than polish one more stick of silver. Mrs. Loveless, damn her suspicious soul, inspected each piece, throwing most back into the tarnished pile after spotting imaginary flaws.

"Mrs. Loveless, it appears you made a mistake. You put perfectly clean silverware in with the tarnished pieces," Victoria said as diplomatically as possible, while trying not to get angry.

"No mistake was made, Sheila, as you well know. Those pieces were not clean. At least not clean enough for my table." Victoria had to stifle a smile, for when Mrs. Loveless spoke, she raised her head, giving an even better view of her now-famous nostrils.

"This silverware is for your own personal use?" Victoria asked, deliberately misunderstanding the woman. Mrs. Loveless had a proprietary attitude about everything in the Grants' home. "And I prefer Victoria."

Mrs. Loveless' cheeks turned a dark red, but Victoria couldn't tell whether it was caused by anger or embarrassment. "The silverware is for the Grants' dining table, Sheila. This continued impertinence will not be permitted."

Victoria knew she had stepped over the line, but the woman was trying to make her angry. She dropped her head so Mrs. Loveless wouldn't see the anger building there, but when she lifted her head once again, her eyes, of their own volition it seemed, zeroed in on those darned nostril hairs that had no business wafting in and out of a woman's nose.

"You know, Mrs. Loveless, I bet I could make you over, and you wouldn't recognize yourself. A little tweeze here and there, a little more flattering hair . . . And I have a little pair of scissors that would work wonders on those pesky nose hairs," Victoria said, rather more loudly than she intended. The kitchen staff, which had been pretending to ignore the scene being played out before them, was suddenly put-upon to show the utmost restraint. A few of the lower servants failed miserably, letting out snickers and snorts. The cook had the good sense to depart the room before letting out a laugh that could be heard through the closed door.

And that was when Mrs. Loveless painfully pinched Victoria's arm. Victoria bore it silently, knowing immediately—even as the words fell from her mouth—that she had insulted Mrs. Loveless. Again.

"I deserved that," she said quietly, so that only Mrs.

Loveless could hear. "Sometimes I don't think before I speak. I *was* only trying to help." The older woman was momentarily confused by the admission.

"You deserve to be fired, *Sheila*. But I'll give you one more chance." And she stalked from the room. Victoria had been given a dozen "one more chances." So many that she thought Mrs. Loveless secretly admired her spunk. Fear of Sister Margaret alone could not be the only reason Victoria still had a job. For the life of her, she did not know why she continued to put her foot in her mouth every time she spoke to that woman.

"You can only have so many more 'one more chances,' " Anne said, echoing her own thoughts. Her eyes were bright, though, with humor.

"I know. I'm going to cool it for a while."

"What're you going to do?" Anne asked, cocking her head a bit.

"I'm going to be a good worker. If I keep this up, Mrs. Loveless will pink-slip me for sure. I'll be good, honest, Anne. It's just that when something pops into my head, out it . . ." Victoria stopped mid-sentence, cocking her head to listen. There it was again! Somewhere in this house, a baby was crying. Or a cat was in heat. But it sure sounded like . . . yes! A baby.

For the past two months, Victoria had kept her ears open for news that one of the elite that visited the Grants had recently adopted a baby. Anne, who had an amazing ability to find out what was happening in other homes, had been her best source. While the two worked side by side, washing endless dishes and scrubbing ever-dirty floors, Anne would talk and talk and talk. Most of her information came from her equally talkative beau, Jerry, who delivered milk almost daily, bringing news of the other households along his route. Through Anne, via Jerry, Victoria had learned of several births, a few deaths, but no adoptions. On her half day off, Victoria headed to the Public Garden off Commonwealth Avenue, hoping to find young families out with their new babies. She walked endlessly up and down the streets of Boston's wealthier neighborhoods, not knowing quite what she was looking for, coming back with her feet raw with blisters from her too-tight shoes. Every time she came upon someone with a baby, her heart beat a bit more quickly. Always, it was the same: The baby was either a boy, too old or too young. But her greatest fear was that she would find her daughter and not know her, she would pass her by.

How long would she try? When would she give up, she wondered. Each night, she'd replay the same fantasy over and over. She was walking down a street and coming in the opposite direction was a nanny wheeling a carriage. She would pause and ask to see the baby, pull back the blanket, and lo and behold, there was the cross, gleaming in the sun. She never took the fantasy beyond that, for once she found her daughter, she had no idea what she would then do. As the weeks turned into months, Victoria's hope waned, but her overwhelming need to see her daughter did not. It was a strange, hurtful longing, as if a part of her heart had been misplaced and she need only find it to feel whole again. No matter how many times she told herself that the tiny baby was not truly hers, the ache in her heart would not dissipate.

"What is it?" Anne asked, eyes growing large. "You look like you've seen a ghost."

Victoria blinked rapidly. "I hear a baby crying. I just love babies, don't you?" she asked, a little too brightly. Her whole body was tense, rigid from the hope she felt and tried to deny. She had heard babies crying in the past two months, but never had her heart responded so violently. "Let's go see her," she said without thinking.

Anne creased her brow. "We can't leave the kitchen, you know that," she said. "And how do you know the baby's a girl?"

"I don't know it's a girl," she said, though her heart told her she was right.

Gertie was having no more luck than anyone else at quieting Emma's tears. Mary, who considered herself to be a baby expert, had tried and even Henry gave his best effort, awkward attempts that drew a smile to his wife's lips. The group was gathered in a small parlor, all sitting but for Jack, who paced madly about the room.

"Do you see what I mean?" asked Jack, desperation tingeing his voice. "Something is wrong. It's not colic. It's been too long. This has been going on for two months now." Jack wiped a hand through his thick hair, already mussed from similar gestures.

"She's a crier, all right," Gertie said, chuckling as Emma let out a particularly loud screech. Laughing was the last thing Jack could think of doing. He loved Emma with all his being and seeing her cry tore at his heart. Gertie had tried all her tricks, nothing worked. Emma was now nestled in her cradle, exercising her lungs as the adults spoke loudly to be heard over her cries.

"She'll outgrow it, Mr. Wilkins. They all do. One day she'll just stop," Gertie said. And at that moment, Emma did, indeed, stop.

All in the room became still as statues, staring at each other as if trying to discern that the silence they heard was not their imaginations. As one, they turned toward the cradle and spied a tiny kitchen maid bending over the cradle, another hovering by the parlor's opened door.

Victoria could not breathe, the pounding of her heart made her deaf to all other sounds, as she gazed upon her daughter for the first time in two months. The cross, attached to her gown with a diamond-studded pin, gleamed in the soft gaslight like a beacon in a dark night. Victoria had just enough presence of mind to not squeal in delight, but she could not take the joyful smile from her lips. Taking one finger, she followed the track of one of Emma's tears, wiping away all traces of wetness.

"My God." Victoria stiffened when she heard a gruff male voice behind her. She had almost forgot she had an audience, so enraptured was she by the baby. She had barely spared the people in the room a second glance when she spotted the cradle. Keep cool, she said to herself, and slowly straightened to confront whoever was behind her.

"Who are you?" Jack could not keep the awe from his voice.

"She's a scullery maid," Mary Grant said, crossing the room to confront the wayward servant. "I don't believe you have any duties in the parlor, do you, miss?"

Victoria met her gaze, not caring that most maids would scurry from the room if faced with Mrs. Grant's steely look. "I heard the baby crying and thought I'd come see her. I like babies," Victoria finished, knowing her excuse sounded weak.

"You may return to the kitchen now, Miss . . ."

"Victoria Ash . . . Casey." Her eyes drifted to her daughter and back toward the man who was looking at her as if she'd grown two heads. With no other choice, Victoria turned to go, feeling as if she were being wrenched apart. She didn't even know who her baby now belonged to and had no idea how she could see her again. With one last look at her daughter, Victoria began to leave the parlor, her throat constricting tightly with unshed tears. As she did, the baby let out a small cry, which Jack recognized as the beginnings of a full-fledged scream.

"Stay." The word was said softly, but it might have been shouted for the effect it had on all in the room.

Victoria turned then, for the first time looking at the man who had asked her identity. She looked no further than his eyes, a deep blue that would have looked black if the room had not been so well lighted.

For what seemed like minutes, Victoria was captured in the intensity of those eyes, almost as if he had the ability to pin her to the spot with simply a look. And indeed, that is exactly what he was doing. Even though his impaling gaze was rather distracting, Victoria managed to notice he had a face found only in aftershave ads: thoroughly masculine, lean, and sexy. And a body to match, she realized with a quick perusal. She hadn't thought they grew them this good in this century. She could almost feel Allie giving her a nudge in the ribs. "On a scale of one to ten, honey, this guy's a sixteen," Allie would say.

"Miss Casey, is it?" At her nod, Jack continued. "I would like you to walk from this room and return when you hear the baby cry."

"Jack, what are you doing?" Mary asked, her eyes lit with amusement.

Jack shook his head. "I don't know. Please, Miss Casey, do as I ask."

Victoria's heart began to beat hard in her breast. It was obvious this guy wanted to see if the baby started crying when she left and magically stopped crying when she reappeared. Fat chance, she thought, knowing how important this moment was. For if the baby followed the script the man had obviously written in his head, Victoria knew she would be at least one step closer to her goal. And if the baby did not cooperate, Victoria's hopes would be dashed. For that reason, she hesitated.

"Miss Casey," Mary said, "please do as Mr. Wilkins asks."

Victoria bristled at her employer's imperious tone, but reminded herself that everyone who asked her to do something sounded imperious to her modern ears. She took one last look at her fidgeting daughter before walking slowly toward the door. Outside the parlor, Victoria spotted Anne hiding by the home's sweeping staircase.

"What's going on?" she whispered. Victoria could

only shrug as she hovered outside the door and waited, holding her breath as if the noise of her breathing would somehow drown out the noise of the baby's cry.

"Cry, kiddo, come on, cry. God, please make her cry," she said quietly. And when she heard that first angry bawl, her heart nearly soared out of her body. "Good girl," she said, closing her eyes and saying a quick thank you to God.

"Would you please come in," Mary said. Victoria could tell the Grants were enjoying the show, but a quick look at Jack Wilkins told her he was as tense as she had been while waiting to hear her daughter's cries.

Victoria immediately walked to the cradle, smiling at her daughter's angry little face. "Shhhh, shhhh." The little girl obeyed. Victoria's smile could have lit up the entire city block. "May I hold her?" she asked, feeling more powerful than she ever had—even more than when she won the Enchantress contract.

"Agoo," the babe said when Victoria lifted her from the cradle, and tested a smile out on her mother for the first time.

Eight

Victoria's brief career as scullery maid was over as quickly as Emma's tears dried. Mary Grant made a weak protest about losing a good maid, but the protest was all show, and everyone knew it. In a matter of minutes, all details of her departure were worked out and her packed suitcase was set at her feet.

"I need to say good-bye to someone," she said, finally asserting some control over her life as she stood at the front door clutching her suitcase. A taxi was waiting for her, the horse stamping impatiently, but she had decided she would not leave until she had said good-bye to Anne.

"Nonsense. The taxi is waiting," Mary Grant said, waving a hand in impatience.

"Mrs. Grant," Victoria said softly, looking Mary Grant in the eye. "If you were me, wouldn't you want to say good-bye to the only person here who was kind to you?"

Two minutes later she was giving Anne a bear hug the girl would long remember and promises that should Jack Wilkins again visit the Grants with her in tow, she would come down and say hello. "A nurse, you say? You'll not be mixing with the likes of me," Anne said, a bit sulky.

"Oh, don't be ridiculous," Victoria said, giving her another squeeze. "Where I come from, an ordinary person like me can meet the president." It was true, for she had.

"Oh, sure, and men will walk on the moon, an' fly around the world, an' machines will wash dishes." As the two were falling asleep in their tiny room, Victoria always played what she had come to know as the "do you think" game: Do you think men evolved from apes? Do you think a woman will be president, that cars will ever go one hundred miles an hour, that a baseball player will earn one million dollars a year? It was fun for the woman who did know the answers, and the one that didn't.

"Hey, I've got one for you. Do you think I would let anything as silly as this ridiculous hierarchy stop me from thinking of you as a friend?"

Anne just smiled, but blushed into her hairline and beyond the little white cap she wore. "Well, good luck to you, Miss High and Mighty," Anne said in jest, giving her an awkward hug before letting her go. It sure would be boring in the Grant house now that Sheila Victoria Casey was gone.

Jack was nearly frantic by the time he heard the taxi arrive outside his three-story brownstone. Emma had returned to her former self the moment the little maid was sent to pack. Flinging open the door himself, much to his butler's chagrin, Jack willed the young girl to hurry, for Emma's tears were driving him mad. The poor little thing wailed as if all the bleakness of the world were hers to cry about.

As Victoria stepped from the taxi, her eyes immediately went to the man standing in the home's doorway, holding her daughter against his shoulder, bouncing up and down in a vain attempt to quiet the ungodly loud screams emitting from his little bundle. His eyes were filled with relief and just a bit of terror.

"She won't stop crying. Hasn't stopped for more than an hour. I was about to fetch you myself when I saw you outside," he said, jerking his head toward the taxi.

Victoria prayed the events that occurred in the

Grants' parlor were not a fluke, for if this man wanted a nurse, he had not gotten what he bargained for. Victoria had never baby-sat for an infant as a teenager, and in the world of high-fashion models, there weren't a lot of career mommies running around. The one friend she'd had who decided to temporarily sacrifice her figure to have a child also had the money to hire a nanny. Victoria might love her daughter, but she hadn't the slightest notion how to take care of her. The only thing she could bring her employer, she hoped, was her ability to get the baby to stop crying.

Act professionally, she told herself as she made her way up a short set of worn marble steps that led to the entranceway. Act like you know what you're doing, as if his fears are unfounded. You, Victoria, are the goddamn cavalry to this man, act like it.

"I'm sure she's just hungry," she said as calmly as possible.

"But she won't eat. She won't take the bottle. I've tried." Victoria smiled at Jack Wilkins, liking him just a little upon hearing the edge of panic in his voice. It was obvious he was trying to keep control, and just as obvious he was about to lose it.

"Let me take her," she said, and was gratified when Emma immediately stopped crying. Looking up at Jack with a satisfied smile and seeing his questioning look, she could only shrug. Somehow, her baby knew her. Somehow, God had decided that they belonged together, despite nearly breaking her vow. No lightning had crashed, no booming voice had called down His displeasure. She was standing in a high-ceilinged foyer beneath a glittering chandelier, holding her baby. Every light on that chandelier could have been extinguished, for in that moment, Victoria's happy glow would have lit the entire house.

Jack didn't care what it was about the girl that made his daughter stop crying, he only cared that the crying stop. Looking at Emma, content and gurgling in the girl's arms, it was hard to believe she had been screaming not two seconds earlier.

"My goodness, Jack, you were right. It is remarkable."

Victoria lifted her head to see one of the most beautiful women she'd ever seen walking toward them. Honey, she thought, the Ford Agency would love to get ahold of you. She was a cross between Demi Moore and Andie MacDowell. Except more beautiful, if that were possible. A perfect match for the perfect man, Victoria thought, believing she was meeting Mrs. Wilkins.

"Suzanne, meet my little miracle," Jack said, his gaze resting warmly on Victoria, who flashed him a crooked smile.

"Victoria Casey," she said, reaching for a handshake. Suzanne offered her only a stony smile, and Victoria withdrew her hand as gracefully as possible, quickly realizing servants evidently didn't attempt to shake hands with their superiors in the 1890s.

Suzanne turned to the butler. "Gibbons, please find Mrs. Winters, and have her escort the nurse to the nursery," she said, dismissing Victoria. She should have been used to being treated like a servant after two months as a scullery maid, but somehow this woman's dismissal bothered Victoria more than Mrs. Loveless's loud berating ever had. Instead of retreating immediately with the butler, Victoria turned her eyes to Jack, instinctively knowing that such a gesture would anger the woman.

"I'll be up to visit Emma later, Miss Casey," he said. Victoria gave him a smile. Nice guy. Too bad he was married to such a witch.

Once left alone, except for her sleeping daughter, Victoria did a quick inventory of the nursery. It was a Victorian dream with an elaborately carved mahogany crib, canopied in frothy pink, dolls lining one wall, a huge white wardrobe, heavy pink and white drapes, and beautiful wallpaper effused with pink and white roses. Victoria couldn't help but smile when she thought about the Wilkinses picking out every detail of this room. It was awfully overdone, an exaggeration of a perfect nursery. As Victoria looked about, she couldn't quite picture the woman she'd met downstairs throwing herself into such a task. Maybe I'm selling her short, she thought.

Victoria sat down in a comfortable rocking chair with upholstery that matched the wallpaper, and held the little bundle in her arms. To her horror, Emma awoke and began to cry. She began rocking her, whispering comforting words in her ear. Nothing worked. Then it dawned on her that perhaps the baby was hungry. The crying abruptly stopped, and Victoria watched in the amazement of someone who has never held a baby as Emma's mouth opened wide at the touch of the bottle's nipple. "Good girl," she whispered. "There's my good girl."

As Emma ate, Victoria sighed with relief. She must not be breaking her vows. She was still alive even though she had fudged the rules a little. "I wonder, Dr. Wing, if you knew all along what would happen," she whispered. She would not push her luck, though. Technically, she had not kept her daughter. She had allowed her to be adopted by the parents she was meant to have. Victoria would not break the other rules. Suddenly, she thought, gazing down at Emma's perfect little face, life was too, too precious to throw away.

After putting Emma in her crib, Victoria drifted off to sleep. A soft knock jolted her awake.

"May I come in?"

A tall, slim woman walked in quickly and spied the baby sleeping in the crib. Raising her eyebrows a bit in surprise, she said, "So the little mite's asleep. You are a wonder . . . Victoria is it? I'm Etta Martin. That's short for Henrietta. Father wanted a boy, but all he got was a passel of girls. Mr. Wilkins wanted me to get you settled into your room."

Etta walked over to a door that Victoria had assumed was a closet. It turned out to be Victoria's new room. Although sparsely furnished, it was large enough to hold a large wardrobe, a bed, and a dresser. Two heavily draped windows bookended the bed, covered with an old-fashioned quilt. Victoria's small suitcase sat upon the bed.

"The bathing room is down the hall. We share that," Etta said.

Victoria prayed this house had indoor plumbing, for the thought of squatting over a porcelain pot was not a part of history she wanted to experience again.

"May I see it? The bathing room, I mean."

Etta seemed to take this request in stride. "Mr. Wilkins is an architect, you know. And even though this house was built nearly one hundred years ago, he's put in all kinds of newfangled things. We were the first house on Beacon Hill to have electric lights. The first to have a telephone, although, honestly, that thing scares me to death. Cold *and* hot running water, even. Oh, when I think of all those cold, cold morning washes, I shiver just thinking about it."

Victoria smiled and gave a little prayer of thanks for landing her in a place with all the conveniences of home. The bathroom was surprisingly spacious, containing a sink, bathtub (oh, would wonders never cease), and the kind of toilet with a wooden tank suspended above the bowl and a pull chain for a flusher. "This is wonderful," Victoria said, looking about her. "You've no idea how wonderful this is."

Etta gave a contented sigh. "Oh, I think I do know. 'Tis one of the most wonderful rooms in this house, sure enough."

When Victoria returned to the nursery, Emma was still asleep, her little fists up by her head, her legs slightly bent, as if held in place by a small spring. Victoria yawned and debated whether to join Emma in her little nap. Nestling in the soft chair again, she drifted off, a smile on her face.

* * *

"She's wet."

For the second time that day, Victoria found herself being jolted awake after having fallen asleep in a chair.

"What, what, what . . . ? Oh." When her mind finally cleared, she found herself staring into Jack Wilkins' frowning face.

Jack had not wanted to wake her. When he walked in the room after tapping softly on her door, he was immediately enthralled by the sleeping figure of his daughter's nurse. Victoria Casey was balled up like a kitten, her curling red-gold hair escaping an ill-made bun, making her look incredibly innocent. Lashes tipped with gold brushed cheeks rosy from sleep, and from her mouth, open just slightly, came just the tiniest bit of drool.

Jack found himself smiling and wanting to bundle her up and tuck her into bed. And the thought of putting the girl into a bed led to another thought— one that made him disgusted with himself, one that made him irrationally angry with Christina. For if she had allowed him his husbandly duties in the past two years, he would not be standing over this Irish girl with lurid thoughts entering his head. He would not be uncomfortably aware that, for the first time in years, he was becoming aroused at the mere sight of a woman.

And that was why when Victoria opened up her eyes, it was to an unhappy man who looked as if he wanted to beat her, not bed her. *What a grump,* Victoria thought as she jumped up quickly, wincing as she realized one of her legs had fallen asleep.

"Is something wrong?" Jack asked. His voice lacked any real concern, Victoria thought uncharitably.

"My leg fell asleep." She shook her leg, grimacing at the pins and needles, and walked awkwardly over to retrieve Emma, who was dangling from his outstretched arms. "Oh, you are wet, poor baby." The diaper was soaked, and Victoria gave one fruitless wish for Pampers before going about the task of re-diapering her daughter, who immediately began wailing. Casting a glance over her shoulder, she noted with a bit of frustration, that Jack was still in the room monitoring her progress.

"Do you want to learn how to do this, or are you just curious?" Victoria asked with a smile. Taken aback, Jack muttered a few unintelligible words before turning sharply and leaving the nursery.

Thank God, Victoria thought. For she had no clue how to use the cloth diapers. It took her three tries before she achieved results that looked moderately like what she thought they should. Emma continued to cry until Victoria again put a bottle up to her greedy lips. "There you go, Emma. I like your name. Did I tell you that? You're such a good girl." Love like Victoria had never experienced before welled up in her heart.

"What am I going to do, Emma? What am I going to do when you don't need a nurse anymore?"

Nine

Jack Wilkins was doing something he rarely did: he was brooding. He stared at the fire, more a jumble of hot coals than a fire anymore, and debated whether to add another log or let the damned thing go out. A nice fire was about the only cheerful thing in this mausoleum that had been his home since his marriage ten years ago to Christina. Slowly, he had modernized the place, installing plumbing, a furnace that ate coal at an alarming rate, and the latest, electricity that was spotty at best. Half the time, it seemed, he heard the familiar hiss of the gas lamps that told him the electricity was out. Again.

At the moment, it did not matter. The room was dark but for the dim glow seeping into the room from the huge marble fireplace. Christina's father had boasted the rare pink-hued marble had been imported from France when he gave the young couple a tour of their wedding present. Jack had been intimidated more than pleased with the huge house, a voice in his head shouting, "you do not belong here." He ignored that voice, thanking his father-in-law so profusely, he'd embarrassed the man. Jack still flushed at the thought of the young man he was, so completely awed by the family he'd married into that he'd made a fool of himself.

Jack was no longer a fool, no longer a naive young man. He was a renowned architect, a shrewd businessman, an often-seen figure at city hall, ballrooms, and men's clubs. And now he was a father.

Jack smiled, thinking about Emma, fast asleep upstairs. He had watched her for several long minutes, amazed at her smallness, her perfection. Her blessed silence.

He heaved a sigh, allowing himself to brood once again as his deep blue eyes scanned the room. Sitting alone, staring at a dwindling fire, was not what he had pictured when he and Christina had discussed adopting a baby. He had pictured Christina sitting on the settee doing needlework or reading, one foot gently nudging a cradle where Emma lay asleep. The lights would be on, illuminating Christina's blond hair, her cheeks flushed with the pleasure of motherhood.

Jack gave a bitter laugh that seemed absurdly loud in the silence of the room. *You do it to yourself, idiot. You build up a fantasy in your head and think you can make it come true.* He could do that with brick and mortar, but Jack could not do the same with his life. Even had Christina lived, that little scene would never have been played out. She had been frightened, she had been ill.

Those thoughts only made Jack frown. For Christina, his frail wife, had not been sick. He was convinced of it after years of doctors and specialists who examined Christina and then came away proclaiming vague maladies and prescribing bed rest. "Hell," he had shouted at one doctor, "bed rest is what's killing her!" Nearly every doctor who entered their house left leaving Christina more convinced than ever that she was dying. That she had been "dying" since she was twelve years old was never considered evidence that her death was not imminent.

It was Dr. James Michaels who had said the words aloud that Jack at the time had been just beginning to contemplate. A young, progressive doctor, well-respected at the age of just thirty-three, he had examined Christina four years ago. The doctor had spent more time talking with his wife than examining her, something that had frustrated Jack. He wanted action, not words. But it turned out Dr. Michaels' words were enough.

"Mr. Wilkins, there is nothing physically wrong with your wife."

At first, Jack's heart had soared. Nothing wrong! But then the words, said so firmly and definitively, began to sink in. Of course there was something wrong with Christina. She was ill, constantly complaining of headaches and weakness and nausea. Certainly she was ill.

"I don't understand," he had said. "You're saying you cannot find something. But that does not mean there is nothing wrong." Even to himself, his words lacked conviction, and Dr. Michaels smiled.

"There is something wrong, Mr. Wilkins. Your wife believes in her heart that she is ill, that she is dying. I'm convinced that when she says she feels ill, she is not lying. But that illness is not physical."

Jack had clenched his jaw and stalked around the library trying to control his anger at the doctor. "You're saying my wife imagines she is ill? Impossible. I've known her for seven years. She's always been frail, sick."

That is when Dr. Michaels told Jack the story about his wife that ultimately convinced him the doctor was probably right. It was a story Jack already knew, but Dr. Michaels shed her life in a new light.

Christina was the youngest child of the incredibly wealthy St. Georges of Beacon Hill. Coddled and smothered with love, she was also sheltered by parents who never thought they would be able to have more children. Christina's mother had been thirty-five when she became pregnant with her daughter, a miracle five years after the birth of Suzanne. Every cough, every sniffle and sore throat resulted in a mad dash for the doctor. Without even realizing it, Christina at a very young age made the connection between illness and being loved, Dr. Michaels explained. When she was sick, her mother stroked her head, her father gave her gifts. Some of her illnesses were real, some she exaggerated a bit knowingly. Because she was so tiny, so pale, her appearance only validated the fact she was fragile, a whisper away from death.

At twelve years old, Christina overheard a conversation that would alter her life. While summering in Mount Desert, Maine, Christina had become truly ill, vomiting with chills and a wrenching stomachache. The family doctor had pulled Mr. and Mrs. St. George outside Christina's room, where she lay miserable and told them what he believed to be the truth. Their daughter would not live to adulthood. She was certain to die. He wanted to prepare them, to be honest and forthright. Christina had overheard every solemn word, every choking cry from her mother, every tortured curse muttered by her father. It seemed at that moment that everything the St. Georges had secretly believed, but had been too afraid to acknowledge, was actually true. Their little girl would die.

"She had a chance before then," Dr. Michaels told Jack. "But hearing such a thing at such an age . . . It was devastating. It was undeniable."

Jack had stared out the window trying to right the world that had just tilted crazily beneath him.

"What can I do?" he had asked hoarsely.

Dr. Michaels had frowned, knowing he could do nothing. "Your wife's ailment is not physical, Mr. Wilkins. And yet I am hesitant to recommend an alienist. So many work in a completely unscientific manner."

"My wife is not insane, Doctor," Jack had bit out.

"I agree, Mr. Wilkins. But nor is your wife's illness physical, and so I cannot help."

Jack took a small sip from his whiskey as he recalled the ugly, tearful scene with Christina that had followed the doctor's visit. In the end, he had comforted her, told her that she was right, Dr. Michaels was a fraud who had no business practicing medicine. Christina had been unaccountably hurt that Jack had for a minute believed Dr. Michaels when so many other doctors had said she was ill. And Jack had not reminded her that none of the doctors had ever diagnosed her with anything specific. He had held her, and stroked her head. And believed in his heart that Dr. Michaels was right.

Jack had loved his wife. But it was a passionless love, one that held no change, no fire, just something constant that beat relentlessly against him, like a drop of water that at first is ignored, but then becomes a maddening thing.

Emma. Jack knew he had probably put too large a burden on the baby upstairs. Christina had seemed so happy about their decision, so willing to accept the baby into their home. He'd tried to make himself believe that once she got over her uncertainty, once she began to love Emma, things would be better. As he stared at the fire's last glow, Jack felt his stomach give a sickening twist, knowing in his heart that what he had been asking of Christina was impossible.

Ten

Victoria was playing in front of the mirror again, testing out her new face. "I'm too sexy for my face, too sexy for my face," she sang, and giggled.

Still laughing, Victoria walked through the bathroom's doorway, only to stop short at the sight of Jack Wilkins, looking as gloomy as ever, heading down the hall. Victoria abruptly put on a straight face, and Jack found himself slightly disappointed that his daughter's nurse immediately put away her smile.

"I thought I'd check in on Emma before retiring for the evening," he said, his gaze going beyond Victoria to see if there was anything in the bathroom that would explain the woman's laughter. Victoria found herself unsuccessfully suppressing a smile at her employer's transparent curiosity.

"I was entertaining myself in the mirror," Victoria said, her Irish complexion blushing furiously. "Making faces."

Jack looked at her as if viewing an oddity in a museum and then again looked behind her, not believing such laughter could have been self-inflicted. "I see," he said slowly, finally.

Afraid he might think her a bit flaky, Victoria quickly worked to put him at ease. "I'm usually very serious, Mr. Wilkins. I'm just really exhausted, and when I get like this, I can be rather silly."

"No need to explain," he said, but he was scowling. Victoria wondered if his face could hold any expressions other than anger, impatience, and disgust. The guy made her nervous, partly because he loomed over her because of her small stature and his large one, and partly because his dark good looks were a bit menacing. Those dark eyes of his, one minute almost black, the next a deep blue that you just couldn't help but stare at if only to see if they really were as blue as they looked. It was downright disturbing. Before Victoria's accident, she was rarely intimidated by anyone. Her height and cool beauty gave her confidence that others usually found intimidating. But Sheila Casey, bless her departed soul, was a tiny woman whose innocent little face probably couldn't intimidate a puppy.

"Will you be needing me?" Victoria asked, praying she could escape to her room. Although she had managed to sneak in two catnaps, she was exhausted and knew she was facing a night of being awakened every few hours by her hungry daughter.

"No, Miss Casey. Good night."

Once in her room, Victoria gave up a huge yawn and eyed her bed with relief. Wishing she had her old flannel nightgown, Victoria stripped down to her petticoat, carefully hanging up her dress. She wrinkled her nose at the thought of wearing the same dress again before it got a well-deserved washing. But wash day was once a week, and with only three dresses, and one meant only for Sunday, she would be forced to wear the same clothes for several days.

"How's Daddy's girl? How's Daddy's beautiful little girl?"

Victoria started, at first thinking that she had left the door between her room and the nursery open. But a quick look confirmed the door was closed, but also confirmed sound traveled remarkably well between the two rooms. It was then she noticed for the first time a grate cut high in the wall, probably so the nurses would hear every peep made next door.

"You are so beautiful. Did you know that? Your daddy loves you very much."

Victoria smiled at the tender words. It was hard to believe the man she met could utter such nonsense to an infant. For some reason, Victoria found herself pleased that he loved Emma. She had thought she would be a bit jealous of her adoptive father's love. True, she longed to say such words to her daughter. She longed to tell Emma that, yes, her mommy did love her. While enjoying the nonsensical chatter from next door, Victoria wondered how she would feel if it were Mrs. Wilkins bending over Emma's crib. Would she be happy then?

"I will have to be happy," she whispered, though her heart ached a bit at that truth.

Four hours later, Victoria cringed hearing her daughter's bleating cries once again. Did she never get enough to eat? she wondered. Heaving herself out of bed, her bare feet trudging tiredly across her thin carpet, a bleary-eyed Victoria made her way through the nursery door for the second time that night. She might tell herself it was her job as nurse to get up and care for Emma, but she couldn't help thinking it would be nice if Mrs. Wilkins at least made a show of concern. Unlike Mr. Wilkins, the wife had not been in to see her daughter, Victoria noted.

"I'm just tired," Victoria told herself, already feeling guilty about her angry thoughts. As grumpy as she was when she again heard Emma's piercing cries, as soon as she picked the tiny baby up, all anger was gone as if someone had waved a magic wand over her head. "Hungry, sweetie? Yum, yum, yum." Shaking her little head like a baby shark, Emma was soon cemented to the bottle, quiet and content. "My little angel," Victoria said, and kissed the very top of her daughter's downy head.

The night seemed endless to Victoria, but somehow morning came all too quickly. Victoria rolled her eyes as Emma let out another shriek. The crying started just as she was getting dressed for the day, and she debated whether to rush in half dressed. Deciding her hungry daughter could wait two minutes, Victoria dressed as quickly as possible, her fingers stumbling over the multitude of buttons that traveled from her waist up to a neck-choking collar. At least, she thought, the buttons are in front. She was halfway dressed when she heard her employer trying to calm Emma.

Next came a smart knock on her door. "Miss Casey, your charge needs you."

Victoria stuck her tongue out at the door. "Yes, Mr. Wilkins. I'm on my way," she said, oozing pleasantness. Forgoing the rest of her buttons, as well as her stockings and shoes, Victoria hurried to rescue her daughter. She found Jack bent over the crib, one finger trapped by Emma's fist, trying to soothe his daughter with a bottle she refused to take.

"Here. Let me try," Victoria said, taking the bottle from his hand and picking Emma up.

Jack smiled as his daughter stopped fussing and took the bottle with vigor. His eyes, gazing at Emma's contented face, were drawn to the small amount of creamy flesh exposed by the nurse's unbuttoned dress. He watched, riveted, as if he had never seen the smoothness of a woman's chest, and he longed suddenly to touch her there, to see if her skin could possibly be as soft as it looked. Shocked by his thoughts, and more by his hand that began to drift upward as if to touch that bit of skin, he brought his eyes to the floor only to be confronted by her tiny, naked feet. *Good God, I've got to get out of here,* he thought as his body reacted almost violently to what even his feverish brain knew was only a meager bit of exposed flesh.

"When you're done, come to the library and we can discuss Emma's schedule," Jack said gruffly.

Victoria lifted her head, surprised by his angry tone, only to see his retreating back.

Victoria warily entered the library an hour later, having fed, bathed, and dressed Emma, who was now blessedly asleep. She didn't knock, and so caught Jack Wilkins staring morosely out a window. "This guy is miserable," she thought, and felt a bit sorry for him.

"Mr. Wilkins?"

Jack was startled from his thoughts.

"Miss Casey, please sit down," he said, indicating one chair. Hands behind his back, he stepped over to look at his daughter, allowing himself just the shadow of a smile, then walked to his desk and sat down. "No doubt you have worked in a variety of situations. I imagine every household is different. I am unsure what your duties are, except, of course, to care for my daughter."

"I believe that is the extent of my duties," Victoria said, venturing a guess.

"Yes. Of course." Victoria was heartened by his uncertainty.

"My wife . . ." he began, then faltered. "Since my wife died, I have been through a series of nurses, all of whom have either quit or been discharged."

"Your wife is deceased? I thought . . ."

Jack immediately realized the girl had assumed Suzanne was his wife. "You met my sister-in-law, my wife's sister. My wife died of pneumonia one month ago."

"Oh, God, I'm so sorry, Mr. Wilkins," Victoria said. No wonder the guy looked so sad. He waved a hand, acknowledging and dismissing her expression of sympathy at the same time.

"My sister-in-law, Suzanne Von Arc, has overseen the care of Emma, and I would like that to continue. Emma should spend a considerable amount of time with her." Jack stopped, searching for a way to say the next.

"My sister-in-law has been a tremendous help to

me, Miss Casey, but she is not Emma's mother and we do not always agree on the best way to raise her. Suzanne tends to dominate people. It is simply her way." He had been looking at the fire, but now he turned his eyes to Victoria. She was such a little thing. How in the world could she possibly stand up to Suzanne? She would eat her alive unless he somehow empowered the girl.

"You should know that I am the only person in this household who can fire you. The instructions I give you will be followed, no matter who instructs you otherwise. Do you understand?"

Victoria inwardly grimaced, but vowed she would not be intimidated by the woman. "I understand," she said, wondering whether Suzanne Von Arc had also gotten a warning about her behavior. Probably not.

"I believe at least one hour with her aunt should be sufficient, although I do not expect you to withdraw Emma as the clock strikes. You may use some discretion. I should like to meet with you daily, say eight o'clock here. Each day, if the weather is fair, Emma is to get some fresh air. This will be the aspect of Emma's care that will receive the most challenge from her aunt. But I believe it is imperative." Jack knew he was making Suzanne sound like a tyrant, but the truth was, Suzanne was a tyrant at times. As far as he knew, he was the only person who could control her, and he believed that was only because she allowed him this privilege.

Suzanne ran his household with efficiency. No longer was he plagued with such details as planning meals and scheduling coal deliveries. In the days following Christina's death, she had taken over and Jack had gratefully let her. At first it had crossed his mind that Suzanne was trying to forge a place for herself in the household and his life, to fill the gap left by Christina. But as the weeks passed, Jack never got an indication that Suzanne was interested in anything more than helping out her sister's husband at a difficult time. And now she was such a part of the household, he fairly dreaded the time she would announce her departure as he was certain she one day would. Had Jack thought that Suzanne held designs on his heart, the situation would have been intolerable. For Jack would not marry. If he was certain of one thing, it was that.

"I'm sure I can handle Mrs. Von Arc. And I can assure you I also have Emma's best interests at heart," Victoria said, letting her gaze fall lovingly on her daughter. She let her guard down in that moment, allowing Jack to glimpse the love she felt for her daughter. That look pierced Jack's heart, for it was that look he had imagined on Christina's face. It had no place on the face of their scruffy little nurse.

"It must be difficult to leave your charges once they are too old for a nurse," he said pointedly.

Victoria looked up, sensing the mild hostility behind his words. I must be more careful, she thought. "Of course it is difficult. But I try not to get too attached. It is my job to care for babies, but I always remember who the parents are." *I must remember. I must, I must.*

Her response appeared to satisfy Jack. "Again, I expect to meet with you each evening after dinner. Good day, Miss Casey."

"Sure. See you la—" Victoria stopped herself short and continued more formally. "I'm sure I'll see you later." And Victoria scooped Emma up and walked out of the room, praying he hadn't caught her mistake.

Where *was* this girl from, Jack thought idly. She seemed to be rather well educated—until she opened her mouth.

Eleven

"**I** suppose my brother-in-law gave you instructions to ignore everything I say, Mrs. Casey. That is all well and good, but you must know that, as a man, he does not always know what is in the best interest of his daughter." Suzanne, dressed impeccably in a blue wool dress, sat upright on a small couch, her back straight and several inches from the rear cushion.

Oh, brother, here we go, thought Victoria. She didn't know what it was about Suzanne Von Arc, but Victoria simply did not like her. She refused to believe it was because Suzanne was so beautiful. If there was one thing Victoria had learned, it was that a beautiful face rarely had anything to do with what was in a woman's heart. Maybe that was it, she thought, maybe it's her heart I don't care for.

Bouncing Emma on one knee and singing the theme song to "Bonanza" just under her breath, Victoria let out a small, rebellious sigh. "Mrs. Von Arc, Mr. Wilkins hired me. He's the one who can fire me. If I want to keep this job, I've got to listen to him, regardless of whether I agree with him or not."

Suzanne smiled what could have been called a pleasant smile, except that her eyes remained cold. She would not have believed this little nobody would stand up to her. None of the other nurses had. She had directed the last nurse to let Emma cry, for clearly the baby was trying to manipulate everyone in the household. If Jack had not been so soft, she could have succeeded in getting the baby to stop its infernal crying. Instead, he brought in this ignorant immigrant. He had hired her without consultation, and now she was supposed to acquiesce to this girl? The very idea incensed her.

"Your loyalty is quite commendable," Suzanne said pleasantly.

Victoria almost laughed at how polite and yet so scathing this woman was. "We don't have to butt heads over this," she said calmly. "You must understand my position."

Suzanne wrinkled her nose at the girl's coarse speech. Most nurses were educated females from good families who for some reason were unmarriageable. They were not former scullery maids whose only talent was an ability to get a baby to stop crying. "If you think my position in this household is so tenuous that I can be usurped by a scullery maid, you are very much mistaken," Suzanne said, dropping all pretense of a smile. "Who do you think was responsible for the firings of the other three nurses? Mr. Wilkins takes my counsel very seriously, Miss Carey. You'd best remember that."

Victoria felt her temper rising and stopped herself from making an angry retort just in time. To do so just might get her fired and certainly such behavior would not have been tolerated from a servant. She took a deep, cleansing breath. "Mrs. Von Arc," she said, smiling politely, "it appears we have nothing more to say to each other on this subject. I'll bring Emma to your suite this afternoon so you can see for yourself that I can care for her."

The hour in her suite had been torturous. The woman had the warmth of a snake and the disposition of one, too. The minute she arrived, she wrapped poor Emma so tightly in a blanket, the baby could do little more than squirm. For all Victoria's promises that she would take charge, it was not all that easy.

"Your hands are like ice," Suzanne said to Emma,

casting a sidelong glance at Victoria. It was obvious the woman was blaming her for Emma's cold hands. Victoria couldn't argue, for Emma's hands did feel cold, but she was sure it was not because she wasn't dressed warmly enough.

Victoria had tried to be understanding at first, for in a way Suzanne was rather pathetic in her attempt to maintain control. But now she was beginning to lose her patience, and she wondered silently how Jack could put up with her. She was beginning to think he was a wimp—at least where his sister-in-law was concerned.

That night, Victoria, holding Emma, walked into the library prepared to be completely honest with her employer.

When Jack looked up, the first thing he saw was his daughter's toothless smile. "Remarkable," he said, getting up from behind his desk and walking toward the pair. "Do you know that is the first smile I have seen from my Emma?"

Victoria beamed, taking credit for that smile.

"Tell me about the day," he said, his eyes still on Emma.

"I'm afraid your sister-in-law and I do not get along. But I guess you expected that. We're in the midst of a power struggle."

Jack eyed his daughter's nurse, a look of perplexity on his face. "You have the strangest speech manner-isms, Miss Casey. And your accent isn't Irish. I thought you were from Ireland."

Victoria had thought she was being careful, but real-ized she would have to be more diligent about her speech.

"Um, my parents were from Ireland. I was born in New York, which is where, I suppose, I picked up some of my expressions," Victoria said, hoping he would accept that explanation.

"I've spent considerable time in New York," he

said, not elaborating, but telling her that he questioned her story.

Victoria nodded. "And I've worked in several houses with several different cultural influences—Dutch, Italian, German," she said, thinking of some of her model friends.

"Yes, well, I wouldn't want my daughter talking like a New Yorker, if you understand me?"

Ahhh, that's where he was going with this, Victoria thought. "I'll try to be more proper," Victoria said, though a part of her wondered just what "proper" speech was. She hadn't thought she'd been speaking all that improperly.

"Now that that's settled, tell me about your first encounter with my sister-in-law."

By the end of the meeting, Victoria was convinced that Jack was as good as his word. He would not, he assured her, make any decision about her employment based on anything Mrs. Von Arc told him. But he also inferred it would be a mistake to allow Mrs. Von Arc to know of their little pact.

"And how is Emma?" he asked, his gaze drifting to his daughter.

"You can see for yourself," Victoria said, and brought Emma over to Jack. Jack placed Emma in the crook of his arm, and suddenly she looked so incredibly tiny that a lump formed in Victoria's throat. She quickly looked away, fearful she was showing too much emotion.

He cradled Emma in his arms, smiling broadly when the baby opened her sleepy eyes to stare intently at his face. "She seems more alert."

"Oh, she is. She's a little cutie pie." Victoria and Jack were both smiling down at Emma when she let out a rather explosive bit of gas. The two broke into laughter, smiling now at each other, and Victoria was struck at how different he looked with laughter in his eyes. He looked . . . alive. She found her eyes drifting to his jawline, strong and well-shaped and incredibly sexy with a day's growth of beard.

"She seems very pleased with herself," Victoria said, turning her gaze abruptly back to Emma. She didn't like the way her heart had responded to the smiling man next to her. Her heart had no business picking up a beat at the sight of his happiness. Her eyes had no business staring at his jawline. When she realized she was leaning over him to look at Emma, she straightened quickly.

"Not very ladylike, is she?" Jack asked, still chuckling.

"Probably because she doesn't know she's a lady yet," Victoria said, praying he wouldn't look at her face, which was heated a brilliant red.

"Probably not."

"Would you like to spend some time alone with your daughter or would you like me to take her back to the nursery?" Victoria asked. She wanted to get away from him, to stop looking at him look at Emma with such love. Certainly that was why her heart was doing flip-flops inside her.

Jack sobered at her words. He did not want to spend time alone with his daughter. He wanted to share her. With Christina, of course. But his own thoughts mocked him. His dream that Christina would warm to Emma had been just that—a dream. Even had she lived, he knew they would never have a close bond. He would have gotten angry if Christina had not expressed such sorrow at her inability to care for Emma. He remembered the night he had ended up reassuring her that he still loved her, that nothing could ever come between them. Christina had seemed so relieved, it was almost unsettling. For the first time, Jack's assurances of love had sounded hollow to his own ears and Christina's obvious relief . . . irritating.

"You can take her back to the nursery. I'll look in on her before I retire."

Victoria took Emma from his arms and practically

ran from the room, leaving Jack feeling more alone than he'd felt in a long, long time.

In her room, Victoria paced madly. Great, she thought, I've got the hots for my boss. Whose wife's been dead all of one month. Victoria shook her head in dismay at her reaction to Jack Wilkins. Sure, he was gorgeous. Sure, he seemed to be kind and gentle, at least when he wasn't grumpy. But he was off-limits. More than off-limits. For all she knew, making love to him could mean her death, not to mentioned it would just be plain wrong. Seducing a man in mourning was sick.

"Allie, I wish you were here. You'd laugh your head off, and then tell me to get my act together," she whispered. She sat down heavily on her bed. Okay, I'm physically attracted to him. But that's it. That's as far as it goes. I will not get myself in the middle of some sick unrequited love scenario.

"I will not," she said aloud. But despite her words, a thread of fear eased its way to her heart and settled there, wrapping around until it hurt.

Twelve

The days passed, blurring together, leaving Victoria bewildered that she was not more disoriented. Her life revolved around Emma, her world no larger than the library and the hallway that contained the nursery and her room. When she first contemplated living a new life, she had pictured herself going out, meeting people, making friends. Instead, she found herself strangely content to care for Emma. She dealt with the diaper rash, the nightly feedings, the crying, and the cooing with the same contentment. Gently wiping away a bit of spit up off her sleeping daughter's face, she still found it amazing that she should feel such a strong tie to her, that she truly felt Emma was her daughter.

Suzanne continued to resist any attempts by Victoria to warm up to her, and the sessions in her room were spent with Etta holding the baby and gossiping about other servants and other households. Strangely, after that first meeting in which Suzanne doted on Emma, she rarely displayed that kind of devotion. The one thing she was devoted to, Victoria discovered, was gossip. Etta and *The Boston Globe* was Suzanne's link to the world of society. Victoria was constantly amazed at how animated Suzanne could get when listening to a juicy bit of talk. *The Boston Globe's* "Table Gossip" section was well-read while the other sections, which Suzanne lamented were filled with the dreary business of the United State's treaty with Spain, were casually discarded.

"The Andrews plan to remain in Newport until Christmas," Etta read, apparently knowing this tidbit would provoke a response from Suzanne.

"I assumed as much," Suzanne sniffed. "Margaret Andrews was jilted by that Penham boy, and she's being allowed to lick her wounds." Suzanne turned to Victoria. "You must read between the lines always. There is always more to a story than the little item they put in the column."

"The Mr. Marcus Galvins are expected home from Europe this week," Etta read.

"Already? Don't tell me they pawned that milquetoast daughter onto some poor unsuspecting title. That girl could bore a clock." Suzanne turned to Victoria again to explain. "Money, my dear Miss Casey, is everything. Absolutely everything."

They would go on like that for an hour—Etta reading some tidbit, Suzanne offering her opinion and then turning to Victoria to explain herself. It seemed to Victoria that Suzanne enjoyed herself immensely. Such talk at first bored Victoria, but soon she began to recognize some names, to understand the subtleties of this stringent society. As much as Victoria wanted to dislike Suzanne, at times she found herself charmed by her. Suzanne's sense of humor was dry as burned toast, her comments about her contemporaries scathing but uproariously funny.

"Mrs. Von Arc, you could have a career as a stand-up comedienne."

Suzanne's mouth quirked a bit, sensing a compliment somewhere. "Just what is a stand-up comedienne?"

"A stand-up comedienne is a woman who makes a living making people laugh. She goes up onstage and tells jokes. But the best are like you. They don't tell jokes, they just make observations about life."

"Making a living on the stage is incredibly vulgar,"

Suzanne said, but it was clear she was pleased that Victoria found her amusing. "And if you can picture me on a stage doing some vaudeville act, then, you, too, are a comedienne, Miss Casey."

Now that they had called a kind of truce, Victoria almost found herself looking forward to her afternoon visits. Feeling guilty, she also recognized that she looked forward to her nightly meetings with Jack.

In her head, she called him Jack, though she was always unfailingly proper when she was with him. So afraid was she that he would detect her growing feelings for him, she acted coolly toward him. But as the weeks passed, Victoria realized she would not be able to stop this disconcerting infatuation. She could certainly make sure she never, ever acted on it. My God, she thought, if he knew she had a huge crush on him, he'd send her packing in a minute. It would be embarrassing for both of them. The meetings were friendly enough, with Victoria giving her report on Emma's progress, on her battles with Suzanne, sometimes embellishing a bit to make a story more amusing than the actual event. Suzanne and Victoria would never have a warm relationship, the daily power struggles assured that, but they could converse without the biting sarcasm both enjoyed so much.

Jack was not fooled by Victoria's enthusiastic reports. He had eyes of his own and saw that Suzanne continued to berate Victoria, and he wondered if his sister-in-law were slowly wearing her down. So far, it appeared the little thing was holding her own. She was so full of energy, so unendingly cheerful that he couldn't help but compare her vitality with Christina's apathy. He loved watching her with Emma; the two seemed to have such fun together. He would have been jealous if he were not so pleased that Emma was, finally, a happy little girl.

It had broken his heart a little bit every time he brought Emma in, happily tucked in his arms, to visit with Christina. She had always seemed disappointed when he brought Emma with him, although she eventually took her readily enough when he offered to let her hold her. If he were honest, Christina did seem a bit more animated just before she died, and had even talked about going to a Thanksgiving feast at her parent's home.

The St. Georges had visited each Sunday since Emma was brought home, goo-gooing over her crib like grandparents should. They continued their visits even after Christina's death. They had no qualms accepting Emma as their grandchild, for they had believed, as Christina had, that she could not bear children for fear it would kill her. They had been told early on by that same old doctor who proclaimed Christina's imminent death, that childbirth would be deadly. And so they endlessly lavished this adopted grandchild with gifts, giving Jack a glimpse of Christina's life as a child.

Emma was robustly healthy, but she might have been a mewling frail thing the way the St. Georges, including their daughter, Suzanne, carried on. She was too warm; she was too cold; she looked peaked; she looked too rosy.

"Emma is fine," he said, picking up his girl and holding her high above his head, making her squeal in delight.

"Oh, mercy, Jack. Must you be so rough with her," his mother-in-law would lament, wringing her hands much like Christina once had. "It's not good to get her overexcited. It would be different if Emma was a boy. But with a girl, you must be gentle."

He'd just laughed and held her high again, sneaking a look of mischief over at Victoria, who had beamed a smile at him. Victoria. She had become his confidant, his partner in crime. Christina, for all her indifference to Emma, had strictly forbidden any outdoor excursions for her daughter. She was strongly backed by her near-hysterical parents, and now posthumously by

Suzanne. But Victoria and he had bundled up the little girl so tightly, the two ended up laughing at poor Emma's scrunched little face that peeked out of mountains of warm material, and went outdoors. The two agreed fresh air was healthful more than harmful, and Victoria seemed to have rather modern views of how diseases were transmitted. "It's the germs that are bad, not the fresh air," she'd said.

He liked her no-nonsense way, how she didn't smother Emma, let her get a bit dusty. He even liked the way she told white lies about her meetings with Suzanne, making them sound like pleasant banter rather than the battle of wills he knew they were.

Night after night, Victoria and Emma marched into the library for a meeting that had less to do with Emma and Suzanne each night. Victoria would give her report, pretending it was the truth, and Jack would listen, pretending to believe her. Their conversation would then naturally shift to other subjects. At first, they talked only about Emma, but slowly they began to talk to each other about life in general. Unlike Suzanne, who read only the *Globe's* society pages, Victoria found herself completely fascinated by the news of the day. So much of what captured the attention of this world would be forgotten, glossed over in history classes, a single question on a hated test.

Victoria found herself reading the newspaper, searching for interesting items she could talk about that evening with Jack. She'd cut out the articles and bring them along. Jack would eye the little stack of clippings, his bemusement growing the larger the stack.

"What have you tonight, Miss Casey. I can hardly wait," Jack said one evening.

Victoria pulled out her stack. "No, Emma," she said as the little girl reached out to play with the papers. Jack offered to hold her—as he did every night—and Victoria began flipping through the clippings.

"Ah, here's an interesting item," she said, peering

at the article. "I'm sure you didn't read this one, but I'm curious what you think of it, as a social experiment. It's an item about New York socialites coming out. 'There is such a big batch of buds to come out, beautiful girls with millions back of them, and the parties that will be given to introduce them will dazzle society.'" Victoria looked up, and seeing no reaction, continued. "'It is lovely to be with these fresh, lovely creatures, with their minds white and sweet, and their enjoyment in everything so pure and undisguised.' Well?"

Jack shrugged. "Sounds like some very nice girls are being introduced," he said innocently, knowing exactly where Victoria was taking this conversation. He enjoyed baiting her as much as she enjoyed provoking him.

"You don't think that description of those women is just a tad condescending. Listen to this: 'with their minds white and sweet.' Just what is *that* supposed to mean? I'll tell you," she said, before Jack could open his mouth. "It means vacant, ready to be molded."

"And your point being?"

Victoria looked at him agape. "My point? You have to ask my point?"

Jack shrugged again.

"Stop shrugging as if you don't know exactly what is wrong with this article! This same paper yesterday had a very nice article about a woman who opened a law school for women and then this . . . this idiot reduces these women to things whose only goal in life is to marry well!"

"As you are an unmarried woman who is a bit long in the tooth, I can understand why you would be so affronted by a young woman who is going about husband hunting and who will likely be successful." He didn't crack a smile when she looked at him agape, but Lord, how he wanted to.

Victoria was about to launch a tirade, when she saw his smiling eyes. "You've got to stop doing that," she said darkly. "I'm trying to have a serious conversation with you."

His smile finally broke through. "Miss Casey, you are a delight."

Victoria scowled at him and then flipped through some more clippings, breaking out into a huge smile. She hadn't been sure she should bring this one along, something a bit devilish made her include it in her stack. "Have you ever heard of Dr. Hallock's Wonderful Electric Pills, Mr. Wilkins? Or perhaps you've even taken them yourself." Victoria pretended to peruse the item as Jack nearly bit his tongue in half trying not to laugh. He knew exactly what Dr. Hallock's pills were and was rather shocked at Miss Casey. Shocked and delighted.

"Ah, here it is," Victoria continued. " 'Guaranteed to cure sexual debility, impotency, involuntary emission.' Oh, that sounds rather serious doesn't it? It says here it 'never fails to restore lost sexual vigor.' Sounds rather potent doesn't it?" She smiled innocently.

"I wouldn't know."

"No? How good for you. Let's see what else Dr. Hallock's potion can do."

"I think we've heard enough about Dr. Hallock's potion, Miss Casey," Jack said, making his voice stern.

"I just thought you'd be interested in the latest breakthrough in science." She tapped the paper. "It says that's what it is, right here. 'The latest breakthrough in science,' " she read.

"Miss Casey!"

"Yes?"

"Have you no idea that this type of conversation between a man and a woman is highly improper?"

Victoria flushed. Jack appeared truly upset with her. "Well, I suppose I figured if it was in the newspaper . . ."

He wanted to continue to pretend to be angry with her, he truly did. For it was not proper at all for a young woman to read such a thing aloud to a man.

But instead he found himself wanting to kiss her. And that, more than the improper conversation, put an end to that evening's discussion.

"I think our meeting is over, Miss Casey."

Victoria stood up, regretting her jokes, and feeling truly miserable. She kept forgetting how puritan people were—or at least how puritan they all acted. "You're not too angry, are you, Mr. Wilkins?"

He shook his head slightly. "I'm not angry, Miss Casey."

She gave him a little smile. "Good, because if you were, then I really shouldn't give you this." She whipped out a bottle of Dr. Hallock's Wonderful Electric Pills and plopped them onto his desk. She'd seen them today in Lofton's General Store and couldn't resist buying them—even though she had hardly any money to spare.

Jack stared at the little brown bottle with disbelief. Then he let out a bark of laughter. "You have no shame," he said, smiling a smile that made Victoria's heart speed up about twenty beats a minute.

"I do, too."

He handed Emma back to her, her infectious grin making him keep his smile a bit longer than was normal for him. "Good night, Miss Casey."

"Good night." Jack.

When she left the room, Jack's smile slowly faded. You've no right, he said to himself. No right to look at her that way, no right to think of her as much as you do. For weeks, Jack had been wracked with guilt, knowing that his feelings for Victoria were changing, knowing that he could stop these meetings at any time. And should stop them.

Christina was dead only two months. Surely her memory was worth more than that. He ignored the voice in his head that reminded him he had not been with a woman in years. And even when Christina allowed his husbandly rights, it was so infrequent and unfulfilling, he might as well have been abstinent.

Christina was deathly afraid of becoming pregnant. When she submitted, she did so with dread, leaving Jack feeling guilty and remorseful. He worked as a release, falling into his bed so exhausted, thoughts of his wife had been driven from his head.

Nothing, it seemed, could drive thoughts of Victoria from his head—or his body. It had gotten to the point where even the sound of her voice could cause a tightening in his loins. For the first time in his life, Jack contemplated a visit to a house of ill repute. Many of his colleagues, even those who professed to be happily married, frequented such establishments. The girls, they reported, were clean and willing. Despite the temptation, Jack found the thought of paying a woman to lie with him distasteful. He knew, without a doubt, that when he drove into a whore, his eyes would be closed but he would be seeing Victoria. Jesus, how had this happened, he wondered. How could it not have? Victoria was wonderfully charming, adorable, and remarkably insightful. He loved her odd way of talking, her bluntness, her kindness. He should stop their meetings, God knew he should. But he could not, and he would not.

"Weak bastard," he said aloud. Jack stared at the door where Victoria had disappeared. He must never let her know how he felt. She'd leave if she knew; she'd be frightened by the intensity of his feelings for her. When had it started, he wondered, when had he allowed mere lust to grow into something more? As strong as his feelings for Victoria were becoming, so was the guilt, as if the two emotions were tied together by a heavy chain.

"Christina, Christina," he whispered, "I don't know what to do. I've tried to be true to your memory. I swore I would never break my vows to you. But I think I'm falling in love." The words said aloud sat heavy on his heart. For hadn't he already broken his vows, wasn't he breaking his vows, being untrue to his wife's memory every time he met with Victoria? Every time he thought of her? Every time he longed to kiss her? And God only knew how he longed to kiss her. How many times had he imagined that one perfect kiss?

He left the library and trod up the stairs toward his room, his gut clenching tightly, the guilt weighing him down and slowing his steps as he remembered one of the last times he had been with his wife before she had become ill.

"Oh, Jack, I'm so glad you're here. Just guess who Mother invited to Thanksgiving and was honored by an acceptance? John Harding."

Jack had smiled at his animated wife, his heart twisting painfully, for she was acting like a young girl again. He'd gathered her into his arms, her eyes widening in surprise. "I love you," he had said against her pale blond hair. "I love you." And his heart had cried out, "Please, God, make it so."

Thirteen

The smoke was thicker than a springtime fog in the tiny pub, but no one seemed to notice. Certainly not Kevin Donnelly as he puffed thoughtfully on his cigar, contemplating the information just given to him by Tom Reilly. Tom was woefully thin and tall for an Irishman, an almost comical contrast to Kevin, whose stocky, muscular frame marked him as a man few wanted to deal with. Some were fooled by Donnelly's boyish handsomeness, those pretty blue eyes and flashing white teeth. He could smile and charm almost anyone into doing almost anything—except, it seemed, Sheila Casey.

"You say she pretended not to know you?" Kevin shook his head, puzzled by Sheila's behavior. "And did you not tell her that Kevin Donnelly was looking for her."

"I did," Tom said. "She said she didn't know any Kevin Donnelly."

Kevin took another puff on his cigar. "Did she, now?" A man who didn't know him would have thought he was taking this news in stride, but Tom knew Kevin, and his gut tightened uncomfortably. He didn't like the look in Kevin's eyes, a sharp glint that could sever a body's soul if they stared too long.

"Well, now, why would she do something like that, do you think, Tom?"

Tom shifted in his stool and took a sip of whiskey.

"I wouldn't know, Kevin. Sheila's always been nice to me."

Tom swallowed, noting Kevin's tightened jaw. "She's betrayed me, Tom. The girl's gone and figured she can do better on her own. Ain't no accident she's working in the same house where the babe's at."

"Maybe she didn't want to give it up," Tom ventured.

Kevin gave Tom a crooked smile, and Tom relaxed. "Ain't likely. Sheila's not the motherly type. She gave the baby up for adoption two months before the mite was born. I'm thinking she's had this planned all along."

"What planned?"

Kevin poured the rest of the whiskey down his throat. "That, my friend, is what I intend to find out. But whatever it is, Sheila owes me. She ain't gonna cash in on those riches without some going in my own pocket."

Eight o'clock. How many times had Victoria glanced at the clock in the nursery, wishing the time would fly by. And every time she did, she chastised herself. She was in the midst of a full-fledged crush, like that not experienced since she was thirteen years old and convinced she was in love with Camp Ugoto's most handsome camp counselor, Dean Harrington. She had every disgusting sign: her heart would quicken at the sound of Jack's voice, her face would redden at the sight of him, and her body would react in a much less innocent way if they happened to touch. She stuttered like a schoolgirl, her body tingling and alive whenever they met accidentally in a hall.

"This wasn't supposed to happen," she told Emma, who sat upon her lap and looked at her as if she just might understand. "The last thing I wanted was to get involved. I just wanted to live, you know, walk down a street without people staring at me. I wanted to be ordinary. I did not want to fall in love."

And I haven't, she told herself. Not yet, anyway. But Victoria recognized all the signs of infatuation. She was starting to notice things about him, the way he rested his chin on one thumb when reading one of his architectural journals, that his eyes were that most beautiful blue of the sky after the sun has disappeared below the horizon. He had a small birthmark behind his left ear, a small scar above his right eyebrow. He had an exquisite butt that would look great in a pair of Gap jeans, and Victoria was beginning to wonder how his derriere would look without anything covering it at all.

These were not the thoughts a nanny should be having, nor a Victorian lady, either. Victoria had never been the type to stare at men, and certainly not the type of woman to mentally strip a man! But Jack . . . Well, it just wasn't fair to have been plunked in such close proximity to such a handsome man, knowing you could never, ever do anything about it. Never. Ever.

Thank goodness Jack had absolutely no desire for her. A couple of times she thought she had detected more than his usual politeness but quickly chalked it up to an overactive imagination. She'd had to fall upon her best acting skills to make certain Jack had no inkling of her feelings. Just the thought of him discovering her ridiculous crush made her face tingle almost painfully.

But when eight o'clock came, she smoothed her skirts and tried to tame her errant curls. Used to stick-straight hair, Victoria hadn't a clue what to do with these unruly locks, so she simply piled them inartfully upon her head. As a result, she usually looked slightly mussed. Tucking a curl behind her ear, Victoria picked Emma up, and made her way to the library, where she would find Jack, more than likely with that thumb pressed against his chin, reading a journal.

"Hello," she said, ignoring the frown that was immediately produced. She was obviously disturbing him. "I'm sorry. Do you want to skip tonight's meeting?"

Jack realized he was frowning and forced a smile. He'd been aware of her the second that knob turned on the library door, and he hated his absurd feeling of elation that washed over him. Things were getting entirely too friendly. If he wasn't careful, he would slip, and he would somehow let her know that he wanted her in an almost desperate way. Yes, they were much too friendly despite the formality they still clung to. She did not call him Jack, although there was something in the way she called him Mr. Wilkins, that somehow seemed familiar, intimate. It was ridiculous, of course. She was always impeccably polite in front of servants and ridiculously so in front of Suzanne. How many times had he been forced to turn away so that his sister-in-law would not see the smile he was unable to suppress.

"Here's your girl," she said, plopping Emma onto his lap. "Did you read about the Fennessy court-martial?"

"Fill me in."

"This Lieutenant Fennessy is getting all kinds of heat because he was critical of his own unit. Apparently his unit gunned down several Spanish prisoners."

"Ah, yes. I remember now. Some in his unit accused him of cowardice because he called the action murder."

"Right. So what do you think? Do you think Fennessy's a coward?"

Jack leaned back in his chair, shifting Emma from one shoulder to the other, a pleased smile on his face. Tonight's discussion promised to be an interesting one.

"I think Fennessy's not the brightest fellow." And he waited, knowing that one simple comment from him would release the flood of comment Victoria was apparently bursting to deliver.

"I think Fennessy showed incredible courage by

being critical of something that he knew he might get in trouble for saying."

"But admitting that your own troops were a murderous lot is not very political," Jack countered.

"I'll give you that much. But the soldiers who are trying to justify killing defenseless prisoners are just getting caught up in false patriotism. I'd bet if you got each one of them in a room separately, they'd all regret having done what they did. Someday they will."

"Reports about what actually happened are conflicting, from what I've read. There is no clear evidence that the Spanish prisoners were unjustifiably killed," Jack countered.

"Then, why would this Fennessy claim they were just gunned down? He's got no reason to lie about it. In fact, he's putting his own career in jeopardy for telling the truth."

Lord, she was an amazing woman, able to discuss war with intelligence, without squeamishness. "Everyone's perception of the truth is different. What he saw as an act of murder, another man might see as a justified killing."

"The truth is the truth, and that's that."

"Not in war."

Victoria knew he was right. History had proven time and again that one country's truth was its enemy's lie.

They were interrupted by the entrance of a young maid bearing a tray loaded with cherry tarts, and both were glad to be ending their intense discussion. "Just out of the oven, sir. Mrs. Roberts thought you might like some," she said, and left the room.

"Miss Casey?" Jack said, offering her a tart.

"No thank you. Do you know how much fat and calories just one of those things has? You can go ahead and clog your arteries, but I'll pass, thank you very much."

Jack examined the tart more closely. "There's nothing wrong with this tart that I can see."

Victoria eyed the confection, biting her lips and calling upon her famous willpower. "I'll live vicariously through you."

Shrugging, Jack shoved nearly the entire thing in his mouth. "Good," he said, the word muffled from his full mouth. "You were saying, Miss Casey, something about truth?" he asked after brushing some crumbs away that had fallen on Emma's dress.

"I bow to you on that point, Mr. Wilkins. But what about Fennessy. Coward or hero?"

"Naïve hero," he answered, his heart swelling when he saw Victoria's pleased smile. Jack leaned back in his chair, enjoying their debate immensely. The topics might change from night to night, but the discussions were always fun. He never knew a woman could be so witty, so well-informed, nor develop ideas so intelligently. She'd almost convinced him two nights ago that women would vote one day. If all women were as bright as she was, they certainly would, and he'd told her that.

"All women are as intelligent as me—or you, for that matter. They just don't know it. They're so used to being told who they're supposed to be, they have nothing left over to discover for themselves who they really are."

"And who are you, Victoria. A scullery maid? I think not."

Victoria's face heated. "I was a scullery maid. Now I'm a nanny," she said firmly.

He looked at her, his eyes intense. "You're no scullery maid, Miss Casey."

"That's what I said. I'm a nanny," Victoria said, purposefully being dense. Victoria smiled. God, she loved these talks, she thought looking at Jack fondly. Her heart immediately began slamming against her chest. "You've got a glob of cherry on your cheek," she said, trying to cover up her discomfort.

Jack swiped at one cheek with a napkin. "No, the other side. Here, let me." *Danger zone, girl,* a voice said. Ignoring the voice, she took the napkin from

Jack's hand, but instead of using the piece of cloth, Victoria took one finger and wiped it away. And then she did something that would cause her face to heat up for several nights just thinking about it, as if wiping the glob away from his face with her finger wasn't bad enough. She licked that cherry from her finger and watched as Jack's beautiful jaw clenched and his eyes grew dark.

Victoria immediately wiped her finger on the napkin, then briskly rubbed any cherry residue from his cheek. "There. All clean."

Had he imagined it? thought Jack as he watched Victoria quickly return to her seat. Had he imagined that look of want on her face? Or was he only seeing his own need mirrored in her eyes? Jesus, how he wanted her. He should go over to her, pick her up, and crush her against him, lift her skirts and . . . *No.*

He should not. He should not even think such things with Christina in the grave not even three months. But if Victoria wanted it, too, if she would allow him. Oh, God, if she would allow him to love her, to hold her so that he could feel her naked skin against his, to kiss her breasts, to put himself inside her. He swallowed heavily, ashamed to think such carnal thoughts, sinful thoughts really. But if Victoria would allow him . . .

He looked over to Victoria and wondered what she would say if he told her he wanted her, if the first thing he would see in her eyes would be fear. His mind rebelled against comparing Christina to Victoria, but he couldn't stop himself from thinking that it would be nice—no, it would be wonderful—to have a woman look at him with desire. It is what he thought he saw in her eyes, but now he was not so sure.

"Why did you do that?" The moment the words were out of his mouth, he wanted to retract them. What did he expect her to say?

Victoria raised her eyes to his, trying to read his veiled expression. Damn, I've broken some backward

Victorian rule about touching a man without his prior consent, Victoria thought after deciding Jack looked more irritated than anything else.

"I didn't want that cherry to go to waste," she said lightly. "There it was, tempting me, and I couldn't resist taking a little taste." Oh, *that* came out rather badly, didn't it, she thought, grimacing inwardly. She hoped he couldn't read the double entendre.

Jack swallowed heavily. Jesus, she doesn't have a clue what she does to me. "It was inappropriate, Miss Casey," Jack said, trying to convince himself that it was better to discourage any physical contact between the two, no matter how innocent such contact was on her part. He simply could not take much more. He knew if she were to come close again, if she were to touch him, no matter how innocent that touch might be, he would drag her into his arms and kiss her senseless. And so he was curt to her, hoping to control his own desire.

Victoria's entire body grew hot with embarrassment. If she'd wanted to know whether he had any feelings for her at all, now she knew. Her skin prickled, and she knew her discomfort was as visible as a neon sign on a dark country road.

"I'm sorry. I didn't realize that . . . I'm sorry," Victoria finished miserably. Oh, what was *wrong* with her?

The need to escape the library and Jack's disapproving look was overwhelming. "I've got to put her to bed," Victoria said, standing abruptly. She walked over and took her daughter, trying to limit contact with Jack, and marched from the room almost colliding with Suzanne.

Jack stared after Victoria, cursing himself. Victoria was not the kind of girl who tried to seduce a man. The gesture had been completely innocent, and it had been his own raging desire that had turned it into something else. Hell, he only needed to watch her walk across the room to want to throw her down and ravage her. Never in his life had his body responded so violently to a woman, never had he been so willing to throw away society's conventions and his own beliefs to bed a woman who obviously had no desire to be bedded. He shifted in his seat, ignoring the near painful need, and readied himself for another litany of complaints from Suzanne.

"Hello, Suzanne," he said wearily.

Suzanne narrowed her eyes a bit, taking in Jack's bleak expression. For weeks, every time she had walked past the library in the evenings, she would hear the sound of laughter. It was unseemly, to say the least. Not only was Jack in mourning, but he was being entirely too familiar with the nurse. It wouldn't do to have him become involved with the girl, for him to become content with a mistress when what he really needed was a wife.

"Miss Casey seemed rather flustered as she left," she said casually.

Jack chewed the side of his mouth. He did not want to discuss Victoria with Suzanne, for he knew where such a discussion would lead.

"We had a small disagreement," he said finally.

"Over Emma's care?" Suzanne asked, and smiled. "Or over something unrelated to your daughter's care?"

Jack, who had become used to Victoria's blunt honesty, became irritated with Suzanne's obscurity. It was obvious she had suspicions. "Just say what you've come to say, Suzanne," he bit out.

One elegant eyebrow rose at his sharp tone. "I know I needn't remind you, but you are still in mourning, Jack. These . . . meetings with the nurse, I fear, will lead to an indiscretion. She is a lovely little thing, but it is entirely inappropriate for you to be spending so much time alone with her."

Jack breathed in through his nose, trying to stamp down the anger that was beginning to burn inside him. "We are not alone. Emma is with us."

Suzanne would have rolled her eyes if that was something she allowed herself to do. Instead, she sharpened her gaze and deepened her frown. She could not say more, else Jack would think she was jealous and that would never do. It was not yet time for her to expose herself, Christina's death was too recent. But she believed if Jack began an affair with the nurse, she would be forced to begin her campaign to win Jack's heart sooner than she liked.

Suzanne's husband had been rich, but when he died there was barely enough money to pay for the extravagant funeral, thanks to her husband's poor investments and unsympathetic partners. Spending that money had stuck in Suzanne's craw, but it was the only way to assure her social circle that all was well. In the two years since his death, she continued to live lavishly, knowing that her well of money was about to run dry. So far, her friends believed she was being a devoted sister-in-law and aunt by staying with Jack, but the truth was she was nearly broke. Her home was on the market, and the proceeds from the sale would go almost entirely to pay debts. Suzanne knew she could not stay in Jack's house indefinitely without people discovering she was a pauper. Nothing was less forgiven than being penniless.

For a time she contemplated living with her parents, something that would mean the loss of whatever independence she had managed to attain. They would welcome her, she knew, and she would become like so many widowed oldest daughters who withered away while taking care of aging parents. It would never do.

She must marry, and the obvious husband for her was Jack. He needed her, was fond of her, and he was wealthy. A perfect match, she had thought.

Suzanne had planned well, but now she found she was floundering, for she had no idea how to get Jack to fall in love with her. A shrewd woman, she knew that no less than love would cause him to break his vow to never remarry. Suzanne knew she was beautiful, that men were attracted to her because of that. But she had been unable to entice a man to love her. Suzanne had never minded before, finding the whole thing a bit distasteful. The women she had seen in love made complete idiots of themselves. It had always seemed to Suzanne a remarkable waste of energy. Until now.

Suzanne straightened her spine to prepare for her assault. "I believe you should dismiss her before things advance too far," she said, her pale cheeks sprouting two spots of red.

Jack leaned back in his chair and looked at Suzanne through hooded eyes. "And what makes you think things have not advanced," he said, baiting her.

Suzanne took a quick breath and pursed her lips. "My sister has been dead not three months. That is how I know."

"Thank you for your confidence in my moral character," he said dryly.

Feeling a bit defeated, Suzanne said, "Jack I don't mean to pry, but . . ."

"Of course you mean to pry. It is what you do, dear Suzanne." He smiled. "You have nothing to worry about. Our little nurse is safe."

His assurances did not satisfy her. "I believe your meetings with her should stop."

He let out a small sigh. "So do I. They will stop, Suzanne."

She had not thought he would agree so readily and that he did was quite telling. He did have lustful feelings for the girl, she realized. At least he knew they were wrong.

"I'm glad, Jack. As much as I find Miss Casey rather coarse, I must admit Emma has thrived under her care. You must think of the girl, Jack. Without this position, she would be back in someone's kitchen. It isn't fair to her or to Emma if . . ." She blushed again, unable to complete the sentence.

"I assure you, I can control my lust," Jack said, his

voice tinged with annoyance when he saw that Suzanne was beginning to shake her head as if that is not what she meant. "Please, Suzanne, I know what you are inferring."

Suzanne looked immediately remorseful. She did not want Jack angry with her, but grateful that she was so concerned about the situation. "I have the utmost faith in you, Jack, you know that."

He bowed his head slightly. "Again, thank you for your faith in my character. Now, if you are through lecturing me, Suzanne, I have some work to do." Jack smiled to take the edge off his words, for he realized Suzanne was trying to help in her own controlling way.

After Suzanne left, Jack sat for a long time, rising only to toss a log onto the snapping fire, and wondered when he had ever felt so alone.

One floor up, Victoria was cursing herself. *Did you expect him to declare his undying love for you, you idiot?* "No," she answered herself aloud. "But it would have been nice."

No, it would be horrid, she suddenly realized. For him to fall in love with her would be tantamount to breaking one of her vows. For if Jack fell in love with her, certainly he would not want to remarry as perhaps history might dictate. "Well, he hasn't fallen in love with me, and he probably won't," she said aloud, and tried to make herself glad about this revelation. She and Jack had fun together, but she was quite certain that someone of Jack's social status would find it rather repugnant to fall in love with a nurse. If he did, it would mean leaving her position, leaving Emma behind. And leaving Jack. She didn't know when it happened, but somewhere along the way, Jack and Emma had become entwined in her heart in a knotted tangle that could not be separated.

"Don't fall in love with me, Jack, please don't," she whispered, her throat constricting with tears, for a part of her wished more than anything that he would. She had thought a new life would mean one without pain, but she was discovering how brutally wrong she had been. It hurt so much, this love she felt for Emma. This love she was beginning to feel for Jack. She let out a little puff of air, almost relieved to have finally admitted to herself that she was falling in love. "But I'm not there yet," she whispered with determination.

She sat upon her bed, cursing as her heart began its crazy pounding when she heard Jack in the nursery whispering his good night to Emma. Her heart almost burst from her chest when she heard a soft knock on the adjoining door. A quick check in her small mirror satisfied Victoria that her eyes were dry.

She opened up the door just wider than a crack. "Yes?"

Jack pushed his way through. "I need to discuss something with you."

"Oh?" Keep quiet, you stupid heart, else he'll hear you.

He wiped a hand through his dark hair. "I've decided that it is no longer necessary for us to conduct our nightly meetings. I can see now that you are a competent nurse, and I trust you to continue in that manner."

That damn cherry glob. "I see."

"Yes. So."

Victoria looked at him, not bothering to hide the disappointment in her eyes, and he would have squirmed beneath her gaze had he been a man who squirmed. "Well, um, should I report to Mrs. Von Arc, then?"

Jack suddenly felt awkward to be standing in her room and very much aware she was in only her robe. Certainly his announcement could have waited until morning when the memory of her finger slowly drifting up to her mouth to lick off that bit of confection had dimmed. He moved to the door. "You should still report to me, Miss Casey. There will simply be no more formal meetings."

"For example, if we were to pass in the hall, I would say, "Everything's going smoothly. Like that?" Victoria couldn't keep the bitterness from her voice, much as she tried.

"Yes," he said wearily. "Just like that."

This is good, Victoria thought, just let it be. "That's fine, Mr. Wilkins. Good night."

He hesitated at the door and looked at her, standing in the middle of her small room, her hair tumbling down her back, and again found himself battling against the urge to drag her into his arms. He had made the right decision, and if she looked hurt and if he was miserable, that was just too bad.

Fourteen

Victoria took a hand away from Emma's forehead and frowned. The little girl had been fussing all day, and now she felt warm—too warm. She let out little whining sounds that grew into cries no matter what Victoria did.

"Do you have a little cold, Emma? Poor girl. Maybe we should tell your daddy you're sick, and he can call a doctor," she said as she wiped the baby's red runny nose. Victoria bit her bottom lip, her face etched with worry. Just a cold, please be just a little cold. "Come on, let's go wait for Daddy."

Night fell, and the house had grown quiet by the time Jack returned home. Victoria, who had even considered consulting Suzanne about whether or not to call a doctor, discovered she was also not yet home from a visit to her parents'. She was just about to send the cook's son to fetch a doctor when Jack returned home. Nearly frantic with worry, Victoria told herself to remain calm, for panicking Jack would do no good. It was probably just a bad cold, after all. The runny nose, the dry cough, all pointed to a mild illness. But Victoria had reminded herself a thousand times that day that the infant mortality rate of the 1890s was much higher than the 1990s. She recalled a high school project in which the class visited historic grave sites. She'd never forgotten all those rows of tiny little tombstones erected for infants.

Victoria had no idea where medicine stood in fighting what she grew up believing were common—and harmless—childhood diseases. By the time Jack walked through the front door, she was convinced Emma was dying of polio or some other dreaded illness.

When Jack heard the sound of Emma crying, his eyebrows rose in surprise. It was something he had not heard with any frequency in weeks. After handing off his coat and hat, his eyes immediately went to Victoria who stood in the middle of the foyer, trying to soothe her little bundle.

"She's sick. I think we should call the doctor." Victoria had been a rock throughout the day, telling herself there was nothing to worry about, soothing Emma as best she could, despite her fears. But the minute the words were out, tears spilled from her eyes.

"Here, let me see her," Jack said trying to calm Victoria. The sight of those tears had a peculiar effect on his heart, for Victoria had never displayed such emotion, and he found it disconcerting.

Once Emma was in his arms, his concern for Victoria shifted to his daughter. "Gibbons, call Dr. Brighton immediately."

Guilt consumed Victoria. "I should have sent for a doctor hours ago, but I thought I was overreacting. She's gotten worse, I think. She's been coughing, and her fever is higher . . ."

"Stop." He lay a gentling hand on her shoulder. "We've sent for the doctor now. I'm sure a few hours has made no difference. And I'm sure Emma will be fine." She must be fine, my little Emma, and he tightened his hold on his daughter.

An hour later, Dr. Brighton was grimly examining the baby. It was as he had suspected, for it was his fourth case in two weeks. Measles. Although two children had recovered, one had died after slipping into a coma.

"Rubella, the measles," he said, glancing into Emma's mouth. "See these white spots in the mouth?

You'll begin to see a rash on her face soon." He sighed seeing the look of dread on Jack's face. "She's a healthy little girl, Mr. Wilkins. As long as we keep the fever down, she should pull through just fine."

Victoria, who had at first been relieved to hear Emma had what she thought was a normal childhood disease, was now fighting back terror. "What do you mean, 'she should pull through.' Measles isn't . . ." She swallowed. "I mean, measles can't kill you, can it?"

Dr. Brighton shifted his gaze to Jack, whose eyes had taken on a bleakness that tore at him.

"I had an older sister who died of measles," Jack said, his voice hoarse. "I don't remember her, but I know that's how she . . ."

Victoria suddenly found it difficult to breathe. "No." Although whispered, that single word held immeasurable pain. Victoria wanted to pick Emma up, to hold her against herself, to draw out whatever disease was attacking her little girl, but she held herself in check. You are just the nurse, stop acting like a mother. Her throat ached, her eyes burned, but Victoria found the strength to compose herself.

"What can we do?" she asked, proud that her voice sounded strong.

"I don't have to worry about you, Mr. Wilkins. You've already been exposed to the virus. Miss Casey, have you ever had the measles?"

She shook her head. "I was immunized as a kid," she said distractedly.

"You were *what*?" Dr. Brighton demanded.

Victoria gave herself a mental shake. Remember where and who you are. She truly had no idea if Sheila Casey had ever had the measles or been exposed to the disease. "Oh. No, I don't know whether I've been exposed or not."

"Then, we'd better watch you carefully. If you've been with her all day, I'd say it's already too late to avoid exposure. I want you and Emma to remain completely isolated from the rest of this household,"

Dr. Brighton said. "Until you have any symptoms, you and Mr. Wilkins are the best people to care for Emma. I want you to keep her in dimly lit rooms, give her warm baths, but be sure she does not become chilled. Try to get her to drink to avoid dehydration."

"You don't have any medicine?" Victoria asked.

"I've just told you the best treatment," Dr. Brighton said. "Should her breathing become difficult, if she suffers convulsions, or her fever goes up, call me."

Pneumonia was the biggest fear, Jack knew. God could not be so cruel to take both his wife and daughter by the same illness. He looked down at his girl, so tiny in her crib, her cheeks dry and flushed. She was finally sleeping, exhausted from a day of crying. He glanced at Victoria and was again startled by the look on her face. Had he a mirror, he suspected he would see the same look of anguish in his own eyes.

"She'll be fine," he heard himself say. Victoria tore her eyes from Emma's sleeping form to look at Jack. Don't cry, she told herself. A nurse would not feel this way, she would somehow manage to be detached. Wouldn't she? But a mother, a mother would try to move heaven and earth to save her child. And that is how she felt, though she knew she could not show it.

"I never meant to love her this much, you must believe me." She turned away, ashamed she had been unable to pretend indifference. Victoria heard him come up behind her, knew before she felt his touch what it would be like to be comforted by him. Hadn't she imagined it a thousand times? She felt his arms wrap around her, strong and solid and warm.

"It's all right to love her," he whispered against her ear.

They stood there, eyes closed, taking strength from each other, not caring that they should not, only caring that it felt good to lean on someone, to share grief and hope. When Jack heard Suzanne down the hall, he drew away slowly, turning Victoria so that she faced him. Her green-blue eyes were dry, but he could still make out the salty tear-tracks on her skin.

"Thank you, Mr. Wilkins," Victoria said, a small smile on her lips, knowing the use of his surname was incongruous, given what they had just shared.

"You're welcome, Miss Casey."

Jack wanted to rip the telephone from the wall. "Unreliable goddamn piece of equipment! Gibbons, send for Dr. Brighton, the damned operator keeps getting me the wrong exchange. Here we are on the brink of the twentieth century, and we can't rely on something as simple as a telephone." Despite his order, he tried ringing the doctor again, only to be frustrated. "Goddamn it!" he yelled, banging one fist against the object of his anger, causing its bell to softly sound. He rested his head against the wooden phone, eyes closed and burning from weariness. Victoria had awoken him from a three-hour sleep, tugging on his arm frantically. Emma was worse. Much worse. Her breathing rattled, and she was hot to the touch. Pneumonia, Jack was certain of it.

Dr. Brighton, looking rather disheveled himself, confirmed Jack's fears. After listening to her breathing, he prodded her belly gently, causing Emma to shriek out in pain.

"I'm sorry, Mr. Wilkins. All we can do is wait. She's a strong little girl." The doctor lay a hand on Jack's shoulder. "She's much stronger than your wife was, Mr. Wilkins. Much stronger."

Jack swayed, hearing those words, catching himself on the edge of the crib. "Thank you, Doctor." He waited until the doctor left before allowing the tears to fall. Victoria sat behind him, huddled in a corner chair, tears silently flowing as she watched Jack's shoulders shake as he wept soundlessly. His hands gripped the crib railing so tightly, she wondered what kept it from splintering.

Closing her eyes against the pain, Victoria fought

the urge to comfort him, but she sensed he needed to grieve alone for now. After long minutes, Jack straightened and lay a gentle hand on his daughter's head.

"She won't die," he said, his voice strong and filled with such conviction Victoria's heart wrenched. "She's so little. Too little for God to want."

Take me, Victoria prayed silently. Take me instead.

Throughout the long night, Emma grew worse. When the doctor came the next day, he did not offer words of hope, for he had just come from the deathbed of a child he'd thought would live. "Try to keep her comfortable." It was all he could say, and it was enough to crush any hope Jack had.

He sat down heavily and let out a bitter, ugly laugh.

"Don't you dare give up, Jack. Don't you dare," Victoria said, unaware that she had used his given name for the first time in her anger. She was so very tired, she didn't care what she said or did. She only cared that Emma get better and believed their faith would make it so.

"She's going to die. I'm just accepting it," he said without emotion.

Victoria saw red. She launched herself at him, a wild woman with hair flying and hands drawn up like claws. With fists flailing, she pummeled Jack's shoulders, head, and arms he held up as defense, all the while screaming, "Take it back. You take it back. She's going to live, you bastard. Take it back."

Finally Jack caught her arms, pinning them to her side, and forced her to kneel on the ground when she began trying to kick him. "Stop it, Miss Casey. Stop it," he yelled when she continued to struggle. Exhausted, Victoria hung her head, breathing harshly through her mouth, her hair tumbling around her.

"You take it back, Jack Wilkins," she said softly, raising her tortured eyes to his.

"Sir? Is everything all right?" Etta shouted through

the closed door, apparently drawn to the nursery by the commotion.

"Yes, Etta. Everything is fine." Jack looked down at the woman before him. He loosened his grip on one arm and raised his hand to the side of her face, pushing back her tangled hair.

"I'm afraid," he said softly. "I've never been this afraid in my life because I know what will happen to me if she does die." Jack stopped Victoria from shaking her head in denial by raising his other hand to her cheek. "Shhh. Shhh."

Victoria closed her eyes, so tired she felt the world swirl about her. His hands were warm on her face, and she was tempted to crawl onto his lap and fall asleep. When she opened her eyes, she saw only the deep blue of his eyes and felt only his firm lips on hers. It was a brief kiss, so short she might have imagined it but for the devastating effect it had on her senses. I'm overtired, she thought, else I wouldn't be this moved.

"Sorry I hit you, but you made me angry. And you still haven't taken it back," she said. She made to move away, but he held her close, making her realize for the first time how intimate their embrace had become. Her hands rested on his thighs, her body nestled between his legs.

Jack looked at her uptilted face, eyes riveted on those lips he'd just tasted, wanting to draw her near, to taste again. Instead he let her go. "I take it back," he said, an odd smile on his lips, leaving Victoria to wonder just what he had agreed to take back.

Victoria stayed where she was for a few more moments. "Good, because she's going to get better. She's going to live."

Exhausted beyond what she thought was possible, Victoria finally agreed to get some sleep. The sun had just risen, giving her room a rosy-gold glow, when Jack gently shook her awake. Her back was to him, and Victoria hesitated, frightened by what he might tell her. Slowly she turned, her eyes going to his face, her heart plummeting when she saw the tears swimming in his eyes. Victoria would have thought she'd be the kind of person to scream out in agony. Instead, she closed her eyes, letting out only a pitiful little sound of denial.

"No. No. Miss Casey. Emma is better. She's going to live." Jack shook her to make her understand.

"What?"

"Emma. She's going to be fine."

Victoria threw herself into his embrace, clasping her arms about his neck in pure joy. "I thought . . . I thought . . . Oh, I'm so glad, Jack. Mr. Wilkins, I mean." They both laughed and cried at the same time rocking back and forth, sharing their happiness.

From the nursery door, Suzanne watched, her face pinched, her eyes cold. This would never do.

Fifteen

"**I** take it Emma is better?"

Victoria and Jack separated quickly at Suzanne's question. Jack, who had been half on the bed, one foot resting on the carpet, felt his face flush to be caught embracing Victoria. But when he turned to face Suzanne, he showed nothing more than bland interest at seeing his sister-in-law standing in the doorway.

"Her fever is gone, her breathing is much more clear. But I'm not certain whether it is safe for you to be in the nursery, Suzanne. Emma might still be contagious," Jack said, his voice even. If Suzanne detected a bit of censure in his tone, she ignored it.

"I doubt *I'm* in any danger," she said walking to the crib, where Emma slept peacefully. "I'm so glad to see her better." Suzanne forced herself to smile. How *could* he act as if it were proper to be discovered embracing the half-naked nurse while in bed! She had worried the entire time Emma was ill that this closeness the two were sharing might evolve into something more intimate, and it seemed her concerns were warranted.

Jack walked into the nursery, closing Victoria's door behind him, noting Suzanne's stiff back. "We were overcome with emotion, Suzanne. Please do not read more into what you saw than exists," he said, his voice low. He refused to remember the kiss, Victoria's soft lips pressed briefly against his. It had been a mistake, one he would suffer because of for several nights. He could not have explained such action to Suzanne; he could barely explain it to himself.

Suzanne lifted her chin, her eyes focused on the flowered wallpaper. "I was married for three years. I am not ignorant about what can happen between a man and a woman, Jack."

Jack grabbed her upper arms and spun her around to face him. "Victoria and I have been through hell during these past five days. How dare you imply that anything improper has occurred. She helped save your niece's life. Don't you forget that, Suzanne."

Suzanne stood still until he was finished, then jerked one shoulder to escape his grip. He instantly released her, balling up his fists by his sides, already regretting handling her so roughly.

"I'm sorry," he said, but it was clear he was still angry.

Suzanne breathed in through narrowed nostrils. "You are tired, Jack. And I am sorry if I implied you had been unfaithful to Christina."

Jack clenched his jaw. "Christina is dead."

Suzanne's head jerked back as if she'd been slapped, and her eyes glittered dangerously. "I need no reminder that my sister is dead. But I can't help but wonder if your behavior would have been different had she been alive."

Jack grew still at her words. "What are you saying, Suzanne?"

Suddenly Suzanne's shoulders sagged. "Nothing. I am saying nothing." This was all wrong. She was supposed to be endearing herself to this man, not alienating him. *I must learn to control my tongue,* she thought. She lay one hand on his upper arm, which grew rock hard beneath her touch.

"Sometimes my loyalty to Christina makes me blind. Please forgive me, Jack. I know you loved Christina. But seeing you holding another woman startled me." Suzanne swallowed and took a breath before

saying the next. "I suppose, I might have even been
a bit jealous."

Jack looked at her, surprised by such an admission.

"Oh, don't look at me so," Suzanne said, truly agi-
tated as she wondered whether it was too soon to
say such things to Jack. "You cannot think the only reason
I am here in your home is because . . ." She turned
away, praying he would not make her say aloud that
she was in love with him, for she did not know if she
could act convincingly.

Jack's eyes widened, realizing that in Suzanne's
stilted way, she was acknowledging that she had more
than sisterly feelings for him. Something close to dread
filled him as he stared at Suzanne's back. He did not
want to hurt her, and yet he did not want her.

"Suzanne. You know I could not have gotten
through these weeks without you. You've been a great
friend, a good sister."

Suzanne's eyes filled with panic, but she masked it
before turning toward Jack. "I don't expect declarations," she said quietly, lowering her eyes the way she
thought would make her look forlorn. She must make
him see her as a desirable woman, and quickly.

"Oh, Jack," she said, throwing herself into his arms
and pressing her cheek against his shoulder. "I'm so
sorry. I've fought these feelings for weeks. I know it's
wrong, and here I've been so hateful by reminding
you that dear Christina is just passed when I've
been . . . I'm so ashamed."

Hearing her tortured words, Jack slowly brought
one hand to pat her shoulder like a man lifting a hand
toward handcuffs. "I don't know what to say, Suzanne.
This is so unexpected." And unbelievable. Suzanne
was not a woman who made declarations, who threw
herself into any man's arms. It seemed so false. Yet
when Suzanne lifted her head up, tears filling her eyes,
he was taken aback by the very real emotion he saw
there.

I must make him love me, she thought, I must. "I

know it is. Jack, Jack, if you only knew how much I need you." It was the truth, she did need him, his social standing, his name, his money. She pressed her lips against his, bringing her hands behind his neck to pull him closer. Jack stood unmoving and unmoved. He grasped her wrists and gently pulled them away, hating to hurt her but unwilling to participate in this dramatic scene.

"Don't push me away, Jack. I love you," Suzanne said, desperation tingeing her voice.

"No, Suzanne, you mustn't. In my mind, I am still married to Christina." But not in my heart, he added silently.

The image of Jack embracing Victoria flashed before Suzanne, and she swallowed a thick clot of rage that formed in her throat. "I know you are still in mourning, Jack. So am I," She said, and rustled the skirts of her black dress. "But someday . . ."

He stopped her. "No, Suzanne. I will never remarry. I'm sorry."

"But if you were to love me," Suzanne said, hating the way she sounded.

Jack closed his eyes briefly to shut himself away from the pain he saw in her eyes. "I don't."

Suzanne's eyes grew dull, as if all hope were draining from them. "Do you love her?"

"Her?"

She smiled coldly. "Yes. Your little nurse. The girl you were embracing not ten minutes ago in her bed."

"I will not discuss Miss Casey with you, Suzanne," he said, his eyes growing hard.

"Oh, my God, you do love her." Suzanne could not help herself. She began to laugh. "Poor, poor Jack. In love with a scullery maid. How absolutely ridiculous. I imagine she's a lusty little creature, hmmm? My goodness, I've been usurped by a servant."

Jack clenched his jaw, the muscles there standing out, sculpting his anger. "That is enough, Suzanne."

Suzanne began moving about the room, her steps

jerky, as if the very effort of doing something as mundane as walking was nearly beyond her. "It is so very coarse of you, Jack. I'd thought Christina's influence would have gone a bit further." It was a veiled reference to his less-than-affluent origins.

A cold smile formed on Jack's hard lips. "My, my. Where has that love you professed for me not moments ago flown to, my dear?"

Suzanne drew up short, realizing she allowed anger to control her, to nearly ruin her plans. "Again I must apologize Jack. But I have just been rejected and am feeling a bit out of sorts." Real tears of frustration appeared in her eyes, making her suddenly look as vulnerable as she sounded.

"I have not rejected you, Suzanne. I have rejected the idea of marriage. It is two different things entirely."

Dashing the tears from her face, she managed a smile. "Thank you for being kind, Jack. I won't embarrass you or myself over this matter again," she said, leaving the room with as much dignity as she could muster. It was as she had suspected. She would get nowhere in her campaign as long as the nurse was tapping into Jack's heart. She would have to be gotten rid of, she must not be allowed to stay and distract Jack from what he truly needed.

Jack muttered an oath, his eyes going to the grating that separated the nursery from Victoria's room. She had overheard every single word, he was sure. He strode to the door and whipped it open, startling Victoria, who hovered beneath the grating, one ear cocked to the ceiling. Crossing his arms and leaning against the doorjamb, Jack waited for Victoria to begin denying that she had been eavesdropping. But she surprised him.

Raising up her hands, Victoria smiled. "Caught red-handed." And red-face, Victoria realized, feeling her face flush. "Are you planning to marry Suzanne?" she managed to ask conversationally.

Jack somehow managed to scowl and smile at the same time. "Of course not."

Victoria tilted her head and smiled, glad to hear him say it aloud, even though a part of her feared his rejection of Suzanne just might have something to do with her.

Victoria bit her lip. "Second question. *Do* you love me?" Victoria said it lightly, as if the answer didn't matter one whit to her, as if her world wasn't careening out of control waiting for the answer. To make matters worse, Jack became serious, and Victoria's heart began slamming painfully against her chest.

"It would be incredibly inappropriate for someone like me to love someone like you," he said, thinking he was being evasive, not insulting. Victoria was definitely insulted.

Her mouth gaped open in surprise. "What a snob you are. I have more money . . ." She stopped, realizing what she was saying.

Jack raised one eyebrow. "Yes?"

Victoria crossed her arms. "Never mind," she grumbled. "But I still think you're a snob."

Jack smiled the smile that let him get away with almost anything with Victoria. "I'll add that to my vast list of faults."

"That list is getting rather long, isn't it?"

"Let's see if I remember correctly. Misogynist, bigot, prude, narrow-minded, snob, of course. Have I missed any?"

Victoria stopped herself from laughing aloud. Barely. "Hypocrite. But I took that one back almost immediately." That one had slipped out during one of their more animated conversations.

"Ah, yes." Jack grinned and resisted the urge to kiss her again. By God, she was the most kissable woman he had ever met. He recalled Suzanne's cold lips that had just moments ago been pressed to his, and he had an almost overwhelming desire to erase that memory with Victoria's soft, warm mouth.

"Oh, my God. Emma! I almost forgot all about her." Victoria brushed past Jack and hurried to the crib, immediately placing a hand on her forehead. Her eyes when she lifted them to Jack were bright with relief. "She's cool." She resisted the terrible urge to pick her up, knowing that the little girl needed her rest.

Victoria bit her lip to stop the tears that threatened to appear. "We almost lost her, didn't we?"

She watched as he worked his jaw before forcing a smile. "We didn't lose her. But I won't be happy until the doctor tells me it's over."

Victoria gave him a mischievous grin, hoping to distract Jack from his worry. "You know, you never really answered my question."

Jack raised one eyebrow. "What question was that?"

She lifted her chin and tilted her head. "You know, the question about whether you love me or not."

Jack pressed his lips together, an unsuccessful attempt to hide the smile that threatened, and left the room without another word.

Sixteen

New Hampshire. He'd be gone for at least a week. A week without Emma. A week without Victoria. Jack stared at the blank paper in front of him and frowned. His mind was as devoid of ideas for this project as the paper was of lead from his pencil. There was no getting away from it any longer. To get any real ideas for this design, he would have to visit the site in the White Mountains. Once there, he knew the image of Joshua Taylor's hunting cottage would burst into his brain, as if it had been hibernating and just waiting for spring.

Jack tapped his pencil against the sheet of paper in thought. Emma was now fully recovered from her bout with the measles, and he could no longer use that as an excuse to Mr. Taylor why he had not gone to the site. The man was getting impatient, for construction was to begin as soon as the thaw set in, and the design was already weeks behind schedule. Jack had hoped he could design the house from the photos of the spot Taylor provided, but his mind was frustratingly blank. He would have to go and leave Emma behind.

Since her illness, Jack had tried to bring as much work home as possible so he could spend more time with his daughter. And, of course, that meant spending more time with Victoria. He could no longer convince even himself that it was only the thought of leaving Emma behind that kept him from going to New

Hampshire. He would miss Victoria more than he cared to admit. And that bothered the hell out of him.

Jack smiled, picturing Victoria sprawled out on the floor, trying to encourage Emma to crawl, her skirts exposing her stockinged legs nearly to her knee. If Emma happily gurgling on the floor wasn't enough distraction, the sight of Victoria's slim leg made it nearly impossible to get a lick of work done. He hadn't complained. Hardly. Instead, he'd leaned back in his chair and watched them play for long minutes while pretending to think. He suspected that had Victoria known that the only thing he'd been thinking about was how trim her ankle was, she'd have bolted from the room. Or else called him to task, her lovely face flushed with anger.

Then it came to him. He could bring Emma along with him to New Hampshire. There was no reason why he could not bring her along. Why, he could bring Victoria along, too. To watch Emma. Yes. Someone would have to watch Emma when he was surveying the site and making sketches. They could all stay at Taylor's small lodge. No one was there now, except for the caretakers. They could be informed that he was coming up to the spot, that a woman and baby would be along. That would make it respectable. Not that he needed anything to make this trip seem respectable, he told himself. It was completely, totally without hidden meaning, this trip he planned with Emma. And Victoria.

Liar.

Jack frowned at his pencil, which left little dots on his once clean piece of paper, and stuck it behind his ear. The pencil was still there two hours later when he hemmed and hawed his way through telling Victoria about his idea for a trip for Emma. As if he were nervous about something. As if bringing Victoria along were not completely and totally proper. They were packed and gone before he thought to tell Suzanne about the trip.

* * *

"It's gorgeous," Victoria said, her breath coming out in a vaporous puff. They stood at the base of Mount Stinson with the snowy White Mountains looming up behind it. This last leg of the trip on a horse-driven sleigh, complete with jingling bells, had been magical. Wearing a fur-lined coat Victoria suspected was a cast-off from Christina, the only part of her that was cold was her cheeks and nose. Jack had wrapped a blanket around her feet, bundled Emma up in a fur wrap so that only her tiny face was exposed to the crisp air, and sat down beside her, a look of satisfaction on his flushed features.

The driver was Mr. Bitters, Taylor's jovial caretaker who talked more to the two horses dragging the sleigh than to his passengers, but who somehow managed to talk to Victoria and Jack through the horses nonetheless. Victoria laughed at his odd manner, feeling wonderful and alive sitting next to Jack and holding Emma close against her. It was easy to imagine, much too easy, that they were a family. It seemed that they were, the way they sat so close, the way their eyes met, the way they laughed together at the older man's banter. When they finally stopped in front of the rustic lodge, white smoke drifting lazily up from a center chimney, it was all just too perfect, and Victoria suddenly had an overwhelming need to cry. Instead she made an inane comment on the view.

"Yes. Very pretty. I'm not sure I'd change a thing," Jack said, but his voice was tinged with excitement, and Victoria knew he couldn't wait to take out his sketch pad.

"Windows."

"Windows?" Victoria asked.

Jack shook his head. "It's already here," he said, tapping his head. "I knew it was. I knew it. The house. Lot's of windows. Stone and shingle. It's . . . perfect."

Victoria smiled at his pleasure. Then her heart wrenched, and she wanted to shout: "Stop it. Stop making me feel like I'm a part of you when I'm not, when I never can be. Don't you see what you're doing to me? Can't you see that I've fallen in love with you?"

She tore her gaze away from his face and made to disembark. He leapt down and helped her, of course, for she couldn't have managed to do so on her own. Not with her holding Emma and her bulky coat and skirts tangled about her legs. He put his hands around her waist, and she could feel the heat of them, through all those layers, through even his thick leather gloves. And then she realized it was impossible, that the heat she felt could only be her imagination. Her boots crunched in the snow. It wasn't as deep as she'd thought. Only four inches of the white stuff.

"I'm going to tend to the horses. You go right in. The missus is there, by the cookstove, likely as not cooking enough food for ten people 'stead of the four that we are," Mr. Bitters said. And Victoria knew right then that the old man loved his wife, loved the fact she would fuss and fret and make too much food. Tears threatened again, making Victoria wonder if she was going a bit daft.

The woman who opened the door looked so much like Aunt Bee from the *Andy Griffith Show,* that for a second she almost asked if it were she. Her voice was different, though, softer and surprisingly cultured, given that the man she married seemed a more common sort.

After politely asking about their trip and commenting on what a good baby Emma was, she went about helping them peel off their coats, mufflers, and gloves as Victoria took in her surroundings. The lodge seemed to consist of one main room, a staircase and kitchen downstairs with a loft upstairs. From her spot near the door, Victoria counted two doorways in the loft—two bedrooms. Mr. and Mrs. Bitters must be staying elsewhere, leaving Jack and Emma and herself to fend for themselves. Victoria's eyes were riveted on those two doors, then she cast a sidelong look at Jack, biting her lip. Had he known they would be alone? He couldn't have. Mr. Oh-So-Proper would never have invited her along if he'd known. Would he have?

"It's not as large as I'd thought," Jack said to Mrs. Bitters.

"That's why Mr. Taylor is building a bigger house, you see," Mrs. Bitters explained.

"Of course."

Jack *hadn't* known. For some reason, Victoria was glad.

"Usually, when there's more visitors, we set up cots," Mrs. Bitters said helpfully. "But it's not very comfortable, and with our cabin just a short distance away, I'm sure Miss Casey won't mind."

"Mind?" Victoria asked.

"Won't mind the short walk." Seeing Victoria's confusion, Mrs. Bitters flushed, obviously wondering if she had completely misread the situation.

A lightbulb went on in Victoria's head. "Oh. *Oh.* You mean I won't mind walking to your cabin at bedtime. Of course not. I hope Emma won't disturb you."

Mrs. Bitters, smoothing down her wrinkless apron, looked immensely relieved. "No, no. I adore babies. I had five myself. Of course they're all grown now and on their own. Not too far away, thank goodness. But not too close, either." And she let out a small chuckle. "I thought it would be better for you and the baby to stay at our cabin than here. It's a bit more homey, a bit more comfortable."

"That sounds wonderful." Victoria was relieved, she truly, truly was. She was afraid that the intimacy of the place, its rustic charm, that huge fireplace with that inviting bear's rug in front of it would chip away at her resolve. Victoria knew it would take only the slightest encouragement from Jack for her to be in his arms and making a complete fool of herself.

Jack was disappointed, although he told himself he

was relieved. He told himself several times, in fact. Then his eyes strayed to that bear rug, and he pictured Victoria there, her skin creamy and glowing gold from the fire, flushed from his touch. Dear Lord, he thought, wiping a bit of sweat from his brow, thank God the old woman is here to keep me in line. Poor Victoria, she'd run like a frightened deer if she knew what I had on my mind, Jack thought. He'd seen her eyes dart up to those bedrooms, and he'd seen her obvious relief when Mrs. Bitters explained the sleeping arrangements. It was more than obvious that Victoria had been scared to death to stay alone in this lodge with him.

And for good reason, Jack thought.

Dinner was a feast of thick venison stew and biscuits slathered with butter that Victoria swore to Mrs. Bitters melted in her mouth. She refused to think about the fat and cholesterol she'd just crammed into her little body as she patted her full stomach appreciatively.

"I haven't eaten that much in years," Victoria said leaning back in her chair, wishing she could loosen her stays.

"It certainly doesn't look like it," Mrs. Bitters said. "I can't believe a tiny thing like you managed to eat two full helpings."

"And I was eyeing a third, but my stomach refuses to oblige. See, Mr. Bitters? It's a good thing your wife cooked for ten. We ate like ten people."

Mrs. Bitters cast her husband a good-natured glare. "He's always complaining about how I cook too much food, but he's the one who's raiding the cold box every night at midnight. And he's got the stomach to prove it."

"Now, Thelma, are you saying that I'm fat?" Mr. Bitters asked, scratching his rather large stomach.

"Yes, Richard, I am," she said matter-of-factly.

The table erupted with laughter, and suddenly, it was all too much for Victoria. Too happy, too much

like a family. Standing abruptly, she mumbled an excuse, grabbed her coat, and headed for the door before the tears that had been threatening all day spilled
over. The cold air stole the breath from her lungs as
she hurried away from the lodge. A wedge of light
sliced into the snow from behind her, and she knew
without looking that someone had followed her out.
Stopping, she hunched into her coat hoping it was
Jack and dreading it was him at the same time.

Mrs. Bitters lay a hand on her arm and gave a
hearty squeeze. "Want to tell me about it?" she
asked kindly.

With a loud sniff, Victoria shook her head. "It's just
that you seem so . . . happy."

Mrs. Bitters smiled at her tragic tone. "And that
made you sad?"

"Yes. Because . . ."

Mrs. Bitters waited for Victoria to continue, giving
her arm another little squeeze for encouragement.

"It's been building for a while." She shook her head
and gave another loud sniff. "I suppose I was in denial. For one thing, I miss my own family, and seeing
you and Mr. Bitters reminded me of home. But I guess
the real reason is that I'll never have that for myself.
I'm just feeling sorry for myself, and I'm the last person on earth who should."

"You're a young woman, Miss Casey. Who knows
what's in the future? Now, if you were some nasty girl
or had awful warts all over your face, I wouldn't try
to give you false hope. But you're a lovely young girl
who's simply feeling very lonely."

Victoria almost argued with her but realized it
would be futile. Mrs. Bitters could never know that
Victoria would never be a part of a family, would
never sit across a table from her husband and playfully
call him fat. In that moment, standing in the snow,
her lungs hurting from the sharp December air, Victoria fully realized what her vow had meant. It struck
her as strange that it hadn't occurred to her before,

at least not with such force. She'd simply wanted an escape from the endless pain, the endless sameness of her life.

"You're right, Mrs. Bitters. I'm sure I'll find someone." Victoria tried to make her voice bright, but she failed miserably.

The old woman took a deep breath. "Are you in love with anyone right now?"

"I can't be," she whispered.

"I see," Mrs. Bitters said sadly, looking back at the lodge.

Victoria jammed her hands into the coat's deep pockets and looked up at a sky so full of stars, it seemed almost hazy. "The man I love is a very kind and handsome man. He'll make someone a wonderful husband. And I am certain that someone will not be me. Now. Let's go back inside. It's like the Arctic out here!"

The two women trudged back to the lodge, where the men waited as men do when a woman runs from a room in tears for apparently no discernible reason.

On the fourth day at the lodge, Victoria spotted Jack's sketch pad on the dining room table and inched slowly over to it. Jack wasn't about, Emma was playing on the bear rug, letting her fingers run through the fur over and over again, and there was the sketch pad just sitting there. Jack had not let her see his drawings and had been so secretive about them, it was almost comical. It was also driving Victoria insane with curiosity. After gushing about windows and stone and shingles that first day, she hadn't been able to get another word out of him about his design.

Victoria stood by the table, casting another look around the room, then walked her fingers over to the pad, nudging it a bit with her index finger. She tapped her fingers on the cover and bit her lower lip. She really shouldn't look. Really, really shouldn't. She positioned her thumb beneath the cover while she continued to tap, tap. Oh, what the heck, just one peek.

"That's not it."

Victoria practically jumped out of her shoes at the sound of Jack's voice coming from the loft.

"Oh. I know it's not the sketch pad . . . Okay." She gave him an impish smile. "So I thought it was. If you weren't so darned secretive about it, I wouldn't be so curious. So, you see, it's really your fault that I've had to stoop so low as to snoop."

Jack shook his head and chuckled, a low rumble in his chest. "Your logic amazes me."

Victoria grinned. "Me, too."

"Instead of showing you the design, how would you like a personal tour?" he asked as he walked down the stairs.

"How could you possibly do that?" Victoria asked, narrowing her eyes.

"Come with me and find out."

After dropping Emma off with Mrs. Bitters, Victoria and Jack headed up a narrow trail behind the lodge. Although they stopped only a few hundred feet above the lodge, the view from the spot was breathtaking.

"I don't know why Taylor didn't build his lodge here in the first place. Probably more work, I suppose. But can you just imagine it? My God, I'm almost tempted to make Taylor an offer for this land, though I doubt he'd take it."

They stood on a grassy flat, looking down on the icy lake and the mountain range beyond. Behind them, the mountain rose lazily, becoming steeper only near the peak. It was a sharply beautiful day, the sky painfully blue, the snow glaringly white.

"It's perfect. Absolutely perfect," Victoria said in hushed tones. "Are you sure you want to build a house here?"

Jack gave her an indulgent smile. "You're thinking that a house will ruin the site. Ah, but this will not be just any house." Victoria rolled her eyes. "This," he continued, ignoring her skepticism, "will be a perfect blend of man and nature. The house will be part of the mountain, the mountain part of the house. Windows, stone, shingle. That's it."

"But you already told me that much," she complained. "Where are we standing right now? Which room?"

"First or second floor?"

"First. And second," Victoria added quickly, just in case he refused to divulge more information.

"You're standing in the great room. Behind you is a stone fireplace big enough for you to stand up in. The walls are mahogany panel, the floor pine. In front of you is a wall of windows stretching from ceiling to floor. To the left and right are slightly smaller windows, from ceiling to deep, cushioned window seats. No drapery. None."

"Hmmm. And upstairs?"

"The master bedroom," Jack said, his voice low. "Again, windows and a stone fireplace. Molded ceilings. A fan. A thick carpet."

Victoria had her eyes closed as his voice built the room in her mind. "You're a decorator, too?"

Jack let out a low laugh. "It's just the way I picture it. Taylor will probably come up with something entirely different."

"That's too bad," Victoria said, turning, not realizing how close Jack was. She was a breath away, so close, the front of her coat brushed his. So close, the vapor from his mouth hit her face in little puffs. "I think I'll take a seat in the great room," she said, and plopped down on a nearby rock.

Jack, his back toward Victoria, closed his eyes and let out the breath he'd been holding in before turning and sitting down next to her. But not too close. They sat in silence for a long moment, both taking in the view, lost in their thoughts of what this site would soon contain.

"I've always been amazed what money can buy you," Victoria said without bitterness. "I know a poor man could build a shack here and have the same exact view, but the rich seem to have access to more beauty than the poor. I suppose you've never thought about it much."

"Why do you say that?"

"Well. It's not as if you're poor, Mr. Wilkins."

"I'm afraid I'm going to have to disappoint you, Miss Casey, if you were about to go into a speech about the evils of money. I have not always been this fortunate. I *was* fortunate, however, to have married a very wealthy woman."

Victoria flushed bright red. "Oh." The dead wife.

"How did you meet her? Christina." Victoria felt guilty even saying the woman's name aloud. Even though she was dead, Victoria felt awful talking about the woman whose husband she was in love with. But she was also incredibly curious.

"I was just out of school and working on my first project. A guest house for a wealthy family's summer cottage."

"The St. Georges," Victoria guessed.

His eyes looked out at the horizon, but Victoria knew he was reliving that summer.

"Christina was so . . . delicate. She would sit on a chaise covered up in a blanket even on the hottest days. At first I just said hello. But eventually we began talking. She was lovely and somehow tragic. Even then there was that about her. I suppose that was part of what I fell in love with. Christina made me feel strong, like the sun rose and set around me. She would look at me . . . No one ever looked at me the way she did." He took a deep breath. "I couldn't believe it when her parents made no objections to our hopes to marry. I never gave the money a second thought. Never. It was only later that I realized how different we were. When her father gave us the Beacon Hill house for a wedding present, I was dazzled."

"Of course you were. It was an incredible gift."

"I embarrassed them with my gratitude." Jack shrugged away the painful memory. "I thought, I don't know why, that I could make Christina better. Somehow I thought if I could give her some of my strength . . . But it didn't work. Nothing worked."

Victoria closed her eyes against what she thought was pain in Jack's face. "You must have loved her very much."

Victoria watched as his hands, folded together across his knees, tightened until his knuckles shone white. "No. I didn't." He said the words so softly, Victoria wasn't sure she heard him correctly.

"I've never said that aloud." There was amazement in his voice. "She was my wife, but she wasn't a wife to me. She needed me so much, she drained me. I . . ." He let out a shaky breath, and Victoria held her own, waiting for him to continue. "I did love her once. I did. And I know she never stopped loving me."

"What happened?" Victoria whispered.

"She was always ill. I know it sounds horrible, it sounds so callous. But you cannot know what it's like to live with someone who is never well, who is always complaining of something. We rarely left the house together. She rarely left her bed. We couldn't have children because she feared she would die. And so we . . ." He straightened his shoulders. "I felt . . . feel . . . so . . ."

"Guilty. You feel guilty."

Jack turned his head to her suddenly, his eyes hard, as if she had accused him of something. And then they softened, and he smiled. "Yes. I feel guilty. Guilty for not being able to love her. Guilty for hating her. I did. Sometimes I actually loathed her, the poor thing. It wasn't her fault. I knew it and that made it all the worse. A doctor told me she wasn't actually ill at all, that there was nothing physically wrong with her. Until that point, I had accepted our life together. But after that, I could hardly pretend. Every time I looked at her sitting in that bed, I wanted to shake her until she admitted she was fine."

"But you didn't. You stuck by her. Didn't you?"

"Yes." But his voice was dead.

Victoria stared at him a long moment before she lifted her gloved hand and clutched one of his. "She never knew how you felt, did she."

"I hope not."

She shook his hand, forcing him to look at her. "Do you see? You're not such a bad person, after all. You're not a saint, and only a saint could not have had the feelings you did. You were angry. You felt betrayed. And you were mad at yourself for building up a dream in your heart that you could never realize. If you've been carrying around this baggage about what a rotten person you are, you should stop it. You are one of the nicest people I have ever met." At his snort she insisted, "You are!"

"I didn't tell you this story to boost myself up," he said.

She looked at him, her eyes drinking in every beautiful feature of his face, fully aware that he need only look to see that she had fallen head over heels in love with him. "Why did you tell this to me?"

He looked away, his eyes scanning the horizon. Instead of answering her, he stood up and held out his hand to help her up. "Let's go home."

Seventeen

Victoria wiped away the condensation on the nursery window so that she could look outside at the gray day. It looked like snow, she thought, hugging her arms around her. Maybe it would be a white Christmas after all. She was suddenly homesick in a way she had not been before now. Not even Thanksgiving had sent her thoughts to her family, for she had been too preoccupied with getting Emma well. Even though she had not seen her parents more than a handful of times since her accident, Victoria had always felt close to them—especially her father. Her thoughts did not drift to the two Christmases following her accident, but to the numerous ones before. Holidays filled with laughter and spiked eggnog and awful sweaters she never wore but couldn't bear to throw away. Time had put a pleasant hazy glow on her memories, and Victoria found herself close to tears and wondering for the first time whether she had done the right thing by taking this new life.

"I miss you, Dad and Mom. I miss you so much," she whispered into the window, which turned foggy with her breath. She continued talking to her parents silently. When Victoria had made the decision to "die," she had been in too much mental pain to realize the full impact of her decision. She had not seen her parents before taking that ride to the lake, but said good-bye over the phone. It had been a normal conversation, dull talk about family and friends. Declarations of love and sentimental words would have rung as loudly as an alarm. And so she had not said the good-bye she had wanted to, only a quickly throat-constricted "love ya" to both parents before she slowly placed the phone on its hook.

"I miss you guys so much," she told them silently. "I never knew how much I counted on you to be there, to listen to me complain. I'm sorry I did this to you." She wiped a tear away, telling herself she should stop this silent monologue; it made her too, too sad. "Merry Christmas," she whispered.

"Victoria." Jack's voice rumbled through her, drawing her away from her melancholy thoughts. He always timed his entrances perfectly, Victoria thought as she turned toward him, her smile genuine.

"You're crying."

"Oh, no. Not really. I was just a bit homesick. Remembering Christmases when my parents were still alive," she said, blinking her eyes to disperse the unshed tears. She wiped her cheeks with her fingertips, then self-consciously dried them on her skirt.

She's lonely, Jack thought. Why have I never considered how lonely she must be? As lonely as I am. That urge to hold her swept over him, suffocated him, but he covered it with a stiff smile. There had been no talk of feelings between the two since their banter weeks ago. They had slipped back into their friendship easily enough, debating the day's issues pleasantly, if impersonally. If he looked at her lips a little too often, if he found himself wanting to bury his hands into her hair, he never let it show. And if she wanted to discover if his thighs were as hard as they looked, if she wanted to know what it would be like to make love to a man who made her feel small and feminine, she never let on. It was impossible, and they both knew it. So they ignored it.

"I've brought you a gift," he said, holding out a thin package.

"Oh." Victoria's smile was like a knife in his heart.

She snatched it from him like a greedy child, smiling mischievously up at him.

"It's nothing . . ."

"It's beautiful," Victoria said, unfolding the deep blue virgin wool scarf and holding it against her face. Just as he suspected, the color brought out the blue in her changeable eyes. "Thank you, Mr. Wilkins."

Etta burst into the room at that moment, a green plaid scarf clutched in her hands. "Ooo. I seen you got yours, too. Ain't it beautiful?" Etta, her cheeks flushed with pleasure, held out the plaid version of the same scarf Victoria held lovingly in her hands. "Downstairs staff got handkerchiefs," Etta said, subtly pointing out their superiority over the others in the household.

Victoria flushed, feeling foolish for thinking the gift something special, something that Jack had picked out specially for her. Even had he been inclined to, he would not have, she knew. "Yours is pretty, too, Etta. But I still like mine better," she said, forcing herself to sound jovial.

Jack wanted to explain, to tell her about the beautiful statue he had wanted to give her, but had been unable to give her. He had been with Suzanne when he spied the statue—a woman holding a child up in the air, her face one of serenity, the baby's one of pure happiness. He had picked it up, wrestling with the urge to put it among their other purchases, when Suzanne had come upon him. He could not buy it without explaining whom it was for, and so he had replaced it, thinking that perhaps he would return later. It was then that Suzanne showed him the scarves she had picked out for Etta and Victoria; the plaid for Etta and a drab brown for Victoria. At least he had picked the color.

"It makes her eyes blue," he said, his eyes intense, willing her to understand but somehow afraid that she might.

"So it does," Etta said, holding the scarf against

Victoria's cheek. Victoria gave Jack a small smile, and he felt redeemed. "Does my scarf make my eyes look plaid?" Etta joked. The three burst out laughing.

Etta went off to flaunt her gift to the rest of the staff, leaving Jack and Victoria alone. "I don't have anything for you. But I guess that wouldn't be appropriate anyway. You being the rich man and me being the lowly servant, that is."

Jack's eyes crinkled, but he managed to make his mouth remain stern. "Oh, no, that's not so. The aristocracy willingly accepts gifts from their underlings with no shame."

"Well, you're out of luck. I've nothing for you." Victoria put one fist under her chin and appeared to think. "Nope. I'm afraid nothing I own is worthy of aristocracy. Ah! I've got it! I will bestow upon you the only thing I have worth anything."

Smiling broadly, enjoying this game of hers, he said, "And what would that be?"

"A Christmas kiss."

Jack's smile froze on his face as his body reacted immediately and fiercely to her innocent offering. And it was innocent—it had to be. For if she gave him any indication it was anything else, God help him, he knew he would not be able to stop himself. His eyes traveled to those lips offered to him so blithely, and shifted to relieve some of the pressure that was building in his loins.

"I think not," he said, his voice tight, his body taut.

Those three words bruised Victoria's heart, leaving her feeling rather foolish. "I'm sorry. I . . . didn't mean anything by it." She closed her eyes, hating the way she sounded, knowing he'd have to be a complete idiot not to see how much she loved him. "I was just trying to be funny."

"You think offering me . . . Your idea of what is amusing is difficult to understand, Miss Casey. You cannot be so innocent to think you can offer a kiss to a man without some sort of . . . reaction."

A smile of dawning realization appeared upon her lips, and her heart lifted. "Ooohhh. I see now."

Jack drew up stiffly, acting affronted. "Just what do you see?"

Victoria wrinkled her nose at him. "You *want* to kiss me, and that's why you're so upset." She knew she was treading on dangerous ground, but carried on as her heart soared with the knowledge that she had not imagined those heated looks he had sometimes thrown her way.

Jack battled the ridiculous urge to run from the little temptress. He knew what would happen should they kiss; he knew, and it scared him. He would no longer be able to ignore how he felt. The game would be over.

He breathed in harshly as she came toward him and flinched when she lay a hand on his chest. She didn't know, she couldn't know what she was doing to him. "Miss Casey, I believe . . ."

". . . So do I." And she stood on her toes, hands on each shoulder, and kissed him, pressed her lips against his and pulled back slowly. He stood there, his body rock hard, hands curled into fists by his side, feeling he would surely die if she pressed up against him any tighter. He was about to congratulate himself on his fortitude when he felt her sweet lips again, pressing softly against his.

Victoria was beginning to feel very foolish kissing him not once but twice, and getting absolutely no response. Not that she wanted a response, she told herself quickly. But he hadn't even kissed back! She was about to pull away when she found herself wrapped up in a steel embrace, her mouth crushed, her neck forced back. He was devouring her with mouth and tongue and teeth, licking, nipping, sucking. He moved her with near violence against a wall, her head banging sharply, but all she could feel was his mouth on hers, his hands molding her buttocks and pressing her against his hardness. Wrapping one ankle around his leg, she pulled him even closer, letting out sighs of frustration, wishing that they were already naked and pressed together flesh to flesh.

Victoria buried her hands in his hair, relishing the feel of him, the taste. Oh, finally, finally to touch him, taste him. All her fantasies could not have conjured up this fire she felt. His hands were hot against her thighs. When had he lifted her skirt? she wondered, then realized her hands were beneath his shirt, clutching his muscled back. They were silent except for the muffled moans of pleasure, the rustling of clothes, the harsh breathing. His mouth was at her throat, biting gently, driving her wild, making her want to scream for him to rip off the layers of clothing that kept his hands from her. When she felt the cool, cool air against her chest, she urged him on. "Yes," she whispered against his ear.

And then he stopped. He was all rigid muscle, granite hard. He might have been a statue but for his heaving chest.

"Suzanne," he whispered. "Hurry." He swung her away from the wall and pushed her toward her room. Dazed, Victoria managed to gather enough wits to command her legs to run from the room, her fingers already at her buttons working furiously to fasten them. She turned to look at Jack as he tucked in his shirt, and would have smiled if his expression hadn't stopped her cold. He did not look like a man who had just enjoyed himself. He looked . . . hunted.

Victoria closed the door behind her and pressed her back up against it, one hand still clutching the crystal doorknob, and squeezed her eyes shut. I shouldn't have come on so strong, she thought, her face heating miserably. Sure, I enjoyed myself, I'm a product of the sexual revolution. But he has probably never encountered a woman as free with her . . . favors. Damn, she thought, beating a fist painfully against her thigh. "What a big . . ."

*   *   *

". . . mistake," Jack said, his arms behind his back. He looked rather like what he was, Victoria thought: a wealthy Bostonian speaking to his servant.

"I agree," Victoria said quickly, not wanting him to think she was mooning over him. She ignored the maniacal beating of her heart at seeing him again. Heck, her heart started its annoying pounding when Etta came to get her because "Mr. Wilkins says he wants to see you in his library immediately." She was quite sure he didn't want to see her so he could kiss her again—if that high impact meeting of mouths could be characterized as mere kissing. "It was a mistake. Definitely."

His head snapped up at her ready admission, but Victoria was disappointed to note that he seemed relieved. "I'm glad we are in agreement," he said, his voice uncharacteristically clipped. Never before in his life had he been so entirely out of control as he had when he'd pressed her against that wall. He dimly remembered a mild "thunk" as her head hit the wall, and then all was feeling. Incredible, impossible sensations driving him to a point where he did not recognize himself. He'd looked in the mirror later that night thinking he would see a stranger there. For Jack Wilkins never, ever had lost control like that. It was, well, it was damn frightening, that's what it was.

And it would not happen again, he told himself forcefully as he gazed at her impudent little face turned up toward his, defiant as all hell. And desirable. God, those lips that could drive him insane with one touch. That neck, smooth beneath his lips, smelling clean and lemony. He felt his body react before he could stop his brain from imagining what this firebrand would be like when he made her scream in pleasure.

"Jesus," he muttered, and turned away angrily, leaving Victoria staring at his back and wondering just what she had done now. A creeping fear began to form: What if he believed it was intolerable for her to remain in the house? What if he blamed the entire episode on her? After all, she was the one who instigated the kiss. She practically threw herself at him. And she certainly hadn't protested when things got a bit hotter than even she had intended. She watched as he jerked his chair out from his desk and sat down. Then he stood up, just as angrily.

"It won't happen again," he bit out.

Victoria swallowed. "Of course not."

He stared at her as if that was not the response he was expecting. "I'm sure you didn't mean . . . That is, when you kissed me, I'm sure that was all you intended."

Victoria bit her lip and practically squirmed. "Well, I sure didn't expect things to explode the way they did."

Jack's brows creased. "I certainly did not explode."

Victoria crossed her arms. "I didn't say *you* exploded. I said *things* exploded."

Jack gave a little grunt that Victoria supposed meant he was somewhat satisfied. "You must understand that I am not a man who . . . dallies with the servants. I have certain codes that I live by, and I have broken one of those codes." He meant to reassure her, to apologize for his bad behavior.

Victoria felt sick with embarrassment. She hadn't realized how important class was until that moment. After all their talks, the laughter shared, the heartache over Emma, even after that incredibly hot kiss, the only emotion he could feel was guilt over "dallying" with a servant. Victoria tried to feel happy that he felt nothing for her, for in her heart she knew it was best. But that same heart felt as if it were being squeezed by a fist. That's what you get when you let yourself fall in love, she thought. She was so heartsick at that moment, Victoria couldn't gather enough energy to get angry at his snobbishness. He must feel sorry for her, the poor little nurse throwing herself at her employer.

Victoria stood up abruptly, her hands clutched in front of her, knuckles white, fingers digging into her palms. "I didn't realize," she said, the last word coming out a whisper as her throat constricted.

Jack's gaze intensified. He couldn't believe what his eyes plainly told him. Victoria had been hurt by his words. *Hurt.* And that could mean only one thing. She had feelings for him. He found himself smiling before he could stop himself, leaving Victoria utterly confused.

He walked toward her, his eyes pinning her to the spot, closing in until she had to tilt her head up to look into those burning eyes. "If I dismissed you, Miss Casey, what would you do?"

Victoria's harsh intake of breath nearly turned into a sob. She was so close to crumbling, to letting out a gush of tears, for a moment she could not speak. Bringing her eyes down, she stared at his neatly tied cravat, concentrating on that bit of cloth so that she wouldn't cry. "I don't know what I'd do," she managed. "I would miss Emma very much. I would . . . not want to be dismissed." Victoria closed her eyes, hating how pathetic she sounded, but realizing she felt rather pathetic at the moment.

She felt his knuckle under her chin as he raised her head to force her to look at him. Her eyes slowly slid upward, finally meeting his gaze.

"Would you also miss me, Victoria?" He watched as her expression became closed, her eyes blank.

Victoria clenched her jaw. Why is he doing this to me? Does he get his jollies out of making a fool of me? Lifting her chin off his hand belligerently, Victoria said, "What do you want me to say to you? That I'll miss you? That I love you? So then you can give me a lecture about how servants should keep to their station in life? Is that what would make you happy? I don't know where you got the idea that you can step on someone's heart just because they don't have lots of money."

Jack stiffened at her words, then immediately relaxed. She had practically declared her love for him. All her bitter words came down to that simple truth. He smiled again, much to Victoria's disgust.

"Go ahead and smile, you pigheaded misogynistic hedonist," she spat.

"Quite a vocabulary for a servant," he said blandly.

She had never been quite so angry in her life. Victoria acted without thinking, swinging her fist full force toward his smug face. But instead of making contact with his hard jaw, she found her fist enveloped by the steel grip of his fingers. She stared at his hand, eyes narrowed, lips pressed together so tightly they nearly disappeared, trying to force that fist through his hand and into his face.

"Stop it, Victoria," he said gently.

Victoria darted a look to his face, and seeing yet another smile there, renewed her effort, this time swinging her left hand toward his upturned lips. He thwarted her this time by wrapping one arm around her waist and pulling her close so that her ill-aimed punch passed harmlessly by his ear.

Victoria struggled against him, but quickly realized her little body was no match for his. She might as well have been tied to an oak tree. And so she stood stock-still, stiff and unyielding.

"I'm pleased," he whispered in her ear.

Victoria had decided not to say another word to him, but her curiosity overcame her. "Pleased with what?"

"That you love me."

Of all the arrogant, vain, egotistical . . . Oh, how the hell did he find out?

Victoria gave him what he hoped was her haughtiest look. "Just what makes you think I love you?"

"You deny it?" Jack tried to make his tone light, as if he were engaging in another bout of light banter, but his insides were twisting nervously.

Go ahead, Victoria shouted to herself, deny it. Deny

it, damn you stupid woman. "No." It was said so softly, he couldn't be sure he heard the word. She lifted her chin. "No. I don't deny it. Pretty stupid, aren't I? Pretty goddamned stupid."

She shoved away, disgusted with herself, heartbroken with the knowledge that she would likely be dismissed. Why did she always have to be so damned honest. Why couldn't she lie just a little? Victoria was marching toward the door, continuing her litany against herself when she stopped dead. *I'm pleased.*

Victoria spun around, her mouth opened just slightly, and stared at Jack with disbelief. "You're not going to fire me?"

Just a hint of a smile appeared on his lips. "No."

Victoria gave him a smile of her own. "Okay. But you have to promise me one thing."

"What's that?"

Victoria took one small step toward him, then stopped. "You must promise to not fall in love with me."

Jack's smile faltered. "Promise me, Mr. Wilkins. Jack. You must."

"I promise," he said. He could keep that promise, he thought, for it was already too late. He had *already* fallen in love with her.

Eighteen

Henrietta Martin shook her foot in an attempt to get the water out of her shoe. It was a fruitless effort, for she still had another four blocks to walk and rainwater was running down the street like a muddy river. She hoped the water wouldn't completely ruin her shoes: they cost two dollars at Houghton & Dutton, and there wouldn't be another two dollars for shoes for quite some time. Clutching her umbrella, Etta skirted around the worst of the puddles. "Would have to pick the nastiest day in the nastiest part of the city for this," she grumbled.

"Hey, Etta! Over here," Tom Reilly called, shielding his hat with a soggy newspaper.

Etta gave him a scowl, but she was pleased to see Tom just the same. She had chanced to meet him two days before, a meeting she had since concluded wasn't chance at all. But Etta didn't mind. Tom had been good to her family, and anything she could do to help him out with his boss, she would do.

"Nasty one, eh? We'll get you inside in a jiffy. A pint in your belly ought to do the trick," he said, coming up beside Etta and taking her arm. "Appreciate this. Kevin's been a might testy lately, and I'd told him you could help. Hope you can."

Tom stepped down an alley and pulled open the heavy wooden door that was flush with the pocked brick wall. Only a small painted sign above the door marked it as a drinking establishment: TIMOTHY'S PUB.

Etta shook out her umbrella and squinted her eyes as she adjusted to the dim interior. Two chandeliers hung from the tin ceiling, stained from years of tobacco smoke, but the light was muted by the light fog of cigar and pipe smoke. The pub was nearly empty at this early hour, but Etta knew that by six o'clock, when the work shifts were ending, the place would be thick with smoke and patrons.

Kevin Donnelly stood politely as Etta was led to his table. "Pleased to meet you, Miss Martin," he said, flashing his brilliant smile and bowing outlandishly. Etta couldn't help but blush and giggle at this Irish rake. She was immediately and completely charmed the instant that handsome devil gave her an admiring glance, despite Tom's warning that he was a tough character.

They talked about the weather, about mutual acquaintances, about a man who was killed in the subway by falling under a train, before Kevin brought up the reason he'd wanted to see Etta Martin: Sheila Casey. Sheila had him completely baffled, and if there was one thing he didn't like, it was being baffled. He liked to know not only what people were doing, but why. And it was the why of Sheila Casey that had him so perplexed. He smiled as Etta babbled on about this servant and that, passing on inconsequential information. Kevin wanted to be careful; he'd directed Tom to tell Etta he wanted to discuss the Wilkins household because he was thinking of letting his little boy work as a kitchen helper there. Tom had balked at first, not wanting to lie to an old friend. But Kevin's eyes took on a dangerous glint, and he immediately agreed.

"And then there's the new nurse. She's something, I'll tell you," Etta said, her cheeks ruddy from her second pint.

Kevin tensed, but Etta was having too good a time to notice. "What about the new nurse?"

"Oh, this is a good one. She's set her cap for the master of the house," Etta said, then giggled. "She's a right enough sort, but she's headed for trouble, that's for sure. The two of 'em's been carrying on, and of course that's got poor Mrs. Von Arc in a snit. See, she's been hoping for a proposal from Mr. Wilkins. But it's not going to happen her way as long as that pretty little nurse is about, I'll tell you that much."

A slow smile spread on Kevin's face as he was beginning to understand, finally, what game Sheila Casey was playing. The wise girl had apparently given up on the short-term deal and was going for something a bit more steady.

"You are certainly an observant woman," Kevin said, pleased to see a flush on Etta's cheeks.

"Oh, yes. It pays to be observant. And, to be honest, Mrs. Von Arc tells me things she ought not to, things that are right embarrassing if you ask me. But I suppose she knows she has a loyal servant in me."

Kevin leaned forward, as if captivated by every syllable coming from Etta's thin lips. "What sort of things?"

"Just that she caught Mr. Wilkins in Miss Casey's bed. They weren't doing nothing . . . yet. But it was quite a shock to her. Poor Mrs. Von Arc practically threw herself at him, so she said, but he wouldn't give her the time of day. It's sad, really. She's a beautiful woman. But that Mr. Wilkins is blind to that. I'll tell you something only I know. Mrs. Von Arc is almost broke. She needs to get married and soon. See? That's the sort of thing I shouldn't know."

Almost broke. Kevin wondered what that meant to someone with the kind of money that the Wilkins had. He leaned back in his chair, the two front legs leaving the dirty floor, his hands folded and resting on his flat stomach.

"Now, Etta, do you think truly that this nurse is the only thing between your lady and a wedding ring?"

"I'm most certain of it," Etta said.

Kevin was silent for a few beats. "And do you think,

perhaps, that Mrs. Von Arc would be willing to pay to be rid of Miss Casey?"

Even in her alcohol-induced haze, Etta grew alarmed at Kevin's menacing tone. And then he smiled, putting her immediately at ease. "Miss Casey's not a bad sort," Etta said. "I wouldn't want anything to happen to her."

Kevin looked affronted. "My goodness, Etta, what are you accusing me of? Do you think I'd wrap her in a burlap bag and toss her into the Charles River like a batch of kittens?" He laughed, nearly toppling his chair backward.

Etta began laughing, too, but it was a nervous laugh. She was beginning to think Kevin Donnelly wasn't the charming man he seemed to be. "No, of course not." She swallowed. "But what could you do?"

Kevin lost his smile, and Etta nearly shivered. "I could get her dismissed like that," he said, snapping his fingers. "But I need to meet with Mrs. Von Arc to discuss compensation."

Etta shook her head. "Mrs. Von Arc has already tried to get her fired, but Mr. Wilkins will have nothing to do with it."

Kevin smiled again, flashing those white teeth. "Believe me, Etta, when I get through telling Mr. Wilkins what I got to tell him, Sheila Casey will no longer be an obstacle to poor Mrs. Von Arc."

Etta twisted her hands in her lap. She liked Victoria, and would feel just awful if she were responsible for getting her fired.

"Etta. Mrs. Von Arc needs you, girl. You're the only one who can help her."

Etta looked at Kevin, her worried eyes shifting to Tom, who nodded nearly imperceptibly. Etta made her decision; she must help Mrs. Von Arc. "Tell me what I have to do."

Nineteen

"Tell me you're joking. Good God, Jack, the girl was supposed to take care of Emma, not you. And to think I was worried you'd end up with Suzanne."

Jack could only grin at his old friend Henry. "What can I tell you? That I planned it? It just happened."

Henry paced in front of Jack's desk, glancing at the door to make sure no one else in the office was about who could overhear. "Fine. Fall in love. Bed her. But you don't have to *marry* her. What are you thinking, man?"

Jack had been reclining in his leather chair, enjoying his friend's dicomforture. But he heaved himself upright at Henry's question. "I'm thinking that maybe, for once in my miserable life, I'll be happy."

Henry widened his eyes in dismay. "But Christina . . ."

Jack let out a puff of impatience. "Christina was never a wife to me, Henry. She was never a friend. I loved her, true enough. But it was not like what I feel for Victoria."

Henry stopped his pacing and stood in front of Jack's desk, hands resting on its top. "Think, Jack. I don't mean to sound like a snob, but think what your friends and business partners will say."

"Of course you mean to sound like a snob. You *are* a snob, Henry," Jack said lightly. "Remember, I'm not exactly a blue blood myself. That was Christina's forte. I married into as much money as Victoria will."

"It's not the same," Henry spat. "You came from a good family."

Jack shook his head in disgust. "You're not only a snob, Henry, you're also a bigot."

Henry threw his hands up. "Fine. Call me what you will. But remember, I'm your friend, Jack. I'm just being honest with you, saying to your face what other people will say behind your back. Think what people will say who are not your friends. Can you face that? Can Victoria?"

Jack clenched his jaw. "I appreciate your concern, but I really don't give a damn what anyone thinks."

"You're lonely, Jack. That's all," Henry said.

"You're right. I am lonely. I've been lonely for years." Jack stood up and walked out from behind his desk. "I know you're concerned. But I'm going to marry Victoria if she'll have me, and you can either be there for me or not. It's your choice."

Henry gave Jack a crooked grin. "You may be stupid, but you're also the only man who can hold his whiskey better than me. How could I abandon that sort of friendship?" Henry grew serious. "Just be careful, Jack. There are women out there who will use you. I'm not saying Victoria is one of those, but a rich man can be awfully intoxicating to someone whose been poor all her life."

Jack shook his head. "Not Victoria. She's got a good heart. She makes me happy, Henry."

"Just be careful," he repeated, and slapped his friend on the back. He'd not abandon his friend, not when he was about to make the biggest mistake of his life.

"Good night, sweetheart," Victoria said, tucking a blanket around Emma, who was making a valiant but fruitless effort to keep her eyes open.

Victoria stepped through the nursery and into her

room, quietly shutting the door behind her. If she was lucky, Emma was out for the night. She felt along the wall for the light switch and pushed in the button, smiling when the bulb illuminated. For the last two nights, the Wilkinses' house had had no electricity. Her smile widened when she noticed a package placed beside her lamp. A small tag had written on it, "Happy New Year, Jack." Just seeing his writing made her heart speed up a beat. He had signed it "Jack," not "Mr. Wilkins," and that made her heart jump a bit more. Taking the box, she sat on the edge of her bed, and laid it on her lap. For several seconds she just sat there, enjoying its weight and the mystery of its contents. Victoria had always loved presents.

She gently undid the ribbon, opened the box, and removed a bit of tissue. Victoria's smile widened. It was a beautiful statue of a woman holding a child. She held it on her palm, looking at it with the same peaceful expression as the stone figure looked at the baby. Victoria bit her lip. It was perfect. How could he have known to get her something so absolutely perfect, something that would touch her heart as nothing else would have.

She placed the statue carefully on her small bed table, adjusting its position several times before it was just so. Before she left her room, she looked back at her present and smiled, then began her search for Jack. A glance at the grandfather clock in the hall told her it was later than she'd thought, nearly midnight. He's probably in bed already, she thought, disappointed, then headed to his study just in case he was working late.

When he heard her familiar footsteps enter the study, Jack smiled into the blueprint he was studying. She's found it, he thought.

"It's beautiful. I love it," Victoria said, standing several feet away to hold herself back from throwing herself into his arms.

When he looked up, Victoria stopped breathing. It

seemed lately she couldn't manage the most basic things when he was around. The men she had dated had been gorgeous, with the right hair, clothes, and bodies. But none had the heat, the pure sexiness of Jack. Or a smile that made her heart swell to ten times its normal size. And now that she knew he could drive her wild with a kiss, it was all she could think of.

"I'm glad you liked it," Jack said, returning his attention to the blueprint. He knew that if he continued to stare at her, he would not be able to keep the desire he felt for her from showing on his face . . . and other places.

Victoria continued to stand there uncomfortably until it became apparent the end of their conversation had come. She'd hoped that gift was Jack's way of bridging the awful awkwardness that had developed between them since she had practically proclaimed her love for him. And then ridiculously demanded that he not fall in love with her. Talk about vanity! In the days since their meeting in the library, Victoria had tried to convince herself that particular scene hadn't been quite so awful as she remembered. Sure, he was pleased that she loved him. What guy wouldn't say that he was, if only to spare a girl's feelings. The more she replayed that conversation, the more his comments became condescending, meaningless, and pitying. And then he gave her the statue, resurrecting her confidence. Until now.

"Well, I guess I'll say good night. I just wanted to thank you," Victoria said, and turned to leave.

"One moment, please," Jack said, lifting his index finger and keeping his eyes trained on the blueprint.

Victoria waited with obvious impatience, watching as his eyes bore holes into that blueprint. Curious about what could keep his attention, she walked quietly up beside him, peeking over his left shoulder.

"Is that the Taylor house?" she asked, her face so close to his, her breath touched his cheek. "What happened to all the windows?"

Jack knew if he turned his head, he would be kissing her soft mouth. And if he started kissing her, he wouldn't want to stop. Jack was no prude, but he believed sex could and should wait until marriage. It was another of his blasted rules.

"Mr. Wilkins?"

"Taylor had other ideas," he said curtly. He felt as if he were on fire with her standing so close, and his only thought was that it was time to break some of his rules.

When he finally turned toward Victoria, it was the most natural of things to go into his arms and tilt her head up for the kiss she knew was coming. Their meeting was an explosion of bodies, soft meeting hard, hands clutching at material, pulling them even closer. Jack's mouth slanted over hers, capturing her with a kiss that was almost bruising. He plunged his tongue into her mouth, stroking her, learning her, loving her. Never in his life had he felt so driven to have a woman. Everything she did, every small sound, every stroke of her tongue made his blood surge. He mouthed her throat, her cheek, feeling as if he could devour her and fill the empty ache in his soul.

Victoria was so completely knocked out by his touch, she could only think that Sheila Casey's body must be supercharged for sex. There could be no other explanation for the feelings he was evoking. She wanted to rip his clothes off, shove him down on the desk, and climb aboard. It was absurd, the kind of madness she'd seen in the movies. She'd always thought such scenes were overblown, the stuff of fantasies. This could not be real, his touch could not feel this way. But it did, oh, God, it did, *it did*.

She felt him raise her skirts, saw the blueprint fly off the desk. Without coaxing, Victoria hopped up on the smooth top and hugged her legs around his hips, never losing contact with his mouth. Her hands were at his necktie, frantically pulling it and his collar away, tearing a few buttons off in the process. She dimly heard them clatter onto the desk as she smoothed her hand onto his lightly furred chest, frantic to touch flesh.

"Oh, God, I can't take much more," she said as he made his way to one breast and licked the sensitive tip. The tingling that began at her breast shot down between her legs in a rush that left her gasping.

And suddenly everything stopped. Breathing harshly, Jack lifted his head. "Victoria, I must know. Are you, that is, have you . . ."

Victoria captured his neck in her hands and dragged him down for another bruising kiss. "Have I what?" she managed. She pulled back to look in his fevered eyes, sensing he needed to know something but unable to make her brain work. Suddenly it dawned on her that he was asking her whether she was still a virgin, and she almost said, "Of course not." Then she remembered who and where she was. "No, Jack, I'm not a virgin. But I wish I was."

"It's all right, sweetheart. It's all right," he said, kissing her. He didn't see the slight crease of worry on Victoria's brow as she wondered why it should matter to him one way or another. His mouth and hands soon had her mind blessedly on other matters.

Victoria pulled him closer with her legs, moaning aloud when she felt his arousal. Jack gritted his teeth, feeling her heat through his pants. Who would have thought this sweet girl could be so incredibly hot? Pushing back her skirt, he smoothed his hand up her silky thigh, relishing the sound of pleasure that came from her kiss-swollen lips. When he found the place he sought, Victoria arched her back and pushed her hips to meet his hand.

"Oh, so good, Jack," Victoria breathed, dashing away her misplaced belief that a man of the 1890s would be a selfish lover. The burning, the wonderful burning began to build, and Victoria's body grew taut with expectation. When the flood of pleasure came, Victoria bit back a scream, burying her head in the crook of his neck. When the tide of feeling subsided, she managed to raise her head from his shoulder and give Jack a sleepy smile.

"Thank you," she whispered.

Jack gave her a wicked smile back. "I'm afraid I have more in store, sweetheart."

"Oh, goody."

Jack shook his head in wonder. How he had managed to not shame himself was quite beyond him. Rock hard and nearly frantic, Jack sheathed himself inside her, his face taut and bathed in sweat.

"Jesus, you feel good," he said against her mouth. And he began to move, driving again and again, losing himself, knowing only that nothing had ever felt like this. Finally he found his release, in a shattering of light that shook him to the core.

"I love you," he said softly into her ear. "I love you so."

Hearing those words, those beautiful, horrible words, Victoria squeezed her eyes shut so he wouldn't see the anguish they brought. She would have to hurt him. Badly. Nothing she had experienced before could have prepared her for the searing pain she felt in her heart. How cruel it was, to finally find love but not be allowed to keep it.

Twenty

Jack took an appreciative puff on his Cuban, and smiled at Suzanne through the smoke. "Ahhh. Thank God for the armistice," he sighed, looking at the cigar with fondness. She'd stopped by his office, surprising Jack, and putting him on his guard. Suzanne had never visited him during the day before.

"Yes. I'm sure all the widows can sleep well knowing your supply of good Cuban cigars has been restored," Suzanne said dryly.

Jack waved his hand, dismissing Suzanne's criticism. "You know very well I supported the war effort," Jack said lightly. "I'm just glad to see things back to normal. Our men safely home and my Cubans in my humidor, where they belong. And who can blame me for being glad to have my supply back?" Jack grinned, and Suzanne pressed her lips more firmly together.

"A smile, Jack? Good heavens, let me fetch a photographer so I might capture this rare moment." Jack's smile widened at Suzanne's uncharacteristic joke.

Jack took another puff on his cigar, wondering whether he should tell Suzanne now of his plans for Victoria. He wasn't fool enough to believe that Suzanne would be happy for him, especially considering that embarrassing scene in the nursery. He looked at Suzanne, impassively noting how lovely she appeared and wondering why she failed to stir his blood the way Victoria did. Certainly, most men would think Victoria plain compared to Suzanne's rare beauty. Suzanne left him cold, while Victoria, ah, she left him anything but cold.

"So, Jack, tell me what it is that makes you smile. No, don't tell me. I believe I know." Suzanne's tone was light, but her eyes were cold, her manner stiff. She stood in front of his desk, fingers pressing the polished wood. "Might your good mood have something to do with Emma's nurse?"

Jack gave her a lazy smile that belied the tightening in his gut. "It just might," he said, keeping his voice even. "If you have something to say to me, Suzanne, please say it."

Suzanne took a fortifying breath. "You must fire her, Jack. It is unseemly for you to be . . . carrying on with a scullery maid in your study. Yes, I know. I believe the entire household knows. Have you no morals, Jack? Have you no sense of decorum?"

Jack stared at her blandly. "This is really none of your business, Suzanne."

Suzanne lifted one hand to her throat. "I'm sorry you feel that way, but what happens in Emma's home is my business. At least I hope that it is . . ." She shook her head, unable to continue. "I know you have temptations, Jack. But it is unseemly for you and her to . . ." She flushed a bright red.

Jack's head began to ache. "You're right, Suzanne. It is unseemly, and I plan to set things straight. I . . ."

"Oh, thank goodness, Jack," Suzanne said on a sigh, interrupting him.

"I haven't finished. I plan to ask Victoria to be my wife."

Suzanne's expression was almost comical, so great was her shock. She sat down suddenly, her eyes wide and disbelieving, her mouth gaping open and closed. "You can't mean it," she whispered. "She's a nobody, a scullery maid. She's a common . . ."

"Watch it, Suzanne," Jack said quietly. "You are about to say something unforgivable about the woman who will be my wife."

Suzanne stared at him for a few moments, and Jack could almost see her mind working. "Is this something you feel you *have* to do, Jack?"

He narrowed his eyes in confusion until he caught her meaning. She believed Victoria was pregnant, for in her mind, she could not believe there could be any other explanation for why he would agree to marry a servant.

"I am marrying Victoria because I love her. No other reason. I am sorry, Suzanne. I do not want you hurt. You have been a great friend to me these past weeks. I could not have made it through without you."

Suzanne stood as abruptly as she had sat, clutching her hands together as if keeping her composure gripped in her fists. "Please spare me your sympathy. It is I who feel sorry for you. You are about to make a grave mistake, Jack. I cannot fathom what you are thinking. I can only think that you are allowing certain aspects of your relationship with this woman to dictate your actions. It has been only four months since we laid my sister in her grave. Four months!"

Jack flushed. Christina's death seemed much longer ago than just four months to him, but to the world, he would seem like a cad if he should declare himself in love so soon after.

"I realize it is soon after Christina's death. I never planned on this."

"Spare me your pathetic excuses," Suzanne spat. "I saw this coming weeks ago. I warned you of it. Oh, Jack, keep her as your mistress if you must. Set up an apartment at the Agassiz, where she can be respectable but won't ruin your life."

"Victoria is giving me my life back," Jack said simply.

Suzanne waved an angry hand, dismissing him. "Oh, for goodness' sakes, Jack, you should hear yourself. You might think your life with Christina was miserable."

"It was. More than you know."

Suzanne looked at him with true anguish marring her brown eyes. "Poor Christina. I'm sure she thought you were happy. I'm sure she never knew."

Jack looked off to the side, as if making sure Christina were not there overhearing these painful words. "She never knew."

"Regardless of the state of your marriage, you cannot mar her memory by taking up with Miss Casey. It's unthinkable. It's insulting. I cannot live in the same house if you plan to continue your relationship with the nurse."

Jack gave her a hard look. "That is your prerogative."

Suzanne walked to the door, one hand gripping the knob. "I think this is only a temporary madness, Jack," she said into the door. "It is the only explanation I can accept." With that, she walked through the door, closing it quietly behind her. He had to give her credit for the amount of restraint it must have taken to leave his office, head held high, her face set with determination. He wondered, not for the first time, whether Suzanne actually thought herself in love with him. If not for that single episode in Emma's nursery, he would never suspect she felt any strong emotion toward him. After that scene, Suzanne and he had returned to their normal relationship, one that held little warmth. It was as if he had imagined Suzanne's declaration of love. Was she actually hurt that he had fallen in love with Victoria? Or was Suzanne simply miffed that a lowly servant could capture his heart when she could not?

As Jack tried to turn his thoughts toward reworking the Taylor project, Suzanne was turning her thoughts toward Etta and her promise. She had not yet agreed to meet with Kevin Donnelly, for such action had seemed completely base. She walked up the marble steps of Jack's home with determination, preparing to take matters into her own hands. The little upstart was likely after one thing—money—and Suzanne was determined to give her everything she had to be rid of her.

Suzanne found Victoria in the sunny little parlor overlooking the gardens, brown from winter. Seated on the floor with Emma on her lap, her curling reddish hair a golden halo, she looked completely appealing. In a coarse, homespun way, but appealing none the less, Suzanne thought, frowning at the vision before her. It was no wonder Jack was attracted to her.

Victoria looked up, and the smile on her lips slowly faded as she took in Suzanne's stern look. *She knows,* Victoria thought, her heart beginning a painful pounding. As suddenly as that thought entered her head, she dismissed it. There was no way that Suzanne could know she and Jack had made love. No way, no sirree.

"It has come to my attention, Miss Casey, that you have been . . . indiscreet with the master of this house," Suzanne said as she looked down at Victoria's upturned face that turned a sudden and rather excruciating shade of red.

"Oh, God," Victoria said, feeling a bit ill. Somehow, it did not matter how, Suzanne knew about last night's frolic. Her entire body felt as if it was on fire from embarrassment at the sudden flash she had of how it must have looked to whomever witnessed their frantic coupling atop Jack's desk.

Suzanne, her lips pressed, her arms crossed, struck a rather superior pose. "Indeed, Miss Casey, it is something to be ashamed of."

Emma let out a little whiny cry, and Victoria jiggled the girl on her lap in an automatic response. She sat up straight and tried to look dignified as she said, "I am not ashamed of what happened, Mrs. Von Arc."

Suzanne turned and walked calmly to the nearest chair, sitting down gracefully, before saying thoughtfully, "No. I don't suppose you are. It was, however, a shameful act. You are aware, are you not, that Mr. Wilkins's wife, my sister, has been gone only four months? That this is a house in mourning?"

Victoria flushed again, damning her Irish complexion. "Yes, I am aware of it. But it wasn't on my mind at the time."

It was Suzanne's turn to blush. "I'm sure it wasn't. I'm sure what was on your mind was something else entirely. It must be difficult being poor," Suzanne said abruptly, and Victoria gave her a puzzled look. "I am not without some wealth, Miss Casey. Enough for you to live quite comfortably, considering what I am sure you are used to."

Victoria gazed at her evenly, finally realizing what Suzanne was broadly hinting at. "You want to give me money so that I'll leave."

Suzanne smiled with satisfaction and relief that she would not have to be more explicit. "I can give you two thousand dollars, Miss Casey, more than you could hope to earn over several years. Enough to buy a modest home."

Victoria narrowed her eyes in disbelief and shook her head. "I'm not interested in your money, Mrs. Von Arc. I'll agree with you that what happened should not happen again. In fact, I am quite sure I will not allow it to happen again."

Suzanne snorted. "Miss Casey, you cannot be that naive. Mr. Wilkins is a good man, but he is just that, a man. And since the two of you apparently have an attraction, it is unlikely you will be able to make good on that promise. It is in the best interest of this household for you to leave. Immediately. I will draw up a draft for twenty-five hundred dollars. You cannot expect more than that."

Victoria set a squirming Emma on the floor, and stood. "I don't want your money. I like my job, and I don't want to leave," she said succinctly.

"I can get you another position. A good one. I will even write you a letter of recommendation."

"No."

Suzanne stood, her face a stony mask of anger.

"You will leave, Miss Casey. I can assure you that I will not abide such goings-on in this home."

Victoria lifted her head a notch. "You really have no say about what goes on or doesn't go on in this house, as far as I can tell, Mrs. Von Arc."

The look of pure hatred in Suzanne's eyes caused a shiver to run along Victoria's spine. She hated to admit it, but at the moment she was very much afraid of Suzanne Von Arc. She realized Suzanne saw her as a threat to her position in this household, to her relationship with her brother-in-law, and it was likely pure jealous rage that was driving the woman to attempt to pay her off. She recalled Suzanne's awkward declaration of love, and sympathy replaced the tingling of fear.

"I don't want you as an enemy," Victoria said kindly, a final attempt to make peace to avoid a war Suzanne seemed intent on starting.

Suzanne raised her eyebrow, recognizing the pity she saw in Victoria's eyes and hating it. "No, Miss Casey, you certainly do not want me as an enemy."

With that pronouncement, Suzanne left the room, fists clenched tightly in the folds of her black skirt. She went in search of Etta.

Twenty-one

Snow fell softly, covering the soot-coated city in white, cleaning the air and softening the sounds of traffic. The day had started out unusually warm for January, and the hearty Bostonians left their homes wearing thin coats without mufflers and winter gloves. But as the day progressed, the skies darkened, the clouds thickened, and a bone-chilling dampness descended, leaving nearly everyone gazing at the sky with disgust as they made their way home.

But to Jack, it might have been a fine May day with the sun shining brightly. In his pocket he felt the pleasant weight of the unbelievably expensive engagement ring he planned to bestow upon Victoria that evening. As he walked, the box banged lightly against his thigh, a heady reminder of the blissful days to follow. Jack was nearly giddy with love and happiness, and amazed to find himself in such a state. Rather than fight it, he welcomed the joy, the lightness, the pure exhilaration of being thoroughly besotted.

How happy they would be, he thought, his feet crunching loudly on the snow-covered sidewalks along Beacon Street. On a night such as this, he and Victoria and their many children would gather in the library talking about their day. And at night, he would turn to her and touch her anytime he pleased. Her curling hair would tickle his nose.

Of course, they could not marry right away. They would have to wait at least a year from Christina's

death. As he mentally calculated it meant waiting another seven months, his footsteps slowed. And when
he realized Victoria would have to move out of the
house, he stopped altogether. Oblivious to the pedestrians who grumpily moved around him, as well as the
softly falling snow that dusted the top of his hat and
shoulders, it dawned on him he would not be able to
touch her, either. "Curse my damned rules," he muttered aloud, his eyes so fierce a woman passing by
gave him a startled look.

He tipped his hat, smiling at the poor woman, and
continued walking, abruptly aware he was making a
spectacle of himself idling on the walkway in the middle of a snowstorm. They could make love, he argued
to himself, simply not as much as he would like. No,
he realized, that would never do. Victoria's reputation
would be too fragile for them to risk pregnancy and
a hasty wedding. It would be difficult enough for her
to be accepted without casting doubts among Boston's
elite as to why Jack Wilkins married his daughter's
nurse. Perhaps they could forgo waiting the full year
after Christina's death. Then they could be together.

His grin widened as he thought about the nightly
pleasures they would share. Ah, Victoria, he thought,
we will be so happy.

Victoria sat on her bed in the very middle, holding
her knees tightly against her chest, as if by doing so
she could stop the ache in her heart. She had never,
ever been quite so miserable, except those first horrid
days in the hospital following her accident. She must
break Jack's heart, and in doing so, would break her
own. Victoria looked up at the ceiling in the general
direction she thought God might be, and wondered,
not for the first time, why she had not been whisked
away. God must have faith that Jack will not continue
to love her, that she will make things right. That
thought should have made her happy, but it did not.

She only hoped that in pushing Jack away, she could remain here with Emma.

In her more hopeful moments, Victoria imagined that perhaps Jack was the sort of man who always proclaimed his love after sex. She squeezed her eyes shut, reliving that moment, the tender sound of his voice, rough with passion, when he told her he loved her. No. Jack was not the sort of man who said only what he thought a woman wanted to hear. She only hoped he wouldn't be too hurt, that he didn't love her half as much as she loved him. He couldn't love her that much, not without Victoria knowing. She'd thought all along there was some sort of chemistry between them, but believed any real feelings were completely one-sided. She'd never suspected he *loved* her.

"Here's the thing," she rehearsed in her head, "this Chinese mystic guy says I'll drop dead if someone falls in love with me—or words to that effect. I'm not about to die just because you won't get married to whoever you're supposed to if I'm around to mess things up. I'm being noble, see?" Oh, yeah, Victoria thought with disgust, that would really work well.

"Just face it, you're going to lose them both, and it's your own damned fault," Victoria whispered to herself. What *had* she been thinking of all those times when she flirted with him. Now she could acknowledge that she had. The cherry glob, those wonderful nights in the cozy little library that she looked forward to. And that Christmas kiss—ugh!—that had been the true start of it all. Stupid, stupid woman! Had she thought it was some sort of game? Victoria hated herself at that moment, knowing that by ignoring what she knew was happening between her and Jack—indeed welcoming it—would leave them both brokenhearted.

A knock on her door interrupted her self-flagellation, and she looked at the door with dread. Don't be Jack, don't be Jack, she thought as she padded over to the door, bracing herself before tugging it open.

"Hello, Mr. Wilkins." Maybe if she went back to normal, pretended the last time she saw him she wasn't sweaty and half-naked and lying on top of his desk, they could go back to the way things were, she thought frantically. And formality had always been her best armor. He looked so gorgeous, freshly shaved, his hair combed back off his forehead. He still wore his coat and tie.

Jack frowned at her use of his proper name. "I'd like you to call me Jack," he said softly, kindly, and Victoria's heart plummeted. "May I come in?"

Victoria backed up to allow him to enter, her stomach twisting at his suddenly serious face and the way he quietly closed her door and kept clearing his throat. He seemed almost . . . nervous.

"I, uh," Jack cleared his throat again. "I have something to ask you, Victoria," he said, and gave her a quick smile. Victoria watched in horror as he got down on his bended knee. Oh, God, no. Please tell me, Victoria thought, that he is not kneeling before me holding out a ring. Please tell me that I won't have to do this to him. Oh, it's too, too cruel, God. He doesn't deserve this.

When Jack looked up at Victoria, his love-blind eyes saw only love, not the frantic disbelief that was slowly dawning. He cleared his throat again, smiling at his own nervousness. "Please do me the great honor of becoming my wife, Victoria, and make me the happiest of men."

How had this happened? Never once had Victoria believed his love could run so deep. Oh, please, please, please, God, I don't want to hurt him this way. She looked down at him, wishing with all her being she could thrust herself into his arms and say, "Yes! I'll marry you." But she could not. She couldn't bear to look at him, his face lit by the joy that comes only with the certainty that the woman you have just asked to marry you will say yes.

She spun around to spare herself, taking three stiff steps away, her eyes on her little statue of a mother holding her babe.

"I'm sorry, Jack. I can't." Behind her, there was only silence until she heard him stand.

"I don't understand," he said, shaking his head in confusion. Of all the things he imagined, her refusal was not one of them.

"I can't marry you," Victoria said looking up to the ceiling, willing the threatening tears not to fall. For he would not believe the next if she were to cry. "I don't love you, you see. I . . . lied."

In two quick strides he was behind her, his hands steel bands on her arms as he jerked her around to face him. "I don't believe you. Tell me. Now, Victoria. Tell me that you don't love me." Victoria had to close her eyes so she would not see the pain in his. When she opened them, her eyes were clear, her gaze direct. "I'm sorry that you misinterpreted what happened between us as love, Jack. But it was not."

"I see." He dropped his hands from her arms, and Victoria suddenly felt so cold. "I'm sorry to have subjected you to such an embarrassing scene, Miss Casey." His face was stony, blue eyes dark with emotion, and Victoria watched as he clenched and unclenched his jaw, fighting for control.

"Oh, Jack, don't." A whispered plea.

He put up his arms as if he were fending off an attack. "Spare me your sympathy," he spat.

He tucked the ring back in his pocket and turned to leave.

"Jack."

He stopped, his head turned to one side so that he might hear her as he foolishly allowed his heart to pick up a hopeful beat.

"I'm sorry."

As he walked out the door, Victoria crumpled to

the floor, a hand pressed painfully to her mouth to silence her sobs.

Jack told no one. It was too damned humiliating. Eventually he would tell Henry and Suzanne, just not now. One day they would inquire about the wedding plans, and he would explain then. For now, he would keep his rejection a private thing, as if by holding it to himself he could pretend it had never happened.

When he had left her room those two nights ago, gripping the ring painfully in his hand, he'd wanted to rush back in and beg her to marry him. Surely she could not have better offers. Surely being the wife of one of the wealthiest men in Boston would not be too big a sacrifice. How could he have so completely misinterpreted how she felt about him? Every time he thought of himself kneeling before her, *begging* her to be his wife, his entire body burned with mortification. After two days of self-hatred, he turned his anger toward Victoria. He pictured himself casting her out, her head held low in shame, wearing only rags, while he pointed an angry finger like God casting Lucifer out of heaven. He let his anger build like bitter bile in his throat.

At night, though, his heart betrayed him, allowing him the sweetest dreams of Victoria lying next to him, smiling sleepily as she cupped his face with one gentle hand. He woke that morning, coming out of such a dream expecting to see her, only to find the place beside him empty. "Goddamn it," he said with violence, punching the pillow. What is wrong with me, he thought, refusing to allow himself to savor the sweetness of that dream.

He sat on the edge of his bed, his arousal mocking him, his body taut with desire. Two days he had not seen her. He had left for work early and stayed late, cowardly avoiding her. But in doing so, he had also missed seeing Emma until long after the little girl had fallen asleep. It was Saturday, and he would be damned if he let that woman keep him from his daughter any longer. He grabbed his pocket watch from his bed stand. Six o'clock, too early for Victoria to be up and about.

Dressing quickly, Jack headed to the nursery, stopping short when he saw Victoria rocking Emma and holding a bottle to the baby's mouth. She was unaware of him, and Jack, hating himself for doing it, gazed at her with a longing he thought he had mastered. The golden morning sun muted the scene before him, giving it uncommon beauty. Victoria's head dipped just slightly, her slender neck caressed by a few curling tendrils, as she watched Emma suck hungrily from the bottle. Victoria's lips tilted up slightly at the corners, her eyes were softened by love. He knew at that moment he would not be able to fire her, and the reasons did not only have to do with Emma. He knew, God help him, that he could not bear to see her go. Not yet. What a fool I am, he thought, disgusted once again with himself.

"I've come to see my daughter," he said, forcing his tone to be hard.

Victoria looked up and smiled, forgetting for a moment that she should not, her heart pounding so hard it might have been a ghost standing there instead of Jack. "I didn't think you came to see me."

"No. I did not." Then, why am I looking at you as if I am starved for you, he thought. Victoria had obviously just arisen. Her hair was pulled artlessly on top of her head, and her face still had that sleepy look that reminded him painfully of his dream. Her feet were bare. For some reason, those feet, toes curling into the carpet, made his heart wrench.

"I plan on spending the day with Emma. Without her nurse. You may take the day off. In fact, you may take the evening off as well. I plan to dine with my in-laws, and several times they have asked that Emma spend the night, so you will not be needed. Please send Etta down for me when Emma is dressed." With that, Jack turned sharply, glad the conversation was over. Victoria blinked away the tears that immediately sprang to her eyes at Jack's businesslike tone. This was awful.

"Jack."

His hand, resting on the doorjamb, tightened its grip. "I think it's best if you call me Mr. Wilkins from now on."

"Oh, Jack, please don't be like this."

He turned with near violence. "Goddamn it, woman, I was not joking! You will call me Mr. Wilkins."

Victoria pulled back in shock, and when Emma let out a small sound of protest, Victoria threw him a look of reproach.

"Is this how it's going to be, Jack, I mean, Mr. Wilkins?" she amended quickly when his face turned red with anger. "You being mad all the time and me feeling guilty?"

"It's the way it has to be if you are to remain here."

Victoria bit her lip—hard—and willed herself not to cry. "We can't just go on? Be friends?"

"If you knew . . ." Jack stopped, not wanting her to see how deep his wound ran, and then he lost his internal battle. "You cannot know what you've done to me, else you would not ask such a thing. I broke a vow for you. I swore I would never marry again, and I believed in my heart that I never would. I was prepared to breach convention for you, to go against my family and my friends for you. And you want to know whether we can remain friends? My God, have you never been in love?" Jack let out a sound of disgust, angry with himself for allowing her to see so much of what he still felt.

Victoria looked up at him, her eyes tinged with worry, and despite himself, Jack had the horrible urge to comfort her. "I never meant to hurt you this way," she said. "If I could love anyone in the world, it would be you. Believe me. But I can't. It's all so complicated, more than you'll ever know. So we won't be friends; I can live with that. But let's not be enemies."

Jack shook his head in defeat. "Fine. Not enemies. Not friends. Please send Etta down when Emma is dressed."

After he left, Victoria looked at her daughter, and her resolve to stay grew only stronger. "Oh, Emma. I've made such a mess. Your mama is an idiot. Did you know that?" Emma beamed a smile at Victoria, completely unaware of her mother's breaking heart.

Twenty-two

Jack was finally beginning to relax as the mist pudding, a lemony concoction, was being served. Suzanne had been unusually quiet, and Jack believed it was because she was still stinging from their last conversation. All throughout the dinner of scalloped oysters, fish balls, and mashed potatoes, Jack had waited for Suzanne to say something to her parents about Victoria. Just as he was about to dip his spoon into his pudding, she struck with such finesse, at first Jack was unaware that he was in danger.

"Guess who I saw today, Mother?" Suzanne asked. "You remember Wally Miller." At her mother's blank look, Suzanne persisted. "He was the pimply boy from Mount Desert who was absolutely mad about Christina. You remember, he was the one who you said resembled a pig." She let out a delicate laugh.

Mrs. St. George creased her brow. "Oh, yes. John and Helen's boy. Isn't he some sort of politician now?"

"He works for the governor," Suzanne said smoothly, taking the tiniest taste of pudding. "He asked after you, of course, and expressed his condolences. He couldn't believe it had only been four months since Christina . . ."

Jack, who had been only half listening, tensed.

"Four months," Mrs. St. George repeated sadly, shaking her head. Jack could see that she was trying to stop herself from crying, and he chanced a look down the table to Suzanne. She met his gaze, telling him with that look that his suspicions were correct. She was about to give him up.

"By the way, Mother, Father. Has Jack told you his good news?" She paused to add to the drama, a hard smile forming on her lips. "Jack, it seems, has fallen in love. He plans to marry."

Mr. St. George slammed his palm onto the table, causing the two women to jump. "What's this about Jack? Absurd! Explain yourself, young man."

"Suzanne is only half right, sir. I did fall in love and asked a woman to marry me. But there will be no wedding." He looked at Suzanne, who stared at him in triumph. "She said no."

All three were momentarily silent, and then seemed to speak all at once. Mr. St. George's booming voice finally broke through.

"Good God, you can't be serious. Christina's still warm in the grave!" Mr. St. George had the habit of shouting everything he said so it was difficult to know when he was truly angry.

Mrs. St. George let out a little shriek, and appeared to be on the verge of a swoon.

"I realize that, sir. But since my proposal has been rejected, there is little to say." At that moment, Jack wished he were anywhere else on earth than where he now sat.

"Little to say? I'd say there is a lot to say. Who is the woman?"

"You don't know her," Jack said.

"Her name is Victoria Casey," Suzanne said calmly. "She's Emma's nurse."

Mrs. St. George held one trembling hand to her throat, as if Suzanne just said Victoria was a prostitute. "Oh, Jack. How could you?"

"I love . . ." He jerked his head slightly. "I loved her. It is that simple. I meant no disrespect to you or the memory of your daughter. I would not want to hurt you. It is over now. Suffice it to say that no one, other than Suzanne and Henry Grant, knew of my plans."

Mrs. St. George appeared to be somewhat appeased. "Will the girl keep quiet?"

"Yes." He was certain of it. "She has little contact with other households."

"You can't mean you haven't fired her. You must, Jack. Now that you have made your feelings known, it is imperative," Mrs. St. George said, her hand once again fluttering near her throat.

Jack breathed a deep sigh. "She will remain as Emma's nurse. She is very good with her."

"A million women could take care of Emma now," Suzanne argued. "Emma is older, and she no longer cries without Victoria about. She's been quiet all evening."

Jack knew Suzanne was right. He could not explain why he did not fire her, not even to himself. While Jack stared mutely at his pudding, Suzanne spat, "Maybe her duties have been extended beyond Emma's care, and that is the true reason she cannot be replaced."

"Suzanne!" her mother gasped.

"I'm sorry, Mother," she said contritely. "I just find this all so upsetting. I apologize to you, too, Jack."

After the meal was ended, Jack bade them good evening as soon as possible, wanting to spare himself and them any more awkward conversation. As he headed for the door, Suzanne stopped him. "I know I behaved badly this evening," she said. "I hope you have forgiven me, Jack."

"Of course."

Suzanne gave him a smile. "You haven't. I know it. But you will when you realize what a mistake you made." She was startled by the pain she saw flash in his eyes at that moment.

"I am already fully aware of the mistake I made," he said. With that, he bowed, placed his hat on his head, and walked out the door.

Suzanne realized then that despite the glorious news that Victoria, for some unknown reason, had rejected Jack, he loved her still. She was glad her plan was still in place. Emma's nurse would be gone in two days.

Victoria was drunk. Not falling down sloppy drunk, but she had a nice little buzz from the three little, bitty glasses of whiskey she had downed. Lounging carelessly on a sofa in the library, she eyed the fourth glass with a little smile, swirling the dark amber liquid around. Left alone the entire day, Victoria had had nothing to do but dwell rather morosely on her predicament. By the time Jack had left the house with Emma, her nerves had been frazzled. Every time she heard Jack's low voice or Emma's coos, her stomach would twist, her heart would pound in her breast.

The thought of seeing Jack was enough to make her stomach give a sickening squeeze, and she wondered whether they could ever return to a "normal" relationship. It will have to be me who is strong, Victoria thought, and inwardly winced. She had not, so far, proven to be a very strong person. Victoria lay the blame completely on herself. Jack and Emma were innocent, victims of a weak will and a strong libido. She let out a laugh that was horribly close to turning into a sob, then shook her head trying to rid it of the alcoholic fog. Sheila Casey had not been one to imbibe; this body definitely was not alcohol tolerant.

A noise at the library door brought her head up, and she found herself smiling before she could stop herself. "Hello, Mr. Wilkins," she said precisely, fearing her words would slur. Jack eyed the glass in her hand.

"I hope that is your first glass, Miss Casey," he said dryly, then he turned his gaze to the partially empty whiskey decanter. "But I can see that it is not." He gave her a closer look, taking in the slightly mussed hair, her dress messily arranged about her, her too-shiny eyes. "Are you drunk?"

Victoria bit her lip, looking just a bit chagrined.

"I'm working on it," she said, lifting her glass in a mocking toast. "This stuff started off tasting just awful, but just about now, it's starting to taste pretty darned good. Why don't you join me?" She slid back onto the couch, unknowingly hiking her dress up in the process. All her problems seemed to somehow have faded away. And though part of Victoria knew it was the alcohol making all her problems seem so distant, Jack's proximity was also just as intoxicating. He was wonderfully handsome in his black dinner jacket, tie, and collar undone, as he stood looking sternly down at her.

"I just came in here because I saw the light. I think you should retire as well."

"Nope. It's my night off, and I intend to enjoy it," Victoria said, shaking her glass a bit.

Jack looked at her a bit oddly, Victoria thought. "Then, I shall take myself off. Good night."

Victoria slumped, disappointed. "What do you think would happen if we kissed? Just that. Do you think that would be okay?" She watched as Jack stiffened, and was immediately sorry for blurting out what she'd believed had been a random thought. *Sober up, girl,* she told herself. You're not *that* drunk.

Jack turned, unable to believe what had just come out of her mouth. What was she trying to do to him? He had already been one step away from pulling her into his arms. Had she any idea how adorable she looked, with her skirts all about and that one damned curl that kept teasing her mouth? It had taken all his will to turn away from her, to force himself to go to bed, when the last thing he wanted was to lie there alone.

"You do not play fair, do you, Victoria," he drawled. "You want a kiss? Or do you want more?" He'd meant to shame her, to make her recall how wanton she had been, how callously she had led him on, making him believe she loved him. Instead, a slow smile spread on her lips, making his entire body clench with desire. *Jesus God, please do not let her know what she can do to me with a mere smile.*

Suddenly Victoria was serious, as if aware of the dangerous game she was playing. She looked at him, her eyes filled with some emotion that Jack chose to believe was lust, and softly said: "More."

Jack swallowed, his eyes searching for some sort of meanness, some ulterior motive. He saw nothing but raw need. "Then, I shall oblige you," he said, stalking over. A part of him wanted to punish Victoria for her hold on his heart and his body, but another simply wanted to taste her again, to feel her in his arms, to hear her sounds of pleasure and let him be damned to hell for being so weak.

He put one hand behind her neck and dragged her toward him, half pulling her from the sofa. When their lips touched, both were lost in their hunger, minds shut from what they were doing. "This is what you want," he said against her lips, his voice a rough whisper. "By God, it's what I want, too."

Victoria let out a little sound, and even she was not sure whether it was a sound of defeat or triumph. All she knew was this was right. His touch set her body ablaze with sensations she'd never experienced before. He half covered her with his muscled body, one knee between her legs creating spiking shards of pleasure from the exquisite pressure. His mouth, his wonderful mouth, warm and wet and hard on hers. He was not kissing her, he was devouring her, licking and biting, nipping at her tender lips. One hand, so warm against her rib cage, rested tantalizingly close to her breast, making her want to beg him to touch her. When he finally moved his thumb against her hard little peak, rubbing back and forth, she let out a sound of pleasure so loud, he chuckled against her lips.

"Oh, God, Jack, I love this," she said, kissing him, drawing him closer. "I love you."

They both froze.

Jack was the first to move, pulling back slowly until

he stood above her, his face partially shadowed in the dimmed gaslights. "So which is it, Victoria. Do you love me or not?"

Victoria swallowed. *Idiot. Stupid jerk.* At that moment, Victoria could have happily ordered her own execution, so disgusted was she with herself. She had not meant to say it, of course, but the declaration, fueled by alcohol and raw desire, had tumbled from her lips before she knew what she was saying.

"I'm sorry. I just got caught up in the moment." Her worried eyes watched as he clenched his jaw repeatedly before speaking.

"I wonder how many times you've been 'in love,'" he said scathingly. "So. It is not me you love, but this," he said, throwing a hand at her, indicating her dress hiked up above her knees, and her buttons open exposing her breasts.

Victoria, her face crimson, jerked down her skirt and quickly buttoned up enough to cover herself. "I know I'm not a virgin, but I'm not a slut," Victoria said.

"Some might argue that point."

Victoria sat up, the red in her face caused by anger now. "Do you think I make love indiscriminately. Do you think that anyone could do what you do to me? Well, if you do, you're dead wrong. I don't like not being in control of my own body. I don't want to make love to you up here," she said, jabbing at her head.

Jack sat down next to her, his body slumped in defeat, elbows on his knees, head propped by his hands. "I don't understand you."

"I don't understand myself, either." Victoria sat next to him in silence for several minutes before putting a hand on his thigh, a gesture of comfort and remorse.

"Don't. Please," he said, his voice raw. "Don't you know what you do to me?"

Victoria removed her hand. Yes. She knew.

"I want you to leave this house," he said, his head

still resting in his hands. Suzanne was right; Victoria must go.

Victoria felt as if he had sucker punched her to the gut.

"No." A whisper, tinged with panic.

"I'm sorry, Miss Casey. This situation has become impossible."

Victoria grabbed one hand, forcing him to face her. "I'll stop pestering you. I promise. I . . . I won't bathe for weeks. I'll stop brushing my teeth and washing my hair. Anything. Oh, please, Jack. Emma needs me," she said in a rush, adding softly, "and I need Emma."

Jack turned away from Victoria, for he could not think when he was looking at her. He closed his eyes, as if he were in pain. He should tell her to go. He should. "You may stay."

Victoria knew what it took for him to say those three glorious words, knew how selfless he was being, and felt a stabbing twinge of shame. "Thank you, Mr. Wilkins."

A ghost of a smile formed on his lips before he stood up and walked from the room.

Victoria opened her eyes slowly, afraid to move, afraid that a hangover was certain after her drinking bout the night before. So far, so good. She sat up, bracing herself for the pounding that was sure to begin, and smiled. Just a slight headache, an ungodly thirst, and a bit of queasiness in her stomach. Got off easy.

She automatically began walking toward the nursery door before realizing Emma was still at her grandparents'. Frowning a bit, she headed to the bathroom to relieve her bladder and wash for the day, her mind a bit foggy from the whiskey. It wasn't until she looked in the mirror that she remembered the previous night's adventure.

"Oh, God," she said to her bleary-eyed reflection. "You, Victoria Sheila Ashford Casey, are the biggest jerk on this planet." And then her eyes filled with tears. For she knew in her heart, despite what she'd told Jack the night before, that she could not stay. He was in love with her and would remain so until she was out of his life completely. To stay would not only be cruel to Jack and to herself, but mostly it would mean breaking her vow. Staring at herself, hair tumbling in tangled curls about her, tears wetting her face, she felt her scalp tingle uncomfortably, and Victoria knew that to stay would mean her death. She truly had stepped over the line. The game was up, and she had no one to blame but herself

Leaning her head against the cool mirror, hands hanging limply by her side, she wept silent tears, watching them drop and splatter onto the tile floor. Today. She would leave today and spare Jack more heartache. But not until she could say good-bye to Emma. Swallowing down a sob until her throat ached with it, Victoria cursed herself over and over, using words she hadn't uttered since coming to this time.

She washed her face in cold water, hoping to take some of the swelling from her eyes, somehow gathering herself together. It would not do to create some slobbering scene. She would have to leave with as much grace as possible. It would be so very difficult to say good-bye. To Jack. To Emma.

Victoria had just been about to leave the bathroom when that thought hit her, and a fresh wave of grief struck her like a blow to the chest. There must be a way . . .

"I can't do it," she whispered aloud. "I don't mean to be ungrateful, God, but it just doesn't seem fair. I'm supposed to have this pure heart, so that must mean I'm a pretty good person. And Jack is a wonderful guy. Shouldn't he be happy? And shouldn't Emma get to be with her mommy?" Victoria knew God didn't care a wit about whether it was fair or not, but she figured she'd make the argument anyway, if only to make herself feel better. "I mean, Jack said he hadn't planned to get married anyway so . . ."

She gasped. *Jack said he hadn't planned to get married!* He'd said so himself, hadn't he? *"I broke a vow for you. I swore I would never marry again, and I believed in my heart that I never would."* Maybe that didn't mean anything, Victoria thought, trying to calm herself down, to keep her heart from racing out of control. But maybe, just maybe, that vow he'd made meant everything. The first time around, Jack had never met Sheila Casey because the poor woman died in childbirth. But this time around, he not only met her, he fell in love with her. Could that mean she could marry Jack without breaking her own vow? History would not change. She would not be preventing him from marrying some other woman because he never intended to get married anyway!

Victoria grinned and then as quickly frowned. What if Jack *did* meet a woman and decide to break his vow to never remarry. After all, it couldn't have been that much of a vow if he'd broken it not four months after his wife's death. Victoria bit her knuckle. Damn. She could not ignore an almost overwhelming feeling that she should leave, that to stay would mean breaking her own vow. She wished she could somehow communicate with John Wing, to telepathically let him know she needed him. Everything had seemed so easy sitting in his office, simple rules, clear-cut consequences, cut and dry. No gray area. Somehow, Victoria thought with disgust, she had managed to find a gray area.

Then she remembered that John Wing had told her he was part of a long line of mystics. He'd talked a great deal about his grandfather. Was it possible that John Wing's grandfather was alive? If he was, he'd still be a child. Perhaps Wing's great-grandfather? Hope began to bloom in Victoria's heart. His ancestors likely were still in China, but there was a chance they were right here in Boston. Would his great-grandfather be able to help her? There was only one way to find out.

Twenty-three

V ictoria was completely and utterly lost. She knew she was in Chinatown, for all the faces she saw told her she was and all the writing she couldn't read was in Chinese. But she had no clue how to go about finding a person she didn't even know existed. And even if John Wing's ancestors had lived in Boston at the turn of the century, the chance he would be able to help her was remote in the extreme. Now she faced another dilemma. The first twenty people she had approached looked at her with fear, contempt, or some odd combination of the two. Every person, from an old lady to a teenage boy, simply shook their heads and hurried on their way. They all seemed to be in a big hurry to get somewhere. It reminded Victoria of New York at rush hour.

The more Victoria wandered the narrow streets, the more she was sure she would never find the person she sought. She was as out of place on these streets as if she'd been plopped down in the middle of Beijing. Finally, she stepped out onto what looked like a main thoroughfare. An outdoor market thrived, even in the bitter cold, and her ears were filled with the singsong of the Cantonese dialect. At least that's what she thought it was. Bundled up against the cold, the women harangued the peddlers, making wild gestures to express their dissatisfaction with the price of their wares. Victoria stood by one stall stacked with several different kinds of fish. One wooden barrel seemed to be completely packed with fish heads, which Victoria eyed with both curiosity and a bit of revulsion. The pungent odor of fish mingled with the scent of blood from freshly killed chickens from the next stall down. Whole carcasses hung on display, scrawny unplucked bodies swinging in the breeze. She couldn't help but wonder what this place would smell like in the heat of summer.

Other than furtive looks, Victoria was mostly ignored. She tried approaching several people, but was either ignored completely or looked at with alarm. Victoria had no idea if anyone she'd spoken to understood English, for no one responded in that language. She suspected that more than a few did, for she thought she saw understanding in their dark eyes before they shook their heads and hurried off. She stopped counting the number of times she'd said, "Excuse me, but do you know where I can find a Mr. Wing." She'd been polite. She'd been patient. But after approaching dozens of Chinatown residents, asking the same question over and over, her frustration was beginning to build. She knew many of these people understood her! Why wouldn't they simply acknowledge her? Why not simply answer her question? It was maddening!

Finally, standing in the midst of the throng of marketers, Victoria put her hands on her hips and yelled at the top of her lungs. "I'm looking for a Mr. Wing! Does anyone here know where I can find him?"

The silence that followed was deafening. One hundred pairs of black eyes looked at her with curiosity for a count of ten. Then, almost in unison, they went about their business. Victoria's face heated with embarrassment at the silence and with anger when ultimately she was ignored. She stood there for a few moments, staring in astonishment at vendors and shoppers who had apparently decided to ignore the crazy white woman in their midst.

Victoria was about to give up and give in to the

tears that began threatening as she realized her last hope was gone, when she felt someone tug at her coat. Looking down, her eyes rested on the most adorable little face peering up at her with solemn interest.

"You look for Wing Miyung?" she asked.

Victoria got down on her haunches, mindless that she was soiling her dress and coat, so she might be at the same level as the little girl. She looked to be about six years old.

"I'm not sure," Victoria said softly.

The little girl held out her hand with a trust that touched Victoria's heart. Taking the hand, Victoria allowed the little girl to pull her along, not questioning for a moment whether she should follow her. She led her through a maze of streets, taking so many turns Victoria knew she'd never be able to find her way back to the market. The little girl was silent the entire way, not even answering when Victoria asked her name.

Finally they turned down an alley by what looked like a small Chinese market. For the first time, Victoria began to doubt the intelligence of blindly following this little girl. When they came to a door, the girl reached up, curling her small hand around the doorknob, and pushed open the door with a little shove of her body. Victoria hesitated, trying to look into the darkened doorway. All she could see was a stairway, which apparently led up to the second and third stories. The little girl held out her hand, her expression so serious, Victoria found herself smiling. The girl remained solemn. Casting one more look up the stairs, Victoria heaved a little sigh and grasped the girl's hand. If she was about to be shanghaied, she'd find out in a few seconds.

On the second floor, Victoria found herself momentarily abandoned after being led to a small room with Western decor. She sat down on a cushioned oak chair, but immediately stood when the little girl returned.

"He will see you now," she said.

"But I'm not sure he's the right person," Victoria said, worried about what faced her. For all she knew, she was about to undergo acupuncture.

"He will see you now," she repeated.

Victoria, clutching her stomach to stop the butterflies, decided to follow the girl once again. She led her through a small kitchen, where an ancient, white-haired woman sat at the table cutting some sort of meat with a viciously sharp knife, and into a dimly lit back room. Victoria blinked her eyes to adjust to the gloominess within, her eyes finally focusing on an old man with wildly unkempt white hair and long, well-combed sparse beard. This, she thought, was what she'd pictured when imagining what a Chinese mystic would look like. He was dressed in black, some loose flowing garment, and sitting upon a large flat burgundy pillow with golden fringe. In fact, this man was so much like what she had imagined, it was as if she had conjured him up from her mind.

"Grandfather wants to know who you are," the little girl said, and Victoria assumed she was acting as the old man's interpreter.

Unsure of the protocol, Victoria eyed a flat pillow across from the old man and at the girl's nod, she sat cross-legged upon it, adjusting her skirts carefully, before answering. She looked into the old man's black eyes and became immediately uncomfortable. It was that same intense look John Wing had given her when she'd first entered his office.

"Victoria Ashford."

He gave a nod, and asked another question through the girl.

"What is your other name?"

Victoria gave the old man a little smile and, although she could not be sure, it looked as if his eyes twinkled just a bit. He was far too dignified to crack a smile.

"Sheila Casey."

"Why are you here?"

Speaking slowly so the little girl could interpret what she said, she spelled out her dilemma. She explained that she knew it would break her vow to marry a man who was destined to marry someone else, but asked if it would be forbidden to marry a man who did not intend to marry.

For several excruciating minutes, the old man was silent, as if he were absorbing her words, not just contemplating them. Finally, he muttered something to the little girl, who again turned her solemn little face toward Victoria.

"What is this man's name?"

She told him, and watched with a small furrow between her eyes as the old man stood without another word and disappeared through a narrow door behind him. "Where's he going?" she asked the girl.

"He must meditate."

"Oh," she said, nodding. She tapped her fingers impatiently on her knees for what seemed like an eternity and was just about to ask how long the old man would be gone when he reentered the room and sat down precisely where he'd sat before.

"He wants you to come closer so he can look into your soul," the little girl said, keeping her expression bland even when Victoria shot her a startled look. Under the circumstances, it didn't seem to be that odd a request, so Victoria slid forward until her knees were almost touching his. He lay a hand on her face, a whisper of a touch, the pads of his fingers moving slowly like a blind man learning its contours. He spoke again, and the little girl interpreted.

"You have been through much pain. You have suffered this love you feel, but you have not stopped it as you know you should have." Victoria felt a knot of anguish build. "These vows you have taken were not taken lightly," he continued. "You know this. In your heart, in your soul, you know this." He stopped for a while, and Victoria wanted to run from the room before the knot unraveled and the tears began.

"But still you love him." Victoria nodded even though he was not asking a question.

"My great-grandson's son must be very wise," he said, and for a moment, Victoria did not realize he was talking about John Wing. "You may marry this man. He is like you. He is pure of soul and pure of heart."

With that, the old man stood and left the room.

Victoria looked at the girl excitedly. "That's it? I can marry Jack?" She stood up wanting to leap with joy into the air, wanting to give the little girl who'd found her the biggest bear hug she could manage. But her solemn little face stopped her. Instead, Victoria looked directly into her black eyes and with tears glinting in her eyes, said, "Thank you."

Only then did the tiniest of smiles form on the girl's lips. "You're very pretty when you smile," Victoria said, hoping to turn that hint of a smile into a full-fledged grin. But her face again grew serious, making Victoria smile even wider. She started to follow the girl out of the room when she remembered something.

"Wait. Do you think your grandfather could do me a favor? Could you ask?" The girl nodded. "If I were to give him something, do you think he would be able to make sure it gets to his great-grandson? Could you go ask him that?"

The girl disappeared, returning quickly. "Yes."

"Terrific. Now, miss, if you could lead me back to a trolley or the subway, I would greatly appreciate it."

Victoria stood outside Jack's elegant old brownstone, noticing for the first time that it was showing its age. Her heart was soaring, and she was desperately trying to focus her mind on something other than what she planned. She couldn't just walk in and throw herself into his arms, declaring her undying love. He would be skeptical, perhaps angry. He wouldn't believe her if she told him she suddenly realized she did love him after all.

Chewing her lip, she turned her back to the house and leaned up against the wrought-iron fence that separated the house from the brick sidewalk, feeling the cold from the bars seep through her thin coat. "I could say that I didn't think I was good enough. That I was afraid of his friends and family, of what they would think," she thought. Victoria allowed herself a little smile. That could work. "And then I'll tell him that last night I realized just how much he loves me and how much I love him, and it just didn't seem right to keep us apart." Lame. But it had to be good enough.

Letting out a shaky breath, she walked around to the informal side entrance—not quite the rear, she told herself—and let herself in. Pulling off her gloves, hat, and coat, Victoria could hear male voices from Jack's study and frowned a little. If he had company, she would have to wait until later to spring her good news on him. Maybe she could just take a peek inside and see who it was. It might just be Gibbons.

"Ah, here she is now," Jack said, nodding in Victoria's direction as she poked her head through the doorway.

Victoria smiled nervously, sensing that something was a bit off, but not knowing quite what it was. The man with Jack was an ordinary sort, shorter than Jack and stocky. He turned when she entered, and her stomach did a tight squeeze when she saw recognition on his handsome face.

Jack, who had been leaning casually against his desk, stood erect, and although he made a great effort to seem relaxed, Victoria knew he was angry—angrier than she'd ever seen him. "Miss Casey, I have had the pleasure of meeting Kevin Donnelly. Your husband."

Twenty-four

"**H**usband." Victoria whispered the word as the horror of what he was saying dawned on her.

Jack's smile was tight. "Yes. Your husband has come to take you home. Said now that he's working again, you no longer need this . . . position."

Victoria's first instinct was to deny that she was married, but she stopped herself. For what if Sheila Casey had been married? She couldn't be! Certainly John Wing would have told her such a vital fact. She shook her head, not knowing what she should say or do, with Jack looking at her as if he hated he and this man claiming to be her husband grinning at her.

"Don't tell me, Sheila lass, that you didn't tell our Mr. Wilkins you was married," Donnelly said smoothly, walking over to Victoria. "I've missed you." His gaze was intense, as if he was hiding some strong emotion, but Victoria was too confused to read what it was.

"I don't think I am married," she said slowly, knowing how ridiculous that would sound to both men.

Donnelly gripped Victoria's arm, giving it a painful squeeze that would look to an observer like a caress. "You are married, Sheila." Victoria tore her gaze away from Jack to look again into the strangely intense eyes of Kevin Donnelly.

Something about this man's appearance didn't ring true, but Victoria knew she was in no position to argue with him. Should she pretend to know him? Insist that she did not? Clearly this man was someone from Sheila Casey's past who had come to claim her. And then she remembered that lanky man who'd called her by name, who'd seemed to know Sheila. At the time, she had been startled, but the incident was quickly forgotten and never repeated. She'd never thought about what she would do if someone recognized her, and now realized how foolish she'd been not to come up with a plan. Always quick to think on her feet, Victoria felt as if she'd been drugged. She tried to will herself to think, but the panic that was building second by second was also shutting down her brain. She felt as if she were going to throw up, right there, right on the cheap shoes of this man named Kevin Donnelly.

"Why are you here? Why haven't you come forward before?" she asked Donnelly in an attempt to gain some control of the situation. He seemed to be embarrassed by her question.

"I didn't think you'd want to see me, darlin'. I can tell you're still a bit angry with me, an' I understand. But it's time to mend our fences, time for you to come home."

Victoria looked from Donnelly's sincere, saddened face to Jack's stony one. If Sheila and Donnelly had had a fight, she could use that to her advantage. "I haven't forgiven you, Kevin. I don't think I can," Victoria said, hoping that whatever it was that Kevin did, it was mighty serious.

Kevin, his blue eyes sparkling, looked at Jack as if searching for some male understanding. "I was a brute," he explained to Jack. "I told her I didn't believe the baby she was carrying was mine. I know now I was wrong . . ." He trailed off, managing to look sheepish and pathetic at the same time. Victoria blanched. *Oh, my God.* She was standing beside Emma's true father!

"Baby?" Jack asked. Victoria felt like dying. This was a nightmare, this could not be happening.

Donnelly lifted up his hands as if to appease Jack.

"Don't worry, Mr. Wilkins. I know the babe's yours under the law. But," he said, scratching his jaw, "I was hoping to get a glimpse of her."

Jack's face turned a horrible gray, then as quickly heated to red as his anger built. He looked at Victoria with murderous rage, causing her to shrink in fear.

"Jack, I . . ."

He stalked toward her, then past her to the library door and out of the room, shouting for Etta.

"What the Christ is going on, Sheila? You've got a load of explainin' to do," Donnelly spat once Jack was clear from the room. The affable, simple man he presented himself to be was gone, replaced by a man with eyes as sharp as nails. Victoria was about to answer when Jack returned.

"I want you out of this house, Miss Casey," Jack bit out. "I will give you five minutes. Five minutes. I have done you the great favor of having Etta collect your belongings, so I expect you will not require the full amount of time."

Kevin Donnelly, who seemed to be enjoying himself immensely, cleared his throat. "Actually, I wouldn't mind seein' the little one first, if you don't mind."

"You're goddamn right I mind!" Jack shouted, fists balled by his side. "I want both of you out of my house. If either one of you come near, I'll have the police arrest you."

"Seein' how the little mite is mine," Donnelly persisted, "I think I'm owed a bit of compensation." Victoria looked at him with disbelief. The man wanted money for his own child?

"So help me God, if you don't get out of my sight this minute, I will kill you," Jack growled. One hand clutched the doorknob, as if that were the only thing stopping him from flying at Donnelly's throat. His gaze then touched Victoria. She would not have thought it possible, but his eyes became even more venomous.

Victoria shook her head mutely. He cannot think

that money is why I am here, she thought. But he did; she knew it.

Victoria began breathing in and out as if the room had suddenly lost all oxygen. This could not be happening. Not when she'd been so happy just moments ago. "Jack, no . . ." The look he gave her acted like a gag. She could come back and explain later. Right now she knew nothing she said would convince Jack that she had not used and betrayed him.

"I'd like to say good-bye to Emma."

"No."

Closing her eyes to stop herself from getting hysterical, she repeated her request, knowing that this time, she could not touch Jack's heart.

"I said no."

Nothing you can do, kiddo. Just get your stuff and leave and come back to try to rectify things later. Don't think about it. Don't think that you might never see Emma again. Oh, please God! Let me see her again.

"Where are my things?" she asked, her voice quavering just a bit.

After Jack snapped that everything was by the front door, Victoria walked woodenly out of the study. She didn't care about the clothes or the small things she had accumulated, she only wanted to make sure her statue was among her possessions. Kneeling on the ground, she began rummaging through her cheap suitcase, the same one Sister Margaret had given her.

"It's not there." She stopped still at Jack's voice.

"It's mine. You gave it to me," she said, her back still toward him.

"I'm sure you can't really mean to keep it now." He is so hurt, Victoria thought, so angry.

Straightening, still not facing him for fear she would burst into tears, Victoria said quietly, "No, I guess not." She watched as Donnelly closed the suitcase and walked toward the door, once again the solicitous, affable husband.

"I'll leave you to say your good-byes," he said, and walked out.

Something was strange here. This man was not acting like a husband who'd been cheated on when certainly there was enough evidence to indicate that's exactly what Sheila Casey had been doing. Wouldn't he even be suspicious?

Finally, she turned to face Jack. And because she knew, finally, that it wouldn't matter, she decided to say aloud what she could not before.

"Do you remember the night you proposed?"

He was silent.

"I told you I couldn't marry you because I didn't love you. I was lying. I do love you." She bit back a sob. "You think I'm this terrible person, but I'm not. You don't know what's happening. I'm not even sure what's happening, but it's not what it seems. Oh, God, Jack, you must believe me."

He stared at her for two beats, then turned and walked away.

"Jack!" She could not keep the tears and desperation out of her voice. "Jack, please!" His steps slowed, then stopped as he waited.

"Tell Emma I love her. Please tell her." She left only when she saw one sharp nod. "Thank you," she whispered, knowing he would not hear.

Donnelly waited for her at the bottom of the steps, his expression one of triumph. Victoria stood on the top step, unsure of what to do. She did not want to go with this man but knew she had nowhere else to go.

"Let's get goin' darlin'. Since this is a such a grand day, I think we'll take the trolley to the subway rather than walk it. I'm feelin' generous." His smile was disarming, but somehow calculated. "Let's go, darlin'," he said, his mouth tightening a bit.

"I'm not sure I should," she said softly.

Donnelly's grin widened. "Is it the take you're after? You get none. Not after breakin' out on your own. Not after gettin' airs and forgettin' who you are.

Did you really think he'd marry you, lass? I'm shamed, I am, what's been goin' on in this house."

Victoria walked down the steps finally, and began walking beside him, curiosity overriding her good sense. From what she'd gathered, someone had paid him to do what he did, and she had a fairly good idea who that might be.

"How much did Mrs. Von Arc pay you, Kevin, for ruining my life?"

"Ha! You're a sly one, that you are, Sheila, me girl. Amount don't matter, since you'll not be seein' any of it."

Victoria pulled her collar up against the biting wind as they waited for the trolley. Victoria had strong suspicions about Suzanne, but having them confirmed, she found herself unaccountably hurt—even though she had not liked the woman. Imagine paying this man to get rid of her!

"You're not my husband," she said, taking a wild stab and praying it was true. He certainly did not act like a husband.

"In all but name, I am. It wasn't a big stretch, was it darlin'? When you disappeared on me, I was worried, lass. You were as big as a house with the baby and I am sorry about what happened that night." He stamped his feet in the cold. "But you got me goin'. You just wouldn't stop."

The trolley came, interrupting their conversation. Kevin hopped up, but again, Victoria hesitated. Her gut instinct told her not to go with this man. She knew what she'd wanted to learn, and now she should disappear. But he grabbed at her arm and hauled her up. "Thinkin' of escape?" he asked cheerfully. "You owe me. Pay me back some of the lost wages, and maybe I'll let you go," he said, his tone friendly, but his eyes dangerous. "I figure you managed to get a pretty penny from that rich one. As I said, I'm feelin' generous, so I'll only ask for half."

Victoria wrapped one arm around a pole as the trolley rumbled down the street, and dug her feet into the warming hay that lined the bottom of the car. "I hardly have any money saved, and you can't have any of it," she said, wondering why he thought she should have more. He seemed to think she had gotten money from Jack for some reason.

Donnelly flashed her a smile that only made her more worried. She wondered whether she could jump off the trolley and escape this man. She didn't know why, but her spine tingled with fear every time he smiled. *I shouldn't have gone with him,* she thought. *What was I thinking?*

At the next stop, Donnelly grabbed her arm and led her off the trolley and down the steep steps into the city's new subway. Air rushed about her as they descended the steps, and Victoria fought with her skirts as they descended, one hand gripping the rail. Victoria hadn't ridden the subway since her trip back in time, but was pleasantly surprised to find it much as she remembered—except everything was shining and new and remarkably clean. Donnelly paid a nickel each, and they waited for the train in silence. Riding the subway was old hat to Victoria, who'd grown up using New York's vast system. But for many of the people around her, this was a great novelty, an adventure to be savored. Victoria found herself smiling at one woman who clutched the hand of a man next to her, her eyes staring down the darkened tunnel as if a monster was about to emerge.

"What were you tryin' to do, Sheila? Look at you, dressed so fine, hidin' your accent as if you're ashamed, and goin' to church only once a month. That's right," he said, taking in her stunned look, "I've been watchin' you, tryin' to figure you out. I know you, Sheila, you were workin' a big one, weren't you? Sorry I ruined it for you, but it serves you right."

"You thought I was trying to bilk Jack Wilkins out of money? That's absurd."

"Ain't absurd, darlin'. It's what you do best. Don't

you forget who you're talkin' to. I just want to know what you planned. Somethin' with the baby?"

Victoria was almost beyond speech. What sort of person had Sheila Casey been? Looking straight ahead so Donnelly wouldn't see the lie, she said, "I was going straight. I was sick of it all. And I wanted to be with Emma."

Donnelly let out a bark of laughter. "Wanted to be with the baby? Now, if that's not a lie, nothin' is. There's not a motherin' bone in your little body."

"Maybe not before, but there is now. I love Emma, and I'd never try to get money for her."

"Ah, darlin', it's me, Kevin Donnelly, you're talkin' to. Sweetheart, there ain't nothin' you wouldn't sell, we both know that. It's why I'm so upset with you. We were a team, darlin'. And you struck it alone. It's not the sort of thing to do to Kevin Donnelly."

Victoria gave him a sour look. "Do you always talk about yourself in the third person? Please listen to me. Things are different now. You've got your money for forcing Jack to get rid of me. I'd say we're even. Now you can go your way, and I can go mine."

His smile was chilling. "Why are you tryin' to make me angry, Sheila?" he asked with deadly calm.

Victoria waited until another train went by in the opposite direction before answering, so she wouldn't have to shout over the noise. "I'm not. I'm just explaining how things are."

"Is that right? Well, that's just fine." His smile relaxed her. "Just come up to the flat with me. You left all your things, and I was about to toss 'em out when I learned where you were."

Again, Victoria wasn't sure she should. This man might have known Sheila intimately, but he was a complete stranger to her. Still, he seemed not to be so angry now, she thought as she watched him wave at a bundled-up little girl who sat on her mother's lap. Victoria's heart wrenched at the sight of the mother and daughter. Donnelly was making the little girl squeal with laughter as he pretended to take a penny from her ear and then handed it to her as a gift. A man who could play with children like that couldn't be too bad, she reasoned. And it would be nice to have more clothes, more personal items of the woman whose body she was using.

A few minutes later, Victoria was beside Donnelly as they stepped into the bright coldness from the subway. With each block they walked, the neighborhood became more and more unsavory, the roads more rutted. Tenements rose up on either side, laundry, stiff from freezing in the January air, moved like so many cardboard cutouts in the slight breeze as it hung from ropes strung between balconies. Ruddy-cheeked children with runny noses, seemingly oblivious to the chill, ran about, barking dogs trailing behind. It smelled of cabbage and beer and unwashed bodies. It smelled as miserable as it seemed these people's lives were.

"Toto, we're not in Kansas anymore," Victoria said under her breath.

Most of the people they passed shouted out hearty greetings upon seeing the two trudging down the street, and Victoria found herself smiling and waving back. Everyone seemed so friendly; Sheila Casey must have been very well liked, Victoria thought. Beside her, Kevin was all charm, throwing out one greeting after another, but never stopping long enough to pass more than a word or two.

Down the street, a huge church was under construction, workers covering the roof like ants on a pile of sugar. Victoria stared with amazement at the lavish project being constructed in such a poor neighborhood.

"Sheila! You forget where you live?" Kevin shouted from behind her.

"Oh. I was just daydreaming," Victoria told him, her eyes taking in their home. Four stories tall, the tenement looked like many of the other buildings lining the street with its gray tar-shingle siding and flat roof. They entered the building immediately, walking up a staircase that was so steep and narrow Victoria had to grip the rail. At the third floor, Donnelly stopped at the tiny landing and opened the door. Turning, he flashed her his best winning smile, and Victoria found herself smiling back.

"Get your goddamn ass in here, woman," he bit out, his face turning ugly. He grabbed her arm painfully and practically threw her inside. Victoria stumbled into a kitchen table positioned in the center of the small kitchen, bracing herself against it.

Turning to look at Donnelly with surprise, she said, "Hey! What the hell do you . . ." Her head snapped back, and her jaw exploded with pain.

"You little cheat! I want what's mine, an' I want it now. Think you can go it alone? You'll not make me into a fool, Sheila Casey." Victoria looked at him with terror as he drew back his fist to hit her again. Raising one arm to defend herself and still leaning against the kitchen table, she was once again screeching in pain as his fist struck her forearm. And then her head snapped back again, his fist driving into her as she stumbled off the table and onto the dirty floor.

Victoria knew only that she had to get away from this madman. She skirted across the floor on her rump, pushing off with her legs, her hands scraping the gritty floor as she went backward in a vain attempt to escape his fists.

"You won't cheat me again. I'll be damned if you do it again. You betrayed me!" With every sentence he uttered, another blow was delivered until Victoria was huddled in a corner, arms covering her head. She felt a sharp kick to her side and let out a loud scream.

"Shut up, bitch! I'll give you a reason to scream, goddamn you. I'll give you a reason." She felt the fists, the sharp boots, the spittle raining from her lips as he spouted his venom.

And then she felt nothing. Nothing at all.

Twenty-five

Victoria came to slowly, aware first of the taste of blood in her mouth, and then the pain, the godawful pain. She opened her eyes and felt a moment of panic when she could barely see, until she realized her eyes must be swollen shut. She didn't move, didn't even want to blink, as she was paralyzed with the fear that Kevin Donnelly was still in the apartment, waiting for her to wake up so he might begin again.

Victoria had no idea how long she had been unconscious, how long she had been living this hell. One day? Two? No one had come. No one had responded to screams that surely the neighbors must have heard. She knew she was badly hurt, maybe even dying. He had kicked her so many times, surely something inside her was damaged beyond repair. There was not a single inch of her that was not bruised. It hurt, oh, God, it hurt so much. Victoria thought back to the time she spent in the hospital recovering from her burns. That had been a worse, but a different sort of pain. And at least she had been medicated, at least she knew the best burn doctors in the world were trying to save her.

She tried to hear past the ringing in her ears for some sound that would tell her Kevin Donnelly was still in this apartment. It was so hard to keep focused, so hard to keep awake. Opening her eyes as much as possible, Victoria saw her left hand, bloodied, her pinkie finger obviously broken. She studied her hand, making her brain work, fighting for consciousness. She lost the fight as she again slipped into blackness.

Sun, bright and painful, met Victoria's eyes the next time she opened them. The swelling around her eyes had gone down a bit, for she could see much better. The kitchen appeared to be empty, but she was still so afraid of moving. For endless minutes, she remained silent and unmoving, straining to hear some sound that would tell her she was not alone. Silence.

He'll kill you next time, she thought. You've got to get away. Slowly she tested each limb, wincing as she did. Her legs hurt, but she didn't think they were broken. Right arm, the same. But her left arm was broken somewhere between her elbow and wrist, for the pain she felt when she moved it just slightly made her whimper.

Her heart thudding, she waited to see if Donnelly heard her cries, breathing only when she was sure he was not here. Later, Victoria would not be sure how she did it, but she managed to stand and then to walk. Holding her left arm against herself, she shuffled to the doorway, hunched over and fighting back the screams of agony that threatened. Somehow she made it down those narrow steps and into the street. Surely someone would help her now.

Victoria leaned against the building, fear of discovery consuming her, but unable to go any farther without resting. People on the street, the same ones who had waved and greeted her so joyfully, now ignored her as if she were something shameful or something to be feared. Ah, she thought, that was it. They will not help me for fear it will get back to Donnelly. Her battered eyes managed to make tears that trailed down her hideously swollen face.

"Please," she said to one passing woman. The word, spoken through cut and puffy lips, was nearly unintelligible. The woman's steps quickened. Victoria did not know how long she stayed there, leaned up against the building, too weak to walk away and scared out of her mind to stay. Finally, she pushed away from the building, only to stumble to the hard ground.

"Jesus, Mary, and Joseph, I can't let her die here on the street, Kathleen. I don't care what Kevin will do. I can't turn away," a man's voice said.

"We can't take her to our flat, Joseph. You know we can't."

Victoria felt strong arms lift her. "Where can you go, Sheila. Where will you be safe?"

Victoria looked at him dully. Where could she go? To Jack? He did not want her. She had nowhere. And then she thought of Mrs. Loveless, who pretended to be a tyrant—and often was one—but who also had a heart somewhere hidden beneath the folds of her heavily starched dress.

"Beacon Street. The Grant house."

Suzanne was back, once again a rock for Jack to lean on. Not once had she gloated, not once had she said, "I told you so." With an ease that was startling, she resumed her place in the household as if Victoria had never entered it. Emma's nurse was not mentioned, at least not by the two of them. As if by tacit agreement, the subject of Victoria Casey was closed, a distasteful episode in an otherwise tasteful life.

It took Jack a week before he stopped lifting his gaze from his desk every time the door opened, expecting to see Victoria. Only a week. Why, in a month, he might forget about her altogether, he told himself. Now, sitting at his table and stabbing his knife into a thick steak, he thought of her again. Victoria didn't eat red meat. And so, of course, he would think of her with every bite he took. It was only natural.

"Jack. Are you listening to me?" Suzanne asked gently.

"Yes, Suzanne, something about a concert or such."

She let out a little puff of exasperation. "Yes, Jack, a concert to benefit the Widows of the Spanish War. I was telling you that, as a member of the committee,

I'll be expected to attend. I was hoping you would
escort me."

"Of course," he said, absently, his eyes drifting to
a tray in the center of the table piled high with cherry
tarts—Mrs. Roberts' covert way of trying to cheer him
up. He hadn't known he'd been quite that obvious in
his misery.

Suzanne eyed him with impatience. "Just what is so
interesting about our dessert?"

Again Jack found himself pulled reluctantly away
from thoughts of Victoria. Why am I not angry? he
thought. I should be murderously angry. But something about the way Victoria had left, something about
her voice quavering as she fought back tears, gnawed
at his resolve to remain indifferent. It was that last
declaration of love that bothered him the most, he
decided. For what purpose had it served other than
to torture him? And he could not believe that was the
only reason she had said it.

The fact that she was married was bad enough, but
learning she was Emma's true mother had nearly sent
him over the edge. He had felt anger then, a
wounding, smothering anger that threatened to drive
him to violence. How he wanted to wrap his hands
around Kevin Donnelly's throat and squeeze the
breath out of him. It was not that sort of anger he
felt for Victoria, although, God knew, he tried to con-
jure up such feelings.

He'd replayed the scene in the study over and over
in his head, remembering her reactions to her "husband," her confusion, her tears, and her pleading.
She'd almost seemed as surprised by Donnelly's appearance as he.

He'd regretted throwing her out and hated himself
for that regret. He told himself she was a conniving
bitch, a consummate actress. She'd betrayed him and
then told him that she loved him. He could still hear
her voice, thick with tears. *"I told you I couldn't marry
you because I didn't love you. I was lying. I do love*

you. You think I'm this terrible person, but I'm not. You don't know what's happening. I'm not even sure what's happening, but it's not what it seems."

Bah! It was all a lie, he thought as he attacked his meat anew, sawing at it with savagery.

"It's already dead, Jack," Suzanne said dryly.

"What?" He looked up at Suzanne, then down at his plate. "Oh. Yes, I know. I'm sorry, I'm a bit distracted."

Suzanne was silent for a few moments. "She's not worth one thought, you know, Jack."

He felt his face flush, embarrassed to have been so obviously caught with his thoughts on Victoria. "I am aware of that."

"Jack," Suzanne said, taking hold of his hand. "Do you think you were the only one fooled by her? She probably does this for a living, ingratiating herself into a household, then trying to bilk the owner."

He hated to be put in a position to defend her, he truly did, but Suzanne was wrong. Victoria had never tried to do anything, he realized, except stay with her daughter. It was sneaky and deceitful, and it was likely the only reason she'd made love with him, he had to admit. But he was convinced Victoria had no other black purpose to her actions. She'd seemed genuinely shocked when her lowbrow husband suggested Jack might pay for the privilege of having adopted Emma. He'd replayed that awful day in his head several times, coming to the conclusion that Victoria had not intended to be found by her errant husband. It bothered him considerably that she had so meekly gone with a man who she clearly had no feelings for. It *was* a bit puzzling, but the answer was not that Victoria had been part of some scam.

"I think, Suzanne, that as misguided as she was, Victoria's intentions were mostly benign. She simply wanted to be with her daughter. In a way, I cannot fault her for that."

Suzanne huffed. "Well, I certainly can. She lied repeatedly, seduced you and everyone else in this household into believing she was a devoted nurse. Tell me, why give the child up if she intended to stay with her anyway? I'll tell you way. Money. I didn't want to tell you this, but now I'm afraid I must. I approached Victoria just a few days before we discovered her perfidy and demanded that she leave. I was concerned about certain . . . activities . . . in the library. She refused to leave at first, but then attempted to blackmail me. I, of course, refused. There, you see, Jack? I didn't want to tell you because you were so besotted with her. But you must know the truth now. She was no angel."

Jack shook his head. "She actually demanded money?"

Suzanne looked down, adjusting the linen napkin in her lap. "Yes, Jack. She did."

Jack hadn't realized it, but part of his heart had held out the hope that Victoria truly loved him. But that, too, appeared to be a lie.

"Mr. Grant is here. Shall I bring him in here or your study, sir," Gibbons asked, interrupting Jack's depressing thoughts. He looked down at his supper, suddenly finding it unappealing, and tossed his napkin on the table.

"In the study. Suzanne, if you'll excuse me."

He found Henry Grant pacing the study, obviously impatient to impart whatever news he had.

"It's Victoria. I thought you should know, Jack. She's been beaten. Nearly killed, I'd say."

The only indication that Jack heard was a slight slowing of his steps as he made his way to his desk. He sat down, pressing his palms against the smooth surface so that Henry would not see that his hands shook. "When?" Christ, it was an effort to get that one word out.

"It must have been the day she left. She's been at my house for nearly a week now. She asked me not to tell you, but I thought you should know. I thought you'd want to know."

Of their own volition, Jack's hands drew into fists. "Who did it?"

Henry watched those fists, knuckles white from the strain, and knew how much restraint his friend was showing. "She won't say, but . . ."

"If you know something, tell me."

"Whoever did this to her is a madman, Jack," Henry said, knowing his friend would seek immediate retaliation.

"Tell me."

"Anne Finley—she works in our kitchen—told me Victoria said it was a man named Kevin Donnelly. Ah, I see you know of him?"

Jack closed his eyes, seeing in his mind Donnelly's beefy body. And Victoria's delicate one. Fear for her nearly consumed him, nearly drove him running from the room to beat the man who had beaten Victoria.

"How bad is she?" he choked out, finally letting Henry see how badly this news had shaken him.

"She was horribly beaten. Her face when she first came to the house was unrecognizable. I've never seen anything quite so awful. Even now it's . . . marred. But she's healing."

Holy God, Jack thought fiercely, I'll kill him. Jack stood suddenly, a fierce expression on his face. "Take me to her," he said, striding toward the study's door, only to be stopped short by Henry's grip on his arm.

"No, Jack. She doesn't want to see you. I have to at least abide by those wishes."

"She doesn't want to see me, or she doesn't want me to see her like this?" he asked.

Henry shrugged. "I don't know. I broke a promise telling you anything. But I know you've been looking for her."

Jack looked up sharply, and Henry gave him an easy grin.

"Hell, Jack, every time we're anywhere, you're looking."

"I hadn't realized," he said, his voice fading away. Damn it, he thought, I shouldn't care that she is hurt. I refuse to care. Henry watched as his friend waged an internal war, ready to assist him when he asked, no matter what he asked. Even if, he decided, it meant breaking another promise to Victoria. "She didn't seem all that convincing when she told me she wouldn't see you. I suppose it would be all right."

"She is being cared for?" Jack asked, keeping his voice even.

"Of course."

Jack rubbed the back of his neck. "Thank you," he said.

"Then, you don't want to see her."

More than anything. I want to see her, hold her, take her pain away. I want her to be the woman I thought she was, the woman I was foolish enough to believe existed. "No, I don't."

Jack took a deep breath, clearing away thoughts of Victoria lying battered somewhere in Grant house. "Suzanne was telling me about a benefit concert. Are you and Mary planning to attend?"

If Henry was startled by the abrupt change in subject, he gave no indication. "We plan to. I suppose you will escort Suzanne."

"I suppose I will."

"I heard Suzanne is back here. Reconciled your differences have you?" Henry asked in his irritatingly knowing way. "Or disposed of an obstacle?"

Jack pressed his lips together. "I hope you are not suggesting that Suzanne had anything to do with Victoria's predicament. And you should be happy for me regardless. I do recall a rather heartfelt lecture from you advising me of the dangers of consorting with a woman of Victoria's ilk."

Henry smiled agreeably. "And I also remember another lecture about the dangers of consorting with a woman of Suzanne's ilk."

Jack let out a soft laugh, shaking his head. "So you did. You've nothing to worry about on both accounts. You are looking, my friend, at a confirmed bachelor." His words, which he attempted to say lightly, were filled with bitterness. He would not lay his heart open again to any woman. He knew two things about love: it was the most wonderful thing that could happen to a man, and also the most dreadful.

The next day, Jack began his search for Kevin Donnelly. He did not plan to kill him, he wanted to beat him senseless, pummel his handsome face until his own fists were bloodied and raw. Then it would be over, a chapter closed. The dreams that haunted him of Victoria calling for him, or worse, the dreams of her sweetly turning to him for a kiss, would end. He was sure of it. Something had to drive her from his heart, he reasoned.

And so he searched, with the help of a hired man, for four days before finding out that Kevin Donnelly, knowing he was being pursued and by whom, had disappeared.

Twenty-six

The pain was less today, and so Victoria knew Doc Brighton would not tsk-tsk when she refused to take the laudanum he had prescribed. For the first time in two weeks, she was able to sit up in bed, wincing only once from her still healing cracked ribs, as she gingerly hoisted herself up against the headboard. She refused to look at her face until Anne proclaimed all the bruises gone. She would never forget the first time she looked at her face after the fire, a hideous vision that still haunted her. She would wait this time until she was completely healed. Through some miracle, neither her jaw nor her nose had been broken.

"I feel like these bruises will never go away," she complained, pushing her tongue against one tooth that was slightly loose from a particularly vicious blow.

"You're still your beautiful self," Anne said. Anne was in her glory, clucking over Victoria like a mother hen, as she plumped pillows, straightened her covers, or tried to tame her snarling locks.

"I don't want to be beautiful," Victoria said carefully, for her lips were still healing. "I just don't want to be a monster."

Anne stepped back, as if considering whether her friend looked like a monster. "More like a ghoul," she said, then laughed at her own joke. "Compared to the way you looked when you arrived, you're a rare beauty."

It was true. Although her bruises had turned a sickening yellow-green, the swelling had mostly disappeared and the blood had long been washed away from her face and hair. The beating would leave no permanent damage, Doc Brighton had told her. When Anne first saw Victoria, so weak she could not stand and covered with so much blood it appeared someone had thrown a bucket of it on her, she nearly fainted. Mrs. Loveless, whom Anne had never seen look anything but stern or angry, turned an odd shade of gray before thrusting out her beefy hand to stop herself from swaying.

Once cleaned up, Victoria began to look more herself, or at least more human. And now she looked almost good enough to see a mirror, or so Anne told her when she entered Victoria's room on the fifteenth day of her stay in the Grant household.

"You look fresh as a daisy," Anne said as she adjusted Victoria's pillows. Somehow, and Victoria was not certain just how it happened, she was no longer considered a mere "servant." She wondered if her elevation had to do with her injury, her former position as a nurse, or her former position as the object of Jack's affections.

Victoria eyed Anne with affectionate impatience. "My pillows really don't need fluffing, you know."

Anne stood back and put on a hurt look. "Fine. If you're too good to have your pillows fluffed by the likes of me, a mere scullery maid." And then she flashed her smile. It was her favorite game, trying to make Victoria feel guilty for her odd position in the house.

"Well, I did notice your hands are a bit pruney, which means you must have just been doing the dishes. I have to wonder whether your hands have gone directly from the scummy dishwater directly to my nice white pillows."

"I'm sure Miss Lazybones wouldn't remember, but

we lowly servants are quite careful about our hygiene."

Victoria grimaced. "I remember." And she wondered whether that would be her lot when she recovered. Many of her long hours of solitude were spent contemplating her future. Sometimes she would be convinced the best thing for her to do would be to travel to New York, where maybe she would feel more at home and be able to start again. But then she would think about Emma, which would inevitably lead to thoughts of Jack, her eyes would fill with tears, and she'd know she would never be able to leave Boston.

"Well, if there's nothing else, m'lady, I best get back to the kitchen else Mrs. Loveless will get on me about lallygagging. Though she doesn't seem to actually mind as much as she enjoys nagging at me." Anne continued her grumbling out the door, leaving Victoria chuckling.

It still hurt to laugh, so she stifled her laughter, much as she'd done with her fire-damaged lungs. Smiling still felt like a foreign thing, and her heart wasn't much in it. Victoria had spent the last days crying far more than laughing. She cried for her mother and father, for Allie, and all that she lost from her former life. And she cried for Jack, who certainly hated her now, for Emma, who would never know her mother, and for herself.

Kevin Donnelly took everything away that day at Jack's house. He took her life, then he took her spirit, leaving behind a different woman. Victoria remembered how devastating the fire was, how it changed her inwardly and outwardly. The fire had burned away the person she was, leaving behind someone who wasn't quite living. Kevin Donnelly had done that, but he also gave Victoria something she'd never had—a fathomless hatred. Victoria had never hated anyone or anything in her life and had shied away from that dark emotion. But now she feasted on it, savoring its bitter taste.

She could still see him hovering over her already broken body, screaming at her, spewing out words meant to crush her. Poor, poor Sheila Casey. What a horrible life she must have had, Victoria thought. She had no doubt that Donnelly had been a factor in Sheila Casey's death. "Now I can avenge us both," she whispered aloud. She had no idea what she would do; she only knew she wanted him hurt, so hurt he would want to die. He would beg to die—as she had done.

"Just kill me, and get it over with," she had said as she huddled in a corner of the kitchen. Victoria could still hear herself pleading with him, believing that killing her was what he intended. She believed she would be dead now, if not for her escape.

She shook her head. She did not want to keep remembering the humiliation of that moment, when he had beaten her down to a point where she no longer cared about anything but ending the pain. She was thinking about Kevin Donnelly, imagining horrid things she would do to him if she could, when Mary Grant walked in the room.

"My goodness, I hope that expression is not meant for me," she said.

Victoria snapped out of her dark thoughts, surprised to see her hostess standing by her bed. As far as she knew, it was the woman's first visit.

"Hello, Mrs. Grant. No, I was thinking about the bastard who did this to me."

Mary flushed slightly at Victoria's language. "May I?" she said, sitting on the corner of the bed. "Please, call me Mary." She paused, looking at Victoria thoughtfully. "You look much better."

Victoria gave her a curious look as she tried to figure out what had brought this visit about. "Thank you."

"My father used to beat my mother," Mary said abruptly into her lap before bringing her eyes back to Victoria. "Nothing as bad as this, of course. I think he would have if not for the public embarrassment such a beating might have brought. I hated him. Truly, truly hated him. And her, too, until I got a little older. I could never figure out why she let him do it." She let out a small laugh that somehow held more sadness than anything else. "I know now she had no choice. For years, I was afraid to get married, afraid that's what all husbands did to their wives. Henry convinced me otherwise. I've never even heard him raise his voice. It can be quite maddening, really. But wonderful, too."

Victoria found her eyes brimming with tears as she gave Mary a tentative smile. "I want him to suffer," Victoria said. "He's an evil man. I . . ." Victoria couldn't continue, and Mary lay a hand on her arm. "I want him to feel what I felt. Not only the pain, but the feeling of complete helplessness. Of knowing you cannot stop it, of knowing if you try, you'll only be hurt worse. It's an awful feeling."

Mary looked down at her lap again. "Please forgive me for asking this, but I'd like to know if you'll tell me. Why did you marry him? Did he hide this part of him from you?"

So Jack had told them. "We were never married. He just wanted Jack to think so, I suppose."

Mary's huge brown eyes grew bigger. "Never married? I don't understand. Jack told us that you were married to this man and that Emma is your child."

"Emma is my daughter, but Kevin Donnelly and I were not married. He told me Mrs. Von Arc paid him to make sure I was fired as Emma's nurse. Of course, naming himself as my husband did the trick. It's all such a nightmare," she finished, bringing her hands up to rub her eyes.

"She *didn't*," Mary said, her mouth dropping open. "Why would Suzanne do that?"

"Apparently Suzanne's in love with Jack. Or at least she wants to marry him. I suppose she figured if I was no longer in the picture, she'd have a better chance."

"Suzanne and Jack? Henry had his suspicions, but I thought he was imagining things. This plot is so melodramatic, I can't believe Suzanne would do such a thing." It was clear from her tone, that she did believe Suzanne could have concocted such a plan. "I can hardly wait to tell Henry he was right," Mary said, clearly enjoying this bit of gossip.

"But there is still something I don't understand. If you weren't married, then why did you go with him? Why didn't you tell Jack then and there that Donnelly was lying?"

Victoria was ready for her answer. Though she hated the thought of lying, she knew she had no other choice. "I never expected to see Donnelly again. When he showed up, I was as surprised as Jack. He was a part of my life that I wanted to forget about. I had been so happy, living a fantasy, I suppose, thinking that my past would never catch up with me. Anyway, there he was—he can be quite charming— pretending to be happy to see me. Jack was so angry. And hurt, I could tell that, too. The look he gave me when I started to deny we were married scared me, so I stopped. He wouldn't have believed me at that point, I'm certain of it. And then Donnelly casually dropped the news that he was Emma's father and demanded that he see her. I'll never forget the look on Jack's face. Never." Victoria's eyes filled with tears once more, and she turned her face toward a sunlit window.

"You love him."

"Yes. But it's too late. He thinks I'm a liar, and he's right, I am. I couldn't tell him about Emma in the beginning. He never would have hired me. And then the longer I waited, the bigger the lie." Victoria shook her head. "Now it's one big mess. And Jack hates me. He hasn't even tried to see me." She waved a hand before Mary could deny that Henry had told Jack she was there. "I never expected Henry not to tell Jack."

"You told Henry you didn't want to see Jack," Mary said with exasperation.

"I know that's what I *said,* but I never expected Jack to listen. If it had been Jack instead of me in this bed, do you think anything would have kept me away if I still loved him?"

Mary seemed to think that over, tapping her index finger against her pursed lips. "Jack is a very proud man, and right now he's also a very angry man."

"I understand, Mary. I was just hoping he'd burst through that door and tell me everything was forgiven. I know that won't happen."

Mary shook her head. "No, I don't think it will." She stood up suddenly, marking an end to their conversation. "Perhaps I'll come to visit tomorrow."

"That would be very nice," Victoria said, genuinely pleased.

In the next few days, Mary was a regular guest in Victoria's room, and soon they were fast friends. Victoria wished Mary and Allie could meet, for she knew the two would have gotten along famously. Gone was the haughty woman Victoria thought Mary to be when she was working as her scullery maid. The two joked about those days, with Mary confessing she never felt comfortable ordering people about, and so acted like she thought she should.

"Really," she had told Victoria, "I sometimes wonder what I am doing in charge of all these people. I look in the mirror and expect to see a young girl. I still feel like a young girl. Instead I see this matronly woman with three children and a husband. How did that happen?"

Victoria couldn't tell her about her own life, so she made things up, sticking as closely as she could to the real thing. She told her about her parents and the excitement of living in New York City—at first being careful about what she said and how she said it. But it was so comfortable talking with Mary, Victoria did slip before she could stop herself.

"I used to fly constantly, rather than take the train or drive," she said one day during Mary's daily visit. "I mean, it seemed as if I were flying on the steamship."

Mary gave her a thoughtful look. "I've never been on a steamship. Henry always said it was too expensive, and a train would do just as nicely. Frankly, I believe Henry gets seasick and is too proud to admit it," she said. "Still, steamship tickets can be expensive. I don't know quite what to make of you, Victoria Casey."

Victoria was practically squirming beneath Mary's intense gaze. "How do you mean?"

Mary pursed her lips. "I'm not certain. But let's just say I cannot believe you were once my scullery maid. Or that you were once with a lowbrow like Kevin Donnelly. There's something about you," she said, shaking a finger at her and squinting her eyes comically.

Victoria shrugged. "Life forces people to make all sorts of decisions," she said, purposely being mysterious and praying Mary would come to some erroneous conclusion.

"I'm beginning to suspect that life has not been kind to you," Mary said, laying a hand on her friend's arm. "I must be honest, and now that we're friends I think I can be, but I'm a bit surprised that things have turned out as they have."

"I assume you mean me being here and us becoming friends."

"Well, yes. And you and Jack falling in love. And Emma being your daughter," Mary ventured.

Victoria stiffened, not liking where their conversation had gone. "I don't want to talk about that." It hurt too, too much.

Mary looked down to hide a smile.

"What are you smiling about, Mary," Victoria said.

She lifted her head, the secretive smile broadening. "What if I were to tell you that Jack was coming to visit this evening. With Suzanne." She made a face. "And Emma."

Victoria couldn't stop the look of hope that sprang to her eyes. Then she frowned. "I don't want to see Jack."

"Then, how about Emma?"

"How?" she asked, leaning forward in excitement.

"I adore Emma. Jack knows that. I thought I could play with her, walk around the house, and perhaps just happen to bump into a certain someone, say around seven o'clock in the breakfast room?"

Victoria leaned forward and grasped Mary's hands.

"Oh, Mary. You don't know how much this means to me." Her eyes filled with tears. "Look at me, crying, when I've never been so happy."

"It's all right to cry, Victoria. I know I couldn't bear to be separated from my children. You've been so brave, but I know you've been going a bit mad not being able to see her."

Victoria wiped her eyes with the backs of her hands. "It's been awful. I miss her so much. I thought if I didn't talk about her, I wouldn't miss her. But it hasn't worked."

"I'll see you tonight, then."

Victoria hugged herself and closed her eyes, imagining already she held Emma in her arms.

Twenty-seven

Victoria stared at the mantel clock as if it were to blame for time crawling by. Had the clock stopped? No, she could still hear it ticking its endless beats. The room was lit only by a single lamp, an extra precaution taken in case someone walked by. Finally, the clock began chiming the hour, and Victoria stared at the door as if Mary would suddenly materialize holding Emma.

One minute past. Two minutes. Oh, where the hell was she? she thought, standing more quickly than she should, for her ribs were still sore and a deep bruise in her thigh continued to bother her. She sat back down, gingerly, biting on her knuckles, boring holes through the carved door with her eyes.

And then it opened, Mary poked her head through, a huge smile on her face. And Emma in her arms.

Victoria rushed to her, sore ribs and thigh forgotten, arms outstretched. "Oh, my little girl, oh, Emma," she said, burying her nose in the baby's neck and breathing in her special scent. "You're so big! Look how big you are!"

Mary stood there, tears flooding her eyes, watching the touching reunion. "Look how she's smiling, Victoria. She truly missed you."

"Oh, I missed you, too, sweetheart," Victoria said, giving Emma the best squeeze she could with her bandaged and splinted left arm. She turned to her friend. "Thank you."

"I wouldn't have missed it for all the world," she said, and then grew fierce. "It's not right for the two of you to be separated."

"Please don't blame Jack. This is all my fault. I wish we could all be together, but we can't." She buried her nose into the crook of Emma's sweet neck. "If this is all I have for the rest of my life, it will have to be enough." She said it, but didn't believe a word of it.

Victoria limped over to a nearby sofa and sat with Emma on her lap. "She's changed so much since I've been gone. I can't believe how much. She's so beautiful. Aren't you, Emma? Look at how much hair you have!" She kissed Emma's chubby cheeks until the little girl began laughing.

"You two are taking your life in your hands."

Victoria and Mary both looked at the door with shock to see Henry standing in the doorway.

"My goodness, Henry, you frightened us nearly to death," Mary breathed, a hand over her heart.

Henry walked into the room, shaking his head at his errant wife. "Just be glad it was me and not Jack. He's the one who was wondering where you and Emma disappeared to. And I, dear wife, knowing you as I do, suspected you were up to mischief."

Mary put her fists on her hips. "It's simply not fair of Jack to keep Emma from Victoria. It's cruel and . . ."

"His decision, Mary. Under the law, Emma is more his child than Victoria's. You know that. You both know that."

Both women looked at Henry belligerently. Mary was about to open her mouth to argue, but Victoria interrupted her.

"He's right, as much as I hate to admit it. You'd better take Emma back before Jack gets suspicious."

"I'm sure he's already suspicious," Henry said, watching Mary take the baby from Victoria's arms. He frowned at the tears that immediately sprang to Victoria's eyes.

Victoria kissed Emma's cheek and held her little hand. "We really should get back," Mary said gently.

"I know. Thank you." Victoria bit her lip to stop the sob that threatened as they walked out the door.

Once husband and wife were headed toward the main parlor, Henry whispered fiercely, "Mary, what you did is possibly more cruel to her than keeping Emma from her entirely, you know. At one time, Jack might have been willing to let Victoria see Emma. But not now."

Mary stopped in the hallway, looking up at her husband with disbelief. "You didn't tell him, did you," she accused.

"That Suzanne plotted against Victoria? That Victoria isn't married to that man, even though she made no protest when he came and claimed his wife? Or that Victoria loves him, after all?"

"You make it all sound like lies."

"They are what they are," Henry said, walking again, making Mary catch up to him, the baby bouncing happily in her arms.

"It's all true, Henry. I know it is. I'll admit I was surprised that Suzanne would actually hire someone to get rid of Victoria, and at one time I probably would have thought she was lying. But I know Victoria now. She doesn't have a mean bone in her body. Except maybe for that Donnelly man."

"We'll talk about this later," Henry said as they entered the parlor.

Jack was standing near the mantel, staring at the fire that was lit more for effect than warmth, a glass of port forgotten in his hand. He nodded occasionally, as if he were actually paying attention to Suzanne's plans for the upcoming benefit concert. Being in this house, knowing Victoria was just one floor above him, was driving him slowly mad. He had been rotten company that evening, on edge, expecting her to bounce into the room at any moment. But now, according to Henry's report, she would limp in instead. She was mostly recovered, her face still slightly marred by the last of the bruises, one arm still bandaged, Henry had told him. And he had simply nodded as if he didn't care, as if his gut hadn't given a twist when Henry calmly told him the limp was barely discernible. My God, the fact that she limped at all was enough to drive him to violence.

If he could just get his hands around Donnelly's throat, he could get over this pathetic infatuation, Jack told himself. The matter would be closed. But now, knowing he had let her go with Donnelly, remembering how she begged to see Emma and pleaded with him to understand, he felt responsible. The only way to rid his mind of her face, her scent, her laugh was to find Donnelly and make him pay. How could a man disappear without a trace?

His scowl was so fierce little Emma puckered her face upon seeing her father, and he instantly smiled.

"Here she is," Mary said, holding Emma out to Jack. Somehow, and Mary suspected the woman must have leapt from her chair to do so, Suzanne was there beside them taking Emma from Mary's outstretched arms.

"I'll take my little sweety," she cooed. Mary gave Henry a knowing look before taking her seat.

"I never knew you liked children, Suzanne. If memory serves, I can recall you telling me you were happy Mr. Von Arc was getting on in years, for that meant you might forgo motherhood." Mary knew she was being awful, but didn't care. She knew what a mother's love looked like, and this overexaggerated act was not it.

Suzanne gave Mary a hard look before smiling. "How could anyone not love this little thing," she said, giving Emma a kiss on the cheek.

Mary looked at Jack from beneath her lashes to see how he was reacting to the interplay, only to find him staring once again into the fire. He looked miserable.

Mary stepped up quietly next to him. "Not quite yourself this evening, are you, Jack?"

"Hmmm? No. Not quite."

Mary gave a furtive look to Henry, who was watching with a jaundiced eye as Suzanne played with Emma, before saying quietly, "She's fine, really, Jack. But she misses Emma. And you." He raised one skeptical eyebrow. "Oh, don't look so disbelieving."

"Why do I have the feeling that you and Victoria have developed a somewhat closer relationship than scullery maid and mistress?"

Mary smiled sweetly. "She's no scullery maid. I've never met anyone like Victoria in my life. You must know what I mean. I cannot put my finger on just what makes her special, but she is." She watched, with a certain amount of satisfaction, as the muscles in Jack's jawline tensed. "When Henry first told me about the two of you, I was as shocked as he. I believed you were suffering from delirium. I'm not as big a snob as Henry, but I still found it hard to believe you actually wanted to marry her."

"I really don't wish to discuss this, Mary," Jack said tightly.

Mary was silent for a few moments, staring at Jack as he stared into the fire. "I believe her, Jack." She watched as he took a deep breath, then she plunged ahead. "She loves you. She isn't married and never was and this was all Suzanne's doing."

Jack stared at the retreating back of Mary, who walked away as if a wild dog were about to pounce. *What the hell did that all mean,* he thought. He wasn't surprised that Mary had claimed Victoria loved him. But the other comments?

"Mary!"

Mary was just about to sit down when Jack's voice boomed from behind her. She froze, a rather comical look of guilt on her face. She flashed a look to Henry, who immediately guessed what the two had been talking about so quietly. To her credit, Mary sat with grace and turned her head inquiringly at Jack, not even flinching at the look of menace marring his handsome features.

"How do you know she is not married?"

"Oh, Mary, you didn't." That from Henry, who looked at his wife with a mixture of exasperation and disappointment.

Mary, ignoring her husband's warning look, sat up straight, ready to defend her friend. "Victoria told me so."

"Ahh. I suppose she also told you she is not Emma's mother."

"No, she readily admits that. And besides, I hired a detective just to make certain. And I'm ashamed that I did. Ashamed that I did not take her word for it."

"You *what*?" demanded Henry.

"Hired a detective. I thought I was speaking quite clearly," Mary said, her sarcasm telling her husband just how angry she was.

"Let me guess," Jack said dryly. "This detective person found no record of a marriage. Emma's birth certificate lists no father. In fact, having looked at my daughter's birth certificate myself, I can tell you what it says. Under 'father' is the word 'unknown.' I think that can mean only one thing, that our Sheila Casey, whose middle name according to that very certificate is Shannon, not Victoria as she claims, does not know who the father is. And you are not so innocent, Mary, to not know what that means."

Mary bit her lip. "It could also mean she did not legally want to proclaim Kevin Donnelly the father of her child. If it were me, I would not."

"Mary, dear, Victoria is using you. Like she used Jack. Don't let her fool you, too," Suzanne said smoothly. "Why would she ask to be brought here? She worked here only a short while. She is here because Henry is Jack's good friend and she hoped to somehow manipulate herself back into our household."

"That's not true!" Mary said. "You just want everyone to hate her because you want to get rid of her."

"Mary." Henry's tone held a warning.

"No, Henry, I won't stop. It's got to be said. Suzanne paid Kevin Donnelly to say he was her husband so you would finally get rid of her."

"Mary!" Henry said, clearly appalled that his heretofore genial wife was making such a public accusation.

Suzanne's reaction was quite different. She laughed. "Oh, really, Mary. I hadn't thought you were quite that gullible." She laughed again.

Mary stared at Jack. "It's true. I know it is." But her words had lost some of their fire. Spoken aloud, the accusation *did* sound a bit implausible.

Jack saw her doubt and felt sorry for her. "Victoria is a liar. You are correct. She is not a scullery maid. She is educated and rather cultured, in an odd sort of way. I can think of only one reason she came to work here in the first place—my friendship with Henry. She must have known it would only be a matter of time before I came to visit with Emma. It is quite a coincidence, isn't it?"

"But she looked for Emma for weeks," Mary said. "She didn't know where she was."

"And found her right here."

"It could happen. It *did* happen," Mary insisted. "Why not simply try to get a job in your house?"

Jack shrugged. "I don't know. But I do know that Suzanne had nothing to do with Kevin Donnelly's appearance."

Suzanne gave Jack a brilliant smile while Mary looked to be on the verge of tears.

"You haven't seen her. You don't know what she has gone through. And to think she still . . . You, Jack Wilkins, are a horrid, horrid man." Mary fled the room, one hand over her mouth in an attempt to stifle her sobs.

Henry took one step toward his wife before turning to his guests. "I must apologize to you for Mary. I don't understand this. I married her because she was so steady, so solid. One month in the company of Miss Casey, and she's nearly hysterical. I'm sure she doesn't truly believe half of what she's said this evening."

"Victoria has a way of getting people to believe in her. Please don't fault Mary too much," Jack said. Henry gave a curt nod before departing the room in search of his distraught wife.

Suzanne put a hand to her throat, where her fingers fiddled with a black velvet bow that decorated her high-necked gray silk blouse. "I knew Miss Casey disliked me," she said, "but I didn't know to what depths."

Jack stared at her so long, Suzanne began to feel uncomfortable. "Apparently she does," he said finally, turning toward the parlor door.

As they walked past the curving staircase that graced the Grant's large entrance hall, Emma, still in Suzanne's arms, pointed a chubby finger to the second floor. "Mama," she said.

Jack jerked his head to look up the staircase, which disappeared into the blackness of the unlit second floor. He saw nothing, but knew she was there. He saw her in his mind as clearly as if a beam of light were illuminating her. He stayed that way for nearly a minute, eyes straining into the darkness, daring her to show her face. And he finally turned to go.

At the top of the stairs, Victoria sat huddled against the banister. "Yes, baby, Mama's here," she whispered. "Mama's here."

Twenty-eight

"**I** want her out of this house," Henry said in his best lawyer voice. He had found Mary pouting in their bedroom. "She's nearly fully recovered. There is no reason for her to continue to occupy one of our best guest rooms."

Mary, now fully in control and getting angrier by the minute, stared at her husband belligerently. "She's my friend. That's reason enough."

"She's our goddamn scullery maid!"

"Don't swear, Henry, and she is not."

"I'll admit that Suzanne is not my favorite person. She's a humorless tyrant, if you ask me. But she wouldn't lower herself to hire a thug to get rid of Victoria. Do you actually believe that cockamamie story?"

Mary folded her arms across her chest stubbornly. "Yes, I do."

"Well, I don't and I say she goes. That's final, Mary. Tell her tonight to leave tomorrow."

"Henry, no. Where will she go? She has no one."

"That is not my concern. What is my concern is she is driving a wedge between myself and my greatest friend, and now apparently between myself and my wife." Henry took a deep breath and jerked down on his vest, all his anger dispersed with that gesture. He leaned forward and put a gentle hand on each of Mary's shoulders, kissing her forehead. "She must go, Mary-mine. In your heart, you know it."

Mary frowned up at her husband. "I know nothing of the sort," she said mildly, but Henry knew he had won. "I don't know how I'm going to break this to her. She was so happy tonight."

"Do what you must," Henry said, straightening and turning to leave.

"Henry."

"Yes, dear?"

"I still believe her," she said to his back.

"Yes. That's fine, dear." He continued out the door, not seeing the scowl his wife was giving him.

The next day, Mary broke the news to Victoria, but left her in a much better position than her husband would have liked. Victoria, wearing a borrowed ivory-colored blouse with a deep brown necktie and brown and ivory striped skirt, greeted Mary with a smile. That smile quickly disappeared when Mary did not return it.

"What's happened?"

"Oh, Victoria, I've made a mess of things for you. I thought I was being so brave, and all I've managed to do is get you thrown out."

Victoria blinked at her friend. "You told Jack I saw Emma?"

Mary grimaced. "Worse."

"Worse?" Victoria asked, with a sickly expression on her face.

"I told everyone that you were never married. And that Suzanne was behind Donnelly's visit."

"You didn't!"

"I did."

Victoria gave her friend a sad smile. "And no one, from what I gather, believed you." Mary gave a sad shake of her head.

"I can't say I'm surprised. How did Jack react?"

"He apparently knew about the marriage. But he didn't believe the part about Suzanne. I have a confession to make. I didn't believe you entirely, either, so I hired a Pinkerton detective to find out if you were married or not. You'll be pleased to know he confirmed that you are not. But Henry's so upset with me for accusing Suzanne, he wants you to leave." She sat down dejectedly at the foot of Victoria's bed.

Victoria grinned. "You actually hired a detective?"

"You're not angry?" Mary asked warily.

"No, just surprised. And a little impressed. I know more than anyone how shaky my story is. And I'm not angry I have to leave, either. I knew I couldn't stay here indefinitely."

Victoria's optimism seemed to have little effect on Mary, who continued to look forlorn. "I know you haven't anywhere to go, so I want you to take a gift. Please don't argue, Victoria. You haven't any clothes except my cast-offs that you're wearing now. Let me give you a few more things. And money. I've got some money. It's my own, so Henry won't mind. At least he'd better not."

Victoria shook her head. "Not money, Mary."

"Oh, but you must! Without money what will you do? You shouldn't have to work as a servant. I thought to give you enough to perhaps get an apartment at the Vendome. It's truly *the* place, you know, very respectable. It would hold you for a while until you were able to get a position more suitable."

Victoria wet her lips. She didn't want to take the money, but she knew she could use it. Not for a fancy hotel room but to hire a detective to find Kevin Donnelly.

"Mary, I'll take some money, but it's a loan only. And I won't be throwing it away at the Vendome or any other fancy hotel. I want to use it to hire a detective. How did you find yours?"

Mary jumped up, excited to be able to help Victoria. "I found him through the *Globe,* and I still have the advertisement in my jewelry case. The whole thing was rather exciting. Jasper Porter was his name, I believe. If you don't mind my asking, what do you need a detective for?"

Victoria gripped Mary's upper arms to signal the seriousness of what she was about to say. "I'm going to find Kevin Donnelly. I'm going to make him pay."

Mary's eyes grew wide. "That sounds too dangerous. Aren't you frightened?"

Victoria shuddered. "Of course I'm afraid. I'm terrified. I think what I'm most afraid of, though, is when I see him I'll freeze, I won't be able to do anything."

Mary swallowed audibly. "You're not thinking of killing him, are you?" Her eyes were so wide, Victoria almost laughed.

"You know, I wish I were the kind of person who could do that and not feel guilty. But I'm not. I just want him to pay. I just want him to know that he can't hurt me and get away with it."

A slow smile spread on Mary's face. "Good. Men like him ought to suffer."

"One more thing. Please don't tell Henry."

"You're afraid he'll tell Jack," she said, frowning a bit, and Victoria nodded. "I won't lie if he asks me directly, but I won't volunteer anything, either. Is that all right?"

"That's fine. You're a good friend, Mary."

Mary looked down at her hands, suddenly shy. "I haven't been such a good friend. I could have stood up to Henry." She looked up, suddenly, her eyes bright with mischief. "But I did stand up to Suzanne. I've never liked her, you know, not deep down inside, where it counts. I suppose I never really saw her until now, though. She is trying to get Jack. It's so obvious that she's using Emma to get to Jack's heart. But I know it's not working."

"How do you know that?" Victoria asked, ignoring the flood of jealousy Mary's words brought.

"Just the way he clenched his jaw when I brought you up."

"Clenched his jaw, did he? Why that's practically a declaration of love," Victoria said dryly.

"Yes, it is!" Mary insisted. "And his eyes are so sad."

"You are such a romantic. He was probably just bored silly."

Mary wrinkled her nose at Victoria. "You are much too practical."

Practical. When had Victoria ever been practical? That description from one of the most practical, strait-laced ladies she'd ever met, was a bit jarring. Life had forced Victoria to be practical, she figured. The last time she had allowed herself a bit of impracticality, she'd gotten drunk and tried to seduce Jack. Well, hiring a detective to find Kevin Donnelly so she could beat the smithereens out of him could not be consid-ered staid or straitlaced. It was decidedly insane. Maybe that's why it felt so good to be planning such an escapade.

Having made her decision, Victoria was already be-ginning to feel more in control of her life. Her body, or rather, Sheila Casey's body, had recovered from the beating. Victoria knew her mind would take much longer to heal. The fear that threatened to paralyze her, she turned into hate. How dare he make her be afraid every waking moment? He was a nothing, a coward who took advantage of those weaker. She told herself that when she woke up from shadowy dreams of him looming over her, shouting, his big fists pound-ing, pounding. And she turned it toward the hate she fed like a spider nesting in her heart.

When she left the Grant manse, it was in high spirits and determination. She wore a smart little blue wool outfit borrowed from Mary with a choking collar and a skin-squeezing waist that made her look wealthy and businesslike. Or as businesslike as a woman could get at the turn of the century. Her cloak, another Mary hand-me-down, was fur-lined and cozily warm, and came with a matching muff. As she made her way down Beacon Street to the trolley stop, she nodded at the passersby and they nodded back to her. It hadn't snowed in weeks, so the walkways were clear of snow, and the air that late February day held just the hint of springtime.

She ignored the stab of fear that lanced through her when she stepped aboard the horse-drawn trolley, remembering the last trip she made was with Donnelly. Digging her feet into the hay for warmth, she looked straight ahead and focused on what she would say to the detective.

Twenty minutes later, Victoria made her way up to the third floor of a rather shabby building, stairs lit only by natural light seeping through large dirty windows at the top of each landing. Reaching the third floor, she found a series of offices with opaque glass doors that had company names etched on them.

She stood before Jasper Porter's office several moments before thrusting out her hand and grabbing the doorknob. She entered a tiny reception area, which had no receptionist, only an old oak desk and a green-leather banker's chair. A door to her left was ajar, so Victoria took a tentative step toward it. A waft of smoke made her more confident someone was inside that office.

"Hello?"

"Come in, come in, door's open." Victoria frowned at hearing the voice. She expected something gruff, something decidedly Humphrey Bogart-ish. Instead came a rather unpleasant, high-pitched nasally sort of voice more like Joe Pesci, but without the New York character.

"Are you Jasper Porter?" Victoria asked pushing open the door cautiously.

"I am," Porter said, standing. Victoria nearly burst out laughing. The voice certainly did not fit this hulk of a man. He was brutish-looking, nearly bald but for a close-cropped gray fringe around his head, which seemed to sit directly on his shoulders without the support of a neck. His eyes appeared almost black, and he had the most ridiculous thin mustache above his nicely shaped lips that seemed out of place in his otherwise homely face.

"I'm Victoria Ashford," she said, using her own name and reaching for a handshake. "I'd like to hire you to find someone for me."

Porter grasped her hand briefly, as if unaccustomed to shaking a woman's hand, and sat his bulk behind a massive desk. "Go on," he said.

Ah, Victoria thought, a man of few words. That was fine with her. "A man named Kevin Donnelly. He's some sort of criminal. I want you to find him for me, but I do not want you to make contact with him. I don't want him to know someone is looking for him."

Porter tapped his fingers on his desk, then calmly and expertly rolled a cigarette, never making a sound, and Victoria wondered if he thought the interview was over. She sat, hands on her lap, looking about the messy office, as she waited for a response. Porter stood and was about to light the cigarette, when he remembered his manners.

"Mind?"

She did, but didn't say so. He lit the thing and took a deep drag while walking over to the room's only window, breathing out a smoky cloud, before finally turning back to Victoria.

"Any idea where I should start looking?" he asked.

"I wrote down the address here," Victoria said, laying a slip of paper on top his desk. "You know, those things will kill you," she said, nodding at the filterless cigarette. He looked at the cigarette with mild interest, and grunted in a noncommittal sort of way.

"I'll have a report in one week. If I find out anything before that, I'll send my assistant to tell you." He sat down, grabbing a fountain pen. "I charge five dollars a day," he said, and getting no expression of outrage, he continued. "Where may I reach you, Miss Ashford?"

Victoria made a decision then and there. "The Vendome," she said. She would stay there at least a week and then search for something more affordable.

The interview finished, Victoria stood and smiled when Porter courteously leapt to his feet. "Thank you, Mr. Porter."

"Good day, Miss Ashford," he said, remaining on his feet as Victoria made her way out of his office. He stood staring after her for a few moments before pulling out a file on Kevin Donnelly that was already a half-inch thick. The name of his client—Jack Wilkins—was scrawled along the top.

Twenty-nine

"**I**s she still there?"

Gibbons moved the curtain aside just enough for one eye to peer out the second-floor window. "Yes, sir. That'd be four hours now."

Jack let out a weary sigh. For three days, Victoria had sat on a bench in the tiny park opposite Jack's home, a book in her hands going quite unread. He wouldn't have known it was her unless Gibbons had pointed her out to him, something his loyal servant was apparently uncomfortable doing.

"She must be freezing," he said, mostly to himself.

"It is quite chilly," Gibbons said. "But she looks to be dressed rather warmly, sir."

What was she doing there, sitting hour after hour. Hoping to get a glimpse of Emma, of himself? Or hoping she would be noticed and somehow thinking they could manage a reconciliation, as Suzanne had suggested? Regardless of her reasons, she was a determined little thing, he gave her that much. It wasn't chilly today, it was downright frigid. He could see how red her nose was even from this distance. The sharp-eyed Gibbons had noticed her two days ago, but had not mentioned it until seeing her again today, not wanting to upset Jack. Who knows how long this vigil had been going on? He guessed for as long as she'd been out of the Grants' house.

"Why doesn't she just walk up to the door and get it over with?" he muttered.

Jack took Gibbons's place at the window, and watched her for several minutes. She stamped her feet, no doubt trying to prevent them from freezing, and then she stood, her eyes seeming to look straight at him. He saw her shoulders heave a sigh and then she sat down again, abruptly, as if she were trying to make herself approach the house then lost her nerve.

"Gibbons."

"Yes, sir."

"Please bring this note to our friend down there," Jack said, scribbling on a piece of paper.

Victoria, nearly frozen in place on the bench, was about to leave when the front door opened revealing Jack's butler. She remained seated, barely breathing, as Gibbons made his way through the small park directly toward her. She'd obviously been spotted, something she was half hoping would happen.

"Hello, Mr. Gibbons."

"Hello, Miss Casey. I've a note to you from Mr. Wilkins," he said, and turned to leave.

"Could you please wait until I've read the note? I might have a response," Victoria called out, and then read the cryptic message.

"If you do not discontinue your vigil, I will contact the police and have you arrested for trespassing. JW"

She crumpled the note savagely and turned her stormy eyes toward the house, where she suspected Jack was observing her. "You tell him this is a public park, and I can sit here as long as I want. I can sit here until June if I want. You tell him he's got no right to order me about. You tell him . . . Never mind, I'll tell him myself, the jerk."

Gibbons looked in a panic. "Oh, Miss Casey, I wouldn't do that if I were you," he said, hurrying after her as she marched across the park and jerked open the wrought-iron gate. "He's been in a dark mood lately. Miss Casey! Miss Casey, please!"

Victoria finally stopped in the middle of the quiet street, and turned to hear what he had to say.

"It's been ugly around here since you left. For all our sakes, couldn't you please just stop coming here?"

She shook her head. "If I could just see Emma . . ." Victoria sagged. What was she doing here? Jack would never let her see Emma. Never. He hated her and wanted to hurt her the way she had hurt him. If she were completely honest, she was also hoping to see Jack, to somehow convince him that she loved him. Seeing him at the Grants' house tore at her. He'd looked haunted and worn, a shell of the man she had made love to with so much abandon. She wanted to wrap her arms around him, to steal his pain, to heal his heart.

"Miss Casey, if you could just leave," Gibbons persisted.

Victoria swallowed. "Please just ask him if I might see Emma," she said, much of her former bravado gone. "Tell him I promise to stop sitting in the park if he lets me see her. Please."

Gibbons turned to walk into the house, a look of doom on his face. He certainly did not want to deliver this message. But as he was about to open the door, it swung open, his angry employer glaring at the woman behind him.

"Please go into the house, Gibbons." Jack moved aside to let him pass.

"I thought you could read," he said. "Wasn't the note clear enough?"

Victoria lifted her chin. She'd not let him know how seeing him again so closely affected her. "Yes, I read the note."

Jack smiled. "Then, why are you still here, Miss Casey?"

"Because, Mr. Wilkins, I want to talk to you."

He looked down at her, taking in her red nose, the flush on her cheeks, the yellow tinge along her jawline left over from what must have been one hell of a bruise. Her eyes were angry, but beautiful as always.

They were green today, he noticed, because she was wearing a bottle-green coat.

"We have nothing to say to one another. Good day, Miss Casey."

"Jack, please listen to me!"

He closed his eyes, cursing himself even as he said the words; "What do you want?"

"I want to see Emma." *I want you to love me again.*

"No."

Victoria let anger override her good senses. Stamping her foot, she shouted, "Why not? She's my daughter. You know I love her. How would you feel if you could not see her, Jack? It would drive you insane, wouldn't it? I know you hate me, and you think you have good reason to, but please don't keep me from her. How can you keep us apart?"

Jack stepped down from the landing to stand with her on the walkway. "Because you've no right to her. She's *my* daughter. You gave up any right to have her when you sneaked in here pretending to be a goddamn scullery maid. How dare you come here demanding to see her?"

Her bluster was gone, like a storm that builds and builds and passes, dropping only a few splashes of rain. Three days of sitting in the cold, of hoping to catch a glimpse of Emma, had finally taken their toll. Victoria, filled with unfathomable despair, put her hands over her face as if she could somehow hold the sadness in. Jack gripped her wrists and pulled them roughly down.

"Don't hide from me!" he shouted, and was mortified by the look of pure terror on Victoria's face. He instantly released her wrists, surprised that he still held them. "Victoria, I'm sorry. I didn't mean to frighten you."

Overwhelmed by myriad emotions, Victoria shook her head violently before she turned and ran awkwardly away. Jack let her go, his heart aching, his eyes filling with tears. "Oh, Jesus," he said softly to himself.

For he realized two things in that moment as he watched Victoria run away from him in fear. He still loved her, and Kevin Donnelly would have to die.

Jasper Porter looked up from his desk, a benign expression on his face in stark contrast to the one on Jack Wilkins's. He stood, extending his hand for a shake, raising one eyebrow just a tad when Jack refused to take it.

"I want to know what the hell I'm paying you for. Have you found the bastard yet or not?" Jack demanded, grabbing his jacket and pulling Porter roughly toward him.

Porter simply smiled mildly. "I was just about to send you a note, Mr. Wilkins. Please have a seat."

Somewhat appeased, Jack released the jacket and sat down. Later, he would wonder what in God's name he was thinking of by confronting a man the size of Porter.

"Kevin Donnelly is back in Boston. If he ever left in the first place."

"Where!" Jack demanded, glaring at the hand Porter raised telling him to be patient.

"I haven't found him yet."

"Jesus!"

"But I'm continuing to look. Word on the street is that he is searching for a woman named Sheila Casey, making threats of some kind against her."

Jack's face turned white. "I take it you know her?" Porter asked.

"Yes," Jack choked out. "Listen, my friend, you have to find Donnelly and quickly. He's already tried to kill that woman once, and I've no doubt he will try again."

Porter leaned back in his chair, reaching for a smoldering cigarette as he did so. "Perhaps someone should warn Sheila Casey."

"I intend to." *If I can find her,* he added silently. He didn't know where she was staying, but he was quite sure Mary would. "Thank you, Porter. And keep searching for Donnelly. It is more critical than ever that he be found. I'll double my payment if you find him within the week. Good day."

After Jack left, Porter called in his assistant. "Deliver this note to a Miss Victoria Ashford at the Vendome, Stuart." An hour later, Porter's assistant returned, the note still in his possession. It seemed Victoria Ashford had checked out and left no forwarding address.

She couldn't do it. She now knew that if she were ever confronted by Kevin Donnelly, she would crumble like a two-day-old corn muffin. If Jack had invoked the kind of stark fear in her heart by simply holding her wrists a bit tightly, how would seeing the man who had nearly beaten her to death affect her? Curled up in an old stuffed chair in the corner of her new room, Victoria didn't know how she was going to live a normal life, fearing Donnelly might find her. But she did know she would not be the one to punish him.

She thought of hiring a thug to do the dirty work, but that was somehow more cowardly than doing nothing at all. And so she decided to do nothing at all, left wondering how in the world she could have thought that she would mete out justice to Donnelly alone. It was the hate that had given her that kind of confidence. She still hated Donnelly, but now she feared him more.

Mary had given her enough cash to live for several months in this little boardinghouse. It was run by Louise Girouard, who reminded Victoria of her grandmother on her mother's side, kind but with strict rules that were followed . . . or else, Mrs. Girouard had told her with a wagging finger. In only two days, Victoria realized that a broken rule would not result in eviction, but she found herself obeying the eight o'clock curfew so she wouldn't hurt the older woman's feelings.

There were other rules: no cooking in the rooms, no hanging laundry from the windows, no loud noises after nine o'clock. One of the women played the viola, and Victoria suspected that rule was mostly targeted to her. And absolutely, positively, no men allowed beyond the front sitting room.

Dinner was served promptly at six o'clock. If you missed it, you missed it, Mrs. Girouard had told her sternly. However, Victoria was told on the sly by more than one of the other tenants, Mrs. Girouard was known to sneak a meal up to a hungry boarder with an admonition not to tell anyone else. And of course that meant that everyone knew about the secreted meal the next day. In a way, the boardinghouse was like a family and Mrs. Girouard was the loving but stern mother who overlooked it all. Some of the ladies had been living in the three-story house for twenty years, old maids who were content to gossip about each other and about the old bachelors who lived in an all-male boardinghouse two blocks away.

Victoria wondered if time would transform her into one of those older women who seemed so content to live a life that had no life. Sometimes it was awfully appealing, but other times it seemed more of a sentence to hell or at least purgatory. If anything, it was safe.

A knock on the door startled her out of her reverie, and with heart pounding, she opened the door a crack, relieved to see the worried face of Louise Girouard.

"Hello, Mrs. Girouard."

"Miss Ashford, there's a man downstairs waiting to talk to you," she said, whispering the words "a man."

Victoria's eyes grew wide. No one knew she was here. "Did he say who he was?" Mrs. Girouard shook her head. "Well, what does he look like?"

The older woman licked her lips nervously. "A big man. Bald and polite. Is everything all right, Miss Ashford?"

Jasper Porter, of course. Victoria smiled, relief

flooding through her. "Everything's fine, Mrs. Girouard. Please don't worry. I'll follow you right down."

She found Porter looking a bit ridiculous trying to fit his big body into a rather delicate-looking chair. He stood as she entered the room, nearly bringing the chair up with him.

"You're quite good, Mr. Porter," Victoria said as she walked into the room.

He nodded, acknowledging the compliment. "I've been searching for you for two days. It seems Kevin Donnelly is back in town and searching for a woman named Sheila Casey. I was hoping you might know her."

Victoria sat down, her legs suddenly too weak to support her body.

"Where is he?" she managed to ask.

"That's what I don't know. But if I can find Sheila Casey, I believe I can find Donnelly. I thought perhaps you'd know something."

Victoria gave him an ironic smile. "You've found her, Mr. Porter." For the first time, he looked confused and Victoria almost laughed. "I'm Sheila Casey."

She watched as it dawned on Porter what she was saying.

"Of course you are," he said, and grinned. "I'll be damned."

"So will I, apparently," Victoria said dryly. "I have to admit, I find it a bit upsetting that you found me as easily as you did. If you can, Donnelly can. How *did* you find me?"

"You're correct, you were easy to find, but only because I knew you had been staying at the Vendome. I'll assume Donnelly would not know you were there, and so would not think to ask the concierge if he knew where you'd gone."

Victoria was vastly relieved. "You're right. Donnelly wouldn't know where to look for me. And if he did, he would ask for Sheila Casey, not Victoria Ashford."

Porter frowned, his unappealing face becoming even more homely. "It would not do to completely take your guard off. If I were you, Miss Ashford, I would watch my back. It will make me feel better to check on you daily. This Donnelly is an ugly character."

Victoria nodded. No one knew that better than she.

Thirty

T
he wind howled like some animal in pain through the rafters of the drafty old house where Kevin Donnelly holed up impatient, angry, and just a little bit drunk on some cheap Irish whiskey. Drinking was about all he could do while he waited for his men to find Sheila. It was still too dangerous for him to venture out. He wasn't being a coward, he told himself, just smart. Word was that Jasper Porter was looking for him, and Donnelly had this awful sinking feeling that it wouldn't be long before he was found.

He already knew Jack Wilkins had hired Porter, and he suspected Wilkins, despite being cuckolded by the likes of Sheila, was seeking revenge on her behalf. Wilkins certainly wasn't looking for him to congratulate him on giving Sheila her due. Donnelly cursed himself for leaving her alive, although at the time he'd no intention of killing the lass. Donnelly took a long swig from the bottle, wiping his mouth with a dirty sleeve. She'd been a bloody mess. Even he'd been shocked when he woke up that morning to see her lying on the floor, hair matted with blood, face swollen and distorted, and as still as a corpse. He'd thought she was dead and had the awful vision of his neck being stretched long on a rope. And then he'd hid, sending his men back to collect the body, only to find that Sheila hadn't died after all. He continued to hide, for even as he discovered Sheila had lived, he'd also learned he was a hunted man.

Damn bitch didn't have the sense to die, he thought now. If she'd died, her body would have been deposited in an unmarked grave and no one would have been the wiser. But she lived, damn her soul to eternal hell.

"I'm not a goddamn murderer of women," he told his blurry reflection as he looked at the darkened window. But now he would be. "Forcin' me to do it. Sheila, you stupid bitch, if you'd just let me in on it, I wouldn't have hurt you, lass. If you just would've died the first time. It would have been an acc'dent." He smiled at himself and raised the bottle in a silent toast. "Sheila, my girl, you bring out the worst in me. You always have."

Footsteps on the stairs stopped his monologue, and he turned his bleary eyes to the door. Tom Reilly hesitated in the doorway, his narrow fingers gripping his hat, wet from the rain.

"I can tell from your sad-dog expression that you ain't learned nothing," Donnelly growled.

"No, boss. No one seems to know where she's gone. Etta told me they're lookin' for her over at the Wilkins's house." Tom swallowed hard. "Word's got out somehow that you're lookin' for Sheila," he rushed out, as if saying it fast would lessen the impact.

Donnelly sneered at him. "Word's got out somehow," he mocked. "I'll tell you how word's got out. I got a bunch of imbeciles working for me, that's how. I told you, you've got to be careful who you talk to. Porter's a phantom, man. I swear I don't know how he finds out the things he does. I can feel him breathing down my back. You'd better watch your step now. Check if you're being followed, especially when you're headed here. We've got to find Sheila before they do. Do you understand me?"

Tom shifted, still standing in the doorway. "Maybe we should forget about Sheila."

Donnelly sat back as if contemplating that suggestion. "Now, that's an idea. Just forget about her. Forget that she betrayed me. Forget that she's a little bitch who tried to keep everything for herself. You know, Tommy, you're not as stupid as I thought you were," Donnelly said, smiling a bit at Tom, who looked about to bust from the tension his words were building. "You goddamn idiot! Get out of here, get your ugly, stupid face out of here!"

Donnelly threw the bottle at him, and Tom ducked as it burst over his head. He scurried out the door, cringing at the laughter he heard behind him.

Victoria meant to be home before the sun dipped below the horizon, leaving the rutted frozen streets dark and forbidding. Her footsteps sounded inordinately loud as she trudged back to the boardinghouse, now only two blocks away. It would have been a pleasant walk had Victoria not stopped every block or so to look behind her, heart pounding from imaginary furtive footsteps she was convinced were Donnelly's getting ready to pounce on her. But every time she looked back, the road was empty or filled with innocent pedestrians who, like her, were hurrying home to get out of the cold.

Her ears almost hurt from straining to hear the slightest sound, her neck certainly did ache from the stress. When quick footsteps sounded behind her, Victoria at first told herself it was someone rushing home and ignored the prickling of fear that spread up the base of her skull. But by the time the person was right behind her, Victoria's ears were roaring, and she was fighting the terrible urge to begin screaming and running. When she reached the picket fence that surrounded the boardinghouse, Victoria was convinced Donnelly's hand was reaching out and about to grab her.

"Victoria!" A male voice that to Victoria's fear-crazed mind had to be Donnelly.

She began running, wildly and without thought, toward the gate that led to the boardinghouse's front door. Frantically she clawed at the entrance, deaf and blind to everything but her hands fumbling at the latch that every other day opened with ease. A hand clamped onto her arm, and Victoria began screaming as she was spun around.

"Victoria, stop! It's only me."

Finally, her fear-blinded eyes focused on Jack, and without thinking, she threw herself into his arms, sobbing and clutching at his jacket, burying her head against his chest. "Oh, Jack. I thought you were Donnelly," she choked out. Her words, said against his coat, were muffled.

He hesitated just a moment, arms extended as if surprised to find a woman sobbing against him, before he wrapped his arms around her, crushing her against him. He murmured soothing words, trying to calm her, all the while holding her against him so tightly, it was almost as if he wanted her inside him so he could completely surround her, protect her.

"Shhh, sweetheart. It's going to be all right."

Victoria began shaking her head, denying his words of comfort.

"No. If you found me, then Donnelly can. Don't you see?" She looked up at him, her tear-streaked face nearly breaking his heart. With two hands, he cupped her face, rubbing the tears away with his thumbs. He couldn't resist kissing her. How could he, when kissing her, holding her, had been the only thing he could think of since she had left? Even when he tried to convince himself he hated her, he could not rid himself of the need to hold her. His mouth touched hers, and Victoria sighed like a person who yearns for an impossibly rich dessert and finally, finally, gets a taste of it.

"I can't believe you're here. I can't believe you're actually kissing me," Victoria said smiling dreamily.

Jack chuckled "I can't believe it, either, if you must know the truth." Victoria stepped back, slightly piqued by his honesty.

"But how did you know I was here? No one knew but . . ."

"Jasper Porter," they said simultaneously.

"Let's go inside, where we can talk," Victoria said, stepping back and opening the gate. Victoria led the way to the house, pausing as she opened the front door. "I have to let Mrs. Girouard know I'm here with" —and she shielded one side of her mouth with a hand— "a man." She rolled her eyes before heading off to find the older woman. Jack took in his surroundings, and couldn't help thinking that this obvious haven for old maids was not where Victoria belonged. She was much too vibrant and young to be sitting in this stuffy little parlor with its flowered wallpaper and delicately carved furniture while sipping tea and working on needlepoint.

Victoria was back almost immediately. "We can be private, but I wouldn't be too surprised if Mrs. Girouard finds an excuse to come in this room," Victoria said, sitting down on a love seat. When Jack made to sit next to her, she motioned to a nearby chair. "You'd better sit there, or my reputation here will be ruined," she said, secretly delighted that she was forced to be so quaintly old-fashioned.

Now that they were seated, both felt awkward, remembering the last time they spoke had been the day outside Jack's home.

"You're looking well, Victoria," Jack said, a polite smile on his face.

"Jack, let's get right to the point and talk about what you came here to talk about—Donnelly."

He shook his head and smiled. "You are blunt, my dear," he said. "Donnelly is somewhere in Boston, and he's looking for you. That's why I've come. I want you to move back into my house. For your own safety, of course."

Victoria's first instinct was to jump up with joy and pack her bags, and she almost cursed herself for having a second thought. "I can't."

"If it's because of what's happened between us, I can assure you that you will be under my protection and as such, will not be . . . harmed in any way."

Victoria bit her lip to stop from laughing. "Harmed, Jack? Is that what you call making love now?" She stopped him from protesting with a raised hand. "Don't worry, that's not the reason I can't go with you. The reason is that Donnelly doesn't know where I am, and I'm sure he's been watching your house, waiting for me to show up. People know me here as Victoria Ashford, not Sheila Casey. I'm far away from you and far away from Donnelly. I feel safe here."

Jack stood, irritation marring his handsome features. "Is that why you screamed when I touched you, why you began running away when I called your name, because you feel safe?" He was nearly shouting, and Victoria cast a worried look to the hallway.

"Will you please stop shouting. I have to live here."

"No you don't have to live here!" Jack yelled toward the doorway, purposefully ignoring her plea.

"Oh, that's very mature, Jack. I'm not moving back with you, and that's that. Now, sit down and tell me how we're going to find Donnelly."

Jack sat, but he clearly was not happy. "We'll discuss your living arrangements later," he said stubbornly. "And I don't believe *we* are looking for Donnelly. I believe I am. I hired Jasper Porter to find Donnelly, and when he does, I will handle things."

"I hired Porter to find him, too."

Jack raised his eyebrows in surprise. "Then, when Porter found out Donnelly was looking for a Sheila Casey, he didn't realize it was you."

"Not until I told him it was me. He came to me to find out if I might know where she was. I assume he passed that information on to you, which is why you're here now." Victoria found herself smiling as a realization hit her. "I know why I hired Porter to find Donnelly, but why did you hire him?"

Jack suddenly looked uncomfortable. "Because

he . . . because he hurt you," he said gruffly. "And I . . ." Was he the fool that Suzanne told him he was? He found himself searching her face for some sign of triumph or mockery. "I want him to pay," he said finally.

Then, he does still care, Victoria dared to think. "Why didn't you come to see me all those weeks I was at the Grants? You knew where I was."

Jack looked away. He briefly thought to tell her he had stayed away because he believed that was what she wanted. But he knew that wasn't the truth. The reason had much more to do with what he was feeling than obeying Victoria's wishes. He decided to be honest.

"I couldn't bear to bring myself to believe you. Because that would mean that what had happened to you was my fault. And I couldn't see you without acknowledging that. I'd be a damned hypocrite, wouldn't I? Sending you off with that madman and then regretting with every particle of my being what had happened to you? What sort of person would that make me?" He let out a sigh and turned his tortured blue eyes to her. "So I stayed away rather than admit to myself what a cad I am."

Victoria left her loveseat and knelt on the carpet beside Jack, one hand on his knee, her deep blue skirt billowing about her. "Are you saying that you're a cad?"

Jack stared at her hand, still resting on his knee, his eyes troubled. "The person I know, the woman I loved, would not have done what you did. That woman would not have been in league with a man like Donnelly, would not have pretended to be Emma's nurse." Would not have made me love her then trod on my heart.

Victoria swallowed past the knot growing in her throat. "I was a different woman when I was with Donnelly." She knew Jack would take her words figuratively. "But I am the kind of woman who would lie to you, who would pretend to be Emma's nurse when I was actually her mother. I'm not particularly proud of what I did, Jack. But I never, ever intended to fall in love with you, to make you fall in love with me. I was foolish," she said, squeezing his leg for emphasis, "but I was never malicious or calculated. I hope you can believe me."

Jack shook his head, not so much denying her words as trying to come to grips with what was happening to him. Her hand on his knee, there for comfort more than anything else, felt warm and solid. And he knew when she took it away, he would feel that hand for a long time, would close his eyes and feel that heat. What sort of man had he become, that a woman could so completely take over his every thought and action. If she told him she could fly, he feared he would believe it.

"I'd be a fool to believe you, wouldn't I," he said finally.

Victoria sighed and sat back on her heels. "Yes, Jack, you would. But you know what? I'm willing to bet you are a fool. How's that for you?"

"I'd say the odds on that bet are about even." His grin made her heart swell. God, he was gorgeous. If she wasn't supposed to be a staid old maid, she'd have launched herself at him, she thought. She gave the parlor door a covert look just to make sure Mrs. Girouard wasn't hovering nearby, and then very primly, and almost properly, sat on Jack's lap.

"I just might kiss you right now, fool or not," she said, her eyes half closed and dreamy.

And before Jack could even pretend to protest, she cemented her lips against his. What began as something playful, soon turned into something much less so. The current that ran between the two surged as they melted in each other's arms. When Victoria felt Jack's tongue thrust into her mouth, she almost cried with the joy of it. His hard thighs beneath her buttocks, his muscled chest, his strong jaw beneath her caressing fingers made her senses cry out for all of him. She wanted nothing more than to see him naked, to see if his stomach were as flat and solid as it felt against the arm that was crushed against it. She wanted to see him stand above her, his eyes dark with lust and love, his male member rigid with passion.

His hand traveled along her stockinged leg, along her sensitive calf, over her knee, and higher, until he touched bare flesh just above her garter. "You are very bold, sir," she said, the way a lady of the 1890s ought to say it as she tilted her neck for his mouth.

"Not nearly bold enough," he said, his voice thick and his mouth hot as his other hand moved to cup one breast.

"That's just what I was thinking," Victoria said, shifting on his lap and making him groan aloud. "Shhh," she said, looking toward the door. "I feel like I'm sixteen and my mother's about to catch me making out."

"Come home with me," he said, fiercely bringing his mouth down hard on hers.

"Oh, Jack. I want to, I really, really, really do. But I . . ."

"I thought you two might want some tea," Mrs. Girouard said from down the hall. By the time the older woman walked through the door, Victoria was sitting primly on the love seat, hands folded on her lap.

"How nice, Mrs. Girouard," Victoria said, casting laughing eyes Jack's way.

"Terrific," Jack said dryly as he placed a pillow on his lap to hide his rather obvious state of excitement. "Would you like to join us, Mrs. Girouard?"

She smoothed her apron in a nervous gesture. "Oh, no. I'll leave you young people to yourselves. I'll be right in the kitchen if you need anything."

"You've done more than enough already," Jack said smiling, surprising Victoria with his wry sense of humor.

After Mrs. Girouard left, Jack's smile disappeared. "I want you to come home."

"Home?"

"Yes, godamnit, home."

"I can't."

Jack stood abruptly. "If you're looking for another marriage proposal, if that's what you're holding out for, then I'm sorry that I cannot oblige."

"Where did that come from?" Victoria asked, clearly surprised by his outburst. "I don't expect you to ask me to marry you again."

Where *had* it come from? he thought. From his heart that with every beat cried out for him to trust her, begged him to again ask her to be his wife.

"Nowhere," he said irritably. "I'd better go."

"Hey! Wait a minute. Before you go, I've got to tell you something."

He turned, unaccountably angry and frustrated. He wanted to make love to her, he wanted her in his bed. Tonight. He wanted to marry her even if that meant he was the biggest fool God created. He just didn't want her to know it.

"What will you tell me, Victoria. That you want to see Emma? Fine, you can see her. I will not subject you to my company to do that."

Victoria looked at him as if he had two heads. "*What* is your problem? I just wanted to tell you to be careful. And I was going to give you a kiss, but you can forget that now. I think you have a split personality. Good Jack and Evil Jack."

He let out a bark of laughter. "I'm sorry. I'm just . . ." He stepped closer to her. "Jesus, it doesn't even seem to affect you. I want you so much I'd almost be willing to take a chance your Mrs. Girouard will walk in on us."

Victoria perked up. "Really?"

"Hell, yes." He did not seemed pleased with that admission.

"Wow," she said with a self-satisfied smile. "Actually, it's just as well Mrs. Girouard did come in, because we were getting sidetracked. We haven't made any decisions about Donnelly yet. And that's why you came here, isn't it?"

"I came here to see you."

"I'm flattered, but I want to come up with a plan to get Donnelly." Her eyes grew stony, her face set. "He hurt me, and I want him to pay. I know I can't do it myself, but now that I know you're willing to help, I figure we can get him together. He hurt me, Jack. Don't think you'll be protecting me by keeping me away. There's only one way I can get over this, and that's to see Donnelly suffer."

If Donnelly had been in that room, Jack would have ripped him apart. He had taken his sweet Victoria and turned her into the hard woman he saw before him. "I don't want you in danger."

"Do you think I want myself in danger? I just want him to pay."

Jack pulled her into his arms. "He will," he said close to her ear. "He'll regret, with every fiber of his being, ever laying a hand on you."

If Donnelly had seen the smile that spread on Victoria's lips at that moment, he would have run as fast and as far as he could go.

Thirty-one

A week later, Victoria suffered such an intense fright, she finally agreed to move back into the house on Louisville Square.

It wasn't that the incident was so very frightening, but it was enough to make Victoria realize she should bow to Jack's near-constant demands. Riddled with so many passionate kisses, Victoria half suspected he was trying to bribe her with them.

She had been buying a hat. Victoria found she simply loved hats and became a regular at Nan's Millinery, where she tried one after another of the delicious confections. This time she couldn't resist and decided to actually purchase one. Victoria could have done without the whalebone corsets, the long skirts, the scratchy stockings, and the too-tight shoes, but she could not have done without the hats. It was probably a hat that saved her life that day.

Victoria had begun to relax. Nothing more had been heard about Donnelly, and Jasper Porter on his daily visit even suggested that perhaps Donnelly had given up. She'd been leaving the boutique, wearing her new hat, the bell above the door ringing merrily above her, when Kevin Donnelly walked by. She could have touched him, so close was he. He even turned his head at the sound of that bell, seeming to look directly at Victoria, before continuing down the street. Still standing in the doorway, Victoria quickly ducked back inside, gulping for air.

"What is it, Miss Ashford?" Nan said, rushing from behind the counter.

Victoria had tried to steady her breathing, but she took larger and larger breaths, panicking when it felt as if she were not getting any oxygen. "Hyper . . ." gasp—"venti"—gasp—"lating." And then she fainted.

She woke up within a minute, opening her eyes to see Nan bending over her and waving something wicked-smelling beneath her nose. "Ugh! Stop it!" she said, pushing the smelling salts away.

"You fainted," Nan said, stating the obvious.

"It's these corsets. I can hardly breathe."

Nan gave her a commiserating look and helped Victoria to her feet. "They wouldn't trouble you so if you didn't wear them so tight," she said.

Victoria shook out her skirts and readjusted her hat in the oval mirror resting on the counter. "Thanks for the advice, Nan."

"Why don't you sit here awhile until you feel better," Nan said, indicating a small cushioned chair behind a hat display. And Victoria did, not because she still felt woozy, which she did, but to wait until Donnelly was long gone before venturing out again. When she did leave, she went straight to her room and packed.

Gibbons made his way up to the second floor, his feet feeling as if they were encased in cement. Miss Casey was waiting in the study, having insisted she be let in and pushing her way past him when he continued to hesitate.

"Mr. Wilkins? Miss Casey is waiting in the study. She insisted that she . . ." He was unable to finish, for Jack flew by him before he could complete his sentence. Gibbons looked after Jack as he ran down the stairs, trying to discern whether it had been a smile or a grimace of anger on his master's face as he rushed by.

Jack skidded to a halt outside the door, then entered smoothly, as if having Victoria call was an ordinary thing. The first thing he saw was a suitcase and a large hat box. He looked up, and there she was, standing by the window, hands twisting together by her waist, looking as if he might actually be angry to find her here.

Looking pointedly at the small pile of luggage, he said, "I take it you expect to move in."

"Yes. That was the general plan."

"To what do I attribute this unexpected visit."

Victoria looked at him agape. "Unexpected! You've been practically begging me to move back here for a week. Don't tell me . . ." She stopped, taking in the smile on his face. "When did you become such a comedian?" she asked, hands on her hips.

"Just Evil Jack showing his colors," he said, walking toward her and taking her into his arms. If she'd had any doubts about her welcome, he put them to rest then and there.

"You think you can do anything you want, just as long as you kiss me afterward, don't you?" she asked sleepily.

"I do. Am I wrong?"

"Not so far, apparently."

Victoria withdrew from his embrace, her nerves a roiling jumble in her stomach, making her feel slightly nauseous. Her hands resumed their painful twisting.

"What's wrong?"

Victoria let out a shaky puff of air. "You're going to get angry with me. You're going to say 'I told you so' in that way that you have that really isn't fair and . . ."

Jack paled just slightly. "Donnelly."

"Well. Yes."

Jack didn't move, but Victoria saw his eyes go swiftly over her, as if making a mental inventory of her. He walked over to a couch and leaned against it, crossing one leg over the other, and waited patiently for her to explain. She would never know the effort it took Jack not to haul her against him and then lock her in a closet for safekeeping.

"I saw him, but he didn't see me. That's all it was. But it scared the hell, um, heck out of me. All right? You were right. I shouldn't be alone. You win!"

He raised one eyebrow at her outburst. "As gratified as I am that you concede you need my protection, Miss Casey, the more important thing from my perspective is that you tell me where and when you saw Donnelly."

"And what will you do, then?"

Jack gave her a tight smile. "I would like to kill him. But I probably won't. Let's just say I'll give him a lesson in life that a man should not bruise his fists on the face of a woman."

Victoria shrugged, trying to act as if the news Jack wanted to personally confront that animal didn't nearly paralyze her with fear. "I saw him on Pitt Street. But I doubt he's there now."

"I'm sure you're right. However, the fact that Donnelly feels safe enough to show his face is interesting news."

"I'm glad you find it interesting. I find it rather disturbing. Maybe you should tell Jasper Porter, and let him deal with it."

"Absolutely not."

Victoria put her hands on her hips, knowing that she couldn't look tough if she tried, but trying anyway. "Listen, buddy, he's my problem. I'm grateful you've taken it upon yourself to be my hero, but it's really none of your concern."

"I see."

Victoria nodded once sharply. "Good. That's settled, then."

"I don't think so."

"Let me be more succinct. Stay out of this, Jack. I mean it, it's none of your business."

"I'm choosing to make it my business," he said, appearing to be slightly puzzled by her behavior.

Victoria threw her hands up in disgust. "Oh, great, I've got to deal with surging testosterone," she muttered to herself. "Okay. Fine. Go out and find Donnelly on your own. Be a big man and get yourself killed. See if I care!"

Both eyebrows went up, and a smile tugged at his lips.

"Don't you dare laugh at me," Victoria said, tears glinting in her eyes. "You don't know this guy. He's sick in the head. He's not all there. He wouldn't think twice about killing you, about killing anyone. You can't reason with him, you can't beg him . . ."

Jack was by her side in an instant, putting his hands on her shoulders, trying to draw her near, but she shook him off angrily. "No, Jack. You can't hug this away." She spun around, dashing the tears from her face with shaking hands.

"Victoria, don't you know what it does to me to see you like this, to know that bastard has made you like this? I swear to God, I could crush his head between my hands right now and be glad about it."

Victoria closed her eyes and shook her head. If he was in danger, it was because of her. "You should hate me," she said finally.

"So I've told myself."

She let out a small laugh and turned to look at him, his beautiful face that had an odd way of healing her. "I don't know what I'm doing here. I shouldn't bring you into this. Everything is all my fault. You couldn't possibly understand, and I can't explain, but someone made a big mistake when they took a look at my heart."

Another breathy puff of laughter erupted when she saw his confusion. "Jack, I am so sorry. I think of myself as this intelligent person, and then everything I do is so completely stupid, I amaze even myself." Victoria rubbed her face with her hands, up and down, then folded her hands in front of her mouth. "I'm a selfish jerk," she mumbled into her fingers.

The sound of the study door opening drew their attention to Suzanne, standing there in beautiful glory, an incredulous look on her face.

"Gibbons told me she was here, but I could not believe it. I refused to believe it."

Victoria stiffened, and Jack gave his sister-in-law a mocking little bow. "Suzanne, please do come in. Miss Casey has decided to visit."

Suzanne glared at the luggage as if it were somehow to blame for Victoria's presence. "I can see that. Jack, I believe we should talk privately. If you'll excuse us," Suzanne said, finally letting her snapping brown eyes rest on Victoria, who stood still as a statue.

"I will not excuse you," Victoria whispered through a throat that hurt so much, she wondered how she managed even that.

"What was that?" Suzanne asked in a manner that told Victoria that whatever it was she had said could be of little consequence.

Victoria took two steps toward Suzanne, then stopped. "I said I will not excuse you. Ever!"

Suzanne's eyes flickered with some indiscernible emotion before she recovered her haughty stare. "As I was saying, Jack, may we speak privately?"

"How could you have done it, Suzanne? Was I that much of a threat to you? What is it that Jack has that was worth my life?"

Suzanne's nostrils flared. "I'm sure I don't know what you are talking about." Suzanne turned her affronted gaze to Jack, who was staring at Victoria with narrowed eyes, and she smiled, thinking he was becoming angry with the veiled accusations.

"Please leave the room, Miss Casey," Suzanne said, as if she couldn't quite believe Victoria was standing there still.

"Was beating me part of the deal? Or only that he make sure Jack hated me? I'm just curious, Mrs. Von Arc. Did you know he would nearly kill me? Did you?" With each sentence, Victoria moved a step closer, until she was just an arm's length away. "Do you know what it's like to be huddled in a corner while a man beats you until you don't feel the blows anymore, until you think that maybe you're dying and that's why nothing hurts? And then you wish you were dead because he's still there and he's balling his fists and you know there's going to be more. So I'm asking you, Mrs. Von Arc, if you knew."

Suzanne's face was ashen. "No," she whispered. And then, as if realizing she had practically admitted to hiring Donnelly, she quickly added, "No, I didn't know because I had nothing to do with it. How dare you accuse me."

Victoria looked at her with disgust. "You must be mighty desperate."

"Victoria, that's enough," Jack said, ignoring the glaring look Victoria gave him, as well as the look of triumph in Suzanne's eyes. He turned to Suzanne. "I'm afraid you have no say in the matter of whether Miss Casey is to stay here."

"That's right. No say at all," Victoria said, lifting her head up. "Because I plan to ask Jack to marry me, and I expect he'll say yes."

Thirty-two

Suzanne and Jack both looked at her as if she'd sprouted wings and had commenced flying about the room.

"Well, I had planned to get down on bended knee, but she made me so mad it just came out," Victoria said, biting her lip.

Jack recovered first, gently taking Suzanne's arm and leading her toward the door. "If you don't mind, Suzanne, I need to speak with Miss Casey alone for a moment."

Her eyes wide with shock, Suzanne followed him complacently, gathering her wits just as he was about to close the door on her. "You've no intention of accepting, of course," she said as the door closed.

He stared at the doorknob for several long seconds before turning finally to Victoria. "I'm sure you said that for shock purposes?"

Victoria grimaced. "Actually, I sort of meant it."

Jack pursed his lips and nodded.

"Well? What's your answer?"

"My answer."

Victoria huffed. "Yes, your answer. Will you make me the happiest of women and agree to be my husband?" she said belligerently.

"Why?"

She gave him a startled look. "Why?"

"We seem to be repeating each other's questions. Yes, Victoria, tell me why you want to marry me."

She closed her eyes and kept them closed, not wanting to see the disbelief in his face when she told him. "Because I love you, more than I can ever say. More than you'd ever believe. I love you because you loved me against your better judgment. I love you because you're such a good father. I want to marry you, Jack Wilkins, because you are the most gorgeous man I've ever met, inside and out. Because I never thought I'd be in love, and it's a wonderful gift that I'd be crazy to let go."

"Is that all?"

Victoria opened her eyes a crack, her heart plummeting. "That's all."

"I suppose I'm to believe you want to marry me because you are madly in love, not because your daughter also happens to be my daughter."

Victoria looked surprised that he would think that. "Yes, you are. I'd be lying if I told you it's not nice that I happen to love the man who is Emma's father. But I'd never marry you if I didn't love you."

Jack walked to his desk and sat down, something Victoria knew was his way of controlling the situation, of turning this conversation into something more businesslike. "Then, perhaps you could enlighten me as to why you rejected my proposal, that is if you love me so desperately. And I won't bother reminding you that at the time you claimed you did not love me."

"Well, I . . ." Damn. Damn, damn, damn.

"Yes?"

The truth, girl, stick to the truth as much as you can. "I couldn't marry you because of Emma. Imagine if I'd married you and then you found out I was her mother. That would have been unforgivable. I fell in love with you—against my better judgment, I might add—and then I couldn't tell you she was my daughter because I thought you would throw me out. And I was right. You did."

Victoria looked for some kindness in his face and

found none, her heart sinking so low she could have stepped on it.

"And then there was the husband."

"I was never married to Donnelly. Never."

He gave her a hard, humorless smile. "But you were his lover."

"Apparently," Victoria said, crossing her arms.

"Apparently? You mean you don't know?"

"He obviously got me pregnant. Emma is his child. But I don't think I could characterize him as a former *lover*. I don't think there was ever anything between us that resembled love."

Jack steepled his hands beneath his chin, giving Victoria the same intense perusal as he did one of his designs. "What if I told you I don't love you anymore."

Victoria looked to the floor. She hadn't considered that, not when he acted like he loved her, not when he kissed her and held her the way he had, demanding that she come home. She lifted her troubled eyes to his. "I wouldn't believe you. You do love me."

He moved a pile of papers on his desk from one side to another. "I do," he said in that same maddening businesslike tone. "But I don't trust you."

"Oh." She couldn't blame him for that, now, could she?

"And it would not do to have a wife I could not trust. It would be . . . foolish."

"I suppose it would." The carpet grew blurry, then clear again as she blinked away sudden tears.

His fingers drummed on his desk. "And I'm not a foolish man."

"No, you're not," she said through a constricted throat.

"Well, let me amend that. I *have* done some foolish things."

She lifted her eyes. "Everyone has," she said cautiously.

"I would dare to say I'm young enough that it's

quite likely I will do many, many foolish things before I die."

Oh, this was maddening! "Such as?"

He stood up and walked to the front of his desk, where he half sat, one leg dangling back and forth. "Such as marry a woman I don't fully trust."

Victoria swallowed the joy that bubbled up. "I don't want to jump to any erroneous conclusions here, but, by any chance did you just accept my proposal?"

He let out a beleaguered sigh. "I believe I have done just that."

"Ooooo!" she screeched, and she leapt into his arms, knocking him flat on his desk, smothering his face with kisses. Then she lifted her head to gaze down at him, eyes narrowed. "You're very mean."

"Only a bit. You did seem so sure of yourself." He touched the side of her face, tucking a curling lock behind her ear. "You broke my heart once. You'd better not do it again." He was smiling, but Victoria's heart wrenched at the raw pain she saw in his eyes.

"Never." She brought her mouth down on his, hoping her kiss could take away the heartache she'd given him. He crushed her against him, feeling that sudden jolt that always came between them whenever they touched, and she groaned aloud with it. Lying atop him, Victoria could feel him harden, and her body responded with a delicious liquid heat that moved from her breasts to between her legs in pulsing waves. She slipped her hand between them to feel him, moving her hand over the hardening bulge that jumped to life at her touch.

"Victoria, my God, you are . . ."

"I'm what," she asked, nipping his lips with her teeth.

"Bold. You are so delightfully bold."

Victoria chuckled, moving her hand again. "You can be bold if you want."

"If I want?" he choked.

Then she kissed him, long and hard and deep, lost

in sensations that left her body languid and somehow electric at the same time. She moved against him as he kneaded her buttocks, pulling her closer still.

"We're on my desk."

"Hmmm. I like your desk." She licked his neck, moving her mouth to his ear and tugging on his lobe.

"Jesus," he breathed. "Victoria. I don't think . . . If you don't stop that, I'm afraid things might get out of control."

"Good."

He was panting, moving his hips rhythmically against her, feeling her heat and wondering how he could take much more. "Ah, Victoria, you're driving me mad. But we must stop."

Victoria lifted her head, clearly confused. "Why?"

"Because," he said as if he were in pain, "an engaged couple does not make love on a desk."

She grinned, moving against him, knowing she was torturing him. "Why not?"

He lifted her off him and put her on her feet with remarkable ease. "Anyone could walk in at any moment, for one thing. For another, it's simply wrong. We're not married."

"Oh, that," she said, waving a dismissive hand at him. "As long as we're in love, God doesn't care what we do. And besides, we've already done it!"

He shook his head in frustration, not quite believing he was trying to convince this incredibly desirable woman that they should not make love. "That's not the point. Now that we're engaged, I'm afraid it is even more important that we act a certain way."

Victoria suddenly realized he was quite serious. "So let's just get married right away."

"I plan to. In just six months . . ."

"Six months!" Victoria said aghast. And then more quietly. "Six months is a long time. Half a whole year." She pulled him toward her by his lapels, and snaked her arms around his neck. "Maybe we could get married in, um, six days," she said, getting playful again. "Or better yet, six hours." She nuzzled his neck with her soft, soft lips, and Jack thought he'd die if he didn't have her.

"I have to wait at least a year from Christina's death, Victoria. Her family would never forgive me, and I'm afraid many of our mutual friends never would, either."

Victoria finally stopped the kisses, sobering at the mention of his dead wife. Even in the 1990s, getting married to someone less than a year after their spouse's death would raise some eyebrows. "You make a good point. But if we were engaged, I wouldn't be able to stay here, would I?"

"No."

"What about Donnelly?" She looked up at him, wide-eyed, knowing she was playing her trump card, even feeling a bit awful when that look of worry creased his brow.

"Jesus, Donnelly. You distract me so much I nearly forgot about the bastard. Forgive me, sweetheart," he said, gallantly apologizing for his bad language.

"Then, what should we do?" Victoria asked, all innocence, trying with all her strength not to smile at her rather obvious ploy.

He saw that smile quirking around her lips and after a brief moment of confusion, he saluted her. He wrapped his arms around her waist, pulling her close so she had to bend back to look up at him. "A difficult quandary I find myself in."

"Not so difficult," Victoria said, playing with the hair at his nape.

"No. Not so difficult as all that," he murmured, his beautiful mouth just inches from her mouth. "We'll simply have to put off the engagement and make you my mistress."

If he expected her to be shocked, he was disappointed. "Fine with me," she said. "Just as long as I go to sleep every night by your side and wake up every morning with you still there."

"That sounds suspiciously like marriage to me."

"I thought the rich always have separate beds."

He kissed her lightly. "I wasn't born rich. I married into it."

"Good. I sleep naked, by the way. I hope that won't bother you."

Jack closed his eyes and gritted his teeth. "It will bother me very much, I'm afraid."

Eyes lit with amusement, Victoria continued her subtle torture. "Well, I suppose I could wear that nightgown with the neck that goes up to here," she said, grasping her neck and making a strangling noise.

"Well, if you're *that* uncomfortable, perhaps I could get used to a naked woman by my side." He smiled again, goofy on this love he felt spreading through him like a brushfire before a brisk wind. She was something entirely different from any woman he had met. The thought that she wanted him as much as he wanted her left him practically giddy. And randy. My God, she was a demon in his soul—one he never wanted exorcised.

"So what's the answer, Jack? Mistress or wife?" Oh, he was that fool he'd described, studying her face with eyes that saw no flaws. He ignored the freckles, the slightly upturned nose, the eyes that weren't quite blue and weren't quite green. Ignored the husband that wasn't a husband, the baby that was definitely hers, and that Irish temper as red-hot as her wildly curling hair.

"You'll be my wife," he told her, his voice hard and uncompromising. He took his finger and traced her jaw, his eyes studying the trail his hand made on that smooth, smooth skin. "I just ask one thing of you."

"What's that?"

"Don't ever lie to me again. Not ever."

Victoria nodded, and prayed she could keep that promise.

Thirty-three

Night was always the worst, laying there as memories, horrid and wonderful, assailed her. She never knew what image she would see, Jack's smiling face moving closer for a kiss, or Donnelly's deranged snarl. Four nights after Jack had pledged to marry her, Victoria turned in her bed in a huff and punched the pillow in frustration. Tonight when she closed her eyes, it was Jack she saw. That burning ache in the center of her was growing hotter and hotter. Unfortunately, Jack had displayed unimaginable fortitude on that front. But she knew he suffered, saw the circles that grew darker every day from lack of sleep. The man was so darned stubborn and so caught up in what he thought was "right" and what he thought was "wrong."

Victoria knew he was a man of his times, but found it amazing that he continued to hold to his convictions when confronted by a woman who encouraged him to act on his baser impulses. Victoria was slightly ashamed of herself for tempting him the way she had, and after they fought, vowed she would stop tormenting him. *And I'm so good at keeping my vows,* she thought sardonically.

Jack, frustration clearly showing, had almost roughly pushed Victoria away earlier that day when she tried to make an ordinary hello into something more, relying, as usual, on Jack's resolve to stop things.

She'd pouted when he broke a particularly wonderful kiss. "Are you testing me, Victoria? Is that what this is about?" He was as angry with himself as with Victoria.

"No." *Yes,* her conscious shouted.

"Well, you are," he'd snapped, stalking away.

It was then that Victoria decided to respect Jack's convictions, no matter how silly they seemed to her modern mind. After all, she reasoned silently, she had chosen to live in this time, and she ought to respect its conventions. From now on, it would be chaste little kisses on closed lips that wouldn't tempt either of them to push things further.

Victoria punched her pillow again at the memory of those lips, folded her arms across her chest, and stared at the ceiling. She was back in her old room, adjacent to Emma, pretending to all that nothing had changed between her and Jack. That had been Jack's plan—it was a way for them to continue living in the same house without inviting gossip, and a way for them to be together. Except, Virginia thought sourly, they rarely were together, so careful were they to not cause gossip. For now everyone, including Etta and Suzanne, were going along with the farce. Her first night back she spent in the nursery rocking chair, holding a sleeping Emma in her arms. She couldn't get enough of her, rejoicing at her tears and smiles alike. Her poops, well, they still stunk to high heaven, but Victoria didn't mind so much.

In the hallway, the old grandfather clock chimed once, and Emma stirred in her sleep. That was enough of an excuse to go and stare at her for a while, her little sleeping angel with her tufts of nearly black hair. Victoria was leaning over her crib, a smile on her face, when she heard footsteps outside her door. They paused there, and Victoria waited for them to move on, her heart hammering in her breast. It had to be Jack. But her mind quickly panicked, envisioning Donnelly skulking there, a demonic look on his face.

Victoria bit her lip. No. Of course, it was Jack. She listened intently for the footsteps to move on, then tiptoed to her nightstand and eased open the drawer, where she kept some wickedly pointed shears. Moving to the door, she pressed her ear against it. She couldn't hear a thing, but she knew someone was out there. She could almost feel his heat through the door.

Jack stood outside the door, trying to convince himself that he should continue down the hallway to his own room. What, he thought, was he doing outside Victoria's door in the middle of the night? He looked down the darkened hall, trying to tell himself to do the right thing, trying to tell himself he did not want to rip open her door, tear off her covers . . . He squeezed his eyes shut. This was doing him no good, he decided, imagining her there just a few feet away, soft in her sleep, warm and lovely, stretching toward him like a cat wanting to be petted. Imagining her breasts, those taut jutting nipples so perfect in his mouth.

She wanted him, she'd made no secret of it. And God above knew he wanted her. No. It went beyond mere want. He needed her, needed to be inside her, to feel her clench around him, hot and . . .

It was difficult to say who was more surprised when Victoria yanked open the door to find Jack standing there.

Victoria jumped nearly a foot when she saw a dark outline of a man outside her door, but she recovered quickly enough. "Hello, Jack."

He stood looking at her as if he had conjured her up himself, his eyes finally registering the cutting shears in her clenched fist. He blinked once. "I was . . . I was," he stammered, feeling uncommonly foolish.

"You were . . ." Victoria prompted, dropping the shears on her bureau.

"Damnit, you know why I'm here," he bit out. Putting one hand behind her slim neck, he dragged her

to him, and then they were kissing, long and deep.
"You win," he muttered, raising his other hand to her.

"Oh, Jack, are you sure? I know I've been just
awful. I've given this some thought, and I think you're
right. I think we should . . ." Her words were cut off
by a kiss that put any words she was about to say far
from her lips.

"Jack, you're so wonderfully bold," she said, slipping her hands around his buttocks and pulling him
close. His arousal brushed her lower belly, and feeling
it pressing against her, Victoria let out a sound that
very much resembled a cat purring. They stood that
way for long minutes, kissing, touching, lost in a hazy
world of their own creation. Finally, Jack lifted his
head, his eyes glittering with passion. "Perhaps we
should go to a bed now," he said.

"Too bad there's no desk in here," she said, nipping
his neck playfully. His thumbs were brushing her nipples through the nightgown, and she arched against
him. "I think I told you I sleep naked?"

"I believe you mentioned that," he said as he lifted
her into his arms and walked toward his bedroom.
With one leg he nudged the door closed and dropped
her feet to the ground, dipping his head to mouth one
nipple as his hands drew her gown up. The material
bunched up around his wrists as his hands met bare
flesh, slowly learning her contours. When he pulled
her gown over the smooth curve of her bottom, he
paused, squeezing gently, before moving one hand between her legs. By the time he began his sweet explo-
ration, his breath was coming out in short little gasps,
and she wasn't even conscious of breathing at all. Victoria moved against him, telling him silently what she
wanted, and letting out a small moan of pleasure when
he followed her instruction.

"My God, Victoria. I've never been with a woman
who wanted . . ." he stopped, breathing in and out in
shaky spurts. "You cannot know."

Victoria's heart swelled with tenderness. Jack was

telling her that he feared he would not please her. And she knew then that Christina had been Jack's only experience with a woman, and it had not been very enlightening. Silly, silly man. Didn't he know he need only look at her to make her want him?

"We can teach each other what we want," she said, kissing him. "We've got forever to teach each other."

He lifted her up then, carrying her like a child to his large, canopied bed. He pulled off her gown, gazing at her as a man might gaze at perfection. Victoria knew she was not perfect. Her body bore the scars of childbirth, her skin was freckled. But Jack's loving gaze made her feel she was perfection. He smiled and pulled off his shirt, revealing a muscular flat stomach and a narrow waist. He had those wonderful muscles that some men had just above the hips.

"Not bad, Wilkins," she said. "Not bad at all."

She lay back as he climbed onto the bed beside her, resting one hand on his arm, as if to guide him to her. He kissed her mouth, her chin, her neck, and then spent long wonderful minutes suckling her breasts while his hand cupped the heat between her legs. He was kissing her belly, making Victoria giggle with those tickling caresses, when she gave him subtle instruction. *Go lower, go lower,* she silently told him. He was between her legs, his mouth near her navel, when he brought his head up to look at her, a question in his burning eyes.

"Yes," she said, and arched toward him, throwing her head back.

"Oh, Jesus God," he whispered before doing what she asked.

Victoria closed her eyes and just let herself feel. And oh, how good it felt. She held him there until she let out a mewling cry, her body gone taut, as she convulsed in pleasure.

Jack lay there for several long minutes, hearing her breathing become normal, knowing if he moved, if she touched him, he truly would explode. Finally he could trust himself to touch her again, and he did, skimming his mouth against her belly and nuzzling her breasts and neck before claiming her mouth. He was shaking, *shaking* with desire for her. And he smiled in masculine triumph at her sleepy-pleased face, before pushing into her slowly and beginning the rhythm that would bring his own release.

Oh, how good he felt, Victoria thought, still lazy and languid from his lovemaking. Her movements slow and luxuriant, she moved her hands up and down his back as he moved against her, making her feel again that heat she'd thought was satiated. They climbed together, building slowly, slowly to that place they both sought, bodies slick, mouths hungry. Until it was there, that blinding, light-filled pinnacle that they reached together, fingers entwined, gripping almost painfully.

"I think waiting four days for that was pretty commendable," Victoria said a little while later. She still held one of his hands, and lifted it to gaze at its masculine strength.

"Indeed," Jack breathed.

Victoria lifted herself on one elbow so that she could look him in the eye. "You know, Jack, I would have waited forever for you. But I'm glad we didn't. You're not feeling guilty, are you?"

He shook his head.

"Then, what is it?"

"I'm just thinking of all I've been missing all these years. You have always been out there for me, and I didn't know it."

Victoria kissed his shoulder. "I haven't been. Not really."

"Emma could have been ours," he said after a long silence.

Her heart wrenched. "She is ours, Jack."

"I think you know what I mean. I would not love Emma more if she were ours. But the idea of us creating her . . ." He smiled. "We can make our own now, I suppose."

Victoria lay back down, her stomach tightening. "No, Jack, we can't. When I had Emma, something was damaged. The doctor told me. I can't have any other children."

Jack was quiet for so long, Victoria finally could stand it no longer.

"Jack," she uttered, staring up at the canopy. "Is that . . . Do you still want to marry me?"

When he didn't answer, she gathered the courage to sit up and confront him. He turned away, but not before she saw the tear tracks on his cheek.

"Oh, God, Jack. I'm so sorry. So sorry." She put one hand on his chest, so afraid he might knock it away.

"Victoria, no, no, no," he said, turning his eyes to her finally. "I'm sorry. For you. And for me. For all the babies like Emma we'll never make." He kissed her, wetting her face with his tears. "I love you so much. It kills me to think what you've gone through. What that bastard has put you through."

Victoria shook her head, her fear for Jack growing. If he suspected that Donnelly had anything to do with her inability to bear children, it would drive him over the edge. She'd been thankful when the doctor told her she could not physically bear children—for that made keeping her vow to remain childless so much easier.

As if reading her mind, Jack's face grew even more distraught. "Did Donnelly beat you while you were carrying Emma? Did he?" He shook her, his grip on her shoulders nearly painful.

What should she say? She'd suspected Donnelly had beaten Sheila Casey, that his abuse had something to do with her difficult birth. Difficult? Hell, Sheila Casey had died in childbirth! It was only through divine intervention that Victoria had use of the poor woman's body.

"He did, but I don't think it had anything to do with what has happened to me," she said quickly, praying the half-truth would be enough. It wasn't. Jack turned white, then livid red.

"By God, the man should die," he said through clenched teeth.

"Please, Jack. I just want to forget about it. I just want to forget about him. He's already taken so much. I don't want him to take you, too."

Through the red haze of rage, Jack heard Victoria's pleas. "He should pay," he persisted.

"He will. I just don't want you to collect that payment."

Jack gave her a hard kiss, then lay down and drew her against him, tucking her head beneath his chin. "I won't let him hurt you again, Victoria. I won't go after him now. But if he hurts you again, I'll kill him."

Victoria gave him a squeeze. "It won't come to that," she said. But she shivered all the same.

Thirty-four

"We've found her," Tom Reilly told Donnelly, his face beaming with triumph.

A smile slowly spread on Donnelly's face. "Where?"

"It was like you said. She went back to Wilkins on Beacon Hill."

"I knew it! Damn, I knew that woman would be back. She's got something going there. She's got that much nerve, givin' it another go after the lickin' I gave her. Brave girl, my Sheila. Never used to be so brave as that." He slapped his knee, his twisted possessive pride not lost on Reilly. "We'll go get her, then."

Reilly shifted. "Won't be easy as all that, Kevin. She don't come out, and there's guards now. She's holed up pretty good, our Sheila is."

Donnelly's brow furrowed. Clearly Jack Wilkins was a forgiving man, the fool. "Won't come out, eh? Well, my friend, we'll just have to flush her out."

Two days later, Etta fingered a note delivered from Reilly, her hand shaking in her apron pocket. It lay there, smudged and folded several times over, silently screaming blame for Victoria's beating. It had, she decided, been all her fault. When she had heard the extent of Victoria's injuries, it had only been her loyalty to Suzanne that kept her from tearfully confessing to Jack her part in the scheme. Looking back, she now realized how foolish she had been to think that

Donnelly was the charming do-gooder he pretended to be.

She remembered the snake of fear that slid up her spine when she met Donnelly for the first time. And recalled how she'd ignored that slithering fear, thinking she was imagining things. How could so handsome and charming a man possibly mean anyone harm? she had thought. Etta stared blindly at the back of Suzanne's head. She now knew the extent of Donnelly's evil, spelled out clearly in the letter that not only threatened Miss Casey but herself as well.

"Etta, where are you today? I've had to ask you twice now to do my hair. You're so fidgety," Suzanne said.

Etta, who had always looked upon Suzanne as a queen of sorts, was beginning to alter her view and was finding it a rather painful process. Etta was willing to take the blame for her part, but it was becoming disgustingly obvious that Suzanne had conveniently forgotten her role in what had happened. She'd even had the gall to wonder if she should buy "that poor Miss Casey" a gift for her convalescence. Etta had looked at her as if seeing the woman she had pledged her loyalty to for the first time. Not once had Suzanne shown remorse for the beating. Somehow she had convinced herself that what had happened was not her fault, but rather an unfortunate incident. Suzanne had not been so heartless to be glad about the horrible beating, but she certainly had not been sorry about it, either.

Now Etta was being asked by Kevin Donnelly, a man she had come to fear, to lure Miss Casey to him. Etta knew in her heart she would do it, too. And that, more than anything, was making her physically ill.

"He wants to see her, ma'am," Etta said softly.

Suzanne looked with impatience in the mirror at Etta standing behind her. "Etta, my hair. And who wants to see whom?"

"Kevin Donnelly. He wants to see Miss Casey, and he wants me to help him."

"I don't see why this should be any of my concern. Unless you are asking my advice? In that case, Etta, by all means, help the man." Suzanne picked up her brush and pointedly held it out to her maid.

Etta didn't move. "But he wants me to . . ."

Suzanne held her hand up to silence the maid. "I don't care to hear the details."

Etta pursed her lips. "He'll hurt her."

Suzanne twisted in her chair to look at the maid directly. "I'm afraid that is not my concern. Nor should it be yours. You've made your bed, Etta, and now you must lie in it. No one forced you to talk to Mr. Donnelly on my behalf."

"I did it for you, ma'am! You were so unhappy. I never thought he'd hurt her. If I knew that, I never would have told you about him. Never!"

"How commendable of you," Suzanne said. "Perhaps you should work for Miss Casey, since you are such a great supporter of hers."

"Oh, no, ma'am. I never meant to say I wasn't happy working for you," Etta said, and began working on Suzanne's hair to prove her point.

"I may not have a choice in the matter, Etta. If things continue as they have, I'm afraid I will not be able to afford a personal maid. You will become a luxury."

"What do you mean, ma'am? Has something happened?"

Suzanne's face grew stony. "You have been distracted of late, haven't you? I would have expected you to know this bit of gossip." Suzanne paused for the drama of it. "They are to be married. That means, obviously, that Mr. Wilkins will not be marrying me."

Etta bit her lip. "Would he have?" She seemed startled that the question had popped out of her mouth.

Suzanne frowned, creating deep lines on each side of her mouth and between her eyes. "Of course. We had discussed it. I felt he was warming up to the idea a bit. But that won't happen now. Unless . . ."

"Unless, ma'am?" She knew what Suzanne was going to say. She knew, and it made her want to vomit, for Etta also knew she would do as Suzanne asked. Their eyes met in the mirror.

"Unless Miss Casey decides to leave."

Etta felt as if the hand of God were pressing down on her, and if she did this thing, His great fingers would begin to close and slowly squeeze—squeeze until there was nothing left of her. It was her fate to sin, she decided as she pulled a few strands of Suzanne's dark hair to curl them by her ear. Her hands no longer shook as a strange calm blanketed her. She was doomed, beyond redemption. What was one more sin to add to all her others? For the first time she wished she were Catholic so she could simply go to a priest to confess her sins.

She moved around Suzanne, checked each curl, sticking in hairpins as needed, so aware of that note in her pocket, she could swear she felt its weight there growing heavier with each step. The note had been quite explicit about what she should do, instructions written simply and horribly clear. And it had been just as clear about what would happen should Etta fail. "Your family will be punished," the note had said. She had no doubt that Kevin Donnelly, who had so charmed her, who had beaten Miss Casey nearly to death, would do as he threatened. She could not let that happen, could not put her family in jeopardy. Yes, she would do as the note asked. Had there ever been a choice?

Etta's heart raced just thinking about carrying out the plan. It was to happen tonight when the house was asleep. God forgive me, she prayed, knowing that even He could not forgive this.

Victoria woke with a start, her heart racing madly in her chest, and then settled back down, nestling into the crook of Jack's arm. Her sleepy eyes took in the soft dawn light showing from behind the drawn curtains. It was early. Early enough to not check on Emma, early enough to enjoy this wonderfully warm and masculine body next to hers. Once Jack had gotten over his rule about not sleeping with his fiancée, Victoria had spent every night in his arms.

She had never been able to sleep all tangled up with a man, preferring to stick to her own side of the bed once the loving was done. But with Jack, it was the opposite. She moved toward him in the night, always touching, always an arm draped across his chest, a leg tucked against his thighs, or her entire body cocooned in his embrace.

The past few days had been blissful, absolutely the happiest days Victoria could remember. She wanted to scream out her joy, to go back to the future like Michael J. Fox had in his souped-up car and thank John Wing for allowing her to have this kind of happiness. She wondered if he'd known all along what would happen, the kind of pure rapture she would feel. She wanted to tell Allie about him, to sit cross-legged on her couch and gush out all the love she had for Jack.

This man. This beautiful man lying next to her was hers to keep forever. They would love and laugh and probably cry together forever. She would wake up like this every day of her life, look over and see his face, those long, long lashes resting on his cheek, that mouth sculpted and so soft in his slumber. His beard-darkened face looked so incredibly sexy, so wonderfully familiar, and yet so new and exciting. He was hers to touch and love anytime she liked. Pinch me, I must be dreaming, she thought.

She hugged it all to herself, not wanting any of this wonderfulness to seep out and escape. They had made love so many times in the past four days, exploring each other, what pleased, what made each other scream, what tickled. The back of his knees, the tender flesh that made Victoria so hot, made Jack let out gales of laughter. The kiss on Jack's earlobe that made him grumble low in his chest and crush her closer, made Victoria giggle uncontrollably. Sheila's body was not her own. Victoria had loved to have her bottom stroked, but her large breasts had not been altogether that sensitive. However, Sheila's breasts, my God, was there a more sensitive part of her body? Well, yes, and they had discovered that, too. Several times, in fact.

Victoria sighed dreamily. The house was completely still, and she could hear the first birdsong outside the window. Victoria strained to hear Emma, thinking she heard a little coo, but then chalked it up to imagination. When she was living in the Vendome, and later in the boardinghouse, she had constantly thought she heard Emma crying. It was maddening.

Jack stirred in his sleep, giving off a sexy sound deep in his throat as she cuddled against him. Victoria tried to still her beating heart, tried to stop straining to hear Emma, but gave up with a little sigh. This was not the first time she'd had an overwhelming urge to check on her daughter, and she figured it would not be the last. As she sat up, Jack's hand clamped onto her wrist.

"Don't go," he said, his voice muffled against a pillow.

Victoria leaned toward him and kissed his forehead. "I just want to check on Emma."

"I'm sure she's fine," he said, trailing a provocative line up her arm with his fingers.

"I'm sure she is, too."

He smiled. "Go check. I'll be right here when you come back."

"If she's awake, I'm bringing her with me," she said in light warning.

Jack let out a mock frustrated groan.

"Oh, as if you're not getting your fair share in *that* department," Victoria said, a smile in her voice.

"It happens to be my very favorite department. But

Emma is my second favorite department," he said, hauling her down toward him for a long kiss. "I hope she's sleeping like a lamb."

"Me, too." Victoria pulled away with regret, but her mind was already on her little girl. Crazy, these impulses to check on her, these heart-racing, stomach-clenching moments.

Victoria opened the door to the nursery, a smile already on her face as she took in the lace-trimmed crib. Then her smile faltered as her eyes grew wide with alarm.

The crib was empty. Emma was gone.

Thirty-five

Two days. Two frustrating, fear-filled, nightmarish days passed with no word. Nothing. No note, no demands. And so the police who had been assigned to the case began to suspect two things—that whoever took Emma was not going to give her back, or the little girl was dead and someone in the house was guilty of murder. They kept their opinions to themselves, not wanting to inflict any more pain to this household. To hint the little girl was dead when it was horrific enough that she'd been abducted would have been entirely too cruel.

Everyone was questioned, Jack, Suzanne, Victoria, as well as all the servants. No one had seen anything unusual.

Sergeant Brisby had finished the last of his interviews, and now faced talking with Jack Wilkins, something he put in the same category as skinning a live alligator. The man was wild with worry and rage, declaring that he knew who was behind the kidnapping, but offering no proof to police. He found him in the parlor, the nanny by his side. They had that look about them Brisby had seen in the eyes of soldiers returning from the war with Spain. It was a sadness so deep, nothing could touch it, a pain so raw, nothing could heal it.

"Our interviews are complete. All we can do now is wait."

Jack did not acknowledge the man's presence but for a slight tightening in his jaw.

The police officer stood in the center of the room, enduring the silence. "We'll have an officer here at all times in case someone tries to make contact with you."

"Someone," Jack spat. "Not someone, Sergeant. Kevin Donnelly. If you find him, you'll find Emma."

"We are looking, sir."

"Well, not good enough," Jack said between clenched teeth.

Victoria sat in a nearby chair, swaying slightly, arms wrapped about her waist, her eyes staring blankly at the carpet. "This corset's so tight," she said, continuing to sway. Jack looked at her, his eyes, impossibly, filling with more pain.

"Why don't you loosen it," he said, his voice gentle.

Victoria looked up sharply, as if she hadn't realized she voiced her complaint aloud. "Oh. Yes, I will. Later."

Jack closed his eyes briefly. "What can we do, Sergeant?"

The sergeant's eyes flickered from the nanny to Jack. "If someone contacts you, you must inform us immediately. In cases like this, more often than not it's money the people want. They set an exchange point, then we make an arrest. Kidnappings are rarely successful."

"And what if no one contacts us?"

"Then, we pray, Mr. Wilkins. We pray."

The day was endless. Police officers and detectives passed in and out of the Wilkins house silently, whispering among themselves, casting sorrowful looks at Jack and Victoria, who sat nearby, pale and distracted. Jack would erupt from his seat each time Sergeant Brisby entered, only to sit down again when the officer shook his head. No news. Never any news. And that could only mean that whoever took Emma had no intention of bringing her back. They meant to keep her. It was a possibility Sergeant Brisby told Jack they must consider.

"One thing is puzzling, though, Mr. Wilkins. Someone stole the baby, that's obvious. But whoever did it, didn't break in. We've looked at all the windows, all the doors. You and your staff say they are always locked. Always. Unless one was left open, there's only one way that baby got out. Someone inside was involved."

Jack gave him a startled look. "Impossible. Everyone on my staff has been with me for years."

"Everyone?" Brisby made a show of looking at his notes. "The nanny. A Miss Victoria Casey. She's only been here five months, give or take?"

Jack raised a hand to stop the sergeant from going any further with that particular line of questioning. "Victoria is not responsible," he said flatly.

"Everyone in this household must be considered as a suspect, even yourself, Mr. Wilkins. We approach this as if everyone is guilty, then eliminate them one by one."

"Eliminate Miss Casey."

Brisby shifted uncomfortably beneath Jack's steely gaze. "I'm afraid I can only do that if the investigation warrants it, Mr. Wilkins. Please understand."

Damn, Jack thought. He hadn't wanted to taint Victoria's reputation by telling the police how he knew Victoria was not involved, but it appeared he had no choice. "Miss Casey was with me the night Emma was taken. All night, Sergeant. Take her off your list of suspects." It was a toss up who blushed brighter, Jack or the officer.

The sergeant stared at his notes for a moment, then made a small mark on his paper. He coughed and cleared his throat. "That still leaves us with a mystery, sir. Someone from inside the house is likely involved. Unless we find evidence to go against that theory, that's where the investigation stands."

It was hard for Jack to believe one of his staff could possibly have been involved in something as heinous as stealing a baby from its crib. But he had found of late he was not the best judge of character. Victoria's accusations about Suzanne had weighed heavily on his mind. Though he refused to discuss the matter with Victoria, he was beginning to believe Suzanne was behind the sudden appearance of Kevin Donnelly. He did not believe, however, that Suzanne had any inkling that Donnelly planned to beat Victoria.

As he walked back to the library, he wracked his brain, trying to think who in his staff could be behind the kidnapping. Brisby had requested a list of employees fired in the past year; it was woefully short, and Jack felt would lead nowhere. The two firings had been twins, identical in looks and laziness. He doubted they would have had the ambition to plot a kidnapping. That left someone still in the house. Someone who needed money or simply wanted to get back at Jack. Or Victoria. The path his mind was taking led him to Suzanne. For the life of him, he could not imagine Suzanne sneaking out of the house undetected with Emma in her arms.

Jack returned to the library, his eyes falling on Victoria, who had sat, unmoving, for hours. Her eyes had followed Jack's progress as he stalked over to Sergeant Brisby, not even turning her head if they strayed from her frame of vision. It was as if she feared moving would break some spell and Emma would be lost forever.

Perhaps, Victoria thought irrationally, if she remained absolutely still, she could stop time, stop an officer from approaching them with bad news. The horrors of what could happen to a little girl, even an infant, paralyzed her. She did not know what Donnelly was capable of, and she was certain it was Donnelly behind the kidnapping. Her greatest fear was that Donnelly had taken Emma for spite, not for money. And that fear froze her in place.

As the windows in the library grew dark at the end of the second day, Jack walked over to Victoria and stood in front of her. When she did not look up, he got down on his haunches, laying a hand on her knee.

"You haven't eaten all day, Victoria," he said. Finally, she allowed her eyes to focus on his, and she blinked against the concern she saw there.

"I'm not hungry," she whispered.

"Not eating isn't helping her," Jack said, and when her face scrunched up, he knew he'd finally tapped into her grief. She recovered instantly, her face once again going stoic and taut. He'd been so consumed with his own thoughts, he'd barely noticed Victoria sitting so still. He took her cold hands into his, pulling when she resisted, and forced her to open her hands, which were clenched into two tight little balls.

"Jack," she said, pulling away, "I just want to sit here. I just want to wait."

"Come into the kitchen with me, and we'll get something to eat," he grabbed her hand again, and pulled her up. She seemed to unbend like a rusty hinge, resistant to the movement. When she was standing, she sagged against him, her weary muscles trembling. She could barely stand.

"Look what you've done to yourself," he said gently, kissing her forehead. He rubbed her arms briskly, then her back, as Victoria leaned silently against him.

"If it's Donnelly that has her, I'm to blame," she said against his chest. "Don't deny it. It's true."

Jack couldn't deny it. Those thoughts, angry and irrational, had entered his head. He'd quickly put them aside, but there was no arguing that what she said was partly true. If Victoria had not become Emma's nanny, perhaps Donnelly would not have shown up on his doorstep. Jack, however, did not dwell on laying blame, but he knew Victoria would. Instead of arguing, he hugged her close. "We'll get her back."

They walked together to the kitchen, Victoria leaning heavily on Jack. The room was empty but for a single maid rinsing out a mop at the far end of the long, narrow room. Jack sat Victoria at the long wooden table the staff ate at for their meals as he would have a child, placing her in her seat as if she might topple off it. He placed food in front of her: a hunk of bread, plate of cold ham, leftover baked potatoes still warm from the missed evening meal, a bowl of butter. Victoria sat there, her eyes wide and unblinking, hands folded on her lap, strangely complacent.

"I feel so lost," she said softly.

Jack stopped, his hand carrying a plate, frozen in the act of placing it on the table. He finished the act, placing it softly on the table in front of her. "Come here," he said, and opened his arms. Victoria went to him, letting out a little sound of anguish. He was so strong. Victoria felt on the verge of falling apart, like she was splintering piece by piece and there was nothing she could do to stop it. Jack held her together.

"I'm sorry," she said.

"You've nothing to be sorry about."

"Yes. There is. I'm falling apart, and you've got enough on your mind without worrying about me." Victoria took a deep breath. "I don't want you to worry about me."

Jack smiled. "Of course I'm going to worry about you. But I would not characterize needing a bit of comfort as falling apart. Falling apart is what Emma's grandmother did this afternoon. You missed it, thank God, but I can assure you that you have been a rock."

Victoria found herself smiling back. "What happened?"

"Let's just say the scream that emanated from my mother-in-law could have been heard from here to California. Then she fainted in my arms."

"You actually caught her?" Victoria asked, picturing poor Jack catching the rather rotund Mrs. St. George.

"Let's just say I broke her fall. My father-in-law was much more composed. He just began blustering and shouting at the police, as if they were the ones who'd committed the crime. That, my dear, is falling apart."

Victoria found herself laughing, then immediately felt guilty. "Thanks for cheering me up. You're one of the good guys, Jack, you know that?" She kissed him softly. "I love you. Now. Let's eat. I'm starving."

They ate the meal, their first of the day, with relish. Finishing, Victoria leaned back in her chair and let out a long sigh. "I hate this waiting. I used to feel so sorry for those parents of abducted kids, those little faces on milk cartons, but I didn't have a clue about how horrible it is."

"Milk cartons?"

Victoria looked up, startled. "In New York they used to put missing kids' pictures on milk cartons."

"Right on the bottle?"

Victoria grimaced inwardly. "No. On the crates the bottles came in. Anyway," she sighed, too tired to think of a better explanation for her mistake. "It's the not knowing, that's the worst. Oh, God, Jack, she's got to be all right. She just has to be." Victoria finally let the tears fall that had been threatening all day. They came in a torrent of hard, chest-racking sobs, and were quickly over.

"Feel better?" asked Jack, who had come to her side when her storm of tears started.

"Much." Victoria glanced at the kitchen clock. Eight o'clock. Emma had been gone less than forty-eight hours; it seemed like weeks. "I'm exhausted, but I don't want to sleep," she said, rubbing her swollen eyes.

Jack lay a hand on the back of her neck and massaged the taut tendons there. "Go to sleep for a while. I'll wake you up if there's any news."

Victoria headed to her room. She couldn't bring herself to share Jack's bed, not when she knew that had she been in her own room, Emma might not be missing. She paused a few seconds outside the nursery, closing her eyes and willing Emma back into her crib. She would never forget the moment when she realized Emma was gone, that feeling of sickening panic that grew as her eyes looked uncomprehendingly at the empty crib. Then came the burgeoning, irrational hope, that someone, for some reason, had taken her out to play, that she was still somewhere safe in the house. And finally, came the realization that the baby was gone.

Victoria, her eyes shiny with tears, walked to the crib, hating its neatness, its unrumpled covers. "Come back, Emma," she whispered. "Mommy misses you."

Thirty-six

"Miss Casey." A harsh whisper, a clawlike hand on her shoulder. "Miss Casey, please, wake up."

Victoria jolted upright, hitting her head on Etta's chin and almost causing the woman to drop her lamp. "Ow!" She rubbed her head, looking at Etta with irritation as she tried to clear her head from its sleepy fog. Etta wore a nightcap, a ridiculous floppy thing, and a pristine white cotton nightgown that seemed to glow like an apparition in the limited light. "What is it? What's wrong?"

Etta stared at her, looking like someone with a piece of fouled food in her mouth who found themselves unable to spit it out. Victoria grabbed her arm, "What is it? Is it Emma? Tell me!"

Etta swallowed audibly. "No! I mean yes. Oh, Miss Casey, I'm in awful trouble."

Victoria looked steadily into Etta's eyes and gripped her arms, giving her a little shake. "I don't understand. Tell me what's wrong."

Etta bit her lip, as if still unsure about what she was doing. "You'll hate me for this. I know you will, and you've a right. Oh, Miss Casey, I've committed a terrible sin. A mortal sin, I'm sure."

Victoria wanted to throttle the woman. "Just tell me what you've done, Etta," she said through clenched teeth.

"Oh, Lord. I've given Emma to Kevin Donnelly."

Victoria sagged back onto her pillow, and laid one arm across her eyes. "You're not serious."

Etta worried her lip some more. "I'm afraid I am. He threatened to harm my family unless I cooperated. I didn't know what to do, Miss Casey. I'm so sorry. I didn't have a choice. He promised not to harm her. He said he just wanted you."

Victoria's face turned ashen, and she lifted her arm to look at Etta to see if the woman was telling the truth or just playing some horrible joke on her. "Oh, God," she muttered when she saw the expression on Etta's face.

"I know, Miss Casey. I know what he did to you. I'm partly to blame for that too. Oh, I'm going to hell, that's for sure," she said, sniffing loudly, tears running sloppily down her face. "I was only trying to help Mrs. Von Arc. I never meant for you to get hurt. And now Emma." Etta buried her head in her hands, succumbing to grief and self-hatred.

"Oh, Etta," Victoria said, shaking her head.

"I know! I don't understand what possessed me to trust that man. He seemed so . . ."

". . . charming," Victoria finished.

"Yes! Exactly. He reeled me in like fish, he did. If ever a moment I suspected he would hurt you, I never would have given Mrs. Von Arc his name. Never! You must believe me."

"Etta, you've lost me. What did you have to do with Mrs. Von Arc hiring him?" Victoria asked impatiently.

Etta told her the whole story, pausing now and again to sniff and bawl. "I took her, the sweet little thing, right from her crib and handed her over to a man who was waiting. Emma slept through the whole thing, little angel. Sweet little angel. I was shaking like a leaf. I know what I've done is awful, Miss Casey. But I didn't have a choice! Not with him knowing where my family lives, not when I know what he'll do to them. He mentioned my sister, my little baby sister Elaine, by name."

"Etta, where is Emma?"

"I don't know. I only know he has her, and he'll only let her go if you go to him."

Go to him. Victoria let the fear wash over her, let it run like shards of glass through her veins, as she tried to focus on one thing. Emma. He was a smart one, Kevin Donnelly. He knew the only way to Victoria was through the baby. Score one point for the man, Victoria thought bitterly.

"How will I know Emma will be safe?" Victoria said, her voice even.

Etta dissolved into another fit of tears. "I'm to go for a walk, and a man will give her to me. That's the story I'm to tell. But actually, I'll go with you to Donnelly, and they'll give me Emma then. He said to tell you . . . to tell you . . ." More tears, and Victoria was growing increasingly impatient.

"He said to tell me *what*, Etta. We don't have time for you to fall apart," she bit out.

Etta raised her red-rimmed, bleary eyes to Victoria. "You're not to try any tricks. No police, no Mr. Wilkins. You're to come alone, or he won't give Emma back ever. He wants money, too. A thousand dollars, he said to bring. And if you tell anyone, he said he'd hurt my family." Fresh tears seeped from her eyes. "That's what he said, and I believe him!"

Victoria chewed on the end of her right thumb while she fiddled with her engagement ring, knowing she had no choice. She'd never been the martyr type, but now Victoria knew she would sacrifice herself to make Emma safe. Suddenly Etta's tears sickened her. The meddlesome woman was apparently behind all her troubles, from Donnelly's unexpected visit to Emma's kidnapping. How dare she wring her hands and blubber about her relatives when Victoria was about to voluntarily go to the man who'd nearly killed her. And was likely planning to again.

"Get ahold of yourself! You're driving me crazy."
Victoria rolled her eyes when her harsh tone only
brought forth another gush.

Sniffing loudly, Etta wiped her nose on her sleeve
and hiccuped.

"When is this exchange supposed to happen?"

"Tomorrow. We're to meet a man in the Park Street
subway. He'll hand me Emma, and you're to go with
him to Donnelly. I don't know where."

Victoria's hands balled into fists. The bastard. The
mean bastard. He planned it out nicely. Coward
wouldn't be in the subway himself, so he was safe if
Victoria disobeyed him and brought police along.
She'd have to go alone and pray she could get away
before he hurt her. Victoria's stomach heaved, and
she clutched it with a shaking hand. Going to Donnelly would be the toughest thing she'd ever done.
But she'd do it. For Emma.

"You'll do it?" Etta asked.

"Yes."

"And you won't tell no one?"

The look Victoria gave Etta made the woman
cringe. "No, Etta, I won't tell anyone. Your family
is safe."

"Thank you. You're a good woman. I knew you
were. I felt just awful about helping Mrs. Von Arc,
just awful. We'll go for a walk tomorrow at noon. I'll
meet you here. Good night, Miss Casey." She even
had the gall to smile.

Victoria laid the diamond and ruby ring on the glass
display. The jewelry store owner raised an eyebrow
and immediately tucked a magnifier into his eye.

"I'd like one thousand dollars for this."

Still bent over the ring, the jeweler said, "My dear
woman, this ring is worth far more than one thousand dollars."

"But one thousand is all I want. Will you buy it?"

The man finally brought his head up to examine the

creature in front of him. "For one thousand dollars?" he asked, incredulous.

"I believe that's what I said. Twice."

Disbelievingly, the man brought the magnifier back up, and again looked at the ring, as if perhaps he'd misjudged the piece the first time. A smile spread on his thin lips. "I'll write you a draft immediately."

"No. I want cash."

Those bushy eyebrows rose again. "I don't have that kind of money in the store. I'll have to go to the bank. If you could come back this afternoon, I'll have it for you then."

"That's not good enough. I need the money immediately."

The jeweler stroked his jaw in thought.

"Or I'll take my business elsewhere," she said when it appeared he was hedging.

He smiled tightly. "One moment please." The jeweler walked to the end of the narrow shop and opened a door that led to a staircase, which apparently led to an apartment above. "My wife will be right down to watch the shop. If you'll be so good to wait, I'll return momentarily with your money."

Twenty minutes later, Victoria left the store with a packet of money stashed in her coat pocket.

When she returned to the house, Jack was talking to a police officer, and her heart sped up in a guilty cadence. You've nothing to feel guilty about, she chastised herself. She wanted to run to Jack and tell him what she planned. She wanted him to stop her from doing what she knew she had to do. I'm so afraid, she thought. Only the thought of what Jack's face would look like when he saw Emma in Etta's arms kept her from blurting out what she knew. Everything would sour if she told Jack the plan. Etta, as skittish as a Chihuahua on a bad day, was hovering about, and she had no doubt she'd send off a warning to Donnelly should Victoria cave in and tell the police.

"Any news?" she asked, trying to keep her voice normal.

Jack turned to her. "Nothing. Jasper Porter stopped by this morning while you were out. He's working on the case as well. Where were you, by the way?"

Was that a censorious look? Victoria wondered. She felt like that man in Edgar Allen Poe's "The Telltale Heart," guilt making her imagine things. "I just needed to get out, take a walk and clear my head," she said.

Jack smiled, making Victoria feel even worse. "That's good. You'll just drive yourself to distraction if you stay here and wait."

Victoria flashed him a smile. "I might go for another walk later." She felt like throwing up. She didn't want to lie to Jack anymore. She'd promised she wouldn't, but here she was spinning a tale, covering her tracks. And for what? To protect Etta and her family. Victoria looked over to where Etta hovered, taking in every word, her eyes darting from Victoria to Jack. Victoria felt like smashing the woman's face.

The sound of the grandfather clock chiming eleven o'clock on the second floor two hours later seemed to seal Victoria's fate. She would do as Donnelly said. She might die, truly die this time. Maybe this was all part of the plan, Victoria thought. Maybe Wing tricked me, convinced me to go back in time to test whether I had the courage to sacrifice myself for another. Maybe this was some sort of purgatory for selfish vain people, where they learned to be selfless, and all that stuff about pure hearts was a bunch of bunk. Shit, Victoria thought, I don't know what to think anymore.

Victoria lifted a shaking hand to her hair and tried to tuck the stray strand back into her loose French twist. She only succeeded in pulling more strands out. Jack watched her, noted her shaking hands, and his heart filled with sorrow and love.

"Here, let me try," he said, pulling her hands down.

That's when he noticed her ring was gone. "Where's your ring, sweetheart?"

"Oh!" Victoria looked down at her naked finger, a guilty flush spreading on her lovely Irish complexion. "I, uh, took it off. It was bothering me. I think it's too loose, and I was afraid it would fall off. I put it back in its box." She didn't look him in the eye, so she didn't see the frown that formed on his face. When she turned her gaze upward, he smiled.

"We'll bring it back to the jeweler and have it fitted, then," he said, bringing her hand up to his lips.

Oh, stop being so wonderful, she screamed to herself. I've got to tell him. I have to. I can't lie again. Then she saw Etta slip past the library, her coat on, ready to meet her down the street as they planned.

"I wonder if another walk will make me feel better," she said.

"I'm sure it will. Your nerves are frazzled." Victoria hesitated only a moment.

"Go on, Vic. I'll hold down the fort."

Victoria looked at Jack uncertainly. "All right. I won't be long," she lied. Pulling Jack aside, she kissed him, a bit too long, a bit too desperately, for a woman just going for a walk. "I love you."

She shrugged on her coat, patted the pocket to make sure the package of money was still there, and walked out the door.

One hundred feet before the Park Street subway, Victoria stopped, her eyes cemented to the opening, yawning like a hungry monster. "Oh, Etta, I think I'm going to be sick. I really think I'm going to be sick."

"Breathe deeply, Miss Casey, it will pass," Etta said, and started to walk away.

"No. I mean it." And then Victoria rushed to the side of a nearby building and retched violently. Etta put a consoling hand on her back. "You're awfully afraid of him, aren't you?" she asked, tears coming to her eyes.

Victoria looked up at her, then turned her head to

spit. "I'm petrified," she admitted. "I've never been so afraid in my life." She bit her lips to stop her tears.

"I'm so sorry, Miss Casey."

Victoria straightened up and gave Etta a fierce look. "Sorry doesn't get me much, does it," she said.

Etta could only shake her head. She put her arm around Victoria and began walking toward the subway where Emma was waiting, where she would get on a train headed to the man who had tried to kill her.

Thirty-seven

The Wilkins house was silent, as silent as it had been following Christina's death. Servants walked about as softly as possible, keeping their tones low, their expressions somber. Nearly three days had passed, and the little baby was still missing. Jack sat alone at his desk, drumming his fingers softly against the polished wood. He glanced up at the mantel clock. One o'clock. Victoria should be returning from her walk soon. He was worried about her. Seeing those shaking hands, the fear in her eyes, was jarring. And there was something else in her eyes this morning, something more disturbing than mere worry or fear, an emotion he could not name.

A door slammed, followed by the sound of running footsteps, and Jack stood, his heartbeat quickening.

"I've got her! I've got her!"

Jack rushed from behind his desk, knocking his chair over in the process. He stepped into the marbled foyer to see Etta standing there, tears streaming down her face, Emma in her arms.

With an animal sound, Jack lunged toward Etta and grabbed the little girl from her arms. He held her to him, rocking back and forth, emitting painful sobs from his throat. "You're home, Emma. Home. Thank God." Emma squirmed in his arms, not liking this great big bear hug from Daddy, and letting out a sound of protest.

Jack laughed and held her up, his eyes shining with

tears, looking her over for signs of injury. Her white dress was soiled, her diaper a sopping mess, and her face had the remnants of her last meal still on it, but otherwise, she was perfect. "Victoria! Etta, Victoria went for a walk more than an hour ago. You didn't see her?"

Etta, still blubbering tears, choked out, "No, sir."

"What happened Etta. How did you find her? Where?"

"A man come up to me and handed her to me. I'd never seen him before," Etta said, her eyes wide. "He had a kerchief wrapped around his face. He just handed her to me out of the blue. Just handed her to me. I don't know nothing else."

Jack's smile was brilliant. "We'll deal with that later," he said, and kissed Emma on the cheek. What a surprise awaited Victoria when she arrived back from her walk! "Let's get my little darling here cleaned up so she's perfect when Victoria gets back."

Emma was cleaned and napping when Jack's stomach gave a queasy turn. Victoria should be back by now. It was so unlike her to be gone for so long, especially with Donnelly still about. In fact, her going out twice in the same day suddenly seemed extremely uncharacteristic. Taking one more long look at Emma's sleeping form, Jack slipped out of the nursery and into Victoria's room, his eyes immediately going to the statue he'd given her New Year's eve. The sight of it calmed him a bit. Next to it was the ring box, as if Victoria was trying to keep everything dear to her in one spot. Jack walked over to the nightstand and lifted the ring box, smiling fondly as he recalled Victoria's wide eyes when she'd finally accepted it. He opened the box to look again at the ring he'd taken so much time picking out.

The box was empty.

"Mr. Wilkins. We've found something." Sergeant Brisby stood at the entrance to the study, looking exceedingly uncomfortable.

Three hours after Victoria had left for her walk—two hours after Emma had been found—Jack had told the police he suspected Victoria was missing. He refused to believe Victoria had disappeared on her own, but the coincidence of Emma being found, her disappearance, and the missing ring were beginning to paint a sordid picture.

"What have you found, Sergeant?"

"Is this the ring?" Sergeant Brisby held the delicate ring in his callused palm. Jack walked over slowly, knowing that the officer would be holding the ring Jack had given to Victoria.

"It is."

"A woman who matches the description of Victoria Casey sold this ring to the jeweler this morning for one thousand dollars. Furthermore"—he turned back to the foyer—"Mr. Porter, could you come in here please?" Jasper Porter's huge bulk filled up the entryway. "Tell him," Brisby urged.

"One of my men saw Miss Ashford, I mean, Miss Casey with a man identified as Kevin Donnelly. My man lost them. She appeared to be accompanying him voluntarily, sir. I'm sorry."

Jack turned quickly and walked to his desk, sitting down with care. He appeared to be about to say something, but stopped, snapping his jaw closed. "Are you insinuating that Victoria would willingly go with a man who nearly beat her to death?" he asked with deadly calm. "Tell me, Mr. Porter, that you are not saying that Victoria is a willing participant in the kidnapping of her own daughter."

Porter looked startled. "Daughter? The baby is . . ." Dawning spread slowly on Porter's flushed face.

"I want them found," he said finally. "I want Donnelly prosecuted. I want Victoria back safely. So help me God, I hold you personally responsible if anything happens to her, Sergeant. I told you it was Donnelly. You wanted proof! You've got your goddamned proof now!" Jack slammed his fist down onto his desk, his face a mask of fury.

Nowhere was there a doubt that Victoria was Donnelly's victim. Even after the sergeant had paled under his scathing look, he had not been convinced of Victoria's innocence, stubbornly repeating that Porter's man had observed the woman was a willing participant.

Sergeant Brisby and Jasper Porter watched silently as Jack Wilkins calmly went to a locked cabinet and removed an ivory-handled pistol. "If you don't find Donnelly before I do, gentlemen, he's a dead man. That's a promise."

He hadn't touched her yet. He'd barely spoken a word. But he'd not taken his eyes off her, he'd not let her get more than a few feet from him. It seemed to Victoria she'd been on every mode of transportation in the city, from cab to trolley to train. He'd been solicitous, opening doors, helping her in and out of their conveyances, smiling gently when she flinched each time he held out his hand to her. She wouldn't take her guard down, wouldn't fall for his lazy charm. Walking the last two miles, they'd taken a circuitous route to the four-storied clapboard building where they now stood outside.

"Home sweet home, my girl. At least until things settle down."

Victoria swallowed the bile that formed in her throat. She turned toward him. "I don't want you to hit me."

Donnelly raised his eyebrows in surprise. "Hit you? Now, why would I do that, sweetheart?" He went to lay a hand on her cheek, but Victoria pulled back, and his eyes grew cold. "There'll be none of that, love. I'll not have some whipped female hanging about my neck. Where's the spunk? Don't tell me I knocked it out of you this last time."

Victoria turned her head away and stared at the building. "It was your doing," he hissed. "If you hadn't betrayed me, girl, I wouldn't have been so rough on you." He chuckled. "Thought I'd killed you, I did. But when I sent the boys to collect your body, you were gone. Always were a tough little thing."

My God, Victoria thought, was that admiration in his voice? That she had somehow survived his brutality had won her points with this monster?

"You're sick," she spat. She couldn't help herself. She tensed for a blow, but Donnelly laughed.

"All spit and fire, are you? That's my girl." He patted her on her back.

They trudged up a set of outside stairs, and entered the building on the third floor. Up another set of stairs, Victoria found herself in a full attic, rafters showing in the ceiling above. It was cold and dark and completely uninviting. Donnelly walked over to a black stove, opened the creaking door, and stirred up the coals.

"Be warm up here in a jiffy," he called to her. "Just make yourself at home."

Victoria gazed around her. Light seeped through two vents on either side of the attic, revealing a dirty mattress, a rusty bicycle, chests overflowing with clothes, a cracked and dusty saddle, and other items that melted into the shadows. Her eyes went back to the mattress, and her stomach churned. She'd die or kill him before she lay on that mattress with him. Victoria searched for something she could use as a weapon. But the only thing in this room she could use against him was in Donnelly's hand—the iron poker. She looked at that strong bit of iron, willing it to fly out of Donnelly's hand and into hers.

He slammed the door shut, leaning the poker against the stove. "Tommy will be by soon with some food. And whiskey. I'm feelin' a bit parched about now. We've got to hole up here for a while. Police are sniffing around like a bunch of dogs. But it'll calm down soon enough, and we can go about our business."

Victoria looked at him as if he were insane. "How long do you plan to keep me."

"Ain't keepin' you, darlin'."

Victoria looked around her and waved her arms. "Just what do you call this? You blackmailed me into coming here. You kidnapped my daughter . . ."

"She's my daughter, too. Can't kidnap your own daughter," he said with an easy grin.

Victoria closed her eyes and counted to five. "Some people would definitely call what you did kidnapping. What do you want from me. Do you want to kill me? Beat me? Well, then, get it over with, because I can't stand not knowing. Okay?"

"Aw, Sheila. You make me sound like a monster. Why would I want to hurt you," he said, walking over to her. Victoria, her head already against the slanting ceiling, had nowhere to go. He trailed a finger along her jaw. She wanted to spit at him, but her mouth had gone so dry, she couldn't have even if she decided to be so rash.

"You never used to be so afraid of me, Sheila. I don't know that I like it much. Used to be more fire in you. Now look at you. Shaking like a leaf, and I haven't even raised a fist to you." He raised his hand as if to strike her, and she flinched. "See that," he said, patting her cheek with the hand that had been poised to hit her. "You're a scared little rabbit." He looked at her with distaste. He took his large hand and placed it full on her face, then shoved her down so she landed hard on the mattress. "You make me sick," he said, mildly. And his hands went to the top button of his pants.

Thirty-eight

Mary Grant stomped one foot and crossed her arms angrily. "I won't believe it of her. I won't!"

Jack was glad Henry had brought Mary along when she began her staunch support of Victoria. In the face of nearly everyone's doubt, including Henry's, he'd needed to hear another defend the woman he loved. He needed to have an intelligent person tell him that his growing fear for Victoria was warranted, and not just his heart refusing to accept he'd been duped. Mary had refused to believe Victoria was capable of joining Donnelly in such a plot, despite the evidence that she had indeed.

Suzanne was there, as well, doubt in Victoria's innocence plainly written on her face, though she remained silent. Suzanne had simply pursed her lips when she'd heard Victoria was gone. Suzanne, looking austere in a black and gray shirtwaist, was silent as Mary began her tirade against Henry.

"Mary." Henry gave his wife a warning look.

"Henry, you saw her after that beating. She hated Kevin Donnelly. She even talked about killing him. Why would she go with him voluntarily?" She walked over to Jack and tugged on his arm. "Tell him."

"Your mother never left your father, Mary," Henry said gently.

Mary stiffened. "My mother was beaten down by my father. It took years for her to become that woman, years of belittlement, of beatings. She never showed the fire that Victoria did. My mother finally accepted her lot, and for a long time I hated her for it. Victoria never did. She's a fighter. She'd never go back to a man who'd beaten her so! I just know it.''

"Please," Jack said softly as he rubbed his forehead. He was so damned tired of trying to convince everyone of Victoria's innocence. "It *doesn't* add up. But then nothing about Victoria ever has. Henry, I have more reason than anyone to doubt her. She's lied to me more than once. But in this, I believe her. She would never put Emma in danger, and she would never go willingly with Donnelly.''

Henry frowned, unwilling to hurt his friend by disbelieving him, and just as unwilling to persist in accusing the woman Jack loved.

"Mr. Wilkins?"

Four pairs of eyes turned to see Etta standing in the doorway, hands twisting in her apron.

"Etta. You should be upstairs airing my wardrobe," Suzanne said rather sharply.

"Mr. Wilkins, I need to speak to you."

"Etta, this is not a good time to discuss the mundane matters of the house," Suzanne said deliberately, her eyes challenging the maid.

Etta hesitated, her gaze going from her mistress to Jack and back. "I need to speak to Mr. Wilkins," she said, her head coming up a notch. Suzanne turned her head sharply away as if Etta had delivered a blow.

"Very well. What is it?" Jack said, a crease deepening between his eyes.

Etta walked into the room in stuttering steps, as if someone were behind her trying to push her forward while she resisted. Her eyes darted from one person to the other when she finally stopped.

"Oh, Lord." Etta bit her lip, and tears formed in her eyes.

Jack suddenly became aware of just how distressed the maid was. In three long strides he was in front of her, his piercing blue eyes pinning her to the spot.

"You know something."

"Of course she knows nothing," Suzanne said with harsh derision, and Jack narrowed his eyes at his sister-in-law.

"You know something," Jack repeated, turning back to Etta.

"Yes," Etta squeaked. "Oh, Lord. I just can't do it. I don't care. I'll tell my family to hide. I just can't do it!"

"Can't do what?" Jack asked with forced calm.

Etta licked her lips. "Oh, Lord."

"Etta, if you don't immediately tell me what you came in here to tell me, I will strike you," Jack said, again using that eerily calm voice.

"She's just a silly little maid," Suzanne said with forced lightness. And she walked over to a nearby chair, sitting down to show everyone in the room just how unconcerned she was with whatever Etta came to say.

"Let her speak, Suzanne," Mary cut in.

The maid took a deep breath. "Kevin Donnelly forced Miss Casey to go with him," she blurted out.

"I knew it!" Mary shouted, throwing a triumphant look first at her husband and then at Jack.

"How do you know this?" Jack demanded.

"Oh, Lord."

"Woman, if you persist on stalling . . ."

"Jack, she's frightened. Can't you see that?" Mary admonished. "Just sit here, dear, and tell us what you know. It's all right," she said kindly, leading Etta to a nearby settee.

"This is ridiculous," spat Suzanne.

"It all started with us trying to get Miss Casey fired because we knew you had your sights set on her," Etta said, looking relieved that she could finally set things right.

"Us? We?"

Etta looked up at Jack and over to Suzanne. "Me and Mrs. Von Arc."

Suzanne stood up as if catapulted from the chair. "Why, of all the . . ."

"Sit down, Suzanne," Jack said, his voice softly menacing. "Continue, Etta."

And she did, telling it all, from her meeting with Donnelly, to his threats on her family, and finally about the kidnapping. By this time, she was sobbing, soaking the handkerchiefs handed to her by Henry and Jack.

"She was so scared, Mr. Wilkins. So scared. She didn't want to go, but she did it for me, for my family. And to get poor little Emma back for you. She was shaking so much walking down those subway steps, I had to help her. I helped her walk toward that devil! Oh, Lord. And the worst of it was . . ." She let out a great gulping sob. "The worst of it was she wouldn't even hold Emma, wouldn't even give herself that. Oh, Mr. Wilkins. She thinks he's going to kill her." Etta dissolved into another fit of tears. "She was so scared, so scared," she said again.

Jack stood during the entire story, but at this last, he sat down heavily. "Do you know where he's holding her?" he said, his voice oddly emotionless.

Etta shook her head, pressing the handkerchief against her dripping nose. And Jack sagged. He had been looking for Donnelly for weeks without success. What were the chances he would find him tonight?

"But I know someone who does," Etta said.

His head shot up, and his blue eyes took on a sharpness, a light that had been gone since Victoria had left. "Who?" He was smiling, but his eyes glittered dangerously.

"Tom Reilly. He'll be at the Timothy's Pub by six o'clock. My father always said you could set your watch by him."

Jack and Henry pulled out their pocket watches at the same moment. Five o'clock. They'd know in one hour.

* * *

Victoria watched with dawning horror as Donnelly began unbuttoning his pants. She had not considered this, not when before he hadn't seemed the least bit interested in sex. He'd only been interested in beating her. Her eyes darted to the poker, resting against the black iron stove, well out of reach.

Setting her jaw, she said with as much conviction as possible, "I won't do this, Kevin. I won't." She chanced a look into his eyes. He was smiling at her. Smiling. A menacing leer wouldn't have been more frightening. Her hands clawed into the mattress, nails scraping the dirty fabric.

On the third floor, a door opened and closed, and footsteps sounded on the wooden steps that led to the attic hideaway.

"We've plenty of time to get reacquainted," Donnelly said amiably, buttoning up his pants. "That'd be Tom with our meal and my whiskey." He gave her a wink, and Victoria flinched the same as if he had drawn back his hand.

Tom Reilly opened the door and walked up the four remaining steps that led to the large room where Victoria was held hostage. He jerked his hat off his head, thrusting it in his back pocket. His brown eyes took in Victoria, sitting on the mattress, arms wrapped around her knees, and Donnelly, just finishing buttoning up his pants. He flushed bright red, but Victoria couldn't tell if it was with embarrassment or anger. But when Reilly set down his package a bit harder than was necessary, Victoria got her answer. This innocuous-looking man was angry, but too afraid to say anything aloud. An ally, she thought, hope burgeoning in her breast.

She watched the reed-thin man, wearing a red-checkered shirt and black vest, as he pulled out a loaf of bread and a covered pot. The room was instantly filled with the wonderful aroma of beef. "Jenny cooked a stew for you. She wants to know if you're feelin' better," Reilly said, his tone slightly less than friendly.

"Tell Jenny," Donnelly said, uncorking the whiskey and taking a long pull, "that I'm still feelin' poorly and won't be able to see her for a while." Donnelly's eyes drifted over to Victoria. "But I imagine I won't be feelin' poorly for long." His eyes never left her as he took another drink; then he lifted the bottle to Tom and smiled, as if he meant the whiskey would make him better.

Reilly opened the stove and threw in a few more small logs, stirring up the coals to create more heat. "Take awhile to heat up," he said into the pot.

"Then, I got time to go take care of some business," Donnelly said. Bottle in hand, he walked from the attic, and Victoria's heart picked up a beat as she realized he was headed to the outhouse to relieve himself. When his footsteps died away, Victoria spoke in low tones.

"He's going to rape me. That's what he was going to do when you walked in." Tom pretended not to hear her, but Victoria saw him stiffen slightly, his hand pausing for a moment while he stirred the stew. "He almost killed me the last time. Did you know about that? Tom?"

The slim man did not turn, but he finally spoke. "Why're you talkin' so fancy?"

Victoria rolled her eyes. "You won't help me because of the way I talk?" she asked incredulously.

He turned to her then, his eyes shifting to the doorway where Donnelly disappeared. "Sheila," he whispered harshly, "you know I can't help you. You, of all people, know I can't. Don't ask."

Victoria slumped against the wall and watched as Tom turned back to the stove, stirring the thick stew as if it needed constant attention. She wanted to call him a coward, to rail at him that he had to help her, but believed that would simply turn him against her. "Tom." He stubbornly continued to stir, the spoon scraping against the bottom of the pot, sounding absurdly loud in the silence.

"You're my only hope," she whispered. The stirring stopped, and Tom's head slumped just slightly. And then, without saying a word, he resumed his stirring. "If he kills me, how will you live with yourself. How, Tom?"

"At least I'll be alive," he muttered.

Victoria let the rage she felt at being so helpless erupt. "You coward. You goddamn pussy," she spat as she heaved herself up off the mattress. What the hell was she doing here sitting complacently on the floor waiting for Donnelly to return? She'd be damned if she sat still while that bastard planned to rape her. She stalked over to the poker, holding it in two hands, empowered by its solid weight in her fists.

Tom looked at her as if she'd lost her mind. "Sheila, what the Christ are you doing?"

"What does it look like I'm doing, you idiot. I'm going to nail him when he gets back, and if you try to stop me, I'll nail you with this thing, too." Victoria shook the poker at Tom, baring her teeth at him.

"I can't let you do it," Tom said, shaking his head in resignation. "I'm sorry, lass." He walked toward her, his hand extended. Victoria swung the pole with all her might, making contact with Tom's extended arm. It connected with a sickening crack.

"Christ!" Tom yelled, his uninjured hand covering the spot just above his wrist. "I think you broke it! Christ!"

Victoria recovered from her initial shock of actually having struck a man with an iron poker and lunged at him again, feinting a blow. She noted his flinch with a satisfied sneer. "Now, back off," she yelled, jerking the pointy end of the poker toward his gut. She turned to position herself by the door, her eyes still watching Tom, and ran smack into Donnelly.

He grabbed the poker easily from her grasp and threw it at Tom, who ducked just in time, the poker glancing off one shoulder. "Jesus, Kevin, what'd you do that for?"

"Because, you sorry jackass, you can't seem to handle one little mite of a woman," he snarled. Donnelly grabbed a handful of Victoria's hair and flung her down onto the floor to demonstrate how easily she could be handled. All the fear Victoria had conquered in Tom's presence came roaring back nearly paralyzing her. She scuttled over to the mattress, fearing Donnelly would lash out with his feet. When she dared to look up, she was startled by the good humor in Donnelly's eyes.

"Got you good, did she?" he chuckled, eyeing Tom's already swelling arm.

"Think she broke it," Tom said irritably. Victoria watched with dread as Tom was reduced to Donnelly's flunky. Any courage he had shown—even the courage to stand up against Victoria—seemed to have disappeared.

"Get your arse out of here and have Jenny look at it for you," Donnelly said almost kindly. Tom stuffed his ragged cap back on his head and slinked toward the door.

"I'm sorry I hit you, Tom," Victoria called out. He hesitated just a moment at the bottom step before thrusting himself through the door. Maybe, just maybe, he would come through for her. As pathetic as he was, he was still her only hope.

Thirty-nine

Timothy's Pub was jammed with neighborhood men, sweaty from a long day's work and ready to drink until they forgot how sore their muscles were. They were a friendly, loud lot of mostly men, although a fair number of wives were downing pints alongside their husbands. Dusty gas fixtures emitted weak light in the tavern, lending the bar more atmosphere than it rightly had.

Jack, Henry, and Jasper Porter, whom Jack had enlisted to join in their search for Victoria, sat at a small table near the entrance, eyes peeled on the plank door for a man that matched the detailed description given to them by Etta. Jack and Henry, with their finely cut suits, clearly were strangers in this crowd and drew a fair amount of hostile looks. But Jasper Porter's large bulk served to discourage any regular who might get overly curious as to why the two gentlemen chose their little pub.

Jack pulled out his watch for the fourth time in a quarter hour, and glared at it. "It's nearly half past," he growled, shoving his watch back into his vest pocket. "Where the devil is he?" He searched the crowd already in the bar, wondering for the tenth time if Tom Reilly were already here, and they had simply overlooked him. Each man sitting at the table had an untouched pint in front of him as they collectively stared at the front door. That, in itself, was enough to arouse suspicion of the men who leaned up against the bar, eyeing the trio with ill will. But it was obvious the men were looking for a particular someone, and not a man in the bar didn't count himself ready to fight if the need arose. Henry looked nervously over the bar, taking in the rough-looking crowd eyeballing the three men, and shifted uncomfortably in his seat.

"I don't think we're welcome here," he said in vast understatement. Jack ignored his friend, and Porter snorted out a smile.

Suddenly, Jack straightened. A tall, thin man with ginger-colored eyes and a sad-looking cap in his left hand, entered the pub. His right arm was bandaged and held in a sling. Jack stood up, but Porter lay a hand on his arm.

"Let me handle this," he said softly.

Porter stood and walked directly over to the man they suspected was Tom Reilly. Jack watched as Porter bent his head in discussion, as the man's eyes darted around nervously. For a moment, it looked like he was contemplating running toward the door, but then his shoulders sagged. Porter, one large hand fully encompassing Reilly's upper arm, led the man back to the table. The men standing at the bar became alert, each abandoning their drinks and straightening their bodies. The roughest of the lot was pushing up his sleeves, exposing muscular forearms.

"Tell them everything's fine," Porter said.

Reilly put out his hand, a gesture telling his drinking friends that all was well, and he sat down in the table's only remaining empty chair.

"Mr. Wilkins, this is your man." With that, Porter leaned back, grabbed his pint, and took a long drink.

It took all the control Jack had not to leap across the table, grab Reilly by the throat, and demand he tell him where Victoria was. But he could see the man was frightened almost beyond what he should have been to be confronted with the three men. Reilly licked his lips, then wiped his mouth with a shaking hand, his eyes going to each man and finally coming to rest on Jack.

"I'll take you to her on one condition," he said.

"No conditions," Jack bit out. "Except I might let you live if you tell me." He was so enraged, he believed what he said.

"He'll kill me," Reilly said, and saw no softening in the eyes of Jack Wilkins, only the glinty steel of fierce determination. Reilly sagged in defeat. "I'll take you there."

"Before we go, I must know one thing. Has he . . ." Jack could not speak past the growing knot in his throat. Swallowing painfully, he continued. "Has he hurt her?"

Reilly's lip quirked, and if Jack wasn't mistaken, it almost appeared the man was trying not to smile. "Did I say something amusing?" he asked.

Reilly shifted in his chair. "No, sir. But, you see, Sheila's the one who did this to me." He lifted his arm, indicating his injury.

A gleam of satisfaction entered Jack's eyes, but was quickly gone. "You didn't answer my question."

"He hasn't hurt her," Reilly said, but the "yet" was as clear as if he'd said it aloud.

"Jesus Lord," Jack said in anguish. "Take us to her, man. Now!"

After Reilly hastily told them where Victoria was being held, the four men stood, each feeling a sudden sense of urgency. As they climbed aboard Jack's carriage, Jack shouted directions to the driver and flung himself inside. His horses were fine, strong animals, but to Jack's frenzied mind, they plodded like so many oxen. He couldn't stop the silent screaming in his head. *Too late. You're going to be too late.*

Victoria watched with distaste as Donnelly ate the thick stew. He scooped up each mouthful with relish, practically shoveling the stuff directly from the bowl into his open mouth. Kevin Donnelly might be a charming fellow when he wished, but he had no manners. He ripped off a piece of meat, beaming a smile at Victoria, his white teeth gleaming in the dim light.

"Sure you don't want any, love. Jenny's a fine cook, she is." He patted his stomach loudly. "She's put a few pounds on these old bones in the past few months. I just might marry that girl yet. What would you say to that, Sheila?"

"I'd say Jenny's a fool."

Donnelly's easy grin slowly disappeared. "Why are you pushin' me, darlin'."

"Sorry," Victoria mumbled, and looked away so he wouldn't see the fear that calm, silky voice evoked. When she looked back, Donnelly was grinning again.

"You're not sorry yet, Sheila. You're not sorry for hurtin' my best man, that I know. And you're not sorry for puttin' me through all this trouble of bringin' you back where you belong. I'd say you're not half as sorry as you're goin' to be, darlin'."

Victoria's body suddenly felt like jelly. She had no joints, and especially no spine. Fear, like a blast from a furnace, burned through her veins. She only knew one thing: She could not survive another beating. She had neither the might nor the will. When she had seen Emma in Tom Reilly's arms, she knew in her heart she would never see her little girl again. She looked only to see if she was unhurt before stepping on the train, glad that Jack would have his baby back, believing in her heart this was meant to be.

On that train ride, Victoria came to some awful conclusions. She had tried to steer fate her way only to find it refused to be directed. All those years ago, a little girl was adopted by Jack and Christina Wilkins. Christina had died, and the little girl had been raised alone by her loving father. The little girl's female influence had probably been her Aunt Suzanne. That's the way it had been. That's the way it would be again. Victoria had come to the cruel conclusion that Jack and Emma would be better off without her.

She told herself that even as the fear built to a point she thought she'd scream. Victoria watched as Donnelly scraped the bowl clean, then licked the side with relish. Getting up, he stretched and groaned in an exaggerated way, and stood by the stove stirring what was left of the stew.

"Sure you're not hungry, love?"

Victoria stared at his back, wishing she could kill him with her thoughts. She stared and stared until her eyes hurt, until she felt the hate fly out of her like an arc of electricity. In her mind, she saw that piercing band of hatred bend toward Donnelly and snap into the base of his skull. She was almost amazed when he continued to stir the stew, part of her crazily believing her hate could have and should have dealt him a fatal blow. He stuck his spoon into the thick gravy and slurped it into his mouth, wiping his sleeve across his smiling lips. How she hated that smile. How she hated him in that moment. Somehow, in that instant of pure hate, the fear dissolved. It simply . . . disappeared.

He let out a belch and chuckled good-naturedly. "Nothing like a good meal to reinforce a man," he said suggestively. Instead of her stomach roiling in fear, it clenched with determination. Victoria didn't stop to think where her fear, which had been plaguing her for weeks, had flown. She looked at Donnelly with contempt. How *dare* he steal her daughter, then think he could take her as well? She hadn't been to hell and back because of this devil to let him defeat her in the end. No, Victoria had never been a good martyr, and she decided she was not about to start now.

Again her eyes darted around the room for a weapon, but now with new purpose. The poker was too far out of reach, and it was likely she'd get only a single good whack in before he recovered and wrestled it from her. She could not think to overpower a bulldog such as Donnelly. She had to outsmart him instead. Victoria searched that room, taking in every item, no matter how innocent, and trying to devise a

way to turn it into a weapon. Her choices were woefully small, and she disregarded most almost immediately. A rope hanging from a nail in the wall could
be used to strangle him, but it was more likely he
would use it against her in the end. The stew pot was
too unwieldy, the spoon too small. And then she saw
it—her salvation. Her horror.

A kerosene lamp.

It was sitting not three feet away, unlit, innocuous.
Its glass globe was slightly sooty, its base white with
little pink flowers painted on it. It might not even be
filled with kerosene, she thought. It probably wasn't.
If she reached over with her hand, she could probably
pick it up and jostle it, just to see if it were full. Just
to see. That's all.

Donnelly opened the stove and threw in a couple
more small logs, closed it, and stood, scratching his
full belly appreciatively. She watched him out of the
corner of her eye as she—as nonchalantly as possible—reached out and picked up the small lamp. It
was full.

Victoria did not know whether she was supremely
happy or horribly afraid. She decided she was a mixture of both. For she knew, even as she placed the
lamp down, even as she judged whether she could get
to the matches before he stopped her, that she would
use the only weapon she had available to her. The
only one with which she was intimately familiar. Fire.

Perhaps this was fate. Perhaps she had been meant
to die that day she celebrated the perfume contract.
"Well, Mr. Fate, I'm gonna beat you this time," she
said to herself. "I'm going to live if it's the last thing
I do." She even smiled at the utter ridiculousness of
that thought.

Forty

"**K**evin?"

"Yes, darlin'."

"We can do it, but I want it to be good."

He looked a bit confused, so Victoria clarified. "I don't want you to force me."

Donnelly put on a shocked expression. "I'd not force you, Sheila."

Victoria forced herself to smile. "I'm sure you wouldn't, but I just wanted to be sure. I . . . I know you're angry with me." She lowered her gaze, looking appropriately meek.

"I'd say I'm a bit more than angry with you, Sheila girl," he said silkily, and Victoria felt her stomach roll. Don't be afraid, she begged herself. Don't let him conquer you. He was silent for so long, Victoria simply had to look up to see what he was doing and immediately wished she hadn't. Donnelly was looking at her through half-closed lids, his glittering eyes holding a danger that made her want to curl up in a ball. He was leaning up against a sturdy oak table, and he suddenly straightened.

"You've changed, Sheila. I don't know you anymore. You're not the girl who begged to come to America with me, who swindled your own father out of the passage money. That girl never would have been too afraid to look me in the eye."

Victoria lifted her chin. "I'm not afraid of you. But

you hurt me, Kevin. You nearly killed me. How do you expect me to react to you?"

He struck his fist against his own thigh. "It's nothin' you didn't have comin' to you. You're always blamin' me, pointin' a finger at me, when you're the one who drives me to do it."

Victoria tried to wipe the look of pure disbelief from her face, but was only partially successful. That Donnelly actually blamed her for the beating was sick. Swallowing to stop herself from blurting out how absurd he was, she instead said, "I know, Kevin. But that last time, you hit me awfully hard."

Donnelly appeared mildly mollified as he crossed his massive arms across his chest. "Well. For that I'm sorry, lass," he mumbled.

Victoria smiled up at him carefully, aware her lips were trembling from the false effort. "Could you hand me those matches, Kevin. It's so dark in here with only that one lamp lit. I thought I'd light this one, too."

Without a word, Donnelly threw the tin of matches to her. Grasping them in one hand, the lamp in the other, she stood and walked over to the stove. She was so afraid she was strangely light-headed, her joints weak. She dared not look at Donnelly, for fear he would see what was in her heart, and so she tried to look casual, as if she wasn't planning to douse him with the kerosene and light him on fire. Victoria made a great show of shaking the lamp. "Oh, darn. I'm not sure there's enough kerosene left," she said, sounding like a bad actress to her ears.

She unscrewed the base from the lamp, cursing her shaking hands, still too afraid to look up to see if Donnelly was looking at her with suspicion. He appeared not to care what she was about as he stood there picking his teeth. But she wasn't sure if those clear blue eyes were on her, and she didn't want to be sure. The lamp made what sounded to Victoria like a deafening squeaking sound as it came loose from the base.

When Donnelly looked up, Victoria was standing not four feet away, the base of the lamp in one hand, a match in the other. It did not register what she was about immediately, and when it did, his eyes widened and he turned fully toward her.

"What're you thinkin', love?"

Breathing out harshly through her nose, Victoria stared at her nightmare incarnate and knew she couldn't do it. She could not subject any living thing, no matter how evil, to the kind of pain she knew awaited him. Oh, God, she thought desperately, I can't do it. I can't.

"Back off or I'll set you on fire," she said, her eyes narrowed and as menacing as she could make them. Donnelly took a step toward her. "Now, darlin' . . ." But whatever he was going to say was cut off when Victoria splashed a generous portion of the kerosene toward him and then immediately lit the match.

"Jaysus, Sheila. Don't do it. Don't do it, girl." It gave Victoria intense satisfaction to see the fear, finally, in his eyes.

"Beg me, Donnelly. Get down on your goddamn knees and beg me."

"You're pushin' your luck, girl. Give me the lamp, you little bitch."

He took another step toward her, and Victoria splashed another generous amount on a nearby pile of clothes.

"Wrong answer." And she dropped the match.

"Holy God." Tiny little flames danced in Tom Reilly's eyes as he stared in confusion, from the still moving carriage, at the flames shooting out of the four-storied building.

"Tell me that's not where she is, Reilly. You goddamn better tell me she's not in there." Jack grabbed Reilly's coat and was tugging on it viciously as the

Irishman's eyes stayed glued to the horrific sight in front of him. Finally he dragged his eyes away from the fire to look at Jack.

"I'm sorry," he whispered.

Jack hurled himself out of the carriage before the driver had time to set the brake, closely followed by the three other men. He could already feel the heat from the flames as he frantically searched the ground for some sign of Victoria, then reluctantly looked back at the building.

"There!" Jasper Porter shouted next to him, his hand jutting past Jack as they ran, pointing to the outside second floor. Something was there, moving awkwardly, slowly on the second-floor landing as sparks flew about them like the devil's sparkler on the Fourth of July.

"Victoria!" Jack screamed until his throat hurt. He took off his jacket as he ran, unaware of Jasper Porter matching him stride for stride. They both reached the stairway at the same time, and for one horrible moment fought each other, jostling for position in their frenzy to get up those stairs. The heat from the blaze was searing, and Jack could only imagine how hot it must be where Victoria struggled, her skirt flapping in the fire-wind caused by the heat of the flames.

Porter reached the landing first, unable to believe what he was seeing. That little mite-of-a-woman was dragging the unconscious Donnelly to safety. Or at least trying to with every ounce of energy she had.

"I'll take him," he shouted over the roar of the inferno, raging above their heads. Porter grabbed the back of Donnelly's shirt and dragged him unceremoniously behind him down the stairs.

When Jack reached Victoria, she leaped at him and clung, her hands clawing painfully into his back. He had one awful moment of panic when he nearly lost his balance, sending them both tumbling down the stairs. But one hand gripped the sturdy rail, saving them. Jack ran down the stairs, frantic to get away from the heat, to get Victoria from the fire, praying with every step that his foolish girl hadn't hurt herself too badly, saving the life of that monster Donnelly.

He ran with her in his arms on the uneven ground until the cold air began to penetrate, to soothe his burning face. Still she clung silently to him as if her hands were permanently imbedded into the flesh in his back.

"Victoria, sweetheart, we're safe now. Safe. Let me see you, Vic. Let me see if you're all right."

"Fire."

That harsh whisper tore at Jack's heart. "We're safe now, sweetheart. Safe."

"Safe."

Jack pulled her to him, then tried again to gently push her away to determine her injuries. Strangely silent, she let him examine her hands, her face, in the light from the fire, which now completely engulfed the building. Her hands were already beginning to blister, but she knew she had suffered no serious injury, even though it hurt terribly.

"We'll get you to a doctor," Jack said softly.

Victoria shook her head. "I want to go home. Please, Jack, I just want to go home."

"All right, sweetheart. We'll go home. Emma's waiting for you."

Victoria smiled, just a tiny tilting of her lips. "Emma."

Victoria's burns were not serious, but they were terribly painful. Her hands were one large blister, her hair singed so much, she had to cut it to her shoulders. Jack insisted the shorter hair was much more modern anyway. Two days after the fire, Victoria still lay abed, her hands tightly wrapped. She could get out, but she was strangely complacent and content just to lay there, back propped by snowy-white pillows, and be waited on hand and foot. It's over, she thought. Now my life can begin.

Suzanne, nearly penniless after spending the little money she had left to hire Donnelly, was neatly and permanently ensconced in her parents' home. When her parents learned of her perfidy, it was only a long and rather pitiable bout of tears that convinced them to allow her to stay. Having a daughter so corrupt made it easier to forgive their former son-in-law for the great sin of falling in love and planning to marry less than a year after the death of their beloved Christina.

Jack had asked Victoria why she had risked her life to save Donnelly's, and she hadn't been able to answer him because she wasn't sure she knew herself. She hadn't set Donnelly on fire that night. In fact, her plan had backfired a bit. When she'd finally flung that match onto the poured kerosene, half the room had burst into flame. She'd thought Donnelly could have escaped behind him through a window, giving her enough time to get away. But the barrier created by the blaze hadn't been enough to stop Donnelly. The poker, however, had been. Seeing her mistake, Victoria had picked up the heavy iron and swung at Donnelly's head with all her might. To her surprise, she'd hit him squarely, knocking him out cold. In a panic to get away from the fire, Victoria had left Donnelly behind and was actually on the ground, looking back up at the black smoke billowing out into the night air, before she'd gone back in for him, calling herself the biggest idiot the entire way.

Jack looked at her with a mixture of bafflement and pride.

"I don't know if I would have gone back into that fire for him," he'd said. "Not after everything he'd done."

"You would have," Victoria said definitively.

"Why do you say that?"

"Because, Jack Wilkins, I know what's in your heart."

Donnelly, fully recovered, was in prison, where he

would stay until he was too old to so much as lift his hand to scratch his vermin-infested head. Reilly and Etta were, if not forgiven, pardoned for finally doing the right thing. Etta was fired immediately, but the little maid had been so grateful not to find herself in prison, she had actually thanked Jack after their brief interview.

Victoria hugged the goodwill to her, knowing that nothing in life could faze her now. What a joyous, horrible, wonderful ride her life had been so far, she thought. She needed to do only one more thing before she could finally close this chapter of her life—let Allie know how she was. Her planning was interrupted by Jack, holding Emma in his arms.

"Hey, you," Victoria said softly, taking in his worried look as his eyes touched upon her bandaged hands. Careful to hold Emma away so the little girl wouldn't inadvertently hurt Victoria, he leaned down for a long, lingering kiss.

"I can't wait to hold Emma," Victoria said, pouting just a little.

"And I can't wait to hold you," Jack said hoarsely, his lips still near hers.

"Oh, that. We'll have a lifetime for that. But Emma will only be a baby for a little while." And then she kissed him, pulling him closer with a wrist on each side of his head, telling him she couldn't wait, either. Emma, not happy about being ignored, began squirming, and Jack drew back, a smile on his beautiful lips.

"We have to wait until we get married anyway," Victoria said primly.

Jack raised one eyebrow. "Oh?"

Victoria nodded solemnly. "I was thinking perhaps we could get married, say in six months. That'd give us plenty of time to get things ready. And there are those social considerations."

"Six months?"

"How about six weeks."

"Better. But I was thinking six days."

Victoria smiled wickedly. "That sounds just about right. Although, to be honest, I was hoping to get it down to six hours."

Jack gave her another soul-wrenching kiss. "And I, sweetheart, was going for six minutes."

Epilogue

Allie held Victoria to her until she knew, without a doubt, that she was gone. A few seconds later, John Wing confirmed her fears.

"She has left us," he said solemnly. He looked through the mist-covered windshield toward the lake.

Allie, her eyes red-rimmed and splashing tears, said bitterly, "Yeah. But where to? Oh, Vicky! Where are you?" And she hugged her friend's lifeless body to her, praying for the first time in years that someone was watching over her. Allie was unaware that her back was soaking wet from the incessant light rain, as she kneeled on the ground and held Victoria to her.

Wing watched her impassively, his hands drifting up and down the steering wheel, allowing Allie to grieve her best friend's passing. "She has not died," he said finally, sounding so sure of himself, it made Allie angry.

"Oh, yeah? Well, she sure looks dead to me."

Wing was silent for a long moment, looking at Allie with such compassion, she wanted to tear his understanding eyes out!

"When I turned twenty-one, my grandfather gave me something that his own father had given to him. He told me a great lady had given him this object and that I was to keep it safe. I was never to allow it to come to harm."

Allie was only half listening, her grief distracting her from Wing's monologue. She wiped her eyes with her fingertips, brushing them along her temple and leaving behind a wet path.

"Yeah? What was this mysterious object?" she said, clearly not interested in some story Wing thought might give her comfort now. She didn't want to be comfortable, she wanted to scream and cry and pull out her hair.

"It was this," he said, taking an object out of his suit jacket inside pocket.

Allie creased her brow at the small silver frame Wing held in his hand. "Take it," he urged.

Allie did, the crease deepening. It was a photo of a family. A man, woman, and little baby girl. The man, uncommonly handsome with his dark hair slicked back, revealing a strong, well-formed forehead, rested a hand on the back of the woman's slim neck. An eternal caress. The woman, a sprightly-looking little thing with an impish smile, held an adorable white-gowned baby lovingly in her lap.

"What is this?" Allie asked, caution tingeing her voice.

"Look on the back."

Allie stared at the picture for another long moment, almost afraid to do as Wing asked. For she knew without being told what she held in her hand. Slowly she turned the small frame over, her eyes suddenly filling with tears. She blinked them away quickly so that she might read the simple inscription that only Victoria could have written:

"Allie Cat—Alive and well and *in love*. Vicky."

SIMMERING DESIRES

❏ **HALFWAY HOME by Bronwyn Williams.** When Sara Young's and Jericho Wilde's paths intersect at the Halfway Hotel, they're both in for a surprise—as passion ignites without warning. Now Jericho is torn between vengeance and caring . . . until he sees that death may come as quickly as this chance for love. . . .
(406982—$5.99)

❏ **THE WARFIELD BRIDE by Bronwyn Williams.** None of the Warfield brothers expected Hannah Ballinger to change their lives: none of them expected the joy she and her new baby would bring to their household. But most of all, Penn never expected to lose his heart to the woman he wanted his brother to marry—a mail order bride. "Delightful, heartwarming, a winner!—Amanda Quick (404556—$4.99)

❏ **WIND SONG by Margaret Brownley.** When a feisty, red-haired schoolmarm arrives in Colton, Kansas and finds the town burned to the ground, she is forced to live with widower Luke Taylor and his young son, Matthew. Not only is she stealing Matthew's heart, but she is also igniting a desire as dangerous as love in his father's heart.
(405269—$4.99)

❏ **BECAUSE YOU'RE MINE by Nan Ryan.** Golden-haired Sabella Rios vowed she would seduce the handsome Burt Burnett into marrying her and become mistress of the Lindo Vista ranch, which was rightfully hers. Sabella succeeded beyond her dreams, but there was one thing she had not counted on. In Burt's caressing arms, in his bed, her cold calculations turned into flames of passion as she fell deeply in love with this man, this enemy of her family. (405951—$5.50)

❏ **HARVEST OF DREAMS by Jaroldeen Edwards.** A magnificent saga of family threatened both from within and without—and of the love and pride, strength and honor, that would make the difference between tragedy and triumph.
(404742—$4.99)

*Prices slightly higher in Canada